BURKE IN THE LAND OF SILVER

Tom Williams

First published in 2014 by Accent Press.

This edition published in 2020 by Big Red.

ISBN 978-1-9162635-2-9

Author's Note

James Burke was a real person, as were many of the other characters in this novel.

His name really was James Burke and he really was a spy.

Any resemblance to any other spy with the initials J.B. is an unfortunate coincidence.

Dramatis Personae

Real People

James Burke: a British spy Boukman: a slave
Thomas O'Gorman: an Irish merchant in Buenos Aires
Ana O'Gorman: his wife
De Liniers: an admiral in the Spanish navy
His Excellency the Marquis Rafael de Sobremonte: Spanish Viceroy in Buenos Aires
Commodore Riggs Popham: commander of the British invasion of 1806
Colonel Beresford: British commander of land forces in the 1806 invasion
Duke of York: Commander-in-Chief of the British Army
Sr de Álzaga: mayor of Buenos Aires
Lieutenant John Thomson: a British naval officer
Maria Luisa: Queen of Spain
Princess Carlota: her daughter
Sir Arthur Wellesley: a British general (later Duke of Wellington)
Admiral Smith: a British admiral based in Rio de Janeiro
Lord Strangford: British ambassador in Rio de Janeiro

Fictional Characters

William Brown: servant to James Burke
Molly Simkins: a whore
Monsieur Goriot: a French merchant in Buenos Aires
Colonel Calzada Castanio: a Spanish officer
Jorge and Gustavo: young men who break windows
Miguel: a slightly older man who encourages them
Paco Iglesias: a ranch owner
Pedro: his foreman
Gomez: a fisherman

Chapter One

The parakeets burst out of the forest in a flash of emerald. James Burke heard their screeching and looked up to see them arcing through the sky. After a month in Haiti, he still maintained his youthful enthusiasm for the novelty of the place and the strange, noisy birds were part of the adventure of being there. He envied them, too. He envied their freedom, the casual way they flew across the abandoned fields, while he and his men stumbled clumsily along below.

Burke brought his attention back to the business at hand. His platoon was moving slowly across the ruins of what had once been a plantation field. The walking was not easy, for the field was covered in the stumps of cotton bushes, and the men were weighed down with their packs and the muskets that they carried. He saw one fellow stumble on a stump hidden in the weeds that were already reclaiming the soil. He heard the faint oath as the man's ankle turned beneath him. It was O'Hanrohan, the youngest in the patrol. Barely more than a boy, he struggled to keep up at the best of times. Burke watched anxiously as he took a tentative step onto his injured ankle and relaxed as O'Hanrohan started forward again with only the faintest of limps.

They had been about their thankless task for four days now. Four days of apparently endless walking across deserted fields in pursuit of an enemy that many of them were convinced would never be found. They were sweating into the thick red coats issued to them back in France and which they were now expected to wear in the tropical heat. Insects buzzed around them, biting incessantly. The powder in their hair clogged with sweat, leaving them desperate to rid themselves of their wretched shako hats so that they could scratch at their itching scalps. Imagining their discomfort, Burke lifted his own hat and scratched at his head.

Although he was not weighed down with pack and musket, Lieutenant James Burke was not privileged enough to patrol on horseback, and the days of walking in the heat left him with an occasional light-headedness that increased the sense of unreality that surrounded the whole expedition. Only a few months ago he had been in France, where every street corner seemed home to some would-be revolutionary declaiming on the Rights of Man. Yet before these dangerously democratic slogans had been given time to work their way into his loyalties, he was sent off to the Caribbean to protect the rights of French citizens to keep slaves. King Louis might be showing himself impotent in the face of rebellion at home, but rebellion in the little colony of Saint-Domingue was to be put down with fire and the sword.

The only problem was, as Burke was becoming painfully aware, that the colony might look small on the map, but it was big enough to conceal a rebel army from any number of French patrols. The slaves would appear from nowhere, burn a settlement, massacre the inhabitants, and vanish away again. Even the most sceptical of the French planters were beginning to mutter about voodoo.

O'Hanrohan had fallen back again. It would not do, Burke thought. The Regiment of Dillon had a reputation to maintain.

'Sergeant Dunnet! Attend to the line!'

Dunnet moved toward O'Hanrohan and, seeing him approach, the young soldier hurried forward to his allotted place. Burke relaxed and brushed a speck of dust from his coat. He had bought his uniform second-hand. His regiment might not be fashionable but it was still expensive for a young officer to kit himself out, and Burke's family didn't have the money to spend on what his father would have called 'fripperies'. But, second-hand or not, Burke intended to look good in his uniform. Before he had left France, he had found a tailor who, for a few sous, had fitted the clothes for him and he knew that he looked every inch the smart young officer. And smartness, whether in his person or in the soldiers under his command, was essential. The Regiment of Dillon served under the French crown but it was formed entirely of British troops – most, like him, escaping the provincial limitations of Ireland. They fought under the cross of St George, and their anomalous position meant that there were always those in the French army ready to pour scorn on '*les rosbifs*' if they fell short in any detail of drill or turnout.

'Jesus Christ! What in the name of the devil is that?'

The exclamation came from a fellow to the right of O'Hanrohan and a pace or two ahead of him. For a moment, Burke could not recall his name, but then it came to him. It was Docherty, a solid man and one not given to over-excitement. Now, though, he was pointing at something on the ground and exclaiming so vehemently that the rest of the platoon had broken off their advance and were clustering around him.

Burke stepped forward as the Sergeants yelled abuse at the men and cuffed them back into order. They moved reluctantly back to their places but remained restless. As he reached them, they settled, coming smartly to attention. The men nearest Docherty moved aside to let him pass.

The charred remains of the cotton bush were no different from the dozens of others that had survived the fires set by the rebels. Tied against the blackened twigs, though, was the body of a chicken. It was white and the brown cords stood out against the feathers. It had been tied with its wings spread, so that it hung like a macabre crucifix, about a foot from the ground. Its intestines were piled in a careful heap in front of the body.

The men nearest to him were shuffling forward, craning their necks to see the source of the excitement. There was some muttering and the men began to fidget, looking nervously around them.

'There's another over here!'

Across the ruined field came shouts as the men found more of the dead birds.

Sergeant Geraghty came and stood alongside Burke. He was the senior of Burke's two NCOs and had served in Saint-Domingue for six months before the Lieutenant arrived. Burke might be new to army life but he knew the value of men like Geraghty.

'What do you make of it, Sergeant?'

Geraghty took a long look at the bird while stolidly chewing the quid of tobacco that seemed to be permanently in his mouth. He paused to direct a stream of tobacco juice onto the intestines and turned to Burke.

'It's voodoo. It's their religion, like. It'll be that Boukman, like as not.'

Just a few minutes earlier, the day had held nothing but the prospect of a sweltering walk to be followed by another night of ration biscuits and sleeping on the hard ground. Now, though, it seemed to Burke full of possibilities. For months, the army had been hunting the rebel leader, the mysterious Boukman. Part priest, part general, Boukman inspired a fanatical loyalty in his followers and fury and dread in the French settlers. The man who tracked him down was made for life. Captain James Burke. Major Burke! General Burke!

With an effort, he forced himself not to smile.

'Are you sure, Sergeant?'

'I can't be certain, sir, but I'd stake a guinea on it, if I had a guinea.'

Now Burke allowed himself the smile and was rewarded with a grin from Geraghty.

Burke gazed thoughtfully at the feathered corpse at his feet. 'These chickens were killed recently. If it was him, he's not that far away.' Shading his eyes he looked across the field to the forest where the parakeets had flown from minutes earlier. 'My guess is that they're hiding in the woods.'

Burke felt the eyes of the patrol on him, waiting for his orders. If they found the rebels, he would be leading his platoon into action for the first time. It was a sobering prospect. The elation that had filled him just a few moments ago was gone now. The lives of all these men were in his hands. He had to get this right.

'Order the men to load.'

Sergeant Geraghty barked his orders and musket stocks crashed against the baked earth. Cartridges were bitten off and powder and ball rammed home. Burke felt the thrill of anticipation in his men. They knew the order to load meant their officer thought a fight was imminent. After all their thankless patrolling, they were spoiling for action.

Orders were shouted and the line broke into three separate groups, each of fifteen men. Burke took the centre with Dunnet on his left and Geraghty on the right.

Burke had drawn his sword and waved it enthusiastically as he led forward at almost a trot. He squinted in the sunlight, fixing his eyes on the forest, hoping to see the rebels hiding in the trees, but there was no sign of them.

They carried on, cursing as they stumbled over the uneven ground, but keeping up with the pace, muskets held at high port, slanted across their bodies.

They were less than a quarter of a mile from the edge of the trees now. The forest stood dark against the brilliant sky but there was no sign of movement there. Burke glanced right and left. His sergeants were in line with him, the men following on.

He looked back at the trees. Still nothing.

The cry from his left had him swivel his gaze back to Dunnet. The enemy was there, almost on them.

Now Geraghty yelled. More rebels had appeared to the right. And now there were black figures running toward him, screaming as they came. How could they have appeared so suddenly? Could he have been so dazzled by the sunlight that he simply had not seen them? For a moment, he almost found himself believing in the stories of Boukman's magical powers.

He shook his head, trying to clear his mind. The figures were almost on them. He had to take control of the situation.

He heard his voice shouting the orders he had practised so often. The words had come out automatically. 'Form two ranks.'

A skirmish line was fine for carrying the fight to the enemy but not the best way to defend yourself from attack. To right and left, he heard his sergeants giving the same order and the platoon closed up, facing the rebels in two lines. 'First rank, fire!'

The first rank's volley poured into the rebels.

Burke watched as the shots struck home. Some of the enemy were almost naked and gouts of blood appeared on the black skin of their chests. Others wore their field clothes – European trousers and ragged shirts staining with crimson. Most of the rest had dressed in a mismatched collection of whatever they had stolen from the farms they had destroyed. A tall man stood stock still as he was hit and then buckled at the knees, the fine beaver hat falling from his head to hit the ground just before he did. To his right a one-eyed villain with a machete wore a waistcoat with a fob watch. Incongruously, one or two of the men wore silk shawls pillaged from the boudoirs of their victims' wives.

'Second rank, fire! First rank, reload!'

The first rank barely waited for the order before dropping to their knees to reload while their fellows fired over their heads.

The first two volleys had dropped a dozen or more of the negroes but the rebels outnumbered them by more than two to one. They did not need superiority in weaponry or strategy. Simple weight of numbers could well carry the day for them.

The first rank had reloaded now and rose to fire, while the second rank bit urgently at their cartridges, but the enemy were already on them, spears thrusting forward, machetes rising and falling. The first rank were firing now, balls ripping into an enemy so close it was impossible to miss, but the rebels showed no fear. Burke had been told that Boukman's followers believed that his voodoo powers meant that they could not die in battle. He had insisted that no man, white or negro, free or slave, could credit such a thing. Now, he saw men who acted as if they truly believed themselves invincible. Though the musket balls tore through their ranks, cutting down their fellows, still the slaves came on regardless.

The patrol was closing into a square, each man defending himself and protecting his neighbour. In the centre, a few were free to reload their muskets but most had drawn their bayonets from their scabbards and were using them as swords, stabbing, twisting, and pulling the blades free to stab and twist again. They fought with the ferocity of the Dublin brawlers that so many of them were, but with the scientific viciousness of trained troops. Yet, for all their ferocity, Burke saw one scarlet-coated figure after another fall to the ground and, though more than twenty of the enemy had fallen, still his platoon was outnumbered. Out in the open, they would be overrun. They needed cover.

The woods were impossible. They would have to fight their way through the rebels and then defend themselves among the trees, where the natives would have the advantage of familiarity. But the only other place to offer them any chance of survival was the village where they had bivouacked the night before. It was a good two miles to the south but its ruins were their only hope.

'Push our southern flank. Get some movement.'

The attack had come from the north so, though the rebels had encircled them, there were fewer men to the south. As the platoon directed its efforts there, the enemy fell away, leaving yet more of their dead lying on the ruined field.

'Fighting retreat. Back to the village.'

Burke remembered an afternoon at the French military academy where he had briefly studied the basics of command before being posted off to a ship for the Tropics. Outside, the mob roamed the Paris streets, but in the École des Cadets-gentilshommes the instructors had remained icily efficient. 'A fighting retreat,' an old infantry colonel had told his class, 'is the most difficult manoeuvre you can demand of an infantry unit.' And then he had told them how it should be managed.

Geraghty was yelling orders. 'First section, bayonets. Second section stand and fire. Third section, fall back and load.'

The square had disintegrated but the enemy had given way to the south. Their attacks still came from the north. Every few minutes, the slaves would rush forward. There would be a confused melee of hand-to-hand fighting before a volley of musketry forced the rebels to fall back a few yards, allowing the platoon to move further south until each group re-formed for the next round of fighting.

Burke saw O'Hanrohan stagger, unable to keep up with his fellows, even as he had struggled earlier. Was it only a few minutes ago that Dunnet had urged him into his place in the line? It seemed like an incident from another life.

He saw Dunnet reach to pull the young soldier forward but the enemy was already on him. Dunnet, seeing his own danger, abandoned O'Hanrohan and ran forward to join the rest of his men. Shot whistled past him as the redcoats fired and the rebels checked – but Dunnet fell with a crude spear in his back.

It was two miles to the village. Each mile was marked with the bodies of rebel soldiers and Irish redcoats lying where they had fallen.

Four hours into that desperate retreat, Burke counted just fourteen of his patrol still standing, while more than fifty rebels continued to harry them as they fled. The village was less than half a mile off but Burke despaired that they would ever reach it.

Geraghty leaned toward him, speaking softly so that the men would not hear.

'We'll not fight our way back there,' he said. 'Best chance – after the next volley, drop the muskets and run like hell. They'll get most of us but a few might make it and they can hide out in the ruins.' He squinted at the buildings, outlined against the light. 'Best bet is the church. They're superstitious buggers – they may leave you alone there.'

Burke gave a grim nod. Geraghty was no fool. It was the best chance they had.

Only a dozen stood to fire the next volley and just three rebels were hit – but it was enough. For a few seconds the slaves' attack wavered and Geraghty gave the order to flee. The pathetic remains of the patrol dropped their gear and ran for their lives.

As he ran, Burke heard the cries of the negroes behind him and then the screams of one of his men as the rebels caught up with him. He didn't know who it was and he didn't turn to look. He just concentrated on running, his whole being focused on the tower of the church in the village ahead.

There were more screams. He felt his arm grabbed and turned in horror, only to see Geraghty running beside him, fresh blood on his bayonet. He staggered on the uneven ground. Geraghty caught at his arm, steadying him before he could fall. Then there was a beaten path under his feet, and they were among the buildings.

He ran on, zigzagging through the ruins. He ran aimlessly, the whole world concentrated into the next desperate step, the next breath tearing at his chest. Dimly, he was aware of Geraghty, guiding him this way and then that, while the cries of the rebels seemed to fade away behind them.

At last, he could run no more. He collapsed against a wall and looked up to see Geraghty grinning down at him.

'You ran well,' he said.

Only then did he realise he was leaning against the wall of the church.

Geraghty pulled him to his feet and into the church. Another soldier staggered in after them.

Burke tried to remember the man's name but found he could not. Just then, though, it did not seem important.

'How many others are there?'

The man struggled to speak, then pulled himself to attention. 'I think I'm the only one, sir.'

Burke groaned: 'Oh, God.'

Geraghty was tugging at his arm again.

'With respect, sir, we need to be getting a move on.'

The Sergeant hustled him through the door that led to the base of the tower. Inside, was a bare chamber with a ladder running almost vertically to a hatch in the ceiling far above them.

For a moment, Burke clutched at the ladder and did not move. Then, before Geraghty could scold him for delay, he started to pull himself, rung by rung, toward whatever safety the tower might offer. Behind him, Geraghty's breath was rasping as he followed. Then came the other man. Burke struggled again to remember his name. Brown, that was it: William Brown – the English lad. Brown stood out in a platoon that was otherwise exclusively Irish. But, though he was young, he was a good soldier. And, it seemed, fast on his feet.

Burke was at the hatch now and he pulled himself into the bell chamber above. The floor was thick with bird droppings, but if he lay in the filth and wriggled forward to the window he could raise his head and peer cautiously out at the scene below.

Behind him, he heard Geraghty and Brown moving forward too, until the three men lay alongside each other. They watched as a group of negroes clustered around something on the ground a block away from them. One swung a machete downward. Burke heard a scream that was suddenly cut off. As he lay there, he was all too aware that they had abandoned their weapons and, if the rebels found them, they would share the fate of the wounded.

They lay silent and still. Burke fought not to sneeze as the stench of the pigeon droppings irritated his nostrils. Gradually, his fear faded, to be replaced by anger. This wasn't how it was supposed to end. He was supposed to make a name for himself, fighting against a valiant enemy on the field of battle. He hadn't joined the army – even the French army – to fight native slaves on some Godforsaken island the other side of the world. The army was there to defend planters who had abandoned their native land long since. Their cruelty to their slaves was alien to European ways – it was as if the Age of Enlightenment had passed them by. And now he was to die because the greed of the slavers had driven their victims to revolt.

He heard the sound of naked feet on the bare earth as a group of slaves started toward the church. He felt his fists clench. With no weapons, they would go down fighting with their bare fists.

A voice called an order and the sound of footsteps moved away.

Now they heard more orders being shouted and then a great cheer. Burke risked lifting his head to see what was happening in the square outside the church.

Below, it seemed as if the rebels were mustering for some sort of parade. The men stood in rows, facing a white building that was much grander than any of the others in this little village. Burke imagined it must have been the town hall. There was a flight of stairs to the door and on the top step stood a gigantic negro, who was haranguing the crowd. Women and children were arriving through the houses to join the men in the square and their voices were raised in the cheers that kept greeting the giant's pronouncements.

Burke struggled to make out what was said, but he found the negro *patois* difficult at the best of times and, at this distance, he could not make it out.

The huge black figure seemed somehow out of place there. Black faces seemed natural here, even though Burke knew that these people had been brought from Africa to work in the white man's plantations. Yet the blacks he had seen before all shared a diffidence that marked them as slaves. Even those who were now free seemed somehow diminished as the children of slaves. But there was nothing diminished about the man below him. He looked like a tribal carving Burke had been shown as a child, a totem from some otherworld of magic and horror. He was dressed in a gold-braided livery, presumably that which he had worn as a servant, and the contrast between his savage appearance and the civilised refinement of his clothes added to the monstrousness of the spectacle that he presented.

A woman came forward from the crowd and passed a cockerel to the giant. He raised it, clucking and flapping its wings, above his head and then, in one single savage gesture, he seized its head in one hand and pulled it clear of its body.

The men nearest to him surged forward, reaching out toward the blood spurting from the still flapping corpse. The negro reached forward with the hand that held the head and daubed those he could reach in the second and third ranks. Even from the tower, Burke could see the blood glistening as it dried on shoulders and heads. He watched in fascinated horror. There was no doubt in his mind that this was Boukman. Here, not a hundred yards away, was the man that the whole army had been seeking for months. Yet he could do nothing but pray that no one would think to search the church until the rebels had moved on.

Lying in that tower, it seemed to Burke that the shouting and chanting in the square would never end but, in time, the cries grew quieter and, looking down in nervous glimpses, Burke saw the crowd slipping away.

Beside him, he heard Brown muttering, 'I think we're going to make it.'

'Best not count your chickens, lad,' Geraghty growled.

Burke knew his sergeant was right but, as he risked another look through the windows, and watched the last of the dark figures below slipping through the houses to make their way northward, he thought Brown might be right.

Even so, Burke decided to be cautious and it was not until he had seen no sign of movement for a full hour that he felt it safe to leave the bell tower.

By now, the tropical dusk was already on them. They made their way down the ladder in a gloom that grew perceptibly darker as he waited at the foot of the tower for the other two to ease their way carefully down to join him. Only when all three were ready did he open the door and step into the church.

There, facing the door, as if waiting for him, a black figure sat cross-legged on the floor of the nave. It was Boukman. For a moment, Burke thought that the strain of the day had destroyed his reason, and that the man was the creation of a fevered brain, but he heard Geraghty gasp behind him and accepted that the figure must be real.

The rebel leader looked up at Burke and spoke. His voice was deep and sweet. Terrified as Burke was, he could hear no threat in the man's tone.

'I have been waiting to speak with you.'

Behind him, he heard Brown's boots as the lad rushed forward to seize Boukman. The young man's hands were reaching for the negro's throat when he seemed to trip and fell, rolling away from his prey.

Boukman gave an almost apologetic shrug. 'I sit within a circle of protection.'

Burke looked down and saw a circle roughly drawn around the man. It was hard to be sure, in the failing light, but it looked as if it had been traced by a fingertip dipped in some red liquid.

It took a deliberate effort of will, but Burke forced himself to remember that he was an officer and a gentleman and that the man he faced was no more than a renegade slave.

'You are my prisoner, sir.' He hadn't meant to say, 'Sir.' It was the day spent terrified, stiff from lying in the tower, hot and hungry, and with no knowing how things would end. He knew he was covered in filth from the floor. He brushed self-consciously at his uniform coat and tried again to maintain his dignity. 'You must surrender to me.'

Boukman simply laughed. It was a gentle laugh, devoid of malice.

Burke moved forward but, as he approached the circle, he felt a stabbing pain shoot down his leg and he staggered to a halt. It was cramp, he thought. But he noticed that Boukman held a figure woven of corn, like the corn dollies that Burke remembered from his Kilkenny childhood. The doll was tiny in the negro's huge hands and Boukman was, almost absent-mindedly, twisting at the leg. He stopped twisting the doll and the pain in Burke's leg eased.

'Lieutenant James Burke, I intend you no harm.'

'You know my name.'

The negro smiled. Like his laugh, his smile was gentle. 'I know many things. Sit, and we will talk.'

The pain had passed, but Burke did not question the order. The negro spoke softly, still with a gentle smile, but his words carried the authority of command. So James Burke of His Majesty King Louis' Regiment of Dillon seated himself on the ground to parley with the rebel slave.

Face to face with the man, Burke was even more aware of his size. Yet, it was not his stature that gave such an impression of power. It was his face. The wide nose that was so common among the slaves was framed by high cheekbones. The eyes were the deepest brown that Burke had ever seen and they held him as if mesmerised.

'You are Boukman.'

'I am, indeed. I was a slave in Jamaica before I came here. My master kept me as a servant in his house and had me help with the accounts of his business. I was an able student and he taught me to read and so I was known to the other slaves as the Book Man. And then my master died and I was sold and sent from Jamaica to toil in the fields of Saint-Domingue. So I have served under the crowns of Britain and France. You and I are alike in that respect. And in some others. I was curious to meet you.'

'How did you know I was here?'

'I know many things. Perhaps it is the voodoo. Perhaps I am just well informed. Perhaps your soldier is just clumsy on his feet. It is not really that important.'

'Then, why?'

'That's a much better question. Why? Because I wanted to meet you.'

'Again, why?'

'Because we have something in common, Lieutenant Burke. It is my destiny to assist at the birth of a nation. And it is yours, too.'

Burke felt his grip on reality slipping. Surely he could not be sitting here, talking with the Book Man about his own destiny? And what nonsense was this about the birth of a nation? Burke had ambitions, certainly. He had abandoned Ireland to find a place in Society. He had joined the Regiment of Dillon because there he could take his place in the officers' mess without the fortune needed to buy a commission in a British regiment. In time, he hoped to progress to the point where he might number an earl amongst his acquaintances. Perhaps even a duke. But he was never going to be a person of that much consequence himself.

The Book Man was watching him with an unexpected compassion in those deep brown eyes.

'You do not do yourself justice, Lieutenant. You will never be accounted a great man, yet you will walk with the rulers of the world and your actions will help to bring forth a nation.'

Behind the Book Man, Burke saw Brown, who had sat quietly since his fall, rising to his feet. The negro half turned his head toward the soldier: 'William Brown, sit down again. I would not have you hurt.'

Brown hesitated and Burke gestured to him to sit. Whether the Book Man really had magical powers or not, the Lieutenant had seen enough not to want to risk Brown's life.

The distraction meant the Book Man's gaze turned away and, as if he was released from a spell, Burke found himself suddenly angry with this rebel leader and the deaths he had brought. He raised his voice to draw the negro's attention back to him and away from Brown.

'You talk of bringing forth a nation, but all you have achieved is death and destruction. You are nothing but a savage.'

The Book Man turned his attention back to Burke. He did not speak for a moment. When he did, his voice was still calm, contrasting with the anger in the young Lieutenant's tone.

'You are not a fool, James Burke. And, for all that you affect indifference, you care for the suffering of those you see around you. You have spent months on this island. You have seen the marks of the whip on the backs of my people. Did you speak of savagery then? We have been torn from our land and our families and all that we hold dear. Did you speak of destruction then? Our rebellion is a thing of destruction and cruelty because destruction and cruelty gave it birth. I pray that such things do not need to be repeated but I know my prayers will not be answered.' He paused and, when Burke gave no reply, he continued. 'We are more alike than you think, Lieutenant. Both of us are exiled from the land of our birth, although you had the luxury to choose your exile. Both of us now fight under alien banners. Both of us despise the station we were born to in life. But I think that your course is, perhaps, easier than mine.'

Caught in the gaze of those brown eyes, Burke struggled to maintain his anger, to rail against this slave, sat in a circle of blood. 'I have nothing in common with you.'

The Book Man's eyes were drawing him in. He tried to remember that the negro was the enemy and that he should hate him, but he felt his anger fading as the rebel leader spoke.

'We are all men, Lieutenant. We share a common humanity. Soon, I will die in the struggle to build freedom here. You will live for many, many years. But perhaps I have, after all, the better life. I know who I am and what I fight for. It gives me peace and strength. You, Lieutenant, change the person you are as you change the company you keep. You will fight for the French against the English and for the English against the French. You have yet to find your path.' He paused, nodding slowly to himself. 'I am glad we have spoken. I am going to my death. I know that I have found my own path and I am ready to follow it.'

The slave leader rose to his feet.

'One week from today, my army will meet with the French. There will be a battle. The French will win. But their war, I know, is lost.'

From a pocket in his jacket, he took a handful of seeds and threw them to the ground.

'As the corn roots in the earth, so may you be fixed to the spot where you stand.'

Then, stepping from the circle, he walked toward the door of the church.

Burke watched him go. He knew he should stop him but his feet seemed strangely unwilling to move.

'Detain that man!'

Geraghty started, as if suddenly awakened, but he did not move from the spot. Brown managed just a step or two before stopping.

The three of them stood watching as the Book Man opened the door and slipped away. Burke knew they should be pursuing him, but it seemed far more natural just to stand there and watch him go.

As the rebel leader moved out of sight, Burke willed himself to step forward. Reluctantly, his foot left the floor and he started toward the door. A moment later, the others followed.

They emerged from the church into the growing darkness. Outside, the square was empty.

The Book Man had been less than a minute ahead of them. But now the little village was deserted.

*

When Burke made his report, he did not mention what had happened in the church. Nor did the others ever speak of it.

He had more or less convinced himself that he had imagined the whole affair when, exactly one week later, the rebel army finally faced the French in open battle. Burke had yet to be assigned a new platoon, so he had been kept in the reserve, close enough to watch the battle, yet taking no part in it. It had seemed like some monstrous pageant, put on for his amusement. He had watched as the rebels had rushed the regiment's lines, a great black tide breaking against a line of red rocks. They had attacked with the passionate fearlessness of the dispossessed but the outcome had never really been in doubt. The disciplined ranks of the Regiment of Dillon had fired and reloaded, fired and reloaded, pouring death into the rebel ranks.

When it was over, one of his brother officers – a fellow from Dublin with all the self-importance of a man from the capital – told him that they had killed the Book Man.

'Huge, ugly fellow. You can see the corpse for yourself. Something to boast about when you get back to Ireland.'

Burke had no intention of ever going back to Ireland and, for a while, he resisted the idea of joining the crowds gawping at the corpse. In the end, though, his curiosity got the better of him.

The body had been strung up from a tree. The great head lolled forward, all dignity destroyed. The body was battered and broken and some of the officers made sport of throwing stones at it.

James stayed just long enough to be sure it was the same man and then he went back to the tent that was his temporary home. Once there, he proceeded to get himself very, very drunk.

He had hoped that the Book Man's death and the crushing of the revolt might bring an end to the fighting. But he had reckoned without the changes under way in France. The king had sent them to Saint-Domingue to strike down the rebellious slaves. Now, the king's power was waning. The revolutionaries were in the ascendant and suddenly the Rights of Man were more important than the property rights of colonialist planters.

The island was full of mulattos – the half-caste children of white masters and black slave girls. Many of these had been raised as free men and they and their descendants had become successful and, often, rich. They owned slaves themselves but, in the eyes of white society, they remained blacks. They might be free but they could not mix with white folk or have any of the privileges of citizenship. Now the Revolution sought to alter that. The planters – many of them from Spanish families that had settled here long before French rule – had so far simply ignored the new French laws. Now, though, things were to change.

Despatches were duly sent from Paris and made their way across the Atlantic. The generals passed their instructions to the majors, who commanded the captains and, in time, the lieutenants were told who they were to be fighting next.

Their response was noisy disbelief.

'It's madness. We've no sooner beaten the blacks than we are to turn on their masters!'

Captain Todd raised his hands for silence. He was a good man and he understood the lieutenants under his command.

'We're soldiers. We are here to fight. And we fight who we're told to fight. The blacks we have been fighting were slaves and rebels. But there are others here with black skins but the rights of free men. And the new government in Paris has asserted that they are entitled to the same rights and liberties as any other French citizen. Rights and liberties which the white planters here deny them. So we are told to fight the planters. And we will fight them with as much martial vigour as we fought the blacks.'

There was some muted cheering at this, but as the junior officers messed together that night, there were mutterings of discontent. Lieutenant Dunne – who traced his family tree back to the Lords of Ui Riagan — went so far as to argue that the order was unreasonable and unlawful. The French king, he insisted, could never have approved it. 'It's those revolutionaries with their nonsense about the Rights of Man. The blacks can have no rights. They're not fit for decent society and everyone knows it. It's in the blood. You can't make a hunter out of a carthorse. Breeding matters.'

Burke thought of his own breeding and how Dunne would despise the household he had grown up in. And then he thought of the efforts he had made to separate himself from his roots in Kilkenny; the books he had read, the attention he had paid to the accents and manners of the mess.

'Breeding matters, to be sure,' he said. 'But the meanest of men can aspire to be something more.'

Dunne laughed. 'Are you sure you are no Jacobin yourself, James?'

Burke heard others laugh with Dunne and he was quick to join in. He cursed himself inwardly for having spoken out without thinking. The talk moved on to safer topics and Burke poured himself another glass of wine and let the conversation wash over him.

Lieutenant Dunne's views were of no interest to the army. They fought the planters with the same disciplined enthusiasm as they had fought the slaves. Their enemies this time were no ragged desperados armed with machetes. The planters had muskets of their own and fought in the towns where the Regiment of Dillon could not use the tactics that made them such a formidable force in open country. Instead, James found himself leading his new platoon in desperate fights through the narrow streets of the island's settlements. Every window could hide a man ready to fire down into the platoon. Every house had to be broken into and searched.

It went on for months. In Europe, summer had long since turned to winter, but, in the Caribbean, they continued to fight in tropical heat. Burke marched his platoon from town to town and in every town there was more fighting and more of his dead to bury. He felt his life reduced to marching and fatigue and blood.

He no longer knew why he fought, but he fought well and reports spoke of him as 'a promising young officer'. Increasingly, though, as he lay to sleep, he would remember, as if it had been a dream, a giant Negro telling him, 'You have yet to find your path.'

*

On February 1st, 1793, France declared war on Great Britain. It was months before the news reached the Caribbean but the planters were not slow to recognise a potential new ally. They sent word to Jamaica that they would welcome British rule and, in summer, the British arrived.

The Regiment of Dillon had been fighting continuously for almost a year. They had fought slaves who wanted to be free. They had fought Europeans who wanted to see the blacks kept in their place. Now, a regiment composed entirely of Irish, English, and Scots was to fight the British army.

The Regiment of Dillon marched out to meet the British with its flags flying and the drums beating but their heart was not in it. In an hour, the battle was over. Three hundred were dead. When the British offered terms, the regiment was ordered to lay down its arms.

Lieutenant Burke thought he would feel shame but instead he felt nothing. He was numbed from months of warfare. His dreams, he thought, were shattered. There could surely be no chance of advancement through a military career now. And then came what seemed like a miracle. The British offered the regiment a choice: internment as prisoners of war or the opportunity to fight under the flag of King George. For Burke, the chance of a commission under King George was all he had wanted. Like so many officers in the Regiment of Dillon, Burke had been driven to the army of France because he could not afford the cost of a commission in the army of England. And now the fortunes of war had made him what he always wanted to be: an officer in His Britannic Majesty's army.

Chapter Two

Tilbury docks stank. They stank of the mud of the Essex marshes and the tar of old ropes and older timbers.

James Burke sniffed, curling his lip with disgust. It was something, he supposed, that his orders came directly from Colonel Taylor, *aide-de-camp* to the Duke of York and the man chiefly responsible for Britain's intelligence of the French. It had been Colonel Taylor who had noticed that one James Burke now owed his allegiance to His Majesty King George, and that he spoke fluent French and acceptable Spanish. So Burke had found himself seconded from his regiment for special duties. He was denied the opportunities for promotion that glory in the field might bring and, instead, sent scurrying around Europe in a succession of commissions that had risked his life and liberty but left him still a mere lieutenant at the age of thirty-three. He lacked the money to buy himself promotion. Without either hard cash or social connections, he still languished as a subaltern, while those who had fought alongside him in Saint-Domingue were already majors.

The bright blue of a girl's dress brought a flash of colour to the grey of the afternoon. Burke watched appreciatively as she made her way along the dockside. She paused, catching his eye with an enquiring glance, but he had business to attend to. Besides, he was an officer on His Majesty's service, and not one to consort with dockyard whores.

'She's a good-looking enough wench.'

Burke turned to his companion.

'William Brown, you are incorrigible. Does rank mean nothing to you?'

Brown grinned up at him. It was over ten years since they had faced Boukman together. Though they never spoke of it, Brown and his lieutenant shared a bond even closer than that of most men who had fought alongside each other for so long. Burke might sometimes stand on his dignity with others, but he and Brown shared the relaxed familiarity of those who had faced death together and trusted each other with their lives.

As they mounted the gangplank, which bounced disconcertingly with their tread, Burke was confident that no one watching would have seen anything but what they were supposed to see: a gentleman and his servant. Burke was (as seemed somehow only proper) the taller of the two by several inches, a difference accentuated by the height of his beaver hat. His dark hair was carefully barbered and his neck was wrapped in a black silk stock of the latest fashion. William followed after, rather as a ship's boat might bob in the wake of an elegant yacht. He was decently but plainly fitted out with a brown coat and trousers over his military pattern boots. The boots, together with the style of his hair – pulled back from his forehead and lacking only the regulation pigtail – gave away the fact that he had recently been in the army, but people would assume that the master must have used his influence to obtain the release of a valued servant from the forces of the Crown.

At the ship's rail, a steward, resplendent in a jacket dripping with gold braid, stepped forward to greet Mr Burke. He snapped his fingers for a cabin boy – barefooted but smart in his blue smock – to lead the gentleman forward, while Brown was despatched to his accommodation in steerage quarters. Burke followed his guide, his long strides easily keeping pace with the boy, while his deceptively lazy gaze took in the details of the scene around him: the crew standing by at their stations on the deck or on the ratlines, ready to loose the sails; the Captain on the low quarterdeck; the gentlemen in a nervous huddle toward the bows, and the servants making their way uncertainly to their quarters aft.

Burke's eye was caught by a figure in a long, dark coat. The man was huddled against the rail, staring gloomily across the murky waters of the Thames.

'It's all right, lad. Make sure my man knows which my cabin is. I'll stay on deck a while.' He slipped a coin into the boy's hand and moved toward the gloomy passenger who had caught his attention. 'Mr O'Gorman.'

The man started as if he had been struck, before turning with a visible effort of self-control.

Burke proffered his hand. 'I recognised you from your description.'

Indeed, the man before him matched Colonel Taylor's description perfectly. 'Shortish, stoutish, red-faced, brownish hair – what there is of it. Wears a rather vulgar gold ring on his left hand.' It was the ring Burke had noticed first. Together with the quality of his coat, and the fine leather of his boots, his appearance marked him as wealthy but his crumpled cravat suggested, to Burke's eyes, that he was not really a gentleman.

O'Gorman hesitated for a moment. Then, as if suddenly aware of the hand, took it and shook it with a desperate compensatory fervour.

Burke extricated his hand. 'We should talk, Mr O'Gorman.'

O'Gorman opened his mouth to reply, but was cut off before he could speak.

'In private, would be best. You can show me our cabin. We can talk there.'

O'Gorman gave a half-shrug of resignation and led the way forward and through the door that led to the passenger accommodation. Burke followed, sensing the other's resentment. O'Gorman had earned his wealth in business and was more used to giving orders than to taking them.

O'Gorman opened the third door leading off to the right of the narrow companionway. Burke moved past him and entered the cabin without waiting for an invitation. His mission depended on O'Gorman's unquestioning cooperation and Burke intended to impose his authority as quickly and completely as he could.

'You have had word of my coming.'

O'Gorman barely had time to nod before Burke was speaking again.

'We are new business partners, you and I. We travel together, sharing this cabin and you initiate me into the secrets of commerce with the viceroyalty of La Plata.'

'I understand all this.' O'Gorman was angry and his Irish brogue, distinct at the best of times, grew broader. 'But I protest –'

Burke cut him off with a gesture.

'Save your breath. We neither of us chose our situation and we must simply make the best of it. We are a nation at war and I am about His Majesty's business. You, sir, will do all in your power to assist me. If you do not, you may expect the excise to busy themselves with every cargo you deliver. And I am told they can be very clumsy in the handling of your goods.'

Both men had remained standing, despite the low ceiling. Now, though, O'Gorman sat himself down. He made to pull his chair up to the table that filled most of the space in the cabin, but it was screwed to the floor, a precaution against foul weather that left the merchant tugging impotently at his seat while Burke gazed sardonically down at him.

O'Gorman struggled silently with the furniture for a few seconds before collapsing back in his chair. 'Very well.' He sounded suddenly weary. 'Tell me what you want of me.'

Burke took the other chair and leaned forward toward O'Gorman. He sat silently, examining the other's features. He had no reason to like the man. O'Gorman was a merchant and not a gentleman. He lacked finesse and was inclined to bluster. His Irishness, too, counted against him. Burke had put Kilkenny firmly behind him and his accent now bore no trace of his origins. But if his mission were to succeed, O'Gorman must be won over.

Burke forced a smile and leaned confidentially toward his fellow passenger. 'I want you to introduce me into the merchant community in Buenos Aires.'

O'Gorman gave a puzzled frown. 'But why is that a concern of His Majesty's Government?'

Burke reached into his pocket and tossed a coin onto the table. It fell heavily, displaying the Spanish coat of arms.

'A Spanish dollar. An ounce of solid silver. Whoever controls the source of that silver controls a large part of the wealth of the world. And it is our belief that Napoleon has his eyes on it.'

O'Gorman picked up the coin and weighed it in his palm, almost absent-mindedly: 'It comes from Upper Peru. Nowhere near Buenos Aires.'

'But the mines are governed from Buenos Aires. The silver is shipped through Buenos Aires. Good God, man, the viceroyalty of Río de la Plata is run from Buenos Aires, and governs half of South America. It's the key to control of the Spanish mines.'

O'Gorman looked again at the coin and up at the young officer opposite him.

'You think that the British can take Buenos Aires before the French do?'

Burke smiled.

'I'm sure they can. My job is to find out the best way to do it.'

*

James Burke had hoped that the voyage, tedious and uncomfortable as it was almost certain to be, would at least offer no immediate hazards beyond those naturally associated with wind and wave. William's arrival at his cabin put an end to that.

William had brought a small sea chest with the essentials required for Burke's comfort on the voyage. Good servant that he was, he insisted on stowing away as much as possible in the limited space available. As he pulled drawers from under the bunks, or opened the cupboards built into the walls, he seemed to be for ever tripping over O'Gorman's feet or clumsily striking him with an elbow, apologising all the time with evident sincerity. O'Gorman bore with it for a while but Burke could see his temper about to break.

'Why don't you take yourself onto the deck, Mr O'Gorman?' he suggested, placatingly. 'It will be your chance to see the last of the Thames.'

O'Gorman's jaw clenched and, for a moment, Burke thought he was about to protest that he should not be forced from his cabin to allow a servant to go about his business. Burke held O'Gorman's eyes in a steady gaze as the merchant opened his mouth to speak and then, as if thinking better of it, rose from his seat, and without a word left the cabin.

Burke and William listened to his footsteps moving down the companionway and then the clatter of his toecaps on the steps that led to the deck.

'I thought he'd never go,' said William.

'You were hardly subtle. I hope whatever you're going to tell me is important. O'Gorman must think I have the worst-trained servant on the ship.'

'Helswig is on board.'

Burke raised an eyebrow. 'Well done, William. That certainly is important. Where did you see him?'

'He's lodged aft with me and all the others. We're packed in pretty close up there but I thought I should just take a look around in case I saw any familiar faces. It can't be just Colonel Taylor that's interested in Buenos Aires. I didn't expect to see Helswig, though.'

'No, that is an unpleasant surprise. It suggests that the opposition is showing at least as much interest in the River Plate as we are. Did he see you?'

William shook his head. 'I just caught a glimpse of him the once and then made sure to keep out of the way. But where there's Helswig, there'll be the Dutchman. And he'll be travelling up front with you. There's no chance of you avoiding him for long.'

Burke did not reply for several seconds but then he spoke decisively. 'Either the Dutchman is deliberately following us or it is a most unfortunate coincidence. In either case, his presence endangers our mission. If he is not currently in the pay of Spain, he will sell the Spanish his services as soon as he is able – and he will identify me as a British agent.' He allowed a spasm of distaste to pass across his face. 'I am afraid it is necessary that both men meet with an accident. And the sooner, the better. No one knows them yet. You said yourself that there's a mass of people there and they will be a while getting familiar with their companions. If Helswig goes over the side now, it's only the Dutchman who will notice.'

Burke drew a watch from his pocket. 'It's barely noon as yet. My guess is that the Dutchman will leave his man to his own devices until he changes for dinner. Then he will want help with his toilet.

When you came aft, you crossed the main deck. Is there any connection below decks between your quarters and the upper class cabins?'

'There's one door, sir, but it's kept locked.'

'Good. Then Helswig is easily disposed of. He will have to cross the deck to serve his master and when he does, we will put him overboard.'

'Won't he be seen, sir?'

Burke opened the cabin door and let William into the companionway. He gestured up to where thick panes of glass admitted light from the deck above.

'Those windows, William, are mounted in a structure that stands a good two feet clear of the deck and there,' – he gestured toward the far end of the corridor – 'are stairs rising either side to allow us the convenience of an alternative exit. Now, if you see someone on deck passing that door and then you see them gone, what do you think? Why, that they have descended the ladder and vanished below. It is only if you were to see an actual attack that you would consider the possibility that they would have taken the other direction. The Thames is a noble river but no one would expect a person aboard a snug little craft like this to be stepping over the side.'

'And how can you be sure no one will be looking, sir?'

'Ah, well, William. That's rather where you come in.'

Burke outlined his plan, which was brutally simple.

William nodded admiringly. 'That'll work – mainly because no one will miss him, 'cept the Dutchman. Do we deal with him the same way?'

'Good heavens, no! The upper-class passengers dine with the officers and he would be certain to be missed. It has to look like an accident. We can't have people enquiring into murder on a vessel this size. And a duel would draw too much attention.'

'There's always poison, sir.'

'Hmm.' Burke pursed his lips in thought. 'Tricky to get him to take it between now and dinner. And it has to look natural enough not to excite suspicion but not resemble an illness that would lead to the quarantining of the vessel.'

Burke stepped toward the porthole and looked out at the grey waters. Gradually he began to smile.

'William, I think I have it. I can dispose of the Dutchman and the Captain himself will assist me in covering up the deed. Do we carry the normal complement of floozies aboard?'

William grinned: 'Twice as many as you would expect, sir. We're bound for Buenos Aires. They say there's a hundred men there for every woman and any working girl who can raise the passage money sees her chance to make a fortune.'

'Good. Then here's what we shall do . . .'

*

Burke's approach to the Captain was deceptively casual.

'Some people say that a voyage such as this can be tedious but I am sure I will find the experience most enjoyable – especially as I am sure I saw an old acquaintance on deck earlier. A Dutch fellow, a little stout but still an eye for the ladies! I look forward to renewing our acquaintance. Do you know which is his cabin?'

'Mr van Harwick? Two toward the stern from your own, sir. But I'm surprised you saw him on deck. He took himself directly to his cabin and asked not to be disturbed.'

'Thank you, Captain. If that is the case, I shall wait before I make myself known to him. Who else do we have travelling with us?'

The Captain rattled off the names of the half dozen or so other passengers travelling in the cabins amidships. He knew better than to bother Mr Burke with any information about the mass of humanity still settling themselves in the stern dormitory. Back in steerage, though, William was, at that moment, making an unusual but lucrative offer to a young lady whose innocent face concealed an admirably calculating approach to matters of business.

Twenty minutes later, Burke was knocking on the Dutchman's door. 'Mr van Harwick,' he called, although he had always known the man by another name. In fact, he had lost count of the names the Dutchman used, although his valet was always Helswig. Burke made a mental note that William should be rechristened for their next mission.

'Mr van Harwick, I have a message from the Captain.'

He heard the sound of the bolt being drawn and pushed hard at the door. In an instant he was in the cabin while the Dutchman was staggering back, off balance.

William had rifled the stores to find a stout bag. Now Burke brought it down over the Dutchman's head. Taken unawares, and his shouts muffled by the bag, the Dutchman struck out blindly. Burke wrapped his arms around his victim and lifted him bodily onto the single bed in the room. Burke was the taller and fitter of the two, and the one-sided struggle left him with time to notice (and resent) that the Spanish spy had a large cabin to himself, while he shared a smaller one with O'Gorman. But there were disadvantages to a private cabin. The greatest of which was that, being private, it was a solitary place to die.

Burke reached for the pillow and brought it firmly down across the Dutchman's face. He pushed hard but not too hard – he had to be sure not to break the man's nose.

As his struggles subsided, Burke cautiously removed the sack. Van Harwick was still breathing – just. Now Burke put on a pair of leather gloves and clamped the mouth shut, while pinching the nose. He held him gently but firmly for several minutes until he was certain that he was dead.

There was a triple knock at the door. Burke opened it and William entered quickly, ushering in a girl of about eighteen whose dark hair was worn loose. The hair and a certain liveliness of expression gave away her line of business but she was simply dressed and, if the neckline was somewhat lower than fashion dictated, it was still respectable. Her sleeves were short, and, as she came into the cabin, it was clear that she wore a minimum of underclothing. She moved to the bed and started to undress the body with an expertise that suggested that, if she had never attended to the dead before, she had plenty of experience with the dead drunk.

'You can leave him to me,' she said over her shoulder, her hands still busy removing clothing. 'Just put the guinea on his dressing table.'

Burke bowed slightly, acknowledging her professional expertise and indifference to the death of England's enemies.

'William,' he muttered as they left the cabin, 'while our country produces young women like that, we have nothing to fear for the future.'

*

Disposing of Helswig was messier but more straightforward.

The Essex marshes were a smudge on the horizon when, an hour before dinner, he appeared from his quarters deep in the stern. As he started along the starboard side of the deck, toward the gentlemen's cabins, O'Gorman, obedient to the orders that Burke had given him just thirty minutes before, made his way to where William was lounging by the rail on the opposite side of the vessel. As Helswig passed one side of the superstructure, on the other O'Gorman started berating William about the condition he had left the cabin in.

O'Gorman was not a natural actor but the embarrassment he felt playing out this charade made him even louder and more aggressive than he would have been had he been truly angry. The few people on deck turned to enjoy the entertaining sight of a servant being put firmly in his place.

Meanwhile, unobserved, Helswig approached the ladder to be met by Burke hurtling himself upward. He seized his victim at the waist and simply kept moving forward. Helswig was half-pushed, half-carried across the few feet of decking between the doorway and edge of the ship.

The ship's rail hit Helswig around the kidneys and he toppled backwards before he even knew where he was. By the time he drew breath to scream, he was already in the water.

The *Rochester* sailed on, oblivious to the struggles of the man drowning in its wake.

*

When Mr van Harwick failed to materialise at dinner, a steward was sent to his cabin. There he found a weeping girl still trying to revive the half-naked passenger.

A glass of brandy in the Captain's private quarters elicited the information that van Harwick had accosted the girl before he boarded and instructed her to come to his room. He had given her sixpence to spend the afternoon with him.

Despite the brandy, she blushed as she explained. 'He was a very active man for his age, sir, and he seemed to be determined to exert himself to the fullest and then suddenly he cried out and he collapsed and at first I thought nothing of it, for some gentlemen are taken like that, but then . . .' and she cried prettily, and the Captain was moved to pat her on the hand, for all that she was a whore, and he promised that it would be taken care of.

And it was. The ship's doctor could see no signs of violence on the body and the Captain agreed that a quiet service early in the morning was for the best. The only passenger who had apparently met the man was Mr Burke and the Captain explained to him that his acquaintance had been taken unwell and died shortly after boarding.

'I am assured by our doctor that it was the result of some excitement – probably the thrill of starting for a new life in the Americas. I fear he was not a young man.'

It was, agreed Mr Burke, very sad indeed. 'I will attend the service, if I may, Captain. He should have someone there to mourn him who had known him in life, if only as a passing acquaintance. I feel it is my duty.'

So James Burke stood on the deck of the *Rochester* as the sun rose over the horizon and watched as they consigned the Dutchman's body to the deep.

No one asked about the servant.

'I'll say this for Helswig,' observed William, later. 'He was devoted to the Dutchman. Now they're both in the same grave, so to speak. You know, in a funny sort of way, I think it's what he would have wanted.'

*

After the stir of the funeral, life on board settled to a steady rhythm. The world was governed by the ringing of a bell that hung from its own gibbet on the mainmast. It struck the watches day and night as the ship made slow but steady progress westward.

James Burke watched with detached amusement as the other gentlemen on board struggled to find ways to while away the monotony of the voyage. He politely declined invitations to join them at cards and he did not seek to improve his mind by spending hours in his cabin reading. Instead he occupied himself with the first stage of his mission: winning over Mr O'Gorman.

The merchant had responded badly to the killing of the Dutchman. (Burke recoiled from the word 'murder'.) It was clear to Burke that the man was not naturally cut out for a life of espionage. Indeed, in the early days of the voyage, it seemed that barely an hour went by without him complaining that Burke had been foisted on him, and that he did not intend to involve himself with the spy's sordid activities. Burke allowed him a day or two to calm his nerves and then set out to charm him into enthusiastic support. He asked O'Gorman his views on the progress of the war, and admired the perspicacity of the merchant's opinions, however ill-informed he privately considered them to be. He scattered his own comments liberally with the names of those of His Majesty's counsellors with whom his own work had brought him into contact. He hinted at the missions that he had already conducted on behalf of the government, and, if he made it all sound a little more thrilling than it may really have been, he felt the embellishment to be in a good cause.

Gradually, O'Gorman thawed. His initial taciturn manner gave way to a garrulousness that was just as much a product of his nerves, but Burke felt that he was making progress. To his surprise, he found he was quite coming to like the man. They would take the air together, Burke strolling along the deck with his easy, lazy stride, while the merchant paced with nervous energy.

At first, O'Gorman's monologues (for Burke seldom found himself able to get a word in edgeways) were about the iniquities of governments in general and of Pitt's government in particular. He damned the French for supporting Napoleon and the British for going to war against him. 'All I ask,' he said, 'is for honest merchants to be left to go about their business. Is that so very unreasonable?'

Burke would nod and sympathise and gently turned the conversation away from the politics of Europe and toward the situation in Buenos Aires.

'Well, officially we're ruled by Spain, of course. But the Spanish made their capital in the south over at Lima. I suppose it's because all they really care about is the silver and the silver's mostly that side of the country. But Lima's the other side of the Andes, so we generally manage our own affairs in Buenos Aires.'

'And you expect no trouble once Spain and England are at war? With Napoleon taking over half of Europe, it's only a matter of time.'

O'Gorman would forget his nerves as he lectured Burke. 'There are almost as many English and Italians – and Irishmen too – trading in Buenos Aires as there are Spanish, let alone French. None of us care what's going on in Europe so long as we make our money.'

'But Spain holds a monopoly on trade.'

The merchant waved his arm in a sweeping gesture that encompassed the whole of the ship. 'Where do you think we sailed from?'

'London, of course.'

O'Gorman grinned and it seemed to Burke that the older man was enjoying the opportunity to demonstrate that in matters of trade he was the master and Burke a mere apprentice.

'You think so? In fact, the *Rochester* was in Cadiz before she sailed to London. So technically, all her cargo was shipped to Spain. Then it was exported from Spain to London.'

'But if Spain were at war with England?'

'Then we will have to ship from Spain to a neutral country and then on to London. We're not living in the eighteenth century now. The world is about trade and war is an inconvenience that we must negotiate our path around.'

Burke remembered why he had disliked O'Gorman so much on first meeting. Although he wore no uniform, Burke was a soldier, answerable to Colonel Taylor at the War Office. All across Europe, other soldiers – English, French, and, by now, half a dozen other nations – were fighting and dying in a convulsion that was reshaping the continent. Yet, to O'Gorman, it was all just a matter of 'inconvenience'. Burke looked at him and, for a moment, saw a smug face that reminded him of the Saint-Domingue planters. They had been drunken, arrogant louts, happy enough to have the army put down the slave revolt but revolting in their turn when they saw a danger of losing their fat profits. Merchants, he was sure, cared for nothing but their gold. He despised them and he despised the grasping commercialism that they represented. At that instant, he would cheerfully have choked O'Gorman and flung his body over the side. But the discipline of his own profession came to his aid and he forced a smile. He was, he had to remember, a spy first and a soldier after. O'Gorman was essential to his mission and O'Gorman was to be placated.

'Do the goods suffer by exposure to the salt winds in all this travelling to and fro?'

O'Gorman returned Burke's smile and assured him that they did not suffer in the least. For the next hour, he explained everything anyone could want to know about the storage and handling of leather goods at sea. Burke let the words wash over him. He had learned all he needed about shipping. What mattered now was to convert O'Gorman's grudging acceptance of his position into a positive enthusiasm to aid the British Crown. Flattery, Burke judged, was the best way to achieve that end. So he concentrated on nodding and smiling and, as the weeks passed, he felt O'Gorman relax. By the end of a month, he was even heard protesting to a fellow passenger that the French could be very devil and that it was time something was done to stop them.

The weather grew warmer as they moved southward. They crossed the line with great ceremony and Burke submitted to the ritual dousing at the court of King Neptune. O'Gorman, as a regular voyager across the Equator was dubbed a 'shell-back' and took a wicked delight in lathering Burke with the mix of soap and slops that Neptune offered as shaving cream. For Burke, the whole affair was less traumatic than he had expected. It was only when a bruised and battered William Brown waited on him that evening that he realised the gentlemen passengers had been spared the full ceremony. William, on the other hand, had endured pelting with rotten vegetables and a 'shaving cream' that included tar and the scrapings of the ship's chicken coop.

'Bear up!' said James. 'Think of England. You've suffered for your country.'

'That's true enough.' William's face split into an evil grin. 'And the fellow who dragged me before Neptune has suffered for the ocean god. I had a word with him afterwards and he'll be walking funny for a while.'

Burke wondered briefly if there might be any repercussions from his valet's behaviour but it appeared that steerage was a law unto itself. Brawls associated with the crossing the line ceremony were not uncommon and the ship's officers were careful to ignore them. Amongst the gentleman passengers, of course, there was no violence associated with the ritual. Indeed, Burke noticed that O'Gorman seemed to have worked out the last of his resentment as he wielded the razor. Burke felt that he had quite won him over. Although the merchant had by now shared all he could about trading in Buenos Aires, the two of them would walk the deck each morning in companionable silence.

At first, Burke enjoyed the opportunity to relax. It took only a few days, though, for him to become impatient. He was ready to start his mission. In Buenos Aires, he would be accepted as an honest merchant. O'Gorman would give him the help he needed, providing a base to operate from and vouching for his being no more than he appeared to be. Now he was anxious to start work. He would be landing again in the New World, the world where he had met the Book Man and been assured that Destiny had a place for him. Perhaps here, in Spanish South America, he might find his path – a path that would lead him to the promotion that had eluded him for so long.

Nine weeks out from Tilbury, his morning promenade was interrupted by a cry of 'Land, ho!' from the crow's nest. He abandoned O'Gorman with indecent haste and rushed to the cabin to retrieve the small but powerful telescope William had unpacked for him. Minutes later, he was at the rail, scanning the horizon for a sight of the land that was to be his home for the foreseeable future.

At first, the coast was invisible from the deck – more than a hundred feet below the lookout – but, as the *Rochester* moved westward with the tide, a smudge appeared between sea and sky. Burke leaned across the rail, as if the few inches gained would let him see the land more clearly, and sighed with impatience as the view through his glass remained a blur. At last, the image took on shape and Burke could see the green of the jungle growing down to a narrow strip of beach that fringed the shore. It reminded him of Saint-Domingue and he seemed to hear the voice of the Book Man: 'Your actions will help to bring forth a nation.'

Carried away with the excitement of that first glimpse of South America, Burke allowed himself, just for a moment, to imagine that he might have some part to play in that continent's history. The days that followed, however, convinced him that he would be a fool to think he could have any impact on a place so vast. For a week, they eased their way along the coast of Brazil. In the lee of the land, the winds were light and the crew were kept busy on the ropes, straining the sails to catch any whisper of a breeze. Even allowing for their slow progress, the land that they had reached was vast beyond imagination. Day followed day as they passed apparently endless beaches, and always, beyond them, the impenetrable green of the jungle.

Burke had William bring an easel onto the deck. A quantity of watercolour paints emerged from the hold and Burke would stand for hours, brush in hand, recording the patterns of light on the water. He was, as with all things he set his mind to, a competent artist, and passengers and crew grew used to seeing him in the throes of creation.

The *Rochester* stopped briefly at Rio de Janeiro to take on food and water before sailing on to Monte Video at the mouth of the

Plate. As they arrived at the first Spanish town they had seen in the New World, Burke was on deck with the dawn. When his fellow passengers grouped round his easel to admire his efforts, he explained that he had wanted to catch the first rays of sunlight glinting on the walls of the city. Several gentlemen commented on the way that he had, indeed, caught the special quality of the light sparkling off the ocean. ('Effervescent,' declared one bewhiskered old buffer and Burke smiled politely, although all the word meant to him was mineral water.) None of his admirers noticed that, masterfully as he had captured the colour of the sky, the painting was otherwise notable mainly for the detail it provided of the defences.

Leaving Monte Video, Burke saw the water change from the blue-green of the Atlantic to the silt-laden dirty brown of the estuary of the Plate. The change in the colour of the water was the only way to see that they had moved from the open ocean, for the far shore of the river was so distant that it was invisible from the deck. The *Rochester* struggled against a wind that had swung westerly and was now trying to push them back out to sea. Only after several hours as the ship tacked to and fro, fighting not just the wind but the current, was Burke able to distinguish a strip of land on the far horizon. O'Gorman was standing beside him on the deck and Burke turned to him and smiled.

'You're nearly home, Mr O'Gorman.'

'Not so nearly as all that. It will take us another day or so to get to Ensenada.'

'Ensenada?'

'Where we take on the pilot.'

Burke nodded. He should have realised that the mud would mean uncertain shoals in the approach to Buenos Aires and the Spanish made sure that the English had no reliable charts. They would need a pilot for the end of their journey.

The following afternoon the *Rochester* dropped anchor about half a mile from the shore. Through his glass Burke saw what looked like a poor fishing village – little more than a collection of wooden shacks – clustered around a fine edifice of white stone with a gilded campanile. The Captain called down from the aft deck: 'I see you're admiring the harbour office, Mr Burke. Would you like to meet the pilot when he comes aboard?'

Burke could see the pilot climbing into a boat that bobbed at the end of the harbour office's own jetty. Even at this distance, the brilliance of the man's gold braid was dazzling.

'I'd be delighted, Captain.'

Burke joined the Captain as the pilot boarded. In the exchange of greetings between the three of them, someone suggested that Burke might sketch the pilot and the pilot, shrugging with an affectation of modesty that sat badly with his grandiose uniform, said that he had no objection. So it was that Burke stood sketching throughout the approach to Buenos Aires, and if his scribbles included detailed notes of the pilot's directions and the shouts of the leadsman as he called the depth of the channel, those notes were concealed in the various studies he made of the details of the pilot's uniform and the outlines of the scene before him.

That night they lay to. As the sun rose the next morning, they sailed the last few miles to Buenos Aires – the City of Good Winds in the place that some called the Land of Silver, Argentina.

Burke was, again, early on deck. O'Gorman had told him so much about this city. It was rich, it was splendid. It was, James had convinced himself, a suitable stage on which he could at last play a role that would get him noticed.

As he looked over the brown waters of the Plate to the miserable dwellings on the shore, he felt his heart sink. The buildings here were shacks, no better than those at Ensenada. And, even where he stood on the *Rochester,* the place stank. There was no clear shoreline. The silt dumped by the River Plate meant that water and land merged into hundreds of yards of mudflats, filled with the garbage of the city, now just a few miles upstream.

As the *Rochester* eased itself along the channels through the shallows, the shacks on the shore (Burke could not think of it as a riverbank) grew larger and less dilapidated. Here and there were substantial buildings of brick or stone. Now, in the distance, Burke began to see the domes and spires of churches standing tall on the horizon. His military eye was also quick to notice the fort jutting from the shore, its batteries of cannon commanding the approach.

The *Rochester* hove to almost opposite the fort, where the buildings were most impressive. The September sun shone on the pale stone of the houses and the towers of the churches. Burke was surprised to see that, although generally Spanish in style, most of the buildings were not white but ranged from pink to deep red. O'Gorman had emerged on deck and stood beside him, looking over the city with a proprietorial eye and Burke turned to him to remark on the colour of the buildings.

'I see your painters favour a roseate hue.'

O'Gorman's face creased with a puzzled frown, which cleared as he realised what Burke was talking about.

'The red? No that's not painters. They mix the plaster with bull's blood, for there's more of it than we can make any other use of, and it does make excellent plaster.'

The mud made it impossible for ships to dock and a fleet of rowing boats was already pulling out toward them to take off cargo and crew. Ashore, a small crowd was gathering along the water's edge, the women holding their skirts high to avoid the filth. There was no wharf but a few piers projected from a track that seemed to have been made simply by throwing rocks and rubble onto the foreshore. Carts manoeuvred unsteadily along the rough surface: the noise of iron-rimmed wheels scraping across the rubble setting Burke's teeth on edge. Aboard, the whores were lining the ship's rails and the shouts of the stevedores rowing toward them suggested that they were already setting their price. Aloft, some of the crew were reefing the sails, while on deck rope ladders were being lowered to allow the passengers to make their uncertain way to the boats below. Merchants were shouting for the hold to be opened and servants were pushing and jostling to retrieve their masters' possessions.

Burke and O'Gorman pushed their way through the crowd of steerage passengers to be amongst the first rowed ashore. William was to follow on with the baggage.

Burke's initial impression of Buenos Aires was of the stink of mud. The smell surrounded them as they were rowed to the ramshackle pier, but then he was scrambling ashore and suddenly there were more important things to notice than the smell. All of his attention was concentrated on the woman he saw standing on the rough planking, apparently waiting for someone on board the *Rochester*.

The first thing he noticed about her was her hair. Thick and black, it tumbled out from the simple sunbonnet she was wearing, framing a face almost perfectly oval. As he watched her, she turned and noticed him, dark eyes appraising him, and then, to his astonishment, O'Gorman strode toward her and, with a proprietorial air, took her hand and led her toward forward.

'Mr Burke, may I present my wife, Ana.'

Burke took her hand and raised it to his lips. 'Mrs O'Gorman, I'm delighted to make your acquaintance.'

'And I yours. Mr O'Gorman wrote from England to say that he was to bring a guest, but he was able to tell me no more. For the past week I've been wondering who it could be. And now, here you are.'

She looked at him quizzically, her head tilted slightly to one side. She was obviously waiting to learn more about her unexpected house guest, but Burke did not judge this the time or place to explain himself. 'I am new to Buenos Aires and a mutual friend asked your husband if he could, most kindly, provide me with accommodation while I acquainted myself with the city.'

'Indeed.' Ana O'Gorman was clearly unconvinced. 'A man of mystery. Well, you will have plenty of opportunity to tell me all about yourself as we walk home. It seemed pointless to drive down in the chaise, as there would be three of us, and my husband,' (she smiled at Burke, as if enrolling him in some long-running domestic dispute) 'objects to the expense of a carriage.'

She had a voice, Burke thought, that sounded as if it were on the verge of laughter. Soft and deep, it had the merest trace of an Irish lilt.

'We do well enough.' Her husband's brogue seemed even stronger in comparison to hers. 'We don't need the show of a carriage.'

O'Gorman led them away from the water and into the town. Once off the filth of the foreshore, the soldier in Burke admired the road, which was well paved and arrow-straight.

It took only a few minutes for them to arrive at O'Gorman's house, for he had business on the water often enough not to want to live too far away. It was immediately apparent that the O'Gormans did indeed do 'well enough'. Most of the buildings they had passed had been two floors high, with narrow windows and high doors the only breaks in their plain facades. O'Gorman's house stood three storeys high, with lamps either side of the grand entrance, and elaborately carved panels on the doors. On the higher floors, wrought-iron balconies stood in front of windows open to catch the whisper of a breeze. It was a home that reflected O'Gorman's standing in the British community. As a young man, Burke had dreamed of living in a house that gave every visitor visible proof of the owner's prosperity, but his father had failed at every commercial enterprise that he had ever attempted and their home had born witness to his wretchedness. O'Gorman might not be a gentleman but this house showed that he was successful and rich and, therefore, not totally to be despised.

The place was built around a central courtyard, the rooms leading off it through French windows. The pattern was repeated on the upper floors, where an interior balcony provided access to the bedrooms.

O'Gorman's wealth was reflected in the second courtyard leading from the first, with a kitchen and laundry room on the ground floor and a floor of servants' bedrooms above. It was here that Burke sought out William on the afternoon of their arrival. He had explained to O'Gorman that his valet would have to have his own room. O'Gorman had objected, on the grounds that it was bound to annoy the other servants, who could expect no such luxury of privacy, but, as far as Burke was concerned, it was essential that William could come and go without notice, so a separate room had to be found. The arrangement also allowed Burke somewhere private to store materials he did not want viewed by strangers. It was an irony of living with another man's staff that the servants' quarters were the only place where you were safe from the prying eyes of the servants themselves. Burke could never lock the maids out of his own room but William could defend his quarters from intrusion as fiercely as he wished.

Burke looked about him. Beside the bed, there was a wardrobe – not for the servant's clothes but so that he could store his master's garments. A washstand with a bowl and a jug were available for grooming and there was even a small mirror tacked to the wall.

'They've done you proud, William.'

It was unusual for a gentleman to explore the servants' quarters but it was reasonable that he might want to be reassured as to the safe arrival of his baggage, and the room provided a private spot for their first council of war. Burke found that he preferred such meetings in a room like this rather than in his own splendid quarters. Somehow, he felt more relaxed here.

'We'll need identities. I'm Mr Burke to O'Gorman and, as he is bound to let slip my name to the English community, I'd best be Mr Burke to all of them. But I'll be a Frenchman to the French. Do you have the visiting cards?'

'I do, sir. There's two Frenchmen available – a count to impress those who favour the old regime and Victor Bergotte for those who prefer their aristocrats decapitated. If you want another alias, we have our Prussian – Captain Otto Witz. He's been a useful gentleman before. Then there's –'

Burke cut him short with a wave of his hand.

'I am sure that Captain Witz will do for the Spaniards and Victor Bergotte for the French. You, I think had best be yourself, at least for now. But you should show some disaffection with your lot. The odd complaint, a bit of surliness. I want you to be able to travel freely among the lower orders and a suggestion of rebellious spirit might help.'

'It will be a pleasure, sir.'

'Hmm. So long as it's not too great a pleasure, William. I don't want your sergeant complaining that I have got you into bad habits.'

'I trust Sergeant Geraghty will never have cause for complaint, sir.'

Burke looked around the room once again.

'Well, you seem settled and I'm sure my quarters will offer everything except security, so we'll to business. I think I'd best start slowly. O'Gorman should give me an *entrée* to what passes for Society amongst the merchants and I must try to build on any acquaintance I may form amongst them. In time, I should acquire some useful connections and then we shall see what is really happening here at the end of the world. Meanwhile, your position as a servant should give you ready access to the working people. Keep your eyes open and let me know if there is anything I should be aware of: rumblings of revolt; secret societies; radical infiltration. If the French have infected this country with their revolutionary pox, I want to know.'

William nodded.

'If anything's going on, I'll hear about it, sir. Servants gossip.'

'Just so, William. And, with any luck, so do their masters. Anyway, tonight I dine with O'Gorman and the lovely Ana. I hope she gossips. She looks the sort who might. In any case, I look forward to a conversation that does not revolve around the price of leather.'

'Very well, sir. I will come to your room before dinner to assist with your dressing but I take it my services are not required at the meal itself.'

'You are, as ever, correct in your assumption, William. I will dazzle the mistress, leaving you, I hope, to astonish the maid – or anyone else you can make an impression on.'

Burke stretched and yawned. 'If I am to impress my hostess, I think I had best rest and bathe: I am sure everything about me smells of salt water.'

*

Burke joined his host in his sitting room for drinks before dinner. O'Gorman had wanted to make the arrival of his visitor an excuse for a gathering of English expatriates around his table, but Burke had impressed on him that he wanted his stay to be as discreet as possible and had eventually prevailed upon him to make it a family meal with just Ana present. Ana, though, was determined to make an impression at the first meal with her new houseguest, so the men were kept waiting while she prepared her entrance. They passed the time sipping sherry that Burke thought remarkably poor for a Spanish province. They had exhausted most of the possible topics of conversation on the voyage, so the two men sat silent awhile. Burke took the opportunity to look around the room, which he judged and found wanting. It confirmed his suspicions that O'Gorman was a man with plenty of money but very little taste. The furnishings, he decided, were unfashionably substantial and the carpet hideous. The heavy velvet drapes were acceptable but they hung untidily. The servants, Burke decided, were unreliable.

When Ana made her entrance, though, he found nothing to complain about at all. Her gown was not of the very latest style but the embroidery – flowers and leaves intertwined across the whole of the fabric – was exquisite and the low cut, trimmed about with lace in a way that no longer found favour in London, showed off her breasts to a degree that was more than acceptable.

Ana's arrival, Burke decided, made the evening a much more entertaining prospect. As they entered a dining room where the table was scarcely visible for the serving dishes crowded upon it, he resolved that he would enjoy his meal.

Burke was confident that O'Gorman would dine well, but he was not prepared for the sheer quantity of food laid before him. First came a meat course – but it resembled no meat course that he had ever seen before. Steaks that would barely fit on the chinaware (itself of the best quality) contended for pride of place with a huge sirloin, glistening in the centre of the table. Then there were meat pies and pastry parcels packed with mince, rack of lamb, tongue, and a ham.

After almost three months of ship's rations, Burke had no need to feign enthusiasm as he sampled dish after dish but he did not allow the food to distract him from conversation with his hostess. Ana, for her part, scarcely touched the food, simply nibbling a little here and there while keeping up a steady stream of questions to her guest. Was it true he was a spy? (He winced at that: O'Gorman could reasonably have been expected to tell his wife, but it was galling even so.) Was he really a military man? How long had he been in the army? Had he been to South America before? Did he like Buenos Aires?

'Madam, I wish I was as skilled as extracting intelligence as you clearly are. If I could only introduce you to the Viceroy's court, I am sure we would gather all the information we might ever need.'

Burke noticed how small her teeth were as she laughed before plunging on with new questions.

'You plan to seek audience with the Viceroy, then?'

'I would prefer to meet him socially. And not, perhaps, in the guise of a British merchant.'

'Then you must get an invitation to one of his Friday soirées. His Excellency likes to think that he is a cultured man and he tries to fill his house with men of discernment. But what will you be, if not British?'

'I have been known to pass as a Prussian, madam.'

She cocked her head to one side as if appraising the upright figure at her table against the ideal of a Prussian.

'You speak German?'

'And French. And Spanish. It is a necessity in my profession.'

'You speak French. How charming. My grandfather was French and my mother raised me speaking the language. It will be so good to have someone here that I can converse with in that tongue. Mr O'Gorman,' (she looked archly at her husband) 'disapproves of the French.'

Mr O'Gorman broke off from attacking the ham to retort, 'English is an honest language for honest men.'

Burke allowed himself a smile: 'That may be true, sir, but I am afraid I am not at La Plata to play the part of an honest man. And if I am to discover the plans of the French, then I will have to speak their language. And I would be happy to take up your wife's kind offer to allow me to practise with her.'

Ana smiled in her turn.

'I would be delighted to assist you, Mr Burke.'

'It is the language of Napoleon,' complained O'Gorman.

'It is the language of love,' replied his wife.

'It is also the language of diplomacy,' said Burke, diplomatically.

Servants entered and cleared the meat dishes, replacing them with a second course of fish, lobster, crabs, and oysters, all reminding Burke of Buenos Aires' credentials as a port.

Ana's appetite appeared to revive with the appearance of the oysters. She put half a dozen on her plate and raised the first to her lips. Burke, almost without thinking, found himself doing the same. O'Gorman attacked a crab.

'There is quite a French community here,' Ana remarked.

'So I understood from your husband.'

'And you, no doubt, will be anxious to . . .' She allowed a tiny furrow to appear on her brow. 'Is the word "infiltrate"?'

James smiled.

'That sounds terribly official. But I will certainly be trying to establish the attitudes of the French community.'

Ana smiled in her turn.

'Then I might again be able to assist you, Mr Burke. My maiden name was Mile Perichon and my name has put me on the best of terms with many of the French community. They will forgive me my English husband . . .'

'Irish!' interrupted O'Gorman.

'A distinction recognised by no one this far from Hibernia,' retorted his wife.

Burke remained tactfully silent. He had not mentioned his Irish birth to O'Gorman and did not intend to do so now. O'Gorman's natural assumption that Burke was an Englishman (albeit with an Irish name) gave him, he reasoned, an element of advantage over the merchant which he had no desire to squander. In any case, his Irish roots were, as Ana said, a matter of no conceivable interest in Buenos Aires.

'In any event,' she continued, 'they will forgive me a husband who owes his allegiance to George III on account of my grandfather, who did not.'

'That's generous of them, given that your ancestors are unlikely to have offered allegiance to the Republic.'

Ana allowed herself another oyster before replying.

'You must remember, again, Mr Burke just how far we are from Europe here. For all either of us knows now, Napoleon could be overthrown and there could be a king again upon the throne of France. It would be months before the news reached here. We cannot afford to take such political matters too seriously.'

So, by the time they reached dessert, it was agreed. Ana would introduce James to the French community, where he would be Victor Bergotte, a cousin from Bordeaux. 'It is best if you say you have no interest in politics but have come here to see if you can introduce the benefits of your French expertise to the viniculture of the country. Do you know your wines?'

'Well enough, madam.'

'Good. In that case, rather than exiling me while you drink port with my husband, let us drink wine together. We have an excellent claret – 1785, I think.'

O'Gorman, now replete, appeared in no condition to argue but sat, nodding gently to himself, while his wife and his houseguest discovered their common interest in the plays of Hugh Kelly, the writings of Jonathan Swift, and the paintings of Gainsborough.

James excused himself early to bed, saying that he was still tired from the voyage. Not as tired, apparently, as his host, who was already snoring in his chair. By contrast, Ana was wide-awake and bid him adieu with eyes sparkling, as if they could have stayed up talking half the night.

*

The next morning Burke accompanied O'Gorman to the warehouses where hides were stored ready for shipping to Cadiz and onward throughout Europe. James looked at the crates stacked throughout the vast shed and was impressed. O'Gorman's business was clearly substantial.

The Irishman was reaching for the corner of a hide, pulling it into the light.

'You see this,' he said. 'It's cow-hide. Flexible, but tough.'

Burke dutifully admired it and O'Gorman moved on to another crate.

'This one's calf. You feel the difference. Glove leather, that is.'

The calf was, indeed, softer and more delicate. Burke could easily imagine it made up into a pair of lady's riding gloves. He wondered if Ana rode. He must ask her.

'There's some kid here somewhere.' O'Gorman was moving from crate to crate.

'Please do not exert yourself on my account,' Burke said. 'I can see that this is an impressive business and I am sure your skins are of the highest quality. But tell me, do you ship only hides or do you also deal in leather goods?'

'Mainly hides. They're easier to transport, being flat. Though we do sometimes ship small items that are made here. Labour's cheap.'

'If I were to buy a saddle, could it be shipped with your goods?'

'If you want to do that, it can be arranged. You'll have to be quick if you want anything to accompany this cargo. The *Rochester* returns to Spain tomorrow and my goods must be loaded before then.'

'I will attend to it immediately. If you will excuse me.'

Leaving O'Gorman to his business, Burke set off for the main square of the town. This was directly in front of the fort, allowing him his first view of the Spaniards' landward defences. These, to his military eye, were wholly inadequate. The grandly named Castillo de San Miguel (the locals just called it 'the Fort') had an impressive gate and even a small drawbridge, but the walls were low. There was a token six-pounder beside the gate, but nothing like the artillery cover that James had observed from the *Rochester*. Worse still, the square was no longer the open space that it must have been when the citadel was first built. A strange colonnade had been constructed directly across it, providing a shelter for the hundreds of peddlers who set up their stalls there. This peculiar structure made a useful focus for the marketplace that occupied much of the square but Burke was quick to notice that it blocked off the field of fire from the walls of the fort.

He shrugged. It was clear that no one ever expected to have to defend Buenos Aires against attack from the land. Given that any invaders would almost certainly travel from Europe by ship, the Spanish logic was clear enough.

He turned his attention from matters military to the necessity of negotiating the purchase of a saddle. Several saddlers were plying their wares in the shelter of the colonnade. Their saddles were in the American style, with high pommels and backs and a broad seat so that you could ride in comfort all day. Burke had never ridden in such a saddle and had no need to own one, but he bought an elaborate example and hurried back to the house with it.

As soon as he was indoors, he rang for William, who took one look at the saddle and nodded, knowingly.

'Is it just for papers?'

'Yes. About twenty sheets. There's the fortifications here and at Monte Video and I was up half the night transcribing my notes on the channel into some sort of order. It should be easy enough.'

'Give me an hour, sir. I'll need to resew a seam and that must be done with care if it is not to show.'

'Good man. I'll send a message to Taylor to let him know where to look.'

While the servant worked on the saddle, carefully opening a seam, inserting the papers, and sewing the saddle together again, the master was writing two letters. The first, elegantly phrased, was an account of the voyage, the pleasure he had taken in O'Gorman's company, the splendour of his host's house, and more inconsequential chatter. The other was written in a faint brown ink that faded almost as the words were produced. It described the saddle and the importance of collecting it from O'Gorman's warehouse in London.

An hour later, Burke was back with O'Gorman, followed by William, struggling under the weight of the saddle.

The day, which had started well, now got even better. His messages for England safely despatched, Burke returned to the house to practise his French with Ana. There being no one else in the house who was fluent in the language, he spent the whole of the afternoon alone with Mrs O'Gorman who flirted gently with him in the language of the enemy. And by the time that her husband returned from his business, it was agreed that Ana would introduce him to Monsieur Goriot, the president of the Societé Francaise, at a meeting to be held in only two days' time.

Chapter Three

Madame Goriot was a good republican. At least, she thought she was. There were rumours that Napoleon was to declare himself Emperor, in which case she would have to shed her republican principles. Really, the whole business of the war was making life difficult, even in Buenos Aires. She had some very elegant centrepieces for her table but they were Staffordshire ware and she wasn't sure if it was patriotic to put them out. But they made such a good show alongside the buffet and she knew her husband would want them to make as fine a display as they could. He had only just been elected president of the Societé Francaise and was determined to make the most of the opportunities it offered.

While Madame fussed over the table arrangements, Monsieur Goriot was rejecting his valet's fifth attempt to produce just the right knot in his cravat. The silk was added to the pile of rejects to be repressed for the following day.

'You're a clumsy fellow, Henri! Do concentrate.'

Henri, his face impassive, started on the sixth cravat.

Five blocks away, at the O'Gormans', James Burke was already immaculately turned out in tailcoat and breeches. He drew his watch from his waistcoat pocket.

'Half a crown says she's not ready in thirty minutes, William.'

William continued to brush over the coat as he replied. 'If you were to say an hour, sir, it might be worth the wager.'

Burke laughed: 'I'm sure you're right. Take yourself off and get some rest before you start the night's business.'

William put down his brush.

'I'll be off, then, sir. And my money says forty-five minutes.'

Burke smiled to himself. William would be right. Brown had studied as assiduously to ensure that he never seemed out of place in his servant role as James had studied the manners and accents of a gentleman. William would know exactly how long a lady might be expected to take to dress.

He strolled down to the sitting room to wait for Ana and, forty-three minutes later, she appeared. It seemed to James that she had been worth the wait. Her dress was of green silk, cut wide and low at the front. The plain – almost severe – appearance of the neckline was offset by elaborate full-length sleeves and a long train that rustled as she advanced toward him. Her dark hair was tied around with a simple ribbon that accentuated the unruly mass of curls – an unruliness that had occupied her maid for most of the preceding forty-three minutes.

James bowed and kissed her hand, addressing her (in honour of the occasion) by her French family name.

'Madame Perichon, you are beautiful.'

'Monsieur Bergotte, you are a rogue.'

'Like all Frenchmen, Madame.'

Ana Perichon's smile was dazzling.

'I do hope so, Monsieur Bergotte.'

He offered her his arm and led her through the front door to where a servant stood holding the horse that pulled the O'Gormans' chaise. As this modest carriage held only two, James took the reins while Ana settled in beside him for the short journey to M Goriot's house. In truth, they could have walked, but Ana's trail was too long and too beautiful to be dragged along the street and the chaise was too elegant to be kept for ever out of site in the mews where it was stored.

That they had done the right thing was apparent on their arrival. The street was a mass of carriages with servants hired specially for the evening hurrying hither and yon to hold restive horses or lead them out of the way to make room for later arrivals.

James Burke took in the show and, for all his foppish air, he was already drawing conclusions about the French community in the city. They were wealthy, that much was obvious, but not too wealthy – there were several chaises like his own, a few landaus, but no coaches such as might be seen at a grand soirée in England. Some of the landaus had coats of arms upon the doors, which had been carelessly painted over. Burke deduced that there were many there who were not committed to republicanism and did not really care who knew it.

Inside, they were greeted by the hubbub of voices all talking just a little too loud and a little too fast. The rooms faced onto an interior courtyard as at the O'Gormans' but they were decorated in a fiercely European style and it was easy to imagine yourself for a moment back at home. Yet something seemed odd. Burke surveyed the crowd. There were many more men than women: the merchant class were more likely than the poor to have moved their families to the Río Plate, but the shortage of women was endemic even here. Those there were fluttered like butterflies in their imported silks, doing their best to entertain so many men with their conversation that the imbalance of the sexes would not be noticed.

It was not the absence of women that had caught his attention, Burke realised, but the absence of uniforms. In any British salon, especially now with the country at war, there would be the red of infantry officers and the blue of the hussars adding to the colour of the room. But here there were no uniforms at all. The French presence was almost exclusively civil. This was a gathering of merchants.

The one exception was a man who stood somewhat apart and who had a distinctly military bearing despite his civilian dress. Burke asked Ana who it was and she answered immediately.

'That's Santiago de Liniers. He was born in France but I don't know why he's here. He's Spanish through and through. He's handsome, isn't he?'

'He's too old for you.'

'I like older men. They're more considerate.'

James had to admit that M de Liniers was handsome, with a strong, aquiline nose and full lips, but he was about fifty. He had stayed with the fashion of wearing a wig, presumably to conceal his receding hairline.

'He's practically bald.'

'He's distinguished.'

'Who is he, anyway?'

'He's an admiral with the Spanish navy. He's in charge of the coastal defences here. Would you like me to introduce you?'

'You know him?'

She smiled at him, coquettishly. 'I have met him here on occasion.' And then, at his expression, 'Why, Monsieur Bergotte, I do believe you're jealous.' And she steered him away from the admiral and back toward the civilians.

As James was introduced to one bland Frenchman after another, his impression that he was at an almost entirely mercantile assembly was reinforced. The ostensible reason for the gathering was to listen to some arias from Rousseau's opera, *The Village Soothsayer,* a choice that (it seemed to Burke) was influenced more by the need to honour the philosopher of the Revolution than by any musical merit it might have had. Judging by the constant chatter as musicians and singers struggled their way through the work, most of the company shared his view.

James found himself alone as Ana joined the women to talk of dresses and bonnets and the impossibility of finding a decent cook in Buenos Aires. He moved to where the men were discussing the price of leather and the potential for growing cereal north of the city.

M Goriot, portly in a green greatcoat, approached him with his hand outstretched.

'A new face in our city. Madame Perichon recommends you to us.'

'I am honoured that she should trouble herself on my account.'

'The honour is mine that you should visit our little society here.'

It crossed Burke's mind that the French never ceased to talk about honour, whilst harbouring revolutionary sentiments quite alien to any English conception of that word. He was careful, though, to allow no trace of his distaste to express itself on his features. Indeed, he was at his most charming as he explained that he was newly arrived in Buenos Aires and intended to set up in business there.

'I am hoping that when, as must surely happen, Spain joins with us in declaring open war on the perfidious English, then I will be able to buy some of the properties that will be confiscated from them here.'

M Goriot responded with an expression of horror.

'I trust that there will be no confiscation of properties here, M Bergotte. The Europeans in this province are thousands of miles from home and we depend on each other far more than on our notional masters in the Old World. The English merchants here are a vital part of our community and, so long as one never dines on their execrable food, they are valued as our friends. I would make no plans that rely on obtaining their assets at a knock-down price.'

James did his best to look distressed at the idea that the English would not suffer and M Goriot, responding to his expression, sought to reassure him.

'There will be plentiful opportunities for improving your situation if Spain joins fully in Napoleon's European experiment. At present, all our goods must be shipped through Spain and pay Spanish duties before being moved on to France. I am sure that eventually Spain will become part of a united Europe, allowing the free movement of goods without payment of tariffs, and this will benefit all of us who are engaged in trade.'

Burke allowed himself a short laugh.

'Indeed. That should see off the English!'

M Goriot allowed himself to join the laughter for a moment before suggesting that M Bergotte might like to address himself to the buffet where the sorbets were already suffering from the warmth of the spring September evening.

James did address himself to the buffet and, for all his national pride, found the array of pastries and iced desserts a refreshing change from the groaning boards of the O'Gorman household. He did not linger over his food, though, but set off to circulate again, wanting to waste no time in assessing the political mood.

All he found was more of the attitudes expressed by M Goriot. The French (like the British, if O'Gorman was anything to go by) were in Buenos Aires as merchants. They had no interest in politics and, indeed, were rather nervous about expressing political views. Given how many people had lost their heads in political arguments since the start of the Revolution, Burke had some sympathy for them. It must be difficult to say the right thing when the right thing to say could change so dramatically from month to month. Only a few years ago, anyone who had addressed Napoleon as 'Your Highness' would have risked death. Burke rather suspected that in a few months, anyone who didn't show that degree of respect would face the same fate.

He sipped his wine (imported from France, of course – as if they could not grow perfectly good vines where they were) and scanned the room again. He was becoming bored. The French here would not fight. They would toady to the Spaniards while Spain was in charge and, if Britain ever invaded, they would toady to the British. So long as their profits were guaranteed, they would toady to anybody.

He noticed a cluster of guests at one end of the room and, in the middle, Ana, flirting with a crowd of men who were behaving as if she were the first woman they had ever seen. Burke watched her with the gaze of a connoisseur. She was, he conceded, not a conventional beauty – her lip had a slight twist to it and her eyes were fractionally closer together than fashion dictated – but she had a natural vivacity that shone the more brightly in this backwater. And (he knew, instinctively, recognising in others the imperatives that drove his own life) she had a definite enthusiasm for sex.

Burke caught her eye and was gratified to watch as she extricated herself from the group of men around her, albeit with much kissing of cheeks and clasping of hands. Moments later, she was beside him.

'You look bored, monsieur.'

'Oh, God! Does it show? I have been doing my best not to look bored these last three hours but I think that by now I have learned all there is to learn and I may retreat, my duty done.'

'Back home so early?'

'Well . . .' He paused. 'Perhaps not all my duty is done. I have yet to exercise your horse.'

'Well, sir, let us exercise him.'

They made their way out and a servant led the chaise to the door. He wore no livery, James noticed. Obviously the Goriots could not keep a large establishment and had simply hired the man for the evening. Still, he seemed smart enough and he hurried to open the chaise for Ana. James tipped him a few pesos and then mounted beside Anna and took the reins.

It was cold by now and Ana had every excuse to press herself close against him.

'Where would you like us to go?'

'Head for San Telmo. It's that way.' She pointed southward, along the river.

The chaise clattered along the cobbled streets. They were moving away from the fashionable centre to the fringes of the town but the streets remained straight. The city was arranged in neat blocks, making it easy for Burke to find his way around, even after so short a stay.

The houses they were passing now did not belong to rich merchants but to the men who worked in the port and made their living from the sea. The streets here were darker, but, as they passed a tavern with a torch burning beside the entrance, James turned to his companion. The light of the flames gave her face an almost terrifying beauty. He had admired her since the moment he saw her. He had been surprised that O'Gorman had been so relaxed about leaving them alone together – behaviour which pushed at the very limits of propriety. It was almost as if he did not care how his wife behaved.

As if reading his mind, Ana spoke. 'My husband is a kind man. But he is always the man of business. He is always calm. Always sensible. I am not like that. I was born under the sign of Aries.' She smiled. 'I am the victim of my passions.'

'And where are your passions taking you now?'

'Ah!' she sighed. 'My passions would take me to places that I really shouldn't go with a gentleman of so short an acquaintance.'

Burke raised an eyebrow and she shook her head prettily.

'No,' she said, 'my passions must be kept in their place. And you, sir . . .' She shook her finger at him in mock reproof. 'You shall take me home.'

Burke turned the chaise and trotted back the way that they had come.

*

James allowed himself the luxury of an extra hour in bed the next morning. His attempt to discover the mood of the French had succeeded beyond his wildest expectations. And Ana's mischievous flirting had added some spice to the end of the evening. He wondered if her flirtatiousness might lead to something more and, if it did, whether this might give problems with Mr O'Gorman. It was difficult to tell. The couple obviously got on well enough together, but Ana seemed bored by her life in Buenos Aires and by her husband. She had avowed herself a passionate woman, but Burke could see no passion in her marriage. The Ana who sat politely at the breakfast table while her husband carved himself a slice of cold beef to start his day was a shadow of the creature who charmed and sparkled at the Societé Francaise. She had been the ideal companion for the business in hand, chattering busily to the other guests while James was, by comparison, inconspicuous as he went about his business. There was no doubt she was a useful ally and, he could not deny, he would be happy to spend more time in her company.

For now, though, he needed to concentrate on his next objective: to infiltrate Spanish society and mingle with the Spanish merchants as easily as he had with the French. He could not rely on Ana's help here. Reluctantly, he rang the bell to summon his valet to help him dress.

William Brown entered the room with an alacrity that suggested he had judged to the instant when he would be needed, and had been waiting ready for the call. Even after all their years together, James was still occasionally surprised by just how sharp William could be. His honest broad face and apparent simplicity had lulled many an enemy into a complacency they had come to regret.

Now he was the perfect valet, laying out breeches, shirt and jacket, all freshly laundered.

'Excellent work, Brown. When you leave the Service, I will be able to recommend you as a valet with a clear conscience.'

'I'm glad to hear you say so, sir.'

'And I'm glad that you're glad. But . . .' James swung himself from the bed and started dressing as he spoke. '. . . I need your more exclusive skills at the moment. We need an invitation to one of the Viceroy's soirées.'

'Would that be another outing for M Bergotte, sir?'

James had buttoned his shirt by now and the conversation paused as William adjusted his cravat. M Bergotte was now an established alias and James was tempted to use him again. On the other hand, relations between France and Spain were uneasy. The French had taken exception to the fact that Spain had made a separate peace with England and the Viceroy would be likely to be on his guard with a Frenchman, even assuming that M Bergotte could obtain an invitation. A Prussian, on the other hand, would be seen as distant from the immediate concerns of the Spanish and hence more likely to have the opportunity to gauge the real state of relations between Spain and the other European powers.

'No, William. I think it is time to resuscitate Captain Witz.'

'Captain Witz? But why should the Viceroy be inviting the Captain to one of his fancy parties?'

'As to that, William . . .' Burke smiled. 'I think I will pray for divine inspiration.'

*

Sunday morning found Otto Witz worshipping at the church of San Ignacio. The oldest church in Buenos Aires, it offered a refuge from the heat and a reminder of the European world that the Spaniards had left behind. Burke, listening to the once-familiar litany, was not sure that he wanted to be reminded. He had abandoned his Catholicism the day that he left the Regiment of Dillon, reasoning (rightly) that Popishness would not help advancement in King George's army. Despite himself, he could not bring himself to take Mass without first attending confession. He winced as he recalled his time in the booth the previous afternoon: 'Forgive me father, for I have sinned. It has been more than ten years since my last confession.' Fortunately, the priest had been no more anxious for the full details of Burke's life than he had been to reveal them but, nevertheless, penance had meant that Burke had spent most of the night on his knees before he had felt that he could turn up to the service without putting his soul into immediate peril.

He tried to distract himself from memories of Sunday mornings in Kilkenny by concentrating on the splendid uniforms and gorgeous dresses that filled the pews. The church was favoured by the Viceroy's court and no one attending from there would miss the chance to dress in their full glory. Burke's inspection saw much to be admired, especially among the ranks of the younger and prettier of the wives. More importantly, it confirmed that the place was not popular among the French. He ran little risk of meeting anyone who knew him as M Bergotte.

Captain Witz may have chosen to forgo his uniform for a visit to church but he was every inch the soldier and, as he clicked his heels and bowed to everyone he met, equally obviously a Prussian.

It was not long before one of the Spaniards in the crowd leaving the church after Mass introduced himself.

'Juan de la Cruz Bringas, at your service. You are a stranger amongst us, sir?'

'Captain Otto Witz, at yours, sir. I am, indeed, a visitor to your country.'

'You are a Prussian?'

'I have that honour, sir.'

'And yet a Catholic?'

'There remain a few adherents of the True Faith in Prussia, sir.'

It was as Burke had anticipated: a Prussian Catholic not only had novelty value but was to be feted as a victory of the Church of Rome at the heart of Protestantism. Thanks to William Brown, Captain Witz had been set up with rooms some distance from the O'Gormans' home. Soon messengers arrived there regularly carrying invitations from the cream of Spanish Society.

As Captain Witz became an established character in the town, so Burke spent more time away from the O'Gormans. Much as he regretted losing the pleasure of Ana's company, he felt that it was, perhaps, for the best. So he was surprised when, on one of the increasingly rare evenings when he was dining at the merchant's house, O'Gorman berated him for his neglect.

'Mrs O'Gorman flourished when you attended upon us almost every evening. Now the poor girl is fading away again.'

Burke looked at Ana, who seemed, to his eyes, the picture of health. He turned back to her husband, wondering if the merchant was joking. But, though the wine glass at his place had been drained and refilled several times during the meal, he seemed quite serious.

'I am sure, sir, that your wife does not lack for attention now that you are returned from Europe.'

O'Gorman drained his glass again before replying. 'I am a dull old stick, Burke. I know my limitations. Ana needs more amusing company than the merchants in this town can offer.'

Ana shook her head, insisting that this was not true. James had the uncomfortable feeling that he was caught in the middle of some matrimonial quarrel that had started long before he arrived in La Plata. Searching desperately for a change of subject, he started to talk about the saddles that had proved so useful for concealing the messages that he sent to London. He had admired the quality of the richly decorated leatherwork, but thought the American saddles ugly. 'I cannot believe that they would be comfortable to ride upon.'

'I can't really judge.' O'Gorman clearly didn't want to talk about saddles, but Ana hurried to keep the conversation on a safe topic.

'No, Mr Burke. You couldn't be more wrong. People put a fleece across the saddle and it is as comfortable as if I were sitting in an armchair by the fire.'

'Then you must have little control of the horse.'

'Oh, that's far from true. The horses are trained to respond to the lightest of touches. Riding is one of the best entertainments available in Buenos Aires.'

Her husband interrupted, grumpily. 'I have never seen the pleasure in riding.' Then his expression lightened. 'But you, Mr Burke, you could ride with Mrs O'Gorman. It would allow you to become familiar with the way that things are done over here, and it would give my wife the entertainment she so desires.'

It was not settled straight away. Ana claimed it would be an imposition on their guest and James insisted that Mr O'Gorman would be a better companion for his wife. But by the time they had finished dessert, it was decided. James and Ana were to spend the following afternoon riding together.

*

The wide, straight streets of Buenos Aires were ideally suited to an excursion on horseback. James had to admit that Ana was right: the saddles gave a more comfortable ride than the European style he was used to and, the horses being responsive to even a light touch of the leg, he still had enough control to canter alongside Ana, kicking up dust as he enjoyed the sensation of the horse moving beneath him.

They had been riding an hour, aimlessly crossing and recrossing the city, when James realised they were taking the San Telmo road that he had followed on the night after their visit to the Societé Francaise. As his eyes met Ana's, he realised she was remembering that night, too.

'I said I was guided by my passions.'

'I remember.'

'Do you want to see where they were guiding me?'

He nodded, as if speaking would break the spell.

She led the way. After a few minutes he saw a building, larger than the others around it, with a gate leading to a courtyard within.

Ana gestured towards it. 'People are always coming and going to the ships – they need places to sleep. So the inns here are very prosperous. And comfortable.'

She rode through the gate and dismounted in the courtyard. A groom ran forward to take the horse.

For a moment, James hesitated. She was his host's wife and O'Gorman's cooperation was essential to his mission. But then she smiled again and he was lost. He swung himself from the saddle and, taking her hand, led her into the inn.

Half an hour later, they lay happily exhausted in each other's arms. Burke watched as she slipped easily into sleep. He thought of the taste of her mouth, the touch of her body on his. She was very beautiful. And very passionate. O'Gorman didn't deserve her. She was worth the risk.

*

The next few weeks allowed Burke little time to spend with Ana. Captain Witz was invited to dine with one Spanish family after another. In truth, he was quite pleased not to be eating at O'Gorman's table. The man seemed careless of his wife's activities – and, for all James' feelings toward her, he could not fool himself that he was her first *affaire* – but Burke still felt uncomfortable dining with the man he was cuckolding. So he concentrated on the business of cultivating his new Spanish friends.

Most of his conversations over dinner were about the weather and (for the men) the organisation of the Prussian army or (for the women) the latest European fashions. Everything seemed rosy in La Plata except that now and then someone would talk about a robbery or windows being broken or the danger of being attacked on the way home in the evenings.

'It's odd,' James remarked to Ana. She had taken to visiting him in Otto Witz's rooms. Burke was more comfortable with Ana when they were not under her husband's roof. Now they lay in Captain Witz's bed. It was October. The days were fast growing hotter and their skin had a light sheen of sweat. He licked Ana's shoulder, enjoying the taste of her.

She rolled toward him. 'What's odd?'

'No one at the Societé Francaise mentioned this spate of criminal activity.'

Ana stopped caressing him for a moment, her brow puckered in thought.

'None of my friends have mentioned anything either.'

'It's almost as if the Spanish are being targeted.'

'Mmmhh.'

Ana's tone made it clear that she had no interest in extending the conversation.

James pulled her to him and, for some while after that, neither of them spoke at all.

After Ana had left, James lay alone on the bed, thinking.

The next day, arriving at the O'Gormans' after the merchant had left for his office, he summoned William to his room.

'Enough of the idle life! I've got work for you.'

William's eyes betrayed his enthusiasm but he said nothing.

'I've met the French and they count for nothing. The English keep to themselves. Yet somebody is attacking the Spaniards. Nothing spectacular: a window broken here; a fire set there; a man attacked on his way home; a woman insulted in the street. So if it's not anything that the French know about and it's certainly not the work of the English, then what is going on here, William?'

'You think there's unrest among the working people?'

'Well there's unrest somewhere. Which, strangely, is what Colonel Taylor told me our government suspected. It seems that, just this once, Pitt and his men might have got something right. Yet I have found no one who admits to any unhappiness with the regime at all. So I think it's time you started asking questions among the servant classes.'

William nodded: 'What I've heard here is that O'Gorman's people are sound because they think he's a good master. But they don't give two hoots for the Spanish. I'll get myself about a bit and see what I can pick up.'

'Will they trust you?'

'They've no reason not to. I did what you said and I've made myself out to be unhappy with my lot. And now I can show myself as taking advantage of your being so much away. I'll suggest I'm ready to throw up my position with you and settle over here. I could talk like those damn Yankees and sound off about "the land of the free" and "being created equal".'

'You could indeed. You could even pilfer some of the silverware to fund the exercise and improve your bona fides with the rougher element. I suggest that the pilferage is genuine, as word of that sort of thing always gets out among the servants. I'll smooth it over with O'Gorman. I'll pay for the mislaid items and explain that it's his patriotic duty not to hound you out of his home. I doubt the call to patriotism will achieve too much, but his mercantile mind will probably be soothed by the prospect of recompense.'

Having agreed their course of action, William set to his task without delay. The butler would gather the silver carefully at the end of every day and lock it in his pantry. William had only to retrieve a picklock from one of the hidden compartments in James' chest, though, and three minutes' work left him with ready access to all of O'Gorman's cutlery. An hour later, he was hurrying from the house with half a dozen silver spoons concealed about his person.

He made his way to a street a discreet distance away (but close enough that he could expect that the other servants would hear of his transaction). The three balls hanging over the shop's entrance was the universal symbol of the pawnbroker and something in the shifty air of the proprietor made William confident that this was an establishment where there were no embarrassing questions about the provenance of the items left as pledges. Equally, though, the business made no pretence of honest dealing.

'One peso is generous, señor.'

'They are solid silver.'

'Yes, señor, but the monogram makes them of less value.' The pawnbroker glanced up at him – a glance that said, 'You stole these from the O'Gormans, whose monogram I see here.'

'One and a half pesos.'

'One peso for these but I give you one and a half if you can find me knives to match.'

William shrugged in acceptance and pocketed the one peso. The money would, he reckoned, hardly cover the drinks he would buy that night but his reputation as a potential desperado was being established.

That night, while James settled down to another domestic evening with his new Spanish companions, William was starting on a night's serious drinking that was to take him from the more respectable taverns near the marketplace to the lowest dives by the wharves. As the evening wore on, he became increasingly loquacious, damning (in turn) his job, his master, the O'Gormans, the Irish, the British, George III, and, finally, monarchs in general. By the end of the evening, he had several new best friends and a reputation as a devil of a fellow.

The next day, master and man compared notes in William's room.

Burke was first with his account: 'Well, my dinner had its entertaining moments. Señor Filiberto has a very beautiful daughter who flirted outrageously throughout the meal. And his wife complained that obscene graffiti – presumably about the same girl, but I didn't like to ask – had been daubed on their walls only last week. Which is far from bloody revolution but yet again suggests something amiss. And how was your evening?'

William grimaced. 'I had five pesos when I started and I can hardly believe I drank my way through all that but there seem to be only half a dozen *reals* in my purse this morning.'

'I hope your head aches like the devil.'

William grinned. 'It did, sir, but I had a couple of raw eggs first thing and I'm right as rain now.'

Burke looked disgusted. 'The workings of your constitution never cease to amaze and appal me. Did you collect anything more useful than a hangover?'

'Not last night, no. But I remember you teaching me that the first stage of any exercise of this sort is to establish a character. And I have been promised one and a half pesos if I can acquire the knives that match the spoons.'

'You're being robbed. I had to promise Mr O'Gorman ten shillings for his missing cutlery.'

The two men sat silent for a moment, pondering the perfidy of Argentine pawnbrokers.

James, for whom ten shillings was a less considerable sum than it was for William, was the first to speak: 'So tonight I continue my rounds of the Spanish community and you steal some more cutlery and go out drinking again. It's early days but I think we are on the trail of something.'

'Something. Yes, sir – but I'm damned if I know what I'm looking for. Begging your pardon, sir.'

'Don't worry, William. We'll know it when we see it. Meanwhile, keep up the good work.'

James rose and opened the door. Pausing on the threshold, he turned to William and, in a voice that echoed through the servants' quarters, cursed him as a fool and a liar.

'And I doubt not that you're a thief as well. If I catch you, you'll be horsewhipped, damn you!'

He slammed the door and stormed off. William sat himself down on the bed.

'That's it,' he said to himself, 'keep up the good work.'

*

It was another three nights before Private Brown's heroic drinking sessions bore fruit.

He was in a bar near the main square. This was a respectable part of town and William did not really expect his visit there to bring any results. But, even though he quietly spilled half of his drink on the ground, his efforts in the three bars he had already visited that night had left him in need of some respite. Near the Plaza Victoria, he reasoned, he could moderate his intake, whilst still appearing a devilish rake.

He found himself sharing a table with a couple of youths who, unlike most of the people he had met previously, were neither Spanish nor French but who had been born in La Plata.

'Doesn't that make you Spanish?' he'd asked, slurring his words in the unfamiliar tongue.

Both men looked disgusted. One said nothing but spat angrily on the floor while the other snarled that he was no Spaniard.

'I was born here. My father was Spanish but after he raped my mother, he abandoned her. She was half-Indian, working as a servant for the white men. I am her son – a son of the Americas. I am no Spaniard.' And, like his companion, he spat on the floor.

'No offence intended, I'm sure,' said William. 'I'm English myself.'

William saw suspicion in the glance the two men gave each other and hastened to reassure them.

'Tell you what,' he said. 'Why don't I buy you a drink?'

An hour later, he had two more friends in Buenos Aires. They drank toasts to England; they drank toasts to La Plata; they drank several toasts to the damnation of the Spanish, and, at William's insistence, one to the damnation of the French.

William heard midnight striking before his new friends rose unsteadily to their feet. One draped an arm over his shoulders.

'Do you really hate the Spanish?'

'Aye,' replied William, 'with a passion.'

'Then come with us.'

They staggered their way out into the street, still pleasantly warm, despite the hour.

They led William half a dozen blocks east and then north toward the sea. Every so often they stopped, arguing between each other or looking about them, as if uncertain which way to go.

William reckoned it must have been a good fifteen minutes before they stopped outside a house that, with its fine doorway and its walls glowing white in the moonlight, clearly belonged to a man of substance.

'This is the one.'

A moment later, they had thrown stones through two of the windows and were off running down the street.

'The thing is,' explained William the next morning, 'they weren't just breaking any old window. They went to that particular house. And it didn't seem as if they knew the house. It was as if they had been told to go there.'

'And did you ask them about that?'

William looked sheepishly at his feet.

'They were off so sharp that I was left behind.'

James raised an eyebrow.

'I'd been drinking for hours and I don't know the streets.'

James shrugged.

'If you go back to the same tavern you'll probably meet up with them again. You can do that tonight. I, meanwhile, have finally received my invitation to meet His Excellency the Marquis Rafael de Sobremonte. Or, rather, Captain Otto Witz has.'

'Well, I'd keep my ear to the ground. See if there's any word about rebellion brewing.'

'Thank you, William.' James cast an icy glance toward his man. 'My brain is not so far rotted that I have forgotten the purpose of this expedition.'

'Sorry, sir. It's just that I think there could be something going on that we could turn to our advantage.'

'You are forgiven. Your enthusiasm never ceases to impress me. Out drinking in the service of the King all night and the perfect manservant in the morning.'

'I do my best to oblige, sir.'

'And you do oblige, William. You oblige very well indeed. The day you started as my batman was a good day.'

The two men looked at one another in silence. For that moment, they were not master and man or officer and private but two comrades, united as only those who have fought and risked their lives together can be. Then James spoke and the moment was gone.

'Onward and upward, William. Things to do, people to see.'

'Yes, sir. Very good, sir.'

James and William went their separate ways. James was to take a bowl of coffee with Ana, while he regaled her with news of the previous evening. Stimulated by the coffee, he passed the afternoon riding with her (she was, he noted, a fine horsewoman), exercising the horses as far as the Plaza Victoria and back. William, by contrast, had to make do with a short walk before taking to his room where he tried to get some rest ahead of his night's work.

The two men met again as James dressed for his meeting with the Viceroy. Although this was by way of business, and he would be presented under an assumed name, James found himself seized with the thrill of excitement he always felt when meeting gentlemen of rank. The Viceroy represented the Spanish king in La Plata. Meeting him was, as he explained to William, practically meeting royalty. He certainly intended to look his best for the soirée. There was no question of his dressing alone in Otto Witz's quarters: he required the benefit of his man's assistance.

When William had finished with him, he was every inch the Prussian gentleman. He wore an elegantly embroidered waistcoat, a high collar, a rather less elaborate cravat than usual, and a dark green tailcoat. He admired himself in the tall mirror, while William finished brushing a few invisible specks from his clothes and presented him his hat.

'Will it pass, do you think, William?'

James waited for William's nod of reassurance.

'You needn't worry, sir. You look exactly as you should.'

'Thank you, William.'

William bowed slightly. He didn't usually bow to his master but it seemed fitting, somehow.

'And, William . . .'

'Sir?'

'Good hunting.'

*

Burke left for the front door, where one of the servants was ready with his horse. William, in turn, headed to the servants' quarters to change into a stout pair of boots.

Burke trotted his horse to the palace, deciding that it would benefit from the exercise. The Viceroy's headquarters were in the fort itself and Burke appreciated the irony of the sentries snapping to the salute as he passed through to reconnoitre the fortifications from the inside.

The palace took up most of the open ground within the fort. The symbolic centre of Spanish power in La Plata was an imposing size but, apart from some decorative towers flanking the main frontage, it was just a single floor. An arcade around it provided shelter from the sun. Beneath its shade, high doors opened directly into the main rooms.

It was an elegant place, reflecting the glory and culture of the Spanish Empire but, Burke couldn't help feeling, hardly an appropriate building to put into the middle of what was supposed to be a military defensive position.

Ahead of him the doors were open, guards in their dress uniforms at attention either side.

Captain Otto Witz presented his card, which not only named his regiment in the Garde-zu-Fuss but noted his membership of the Prussian Academy of Sciences. A Prussian in Buenos Aires was a rarity but a member of the Academy of Sciences was a treasure Burke was confident that the Viceroy would be unable to resist.

Captain Witz passed through to the Viceroy's grand salon. It was a magnificent room, the huge crystal chandelier dominating a perfectly proportioned chamber. Landscape paintings showing the beauties of Spain dominated the walls except opposite the entrance door where French windows opened onto a small internal courtyard. More guards, in their immaculate white coats and breeches, stood by the door, reflecting the Viceroy's status as representative of the Spanish Crown. Liveried servants passed among the guests with tapas and Spanish wine, while a chamber orchestra struggled to make itself heard over the chatter of the room.

The Viceroy's soirée was clearly the heart of fashionable life in Buenos Aires. James Burke looked about him at the elegantly dressed men and, here and there, the women in rather grander gowns than those he had seen displayed in the city before. He nodded approvingly. It was right that the guests of the representative of a king – even a Spanish king – should be the most splendid company that Society could offer.

Several of the guests here were wearing uniforms. Most were in the blue and red of the Guards regiments, though he noticed a few sailors, their lapels trimmed in gold braid. He recognised Santiago de Liniers and saw the admiral glance at him, as if uncertain whether he had seen him before. Burke turned away and moved toward the Viceroy. He had no desire to explain to de Liniers why he should have met a Prussian at the Societé Francaise.

His Excellency was standing near the windows, talking (as was only proper) to the prettiest woman in the room but one of his aides detached himself from the group around the Viceroy and approached Burke.

'Captain Witz?' He spoke German but with a Spanish accent.

'I have that honour.' James bowed. 'Would you prefer to speak in German or Spanish?'

The Spaniard looked relieved. 'I would prefer Spanish, if you are comfortable with it. My German, I am afraid, is not as good as it should be.'

'I am sure that is untrue,' Burke replied, taking care to infuse his Spanish with a German accent.

The aide returned his smile and started a conversation about Captain Witz's experiences in the Prussian army and his scientific interests. It was done politely but he was obviously being vetted. Fortunately, Burke had made a study of the Prussian military and his knowledge of their army and his own scientific interests were clearly convincing. Before long, he was one of the group standing with the Viceroy.

In the course of the evening, Captain Witz exchanged only a few pleasantries with his host but he listened carefully to all the conversation around him. The talk was all of improving trade, the absence of good servants, the quality of the horses that you could obtain locally, and the likelihood of a hot summer. One older man did mention a robbery but an aide of the Viceroy stepped in with a remark about Italian opera and the robbery was never returned to.

Otto Witz had the distinct impression that de Sobremonte did not want to hear bad news discussed at his soirées and that if anything were amiss in Buenos Aires, the Viceroy's palace was the last place to find out about it.

There were, admittedly, one or two remarks about the war in Europe. Indeed, one of Captain Witz's few contributions was when he expressed the view that Napoleon was likely to over-extend himself and should not be relied on as an ally – but the men around the Viceroy seemed to regard this as an issue of minor interest. Only one of them, wearing the uniform of a colonel, showed a flicker of concern about the likely fate of the French armies. As the party broke up, Captain Witz made sure that he and this officer left the room together. The groom was slow in bringing Witz's horse to the door and, by the time it arrived, Colonel Calzada Castanio and Captain Otto Witz were laughing together like old friends and the colonel was insisting that Otto must join him for dinner that very week.

*

As Burke set off home from the fort, William was ensconced in the nearby tavern where he had met Jorge and Gustavo the night before.

It was well past midnight before he saw the two again and called them over to his table.

'C'mon lads. I'm buying.' He tapped his nose, knowingly. 'Came by a bit of extra cash.'

Jorge and Gustavo smiled a little nervously.

'We're sorry we left you, William,' said Jorge.

Gustavo agreed: 'We thought you'd keep up.'

William beamed and waved a bottle of wine at them.

'Don't worry, lads. I'm fine. Drink up and relax.'

The two men sat, still somewhat nervous, while William poured wine for the three of them. They seemed to him to be barely into their twenties and if they were part of some revolutionary movement, they must be a very small part indeed.

At first, William was careful to make no reference to the events of the previous night. They talked about women and the price of wine and William made sure that he passed several comments about the unfairness and unkindness of his master. After an hour of steady drinking, though, he felt it was safe to return to the subject of their nocturnal adventure.

'Lads,' he said. 'Why don't we go and break another window?'

The response was what he had expected, but he was still surprised by its vehemence. Jorge and Gustavo were nice lads and they were shocked at the suggestion that they go out on a spree of random destruction.

'You could break my master's window. I'd go in, so he'd know it couldn't be me, and you could break the window.'

William hiccupped.

'It'd be fun,' he slurred. 'Then tomorrow night, you could go home and I'd break *your* master's window.'

The two were horrified. They had no desire to see their master's window broken.

'But you break windows.' William appeared to be having trouble grasping their objections through an alcoholic haze. 'Why can't you break my windows?'

Jorge and Gustavo tried to explain. The Englishman was clearly the worse for drink so they had to explain it several times to make sure he understood. They didn't just break any windows. They weren't common criminals. They only broke the windows they were told to break and that was for a Cause. They were part of a movement for a free republic.

'So who tells you what windows to break, then?'

For a wonderful moment, William thought they were going to answer him but, drunk as they were by then, they weren't quite drunk enough. They couldn't tell him.

'We're supposed to be mates, you and me. Mates don't keep secrets.'

Jorge looked helplessly at Gustavo. They were mates, he explained, but they'd sworn an oath.

Then Gustavo had an idea. Perhaps William could come with them on their next mission. Then, if Miguel approved, he could join them.

'That's a grand idea,' said William. 'That's what mates do.'

Jorge and Gustavo agreed that that was what mates do.

'Let's drink to mates,' said William.

They drank to mates, to women, to the damnation of Spain, and to anything else William could think of. Only when they could think of no one else to toast did he stagger home.

His head ached already.

Tomorrow he would start to track down Miguel.

*

'There's definitely some sort of plot, sir. Whether it's real rebellion or just a few kids letting off steam, I don't know. But I think it's worth trying to find out more.'

'I agree. So far, we've got little good news for Pitt and the government. La Plata is a model colony of contented citizens and happy merchants. The town is barely defensible from land but as any enemy might reasonably be expected to come by sea, that's not necessarily a great consolation to us. If we are to take home useful information we need to find some of these rebels that Pitt is so convinced are ready to rise against Spain.'

'I'll be out drinking for England again then, sir.'

James nodded his approval. He was confident that William's head could survive any amount of wine drunk in a good cause. He would probably even enjoy it. So that night, and every night thereafter, saw William off to get drunk with his new friends with his master's solid approval. The amount of liquor consumed exhausted any sum that could realistically be obtained by pilfering spoons, but William's reputation as a reckless knave was now so well established that his drinking companions took it for granted that his affluence was the result of larceny on a magnificent scale. A reputation, once acquired, tends to maintain itself without any need for further evidence, so Burke felt it unnecessary for William's thieving to continue. William's drinking money was now dispensed by Burke directly from Colonel Taylor's funds. Ana welcomed the new arrangement as the continual complaints of her butler, who counted the silverware religiously, were getting harder to deal with. What Colonel Taylor would have thought about it didn't much worry Burke, as he had no intention of telling him exactly how his money was spent.

For a week, William came no nearer to discovering who Miguel was. Then, on a Tuesday night, Jorge and Gustavo appeared earlier than usual and in high spirits.

'One drink and then we'll go out. You can come with us.'

William nodded solemnly and they took their drink as if they were soldiers bracing themselves for battle.

Jorge and Gustavo led the way through the streets to another fine house. They glanced around to make sure that only William was watching them and then each, with a dramatic flourish, produced a lump of charcoal. William sighed. Graffiti! Well, that would bring the Spanish to their knees. He tried to look on the bright side. At least it wasn't just breaking a window and running away this time.

While William kept guard, Jorge laboriously daubed up the slogan that Gustavo read to him, letter by letter from a piece of paper he held in his hand.

'DEATH TO SPAIN!' it finally proclaimed. 'GLORIOUS VICTORY TO THE FREE PEOPLE OF AMERICA!'

The letters were somewhat uneven but the sentiment, William had to admit, was clear.

Jorge stepped back to admire his handiwork but, at that moment, a well-dressed Spaniard, accompanied by a manservant, appeared around the corner of the block.

'Hey!'

Judging from the anger in his voice, he seemed to be the owner of the house. Jorge and Gustavo turned to run but, to their horror, William made no attempt to run off. Instead, he started to walk deliberately toward the newcomer.

With his servant beside him and Jorge and Gustavo remaining at a safe distance, the stranger was confident that he was in command of the situation.

'What do you think you're doing?'

William gave an amiable grin.

'Decorating.'

The Spaniard stepped forward and, as he did, William suddenly closed on him. There was a blur of movement, a cry of pain, and then the Spaniard was lying on the ground. The footman, who seemed hardly to have had time to react, now moved to aid his master but, while he was still trying to take in the situation, William grabbed his arm and swung him into the wall. As the servant staggered to balance himself, William hit him hard in the stomach. The man doubled over and fell beside the first victim.

The whole thing had taken less than a minute and already William was kneeling beside the master, removing his cash and his pocket watch. He worked a signet ring from his hand and tossed it to Gustavo.

'Here,' he said. 'This is for you.'

The two youths were staring as if they could not believe their eyes.

William straightened to his feet.

'Come on then, lads. Best be off, eh?'

He set off the way they had come at an easy walk, whistling through his teeth.

After a pause, while they seemed to struggle to come to terms with what they had just seen, his companions followed.

*

Captain Witz enjoyed his dinner with Colonel Calzada Castanio. He had again ridden over to the fort, passing through the remarkable colonnade across the Plaza Victoria. He had learned that it was called the *Recova* and it seemed to demarcate the boundary of 'official' Buenos Aires, with the military and the Viceroy's household holding sway to the east while the general population dominated the western (and larger) part of the square.

He clattered across the bridge into the fort but this time he was stopped just inside the gate and directed to the quarters of the colonel. These were in a separate block from the palace – a more workmanlike building from the days when the fort was a real defensive position. The rooms, though, were pleasant enough and the colonel's servants had laid an impressive meal out for their commander and his guest.

The colonel was joined by two of his captains, and conversation over dinner was the typical talk of soldiers from different armies discussing their profession. After some introductory remarks about their respective military careers and the superiority of Prussian troops over French, the conversation had moved on to the experience of garrison life in Buenos Aires. The food was good, the Spaniards conceded, and the climate pleasant – not unlike that of their native country. The absence of women was an irritation and the consequently limited social life left them with too much time on their hands.

'The men gamble,' said one captain.

'So do we,' acknowledged the other.

'But the men can't afford to pay their losses and then there is violence. We have to stamp down on gambling all the time.'

'Which is a bore,' conceded his friend, 'as every so often it is suggested that we set an example.'

The colonel shook his head exasperatedly. It was clear that any suggestion that the officers might lead by example had come from him and that his subordinates were gently teasing their commander.

'As for myself,' he said, 'I find the study of military history passes the time more than adequately.'

'So there is gambling or a study of Caesar's Gallic Wars,' summarised one of the captains. 'What else is one to do in this backwater? There's no theatre, no opera. We have no bull-ring and there is no game for us to hunt.'

'What do the locals do?'

'Most of the decent people in the city are in the same position. The English gamble, the French seduce any women whose husbands are stupid enough to bring them here. We Spanish fawn on the Viceroy and pray for a posting back to Europe.'

'But there must be people who have made their lives here.'

'Oh, the criollos.' His tone was dismissive. 'They gamble money they haven't got and kill each other for not paying their debts. They sentimentalise at the least opportunity, frequent whores, and fight. And they plot revolution.'

'Revolution?'

The colonel coughed meaningfully. Soon after that, the meal was finished and the two junior officers made their farewells.

The colonel poured more wine for himself and his guest.

'You do not like to hear talk of revolution, I observe,' remarked Captain Witz.

'That's because, officially, there is nothing to talk of. But ever since the English allowed the Yankees their independence, every man jack with a grievance plots against Spanish rule.'

Captain Otto Witz feigned astonishment.

'How can such sedition be plotted here? I heard no word of it at the Viceroy's soirée.'

Calzada Castanio grimaced.

'No, you wouldn't. His Excellency is an intelligent and amusing man but a complete fool when it comes to matters military. His concerns are improving the commercial return on Spain's interests in this area and improving the personal career of His Excellency – and not in that order. He has no interest in the views of the criollos and assumes that, because we have an army and they do not, their seditious views are of no account.'

'And is that not true?'

The colonel drained his glass and reached again for the bottle.

'It's true that there is not much danger of a revolutionary uprising such as the English faced in their American colonies. The criollos are scattered and have no organisation. But they can make a nuisance of themselves. In the town, it is window breaking and slogans daubed on walls. Sometimes people are attacked. Only last night, for example, Don Fernando – a most respected citizen – was attacked and robbed by three ruffians. There is no doubt that it was political: his home was daubed with revolutionary slogans.'

Otto Witz was duly shocked at the news.

'It's worse in the country. The criollos there have more Indian blood and cannot be trusted. They strike from nowhere and vanish away. A government post is burned here; a tax collector is murdered there. We send out patrols but La Plata is a big place. Wherever we are, the enemy is somewhere else.'

'And this is organised?' The Captain's voice trembled with Prussian outrage.

'The rebels are well organised and worryingly well informed, but we have no idea who is responsible.'

Witz tutted in sympathy and diplomatically changed the subject. He told a very long and complicated joke involving a bear and a woman of easy virtue. It was a Prussian joke and not very funny but the colonel had by then drunk enough to be easily amused. By the end of the evening, James was confident that the Spaniard would have forgotten just how indiscreet he had been in his conversation with his charming new friend. James, by contrast, remembered every detail and recounted them all to William the following day.

'You need to win the confidence of the rebels. If we can find their leaders, we can work with them to further England's cause at the expense of Spain's.'

'I'm doing my very best, sir. I'm hoping that last night's adventure may mean that I rate an introduction to Sr Miguel.'

William's hopes were to be fulfilled that very night. Jorge and Gustavo appeared later than usual and explained that they had been summoned to Miguel. News of the attack on Don Fernando had spread across the town and Miguel wanted their account of what had happened.

Gustavo was full of excitement.

'He said that we had done well and he wanted to meet the Englishman who was with us.' He grinned. 'That's you,' he added, apparently concerned that William might have forgotten.

William allowed himself to appear to share their exhilaration. In truth, the idea that he might be one step closer to discovering who was behind the unrest was more exciting than any amount of window breaking could ever have been. Jorge and Gustavo led him away from the Plaza Victoria toward the edge of the town, to the taverns where the gauchos drank when they rode in from the country. With their swaggering gait and wide-brimmed hats, these cowmen from the pampas were a different sort of person from any of the men William had drunk with before. They spoke Spanish but quicker than the city folk, swallowing the end of their words as if in too much of a hurry to bother finishing them properly. They all seemed to know each other, jumping to their feet as every new customer entered the place and embracing them with loud cries of greeting.

Toward the back of the room sat a young man whose indoor pallor contrasted with the healthy tans of the gauchos. Even before he leapt up, waving a greeting, William was sure that he was Miguel.

The young man pulled William to him and kissed his cheek. Miguel's chin was stubbled and he smelt of garlic. William was unimpressed but at least he was working his way up the chain of rebels so he hugged and kissed back with enthusiasm.

'Hey, *inglés*. You fight with us for our freedom. But why?'

'You're good lads. You're fighting the masters. Well, I know what it is to serve a master and I'm all in favour of the man who will stand up and fight against him.'

Miguel banged his glass on the table in appreciation of this speech, while William gave an inward sigh of relief. He had been worried that his crude rhetoric would have failed to convince but it seemed that here, where the French liberty bonnet was still an object of admiration, such revolutionary platitudes still carried conviction.

Miguel rose from the table and moved toward a door at the back of the room. Jorge and Gustavo followed him, hustling William with them.

The room beyond was small and tightly shuttered, despite the warmth of the night. A single candle, standing in a pool of its own grease, gave the only light. Two chairs were pushed up against a small table and Miguel took one while William was gestured to the other.

'Do you truly wish to join us in our struggle?'

There was something in Miguel's voice that suggested that he was asking the opening questions of a ritual.

Oh Lord, thought William, it's a bleedin' initiation ceremony.

He was right: it was indeed an initiation ceremony. Questions were asked and William was prompted to give the correct replies. Solemn pledges were sworn and then, as William had somehow known would happen, his palm was cut so that he could mingle his blood with those of his fellow conspirators.

Finally, the main business dealt with, a bottle of wine was produced and toasts were drunk to their success and to the freedom of their country.

Although many terrible oaths had guaranteed the secrecy of their organisation, it seemed that when they returned to the main bar everyone was aware of what had transpired. There was some ironic cheering and William's hand was shaken by everyone he passed. At some stage, the cut was reopened and he dripped blood onto his well-wishers, which only added to their good humour.

Jorge and Gustavo seemed embarrassed by the attention and were soon insisting that they must be on their way home. William, though, settled down to drink with Miguel and his new friends and, by the end of the night, it was generally agreed that he was the devil of a good fellow and that he would join them again the following evening.

William spent much of the next day sleeping with a damp cloth over his head, but by nightfall he was ready to drink with the gauchos again.

When he reached the tavern, soon after ten, it was already crowded but there were welcoming smiles as he pushed his way into the room.

In one corner, a group were throwing dice in an elaborate gambling game. William joined them and made sure that he lost slowly but steadily throughout the evening.

As on the previous night, the talk among the gauchos was mainly of horses and cattle. They lived in the saddle, working day in, day out with their herds, often sleeping on the ground with just a blanket for shelter. They knew too much of the reality of life on the pampas to share the sentimental attachment to Romanticism that was sweeping England. Yet, when they spoke of the estancias – the great farms where they lived isolated in the eternal plains – they spoke with the passion of those who have discovered their own place on earth and, it seemed to William, those who would fight to defend it. Sometimes he would hear a remark about the Spanish troops who might make an occasional half-hearted patrol around the province or Spanish bureaucrats who would assess the farms for taxes. Then the voices of the gauchos would drip with contempt and, unthinkingly, hands would drop to the hilts of the knives that all of them carried in their belts. For the English, by contrast, they seemed to have some degree of affection and, as long as William kept buying the odd drink, they seemed happy to have him share their night with them.

Miguel arrived at about midnight and made his way to the private room, beckoning William to join him.

After the inevitable embrace and kiss and the no less inevitable bottle of wine, Miguel turned to business.

'I am glad you are here, William,' he confided. 'Jorge and Gustavo are good lads but they are fit only to break windows and frighten old men and girls. They're not ready for a real fight, like us.'

William looked at Miguel's narrow chest and the bony wrists that he waved excitedly as he talked. Miguel looked in his early twenties, scarcely older than Jorge and Gustavo. For all that he liked to frequent a gaucho watering hole, he was as much a city kid as the other two and not a particularly striking physical specimen. William doubted if he would last a full minute in a real fight but he said nothing.

'We've been planning to take our battle to the heart of the enemy,' he said, with all the conviction of a general planning a summer campaign. 'We have attacked some of the oppressors from the merchant class but our leader says we should engage the military.'

William said nothing.

'*Mano a mano*,' said Miguel.

It sounded impressive but William doubted they had muskets to hand, so any attack could hardly be anything but *mano a mano*.

'What did you have in mind?' said William.

'Some of the soldiers have taken to drinking outside the barracks. We know where they drink. We wait outside and then attack them when they leave.'

Simple, thought William. Brutal but effective. Whoever came up with this plan (and it clearly wasn't Miguel) had no romantic notions about the revolutionary struggle, but they certainly understood how to make an army uncomfortable.

'I'm in,' he said.

*

James had decided that Otto Witz should retire from Society for a while before people began to bore of their Prussian, which meant that he was spending the night in his room at the O'Gormans'.

William, once again the perfect manservant, presented himself at James' bedside the next morning with his master's breakfast cup of tea.

James groaned at the light streaming in through the window that William had just unshuttered. He extricated himself from the sheets enough to sip at the tea while William reported on his activities of the previous night.

'Not much to it, really. A couple of the gauchos joined us and we made our way to that drinking hole on Arze.'

James knew the place he meant: a nondescript place near the river and just the sort of tavern that enlisted men would make for when they slipped out for an illicit drink. The officer in James often despaired of the predictability of the common soldier but he had to admit that it made his life easier.

'Anyway, we hung around there for a bit, telling dirty stories in Spanish – which did wonders for my vocabulary – and then a couple of chaps come staggering out dragging along a mate who's pretty well passed out with booze and . . .' William hesitated.

James sensed that William was uncomfortable with what had happened next and prompted him to continue his account: 'You fought them.'

'It wasn't hardly a fight, sir. There was four of us, for all that Miguel wouldn't be much use in a bun fight at a vicar's tea party, but the gauchos are hard men. And there was just two of them in any state to stand unaided, let alone to fight. And it was dark and we came at them by surprise.'

'How badly hurt were they?'

'Ah, well, sir, you see, the gauchos had knives.'

'Ah.'

The two men sat in silence while James finished his tea. Finally William spoke.

'They didn't stab the one that was drunkest. He just fell over when it started and I think they drew the line at killing him as he lay there. And one of the others might live.'

'We're in a dirty business, William. You did your duty.'

'Yes, sir.'

'Let's hope something comes of it.'

*

Over the following weeks William joined another attack on a group of drunken soldiers (after which Colonel Calzada Castanio put the garrison under curfew), threw stones at an army patrol (and ran away, pursued by six armed men, whose kit fortunately made them slower in a sprint), and started a fire on one of the piers, which was not a success as the general dampness of the surroundings stopped it from spreading. Although Miguel applauded all these efforts, none of them appeared to warrant an introduction to Miguel's own mysterious leader.

'*Someone* is giving him his instructions,' complained an exasperated Burke. 'He admits as much to you. But we still have no idea who it could be.'

William was, again, bringing him his morning tea to provide an inconspicuous opportunity to discuss progress.

'This Miguel,' Burke said. 'Would you say he was an NCO type?'

'I suppose so, sir.'

'If this conspiracy is as organised as it seems to be, he must report to an officer.'

William nodded.

'I don't see how that gets us any further forward, though, sir.'

'I think the secret is to provide a potential officer recruit. I doubt Miguel will be allowed to deal with such a man himself.'

'So are you going to join me in trying to start bonfires on the piers?'

'No, William. I think we can be a bit more sophisticated than that.'

He put aside his tea.

'Here's what you have to do.'

*

Molly counted the pesos carefully. She still thought of them as 'pieces of eight'. It hardly seemed real money – not like the golden guinea she'd earned on the *Rochester*. She had to smile when she remembered that. It had almost been like a game, for all there'd been killing involved. But Mr Burke's man, William, had explained she was doing it for the king, so she'd really been doing a good deed as well as making a guinea. And she'd found she enjoyed the pretending. After all, most of what she did for a living was pretending. The moaning and the screaming and 'You're the best,' and 'I always feel happy when you call.' But never happy enough to forget to take the money.

She wrapped the coins in an old stocking and returned them to their hiding place under the floorboard. There was a prodigious amount of silver in the stocking. The voyage had been a long one but coming to a country where men so outnumbered women had undoubtedly been a good move.

There was a sudden knocking from the door on the street below. She heard her landlord answer. She paid him well – in cash and in kind – as her protector and he took his duties seriously.

'Gentleman says he knows you but I haven't seen him before.'

Molly opened the door an inch or so and peered through the gap at the mirror strategically placed at the top of the stairs, affording her a view of anyone waiting below. To her surprise, she saw William. Well, she thought, he'd seemed too self-contained, somehow, to be calling on her but it took all sorts . . . And he was a good looking enough young man. She judged him to be still in his twenties, though he carried himself with an air that made him seem much older.

'Send him up.'

She had just time to run her fingers through her curls and arrange herself on the bed when William entered the room. He took one look at her and the bed and the shutters closed against the daylight and he hurried to disabuse her of any expectations she might have.

'I'm not what you might call a customer, Molly. I've another little bit of business you might be interested in.'

As he explained what he wanted her to do, she found her heart beating with the thrill of it. Another chance to serve her king, playing a part to fool some foreigners. And this time with real excitement, almost like a Drury Lane play. And another guinea for her trouble.

As William explained the details of her role, she found herself admiring his broad chest, his well-shaped calf in his tight breeches.

'It could be dangerous,' he was saying. 'Will you do it?'

He had a lovely voice, too. She realised that he was waiting for her to say something and tried to concentrate on what he had been asking.

'Well?' he said.

'And you will give me a guinea?'

'A guinea now and a guinea when it's done.'

Two guineas!

Molly allowed her eyes to run over that chest again. Those calves. And his hands. They looked like strong hands.

Molly knew the value of what she sold her customers. And she knew the importance of never allowing herself to give away what should be paid for.

She patted the bed beside her.

'Come and sit next to me while I think about it.'

'I told you I'm not a customer, Molly.'

'That's unkind, William,' she said, pouting.

'I wouldn't want there to be any misunderstanding.'

'Then you can stand while I consider.'

So he stood and she sat on the bed and looked up at him and thought, 'This is ridiculous,' and yet, in her line of business, what else could she do? And so, at last, she said, 'I'll do it,' and William thanked her gravely and said she was a brave girl and left.

She waited in silence until she heard the front door close behind him.

Then, 'Damn!' she said.

She lay back on the bed.

'I'll have sixpence out of you yet.'

*

Colonel Calzada Castanio was taking his regular morning walk from the fort to the new cathedral and back when he met Captain Witz. The men greeted each other warmly and expressed surprise that they should so fortuitously happen to meet.

'I trust you are still enjoying your stay in our city,' said the colonel.

'Ach! In truth, I am enjoying it somewhat less than I was.'

The colonel was concerned and asked his friend what was wrong.

'I was robbed. My purse was taken.'

The colonel was solicitous. How had it happened?

Otto Witz was embarrassed. It was a stupid tale. He did not want to weary his friend with it.

Gradually it came out. He had been walking late at night in an insalubrious part of the town. He had been accosted by a woman.

'She asked me for money. I thought I would give her a few *reals*.' He paused. 'As an act of charity.'

By God, thought the colonel, I could swear he's blushing. Aloud, he said, 'Yes, of course. A simple act of charity. It is to be commended.'

'Anyway, this woman then embraced me.'

By now, the blush was unmistakable.

'Embraced you?'

'I assumed she was expressing simple gratitude.'

'Of course.'

'I pushed her away. I told her I wanted no gratitude.'

The colonel nodded solemnly: 'Any act of charity should be its own reward.'

'And then, when I got home –'

'Your purse was missing.'

Captain Witz admitted that this was so.

'I went back the next night – last night – and confronted her. She denied it. She said someone else must have stolen it. She made . . .' He could hardly meet the colonel's eye. '. . . certain allegations.'

The colonel laughed and clapped his friend on the shoulder.

'Don't you worry about it. Where was this?'

'About a mile east of here. There was a tavern with some sort of winged figure painted over the door.'

'The Angel. Yes, I know the place. And you say she was there last night and the night before.'

'I think she's there every night, my friend. But not until late. She arrives sometime after one in the morning. I have never seen her there earlier.'

You sly dog, thought Castanio. You must have been practically camping there.

'I'll make sure the patrol picks her up tonight. Don't worry, Captain. We'll get your purse back for you. You must dine with me again on Wednesday and I shall have the pleasure of returning it.'

They made their farewells and parted.

James felt quite sorry for Otto Witz. He would never get his purse back.

*

That night, William introduced a new companion to Miguel and his other friends at The Angel.

'Mr Burke hails from the United States. I met him at the dock where he had but newly come ashore.'

James shook hands enthusiastically with everyone in reach.

'I'm pleased to make your acquaintance,' he said, in a passable American accent. 'I'm hoping to learn how you guys run your herds on open country to see if there's any lessons I can apply in the north.'

As the gauchos realised that the stranger was a cattleman, they crowded round to offer advice. The talk ranged over cattle diseases, livestock prices, and the number of men you needed for each thousand head of cattle you were running. The Yankee listened carefully to their opinions but soon they were asking him questions about the history of the United States. Had any of his family fought in the War of Independence? ('My father, sir, died that his country might be free.') What provision did an independent country have to make against military attack by the colonial powers? ('A militia is essential to the freedom of our country but we do not hold with standing armies and the tyranny that can carry in their wake.') Could an independent country in the New World compete in international trade? ('I am here, sir, as you see. I am confident that you will see citizens of an independent United States trading in every country of the world in my lifetime.')

By one in the morning, James was settled at a table with a clear view through the barred grating that served for a window. Soon after the clock struck the hour, he saw Molly take up her place opposite the tavern, displaying a shapely ankle to anyone passing in or out. Even at that hour there were enough drinkers coming and going for several to approach her but, as they had agreed, she demanded a price higher even than the men of Buenos Aires would pay. James noticed that some seemed to be giving the prospect serious consideration, even at Molly's inflated rates, and he hoped that she would not be waiting there too long.

In fact, barely ten minutes had passed when he heard the tramp of feet and a file of Spanish soldiers moved into view from the left. Their sergeant saw Molly almost immediately and started toward her. Burke didn't hear what was said but he saw Molly raise her hand to strike the man and then the Sergeant had his arms about her and was holding her in a great bear hug with her feet kicking uselessly in mid-air.

'We'll have some fun with this one, lads,' he called and threw her toward the patrol. As she fell, one of the soldiers grabbed at her dress, tearing it open. One of Molly's ample breasts spilled out through the rip and her scream was almost lost in the laughter of the troops.

The patrol had been there less than a minute and things were already getting out of hand. While the other drinkers were just beginning to be aware of some commotion outside, Burke was already heading for the door.

As James stepped out into the street, he saw Molly, now back on her feet, being pushed from soldier to soldier with each pulling at her dress. Two of the men held her by her arms as the Sergeant stepped forward and seized her breasts in his hands. At once, James was on him. A wicked knife had appeared in his hand. The Sergeant went to draw his sword but, before he had it halfway from its scabbard, James' knife had slashed open his arm and he released his grip on the hilt with a shout of dismay.

Their Sergeant's cry seemed to galvanise the patrol. They had no time to load their muskets but came onto James, swinging their guns like clubs. James ducked under the first wild blow and stabbed upward. As blood splattered a brilliant red on his white breeches, the man fell backward into those behind him and James slashed twice more in the confusion.

Any military discipline the patrol might have possessed at the beginning of the night's excitement had been lost by now. The Sergeant was still clutching his arm and leaned against a wall, moaning. His men were spreading to attack James from all sides.

William, obeying the orders he had been given that afternoon, stood ready to join in if it seemed that Burke would be overwhelmed. For the moment, though, the speed and surprise of his attack had given James the advantage. He bent to grab the Sergeant's fallen sword and now swung that before him with his right hand while he held the knife ready to stab with his left. The men in front of him fell back but one stumbled on the cobbles. Burke slashed at him as he tripped and he did not get up again.

Two of the enemy had edged round James and now they rushed him from behind. Burke was listening for their boots on the road and as they were almost on him, he whirled about, the sabre carving a deadly arc that left one screaming as blood flowed from his chest.

The other was luckier or more skilful and blocked James' swing with his own sword. James made to thrust the knife below the man's guard but his opponent countered expertly. James had the advantage of two weapons but there were still two others in the fight. From the corner of his eye, James could see them holding back. In part, this was probably simple cowardice but it seemed as if they had some confidence that their comrade would finally end things on his own.

The Spaniard smiled and his sword spun through the night air, striking at James' blade and driving him back onto the defensive. James tried again to stab forward with the knife but the other blocked it with an almost casual sweep of his weapon. James feinted again with the knife but then twisted and lunged forward with his sword. His opponent swerved aside at the last moment and the blade cut through his sleeve but left him uninjured.

James cursed the bad luck that had pitched him against a soldier who knew how to use a sword. Most infantrymen simply hacked at their opponents, relying on the weight of numbers to crush their enemies. But this man fought almost like a duellist, parrying, feinting, and lunging as James desperately tried to get through his guard. He was confident that he could win in time but time was what he didn't have. His whole strategy relied on his hitting hard and fast to carry the fight. Already the last two unbloodied soldiers were edging forward, and at any moment they might rejoin the fray. Soon, too, their sergeant would regain enough of his wits to get his men into some sort of order. Then they would take Burke down.

Even now, one of the two, rather than join in the swordplay, was raising his musket to fire. Before he could take aim, William, who had been watching for just such a move, threw his own knife, which sliced open the man's neck before falling with a clatter on to the street.

The death of another of his companions, far from intimidating James' opponent, seemed to drive him to greater efforts. He rushed forward, his sword blurring. His enthusiasm, though, was his undoing. James stepped a little to the side, as if adjusting his position in the fencing hall, and thrust once below his opponent's blade.

For a moment, it seemed that the Spaniard was unhurt. He took one more step but his sword was already moving more slowly. With his next step, his arm fell to his side and the sword dropped from his grip as he pitched forward on his face, blood already pooling around him.

James turned on the last man in the patrol who stood staring as if he could not believe what he had just seen. As James advanced toward him, he let his musket fall to the ground and ran for his life. For a moment, his sergeant, his sword arm useless, looked as if he would, nonetheless, try to make a solitary stand. James did not attack but waited, offering the wounded man a chance to escape.

The Sergeant looked at James and at the crowd of gauchos who had gathered around the fight, fingering their knives. There was a moment of stillness and then the silence was broken as Molly, her torn clothes soaking the blood from the street, screamed.

At her cry, the Sergeant turned and fled.

'They'll be back,' said one of the gauchos. 'You'd best be off.'

William looked at Molly, still standing in her bloodied clothes, and hesitated, uncertain whether to stand by his master or see to the girl's safety. Before he could decide on what to do, Molly, as if suddenly aware of her situation, turned and vanished away down the road. As she did so, Miguel stepped forward from among the gauchos.

'I know a safe place. Follow me.'

It was clear to both James and William that they needed no safe place. It would be some time before reinforcements arrived and they could by then be drinking innocently anywhere in the city or, indeed, just go home. But they were more than happy to follow Miguel.

He led them to a stable block, just three streets from where the fight had been. Burke had no intention of staying there. It was too close to the scene of the fracas and three men lurking in a stables would be obvious suspects where the same three men relaxing in a bar might be overlooked (for all that one had blood on his sleeve from elbow to wrist). For the moment, however, he was happy to wait, giving Miguel a chance to decide what to do next.

Miguel himself seemed to have no idea what to do. Having bolted the door behind them he started to describe the fight, thrilling over every blow Burke had inflicted, whilst explaining that he himself had been ready to join in had his efforts been needed. After he had run through this narrative twice, as if to convince himself that he had really seen it happen, he sat silent in the dim light of the stable for a while.

William decided to see if he could move things along.

'It seems Mr Burke would be a valuable addition to our forces,' he said.

Miguel started, as if the idea had taken him by surprise.

'We certainly need men like him,' he said.

James appeared to give the matter some thought.

'Well,' he said, 'I'm only in the country for a few months but I'd certainly be pleased to assist you gentlemen in any way that I can. If the way those soldiers behaved to that poor girl tonight is any indication of the state of affairs here, any lover of freedom will be more than happy to put himself at the service of your struggle.'

There was a pause while Miguel again seemed to be struggling to work out how he should respond.

This time it was James who prompted him.

'I'd sure be proud to meet your leader.'

'I'm not sure.' Miguel had never dealt with a situation like this before and obviously had no idea how to proceed. 'Our leader's identity is a closely guarded secret.'

'But you know who he is?'

Miguel bristled. 'Of course I do. He trusts me to pass on his commands to our comrades in the city.'

Calzada Castanio's comments and the fact that Miguel seemed to have made his headquarters in a gaucho haunt had already made James suspect that the subversion was being organised from the countryside but he welcomed Miguel's unwitting confirmation of this.

'Well, I'd love to meet up with him,' he drawled. 'It's certainly going to be difficult to sign up to the fight if I don't.'

'You could sign up with me.'

Burke surveyed the young man with a lazy smile on his lips.

'I don't think so, son. No offence.'

It was difficult to be sure in the poor light but William was almost certain that he saw Miguel blush.

'I'll speak to my leader.'

'Well, when you've spoken with him, you let me know. I'd best not be seen around The Angel for a bit but I'll keep in touch with William here and he'll pass on any messages.'

Burke unbarred the door.

'I guess I'll be on my way now. It's been an entertaining evening.'

And, leaving Miguel staring into the night, he was gone.

Chapter Four

A week after he met Miguel, James was woken early by William, who entered his room carrying a tea tray.

Burke accepted a cup appreciatively. 'If you keep bringing me my morning tea, O'Gorman's man is going to get slack.'

'He's slack already. After he reckons he's cleaned your boots, I clean them again.'

'I thought I detected British Army spit and polish. Consider your efforts appreciated. But where does O'Gorman's man fail on the tea front?'

William poured a cup and passed it to his master.

'Doesn't warm the pot. But that's not why I'm here.'

'I had surmised that. I imagine you have heard from Miguel.'

'He reckons it's safe for you to show yourself at The Angel again. He says to be there tonight and you'll meet the man you need to see.'

James sipped at his tea.

'I'd better be there, then, hadn't I?'

*

As Burke entered The Angel there was a sudden hush, followed by wild cheering and applause. He had to push his way through the press of men reaching to shake his hand before he got to Miguel who was sitting with a gaucho he had not seen there before.

'This is Pedro.'

'Good to meet you, Pedro.'

James sat down. The two men eyed each other, weighing up what they saw.

Pedro looked like many of the other gauchos. His leather belt was decorated with silver coins, showing him to be a man of moderate wealth, but his clothing suggested that he was by no means rich. He seemed to be in his thirties but his tanned and weather-beaten face made it hard to be sure of his age.

'You want to join our struggle?'

Miguel had put a glass in front of James, who took a sip before he replied.

'I am in this country only a short time but I have told young Miguel here that I would be willing to assist in any way that I could.'

'Miguel tells me you're a fighting man.'

'I try to be a peaceable person but I can fight when I need to.'

'And you feel you'd be wasted on breaking windows.'

James made no reply but simply smiled. He and Pedro, it seemed, understood each other.

'Tomorrow I'll be riding to the estancia where my commander in this struggle would be delighted to make your acquaintance. Do you have a horse?'

'I can hire one.'

'That will not be necessary. Can you find the stables where Miguel took you?'

So Miguel had taken him to a stables used by the revolutionaries. James despaired at the efforts of amateurs in affairs like this.

'Meet me there an hour after dawn.'

It seemed to James that all that needed to be said had been said. He finished his drink and left.

An hour after dawn he was at the stables. He was alone. In his Yankee persona, there was no reason why William should accompany him. James had left him to rest for a few days and to ensure that Molly was well recovered from her ordeal.

Pedro was waiting with two horses in broad, high-backed saddles like the one that James had bought the day after his arrival in Buenos Aires. The saddles were covered in a sheepskin, providing a sumptuously comfortable ride. At first, James thought this an unnecessary luxury but in the hours that followed he was to realise that it was a simple necessity given the distances that had to be covered in this vast country.

They set off to the north-west, following a road for the first ten miles. After that their route branched off onto what was little more than a wide cart track. They moved on for hours at a steady trot, meeting no one and seeing no sign of habitation until late in the afternoon. Then, miles ahead over the plain, Burke saw a cluster of buildings. As they grew closer, he could make out the post house that marked the centre of the settlement. There were a couple of other buildings. He recognised a military guard post with a watchtower and judged the other ramshackle structure to be an inn. The whole place was hardly even a hamlet, but it marked the point at which Pedro swung off the track to head across the pampas. Here the sea of coarse grass, growing nearly to the horse's belly, stretched forever ahead. Their path was simply marked as a gap in the waving green. They swung their horses' heads to the west and trotted on, chasing the setting sun across the open plain.

As the shadows lengthened, Pedro pushed them faster, anxious to reach the farm before dark.

James' first view of the estancia took his breath away. He had been expecting some solid farmhouse, such as he might find in England. Instead, he saw a long, low building, its brilliant white plaster caught by the last of the sun. Two wings projected toward him and, between these, a red tiled portico stretched the whole length of the building. In the centre was a tower, built not for display but as a watchtower. A guard standing atop it was already shouting to announce their approach.

The building was surrounded by a low earthen embankment and a shallow ditch and, to James' astonishment, he saw small six-pounder cannon mounted at the corners. The effect was more that of a small fort than of a farm. Indeed, the only immediate evidence of agricultural activity was a kitchen garden beside the track, but this looked scarcely big enough to supply the people who lived there. The money the farm made came from the cattle, some of which he saw in the distance.

As they approached, Burke saw a tall man with a dark, lean face and a hawk-like nose appear from the house. Something about the way he held himself made Burke sure that here was the owner of the estancia.

The man waited as they approached and stood beside James' horse as he dismounted. As James eased himself gratefully from the saddle, his host stepped forward to greet him, embracing him and kissing both cheeks.

'Señor Burke, I am Paco Iglesias. I have heard of your enthusiasm for striking against our oppressors, and I welcome you to my home. You have travelled far and must be hungry, so let us first attend to that.'

He turned and, an arm around James' shoulders, led him toward the house. Pedro shouted a farewell as he wheeled off around the main building to one of the scattering of outbuildings that lay behind it. Sr Iglesias explained that Pedro would eat there in the canteen with the rest of the men but James was invited to join the *patron* and his wife in the main house.

Señora Iglesias was a homely, rather plump lady, whose appearance contrasted with that of her husband. Paco Iglesias introduced her with obvious pride and then four children, all under six, were paraded for James almost like soldiers turning out for inspection. James made appropriate admiring remarks and Señora Iglesias beamed at each compliment until her husband declared that it was time they went to bed and his brood trooped out.

Sr Iglesias, his wife, and their guest ate alone. Sra Iglesias plied James with questions about fashions in North America, how he liked the country and whether or not he was married, while beef in every guise was thrust before him. Each of the dishes was carried in by a maid who was the first full-blood Indian that James had seen. He was uncomfortably reminded of the negroes that he had seen serving the planters in Haiti. The thought made him uncomfortable and he asked, as tactfully as he could, about relations with the Indians.

Sr Iglesias sighed. 'In truth, relations are not good. The whites take their land for cattle and they move away. If they resist, the army comes and they die. Soon, none will be left. I do not say this is right or this is wrong but it is the way that the world goes.'

'But I see many people in Buenos Aires who have Indian blood.'

His host shrugged.

'Of course. When the first settlers arrived, they brought no women with them. And relations with the Indians are not always bad.' He gestured toward the maid. 'Theresa seems happy working here. But she will probably end up living as the wife of one of my gauchos and their child will be brought up as a white. So, whether we kill them or cleave to them, their nation will still be doomed.'

'So they will all end up Spaniards?'

'No!' There was sharpness in his tone as he spoke. 'They will not be Spaniards. They will be the children of this land – not any part of the Spanish Empire. It will be a free country ruled by those who live and die here.'

Sra Iglesias sighed. It was clearly a speech she had heard before and her husband checked himself. 'But such talk is not proper for the dining table. We will eat and make good fellowship. Business will wait. Tomorrow I will tell you of our dreams for the future and how we plan to make those dreams come true.'

*

He slept that night on a feather bed, and woke soon after eight, still stiff, but with some of the aches from the previous day's long ride now easing. He followed the smell of coffee to find Sra Iglesias busy in the kitchen. Her husband was, she said, already about his business, but would come back soon. She put coffee and bread, fresh from the oven, on the table, but James had hardly time to finish his mug before Sr Iglesias returned to the farmhouse with all the energy of a man who had been up since dawn and was anxious to complete the mornings chores before the sun was much higher in the sky.

He slapped James on the back in an enthusiastic greeting that nearly had his guest choke on his coffee.

'You are refreshed, I hope. Drink up. I want to show you how we do things here.'

Iglesias led Burke to the rear of the house, where he had seen Pedro heading the night before. In the daylight, he realised that what he had thought of as a few buildings round a farmyard was more like a miniature settlement. Buildings were dotted around with neat paths between them. There was even a tree – the first that Burke had seen since leaving Buenos Aires. His host noticed that he was looking at it. 'El Ombu,' he said. 'The only trees that can live here. I think that my grandfather probably built here because of that tree. They're impressive, huh?'

James agreed that it was impressive. It stood only some thirty feet high but it must have measured the same around its enormous trunk. It marked the centre of the group of buildings and Sr Iglesias stood in a shade as he pointed to each in turn.

'Foreman's house; blacksmith; barns; mess hall – with the kitchen block and the well next to it; stables are over there. There's a corral round the back.'

Leaving the ombu tree, Iglesias led James to a long wooden building, neatly painted in white like all the others. As he opened the door, James saw what was obviously a bunkhouse. Beds were arranged along the length of the building, most with small chests in the spaces between them and spare clothes neatly hanging from pegs on the wall.

'You'll be sleeping in here.'

James nodded. It was hardly the comfort he was used to in Buenos Aires, but it would serve well enough. The beds, as far as he could tell from looking at them, were comfortable and the place was spotless. It looked as much like a barracks as a ranch bunkhouse. He noticed, too, that there seemed to be more accommodation than he would have thought needed for a ranch such as this. He thought of the cannon that guarded the front of the house, the sentry who had warned of their approach, and the brisk efficiency of the few men he had seen around the place. Altogether, he felt more as if he were in a military headquarters rather than an agricultural establishment.

As they left the bunkhouse, James noticed two big trail wagons, standing in a corner between the buildings. They seemed incongruous, reflecting a pioneering age that the rest of the estancia seemed to have outgrown. Iglesias saw the direction of his gaze and smiled.

'We have no need of those wagons now but I cannot bring myself to part with them. Those were the wagons my grandfather brought out here when he laid his claim to this land just two generations ago.' He swept out his arm in a gesture that encompassed the whole farm and the land around it.

'We built this. My grandfather. My father. Me. The gauchos and the Indians like Theresa. This is our land: a land that could be rich beyond imagination. The Spaniards call it La Plata but we call it the Land of Silver – Argentina. And we will fight to make Argentina free – just as your father fought for your country, Yankee.'

James looked at the buildings about him and the grassland stretching to the horizon. It was as unlike the countryside of Kilkenny as could be imagined.

He realised, with a start, that this was the first time he had thought of Ireland since his visit to San Ignacio. His childhood home belonged to a life that he had put behind him. And yet, when memories of the place did come unbidden to his mind, he felt the faintest tug. It must be a fine thing, he decided, to love your country so much that you would be happy to die for it.

He turned back to Iglesias. His grandfather had been born in this country and his father. His children would grow up here and there would be land enough that none of them would be forced abroad to seek his fortune. It seemed to James that La Plata was a land of opportunity and Sr Iglesias one of the luckiest of men.

'I understand,' he said.

There was a moment of silence and Iglesias seemed lost in his own thoughts as he gazed out across the pampas.

Pedro appeared from the direction of the corral, and, with an almost visible effort, Iglesias brought his attention back to the moment.

'I will leave you with Pedro. He is my foreman here. You said that you wanted to learn something of how we run cattle here in La Plata. You can do no better than to ride with him for a few days. That's the best way to learn how we make this place pay. Then we will speak again.'

He shook James by the hand and turned abruptly back to the house.

Pedro smiled reassuringly. 'That's the boss. Always busy. Don't worry – he's left you in safe hands. Let's get you on a horse and we'll see how well you do.'

Pedro led the way to the stables and picked out a bay stallion. James tacked him up and mounted.

'OK, Yankee, let's ride.'

Pedro touched his heels to his horse and it set off from the stables at a sharp trot.

James followed him confidently until Pedro turned and said, 'Now we do some real riding.'

At once, his horse was running at full gallop and he was twenty yards ahead before James discovered his own animal had been trained to move to the gallop almost from a standstill.

Thus began an education for the supposed Yankee. Pedro set off to ride the range, checking the location of three separate herds of cattle scores of miles apart. It soon became obvious that his horsemanship was in a different class from that of any other person James had met. He kept up a relentless pace but, even at the gallop, he sat easily in the saddle, reining the horse just with his forefinger and thumb. When James, fists bunched around the reins in approved army style, remarked that his companion must have considerable faith in his mount, the man laughed.

'He's not a bad horse but I rely on my skill rather than his,' and, so saying, he reined the horse violently to the left, bringing it down on its knees. As the horse fell, he remained upright in the saddle and, pulling again on the reins, urged it to its feet and cantered on.

James, who had an Englishman's sentimental affection for horses, was shocked to see an animal so casually brought down, but when he remonstrated with his companion, the gaucho looked puzzled.

'Look around you, *amigo*. There are horses everywhere. They have no value.'

And, indeed, as they rode, every few miles they would pass a group of wild horses which, on their approach, would gallop into the distance.

Sharing the land with the horses were the cattle of the estancia. They did not run as a single herd, eating out all the pasturage in one place, but were split into small groups. As they approached each of these, Pedro would ride around the animals, casting an expert eye over them. There would be two or three men keeping watch and he would speak to them, perhaps suggesting that the herd be moved if the grazing seemed to him to be thinning.

It was late in the afternoon when they approached the last herd.

'The fellow watching these is Julio,' said Pedro. 'He's a good sort. We'll stay the night here.'

Julio welcomed them and Pedro asked him about the condition of the herd before explaining that they would be joining him for their meal.

'We'd better kill a bigger bull then,' laughed Julio.

James looked surprised and Pedro explained, in the tones of a teacher to a bright but ignorant child, that gauchos never ate dried or salted meat if their own cattle were to hand. Instead, they would slaughter a fresh beast every day, roast it over their campfire and leave any remains for the scavengers to pick over as the herd moved on the next day.

James was about to remark that such an approach seemed wasteful when he remembered Pedro's comment about the horses. Out here on grasslands supporting thousands of cattle, he could see that it would make no sense to the herdsmen to eat any but the freshest meat.

As he watched, Julio uncoiled the lasso that rested against his saddle and rode slowly toward the herd. He flicked it without apparent effort toward one of the smaller bullocks and the noose fell easily around its head. At once, the animal tried to escape but, tethered by the rope, the other end of which Julio was making fast around his pommel, it ran in a circle around the horse. The horse turned on the spot, keeping pace with the stricken animal so that the lasso never wrapped around the rider who, had he been caught in the rope, would have been killed as surely as a man trapped by a boa constrictor. After running several times around the horse, the panicked steer fell to its knees and, in an instant Julio was out of the saddle and his knife was stabbing down into the beast's neck, severing its spinal cord. The beast dropped as if struck by lightning. Then, with the blood still pouring from the wound, he started to butcher the animal, cutting off pieces of flesh with the skin still on it to make their supper.

They ate together around the fire, roasting the slabs of beef with the hide resting on the embers of the fire. They ate the meat off the skin, which formed a natural saucer, so that none of the gravy was lost. It was the first time James had eaten the gaucho staple of *carne con cuero* and he decided it was the finest meat he had ever tasted.

Later, lying beneath the stars, James reflected on the casual brutality of life here at the edge of civilisation. Against the practical reality of these men's knives, he thought, the Spaniards did not have a chance.

*

The secret of successful disguise, according to Burke, lay in truly becoming the person that you were pretending to be. If you were a Prussian, you had to think like a Prussian. Burke often wondered if it would help him get into character if he could just pick a quarrel with some hapless passer-by, demand satisfaction in a duel, and kill him – but instead he studied Goethe and listened to Beethoven until he could honestly say that he understood the one and enjoyed the other. Being French was easier. Seduction came naturally to him – so much so that he had almost convinced himself that he had some French blood in his veins. Now, as a Yankee cattleman, he settled down to learn about cattle with the thoroughness that he associated with the commercial men of Britain's one-time colony.

He would wake with the dawn, wrapped in the poncho that Pedro had found for him. There would be coffee and then they would saddle up and check that nothing untoward had happened overnight. At first, he was nervous around the bulls, but he saw the amused glint in Pedro's eye and realised that a bull surrounded with cows posed no danger – only a bull on its own was potentially lethal. There would be calves born in the night that had to be brought down with a lariat and examined for their health. He learned when a calf was too weak to flourish and how to kill it quickly with one of the long, straight bladed knives the gauchos all carried in their belts. He came to recognise the symptoms of liver fluke and was taught how to treat it. He asked about the prices that the cattle fetched and, under Pedro's tutelage, he learned how to judge their quality and estimate their price at auction.

With every day, he knew he was learning more about cattle but it was only after a few days that he realised he was also learning to love the land. He came to cherish its open plains, its prodigal fertility, and the easy fellowship of the gauchos.

After a week living as a cattleman, Paco Iglesias again asked him to dine at the main house.

Over dinner, they talked about his experiences on the pampas and how these compared with the way that cattle were run in North America. James bluffed gamely – for, in truth, he knew no more about cattle ranching than he had learned during his stay – but from time to time, he thought he saw a glint of sardonic amusement in his host's dark eyes.

After dinner, Sra Iglesias withdrew, saying that she had some sewing to attend to, leaving the men at table. Sr Iglesias opened a fresh bottle of wine and poured a generous glass. It was thick and sweet – almost like a Sauterne.

'Produced here in La Plata,' he announced with a flourish.

James sipped it carefully and pronounced it excellent.

Sr Iglesias laughed.

'I am not sure that I altogether believe everything you say, *amigo*. I don't think you like the wine.' He paused. 'And I don't think you're a cattleman.'

Burke took another mouthful of wine and said nothing.

'I live with cattle. I know cattle. And I know a man who knows cattle. And you don't.' Another pause. 'But I think I trust you. And Pedro has watched you for three days and he trusts you. We don't know why you lie about the cattle but we know how you struck at our oppressors in Buenos Aires. I think you are sincere when you wish us well in our struggle for freedom.'

Burke raised his glass in salute to the sentiment.

'You said that you would love to fight beside us. Do you still want such an adventure?'

'I do.'

Iglesias smiled.

'Tomorrow, the Collector for Córdoba will be travelling toward Buenos Aires. There will be two mules with him, both carrying silver. The taxes for Córdoba are not high, so the amount justifies a guard of just four soldiers.'

'You are well informed.'

Another smile.

'And we will use that information to our advantage.'

Now it was Burke's turn to smile.

'When do we ride?'

'Tomorrow, at dawn. We could attack their camp when they are sleeping but we are not cowards. We are men and we will fight them like men. And we will be victorious.'

The two raised their glasses in mutual salute, drank, and left the table.

James excused himself early and made his way to bed. Tomorrow his brief holiday (for that was what it had seemed) would be over. He would, once again, be going to war, this time to kill some Spanish tax collector. He shrugged to himself as he blew out the candle and settled to sleep. But his last thought, as consciousness faded, was that he would as soon fight beside Pedro and Sr Iglesias as in any other cause he could imagine.

He woke an hour before dawn, dressed, tucking a knife into his belt in true gaucho fashion, and made his way to the stables. Paco Iglesias was already waiting there with Pedro and three of his men. They smiled broadly at James, welcoming him with handshakes that seemed strangely formal in the darkness of the stables.

The horses had already been saddled and, as the sun rose across the plain, they started out. They moved without haste, seldom faster than a trot. After an hour, they came to a river, the waters shallow in the summer heat. Iglesias forced his mount to splash along the riverbed and they followed him for some miles.

‘It’s probably not necessary,’ said Paco. ‘But anything that makes our tracks less obvious is to be encouraged.’

For the same reason, whenever they came across tracks left by cattle or wild horses, they would follow them for a way, even if it took them off their route. All the time, though, they headed more or less north and all at the same easy pace, keeping their horses fresh.

It was almost noon when they first made out a small party of horsemen in the distance. Paco moved into a lazy canter and slowly they drew closer to their prey, who had yet to notice them. Only when scarcely more than a mile separated them from the other riders did their quarry realise the danger they were in.

By now, James could easily make out five mounted figures and two baggage mules. The soldiers were striking at the mules, urging them faster, but, weighed down as they were, the beasts could not outrun the steady canter of the bandits.

As the guard realised the futility of trying to escape, they wheeled their horses and came on towards their attackers. The midday sun glinted on their sabres.

Paco Iglesias smiled and began untying the bolas, which he had fixed to the saddle, alongside the lasso.

James looked on, curiously. He had heard of bolas, but had never seen them before. They were made of three small wooden balls tied to leather thongs that crossed in a running knot at the centre. Paco took the smallest ball in his hand and, whirling the others around his head, rode directly toward the troopers. As the first soldier was almost upon him, he loosed the balls, which flew toward the horse’s legs, entangling them and bringing the beast to the ground.

The other gauchos were already riding forward, swinging their own bolas. Only now did they kick their horses to the gallop. They closed on their enemy at full speed, standing in the saddle to keep their bodies perfectly still as the horses raced below them. With one hand holding the reins, the other whirled the balls until they were released toward their targets. In seconds, the four guards were down and the gauchos were upon them.

Although they had approached their foe at a full gallop, all six horses stopped instantly beside the fallen men and the rebels were out of their saddles with their knives busy despatching the soldiers almost before James could take in what had happened.

One remaining horseman had stayed with the mules as the soldiers had turned to charge. This, James reasoned, would be the Collector and, as Iglesias's men were attending to the guards, he started toward that individual. The Spaniard saw him coming and, abandoning the mules, he spurred his horse into a gallop.

James grinned. After three days of riding with gauchos, he was confident that he could catch the Spaniard. He spurred on his own horse – still relatively fresh from the easy ride of the morning – and it surged forward. Ahead of him, the Collector turned his head and, seeing James close behind, he reached to his saddle and drew a pistol.

James moved closer. He could tell that the Spaniard was far from an expert horseman, and with his steed running full pelt under him there was no way that he would be able to hold the gun steady enough for it to be a serious threat.

As he closed on his foe, he heard another horse galloping behind him. Turning, he saw Paco swinging his bolas toward the Collector. Almost instantly, it seemed, the man's horse staggered. James reined himself to a halt and, if the result was not as dramatic as when the gauchos stopped from a full gallop, it was still impressive. The Collector rose to his feet, pointing the pistol toward his assailant, but James was already on him. He swerved his body to the left as the weapon fired. He was barely fast enough and he felt the ball pluck at his collar as it passed. The Collector dropped the now useless pistol and reached for his sword but too late. Before he could draw it, James' knife was slicing into his throat.

Paco, still mounted, looked down on him.

'*Bien,*' he said. '*Muy bien.*' Good, very good.

James looked at the body on the ground. He was a man in early middle age, running to fat. He had a moustache and a small scar on his left cheek. He probably had friends in Buenos Aires who would be waiting for him at a tavern in a few days. They would have a long wait.

Burke bent to the body and cleaned his knife on the man's coat. He was careful about details like that. If you had to spend your life killing people, he felt, you could at least be tidy about it.

He raised the knife and sketched a salute to the corpse. The Collector was a victim of the turmoil of his age just as much as the Haitian slaves or the French Royalists or his comrades in the Regiment of Dillon now, for all he knew, fighting and dying somewhere on the other side of the world. The dead man was a Spaniard. If Spain weren't already at war with Britain (and with Europe three months away, they could already have been at war for weeks), then it soon would be. And the men he rode with were at war with Spain as surely as the Yankees had been at war with England. In aiding them, he served his king, like the soldier he was – and as the Collector had served his.

He mounted and rode to where the others had gathered around the mules. They were forcing open the packs that the animals carried and, as James arrived, he heard them cry out as they saw the silver within.

Paco saw him approaching and shouted, 'We've done well. There must be ten thousand pesos in there, more than we were expecting.'

'And jewels.' Pedro scooped out a handful of necklaces and a great ruby set in a silver brooch. 'Someone couldn't pay and the bastards took his wife's jewellery.'

There was a pause while the gauchos considered the enormity of such an unchivalrous act. A moment later, though, they were scooping their plunder into saddlebags.

'Why not leave it on the mules?'

'If the Spanish trouble themselves to follow the Collector's route, they will find that the attack took place here. The mules are heavy and leave clear tracks. I don't want those pointing toward my estancia.'

As he spoke, Pedro was scooping earth into the empty packs on the mules, while the others were unwrapping the bolas from the horses they had brought down. As each horse was freed, it was driven off and, frightened after their experience, they galloped away, leaving their tracks through the pampas grass – tracks that did not lead to Paco's home.

'If the Spaniards had proper trackers with them, this wouldn't fool anyone. But, if they send anyone, they will send regular troops. They will find a mass of different tracks in different directions and they will give up.'

To be on the safe side, Paco's men started away from home, driving the mules (now weighed down with earth) before them. They carried on, leaving a clear path for an hour, before peeling away one by one, leaving the mules to fend for themselves.

They rode in a great arc, heading toward home only as the sun marked the middle of the afternoon. It wasn't until after nightfall that they met up, arriving back at the estancia by moonlight.

Sra Iglesias was waiting for them. That night, none of the group ate in the canteen. They feasted together in the main house, their plunder piled carelessly in a corner of the dining room.

'What will you do with the money?'

Paco Iglesias looked sharply at James.

'Do you want some of it?'

'Lord, no! It just seemed a lot. What will you spend it on out here?'

Paco laughed.

'You're right, Yankee! What could I spend it on out here? No, this money will make its way to Buenos Aires, where it will be put to good use.'

The intelligence that had guided their attack suggested that Iglesias was himself getting instructions from elsewhere. Now it looked as if the next layer of this secretive organisation might well be concealed, not in the pampas, but back in Buenos Aires. James would have given much to know where exactly in Buenos Aires the plunder was headed. It was clear from Paco's manner, though, that any more questions would be unanswered and might lead to suspicion as to what the counterfeit cattleman was really after.

The next morning, the money was nowhere in sight. Nothing was said about the robbery and life on the estancia resumed its normal rhythm. Paco suggested that James stay on for a week or two:

'There might be something happening that will interest you,' was all he would say. James passed the time helping Pedro with his regular tasks and trying to improve his own skills as a cowman, often to the amusement of the gauchos. His efforts at throwing the bolas caused especial hilarity. As he whirled the balls around his head, one struck a bush and fell to the ground, catching the hind leg of his horse. The sudden tug pulled the whole thing out of his hand and it promptly wrapped itself around his horse's legs, bringing it to a dramatic stop. Luckily, the horse was an old, practised animal and simply stood without kicking, allowing James to retain some dignity as he dismounted and untangled the cords while the gauchos roared with laughter. Later, Pedro said that he had seen every sort of animal caught, but had never before seen a man caught by himself.

James had been at the ranch for almost two weeks, and was just wondering if he would learn anything more there, when Paco announced that Pedro and his men were to cut out two hundred head of cattle and drive them to Buenos Aires.

'You and I, James, will accompany them.'

They started late in the afternoon. James was surprised at this apparent tardiness but Pedro explained that it would allow the cattle an easy first day, which would help to keep them fresh.

That night, Paco joined in their feast of *carne con cuero* and slept with them beside their fire. The next morning, he took James and four of the other men aside.

'Pedro has things well under control now. We're going to leave the herd to drive to the city while we go about some other business.'

No one asked any questions and James had little doubt that this was what Paco had suggested he stay on for. Whatever it was, he was confident that the Spanish would not like it.

Early the next morning, after the coffee that was brewed every day almost as a religious rite, the gauchos began to move the herd on its way and James followed Pedro and the others as they slipped off to the south east. Once they were clear of the herd, Pedro put his spurs to his horse and they rode hard across the prairie. It was not until they stopped for a brief break at midday that he told them where they were going.

'There is a military post-house on the road to Punta Rasa, where the Plate meets the sea. It's a day's hard ride from Buenos Aires and there's nothing else there – just the military use it. They have stabling with fresh horses and less than a dozen men to keep some sort of guard on the place.'

James saw grim nods from the men around him. The post-houses, allowing the Spanish to maintain communications across the pampas, were an obvious symbol of Spanish rule. There would be stabling, accommodation for the couriers, and fresh horses – a tiny Spanish outpost, isolated in the midst of what the gauchos saw as their own land.

'Our plan is simple. We'll arrive after dark. We'll set it on fire. We'll leave.'

James, the military man, admired the straightforwardness of the strategy. As a guerrilla action, it was perfect. The place would be isolated and built of wood. The stabling, packed with straw and hay, would burn in minutes. In the darkness, the rebels could strike and be away almost before anyone knew they were there.

In the event, like most military actions, this was less straightforward in practice than in theory. They travelled until they hit the road to Punta Rasa late in the afternoon. It was ungravelled but the earth was packed down by the passing traffic and they were able to make good speed. They rode steadily for the rest of the day until they saw their destination on the horizon an hour before sunset.

Paco reached into a saddlebag and drew out a spyglass, through which he examined their target. James was, again, impressed with the professionalism of the operation. This was no ramshackle group of malcontents. Their intelligence was good and their expeditions were carefully prepared and well planned. James felt that there must be some organisation behind this that went well beyond Paco Iglesias. That organisation, he decided, was where the silver captured the previous week would end up.

Not for the first time, James wondered about that silver.

When the cattle drive had started out, it had been joined by one of the trail wagons. James had seen sacks of dried beans and various bits of harness loaded aboard and had, at first, thought nothing of it. But they had eaten no beans last night. No one had slept in the wagon. Surely it was not there simply to carry some spare harness? The more James considered it, the more he was sure that was where the silver had been hidden. But where was it to go once they reached Buenos Aires?

A muttered oath from beside him brought his thoughts back to the present.

'There's a guard tower and some officious son-of-a-bitch has set a guard up there. We should leave the road and ride northward in the pampas. With luck, he won't have seen us and, if he has, he'll think we're just gauchos about our business.'

They rode for five minutes until Paco was comfortable that no guard would notice them. Sitting in the long grass, they would, in any case, be invisible and their hobbled horses would just be another small group of animals roaming the grassland.

'We can go no further until dark.'

They sat quietly. Some of the men chewed tobacco; others just stared ahead. Paco issued strips of dried beef for their supper. They could not smoke or light a fire in case they drew the attention of the guard.

They waited until the sun was well below the horizon before mounting and riding back toward the post-house. They stayed in the grass where their silhouettes stood out less against the horizon and, half a mile from the buildings, they slipped silently to the ground.

By now, it was almost completely dark: the guard tower was just a distant shadow against the night sky. As they neared the buildings, they sank to their bellies, the only sign of their progress the waving of grass and a susurration on the night breeze.

The post house was like a miniature version of the estancia. A shallow ditch surrounded a cluster of buildings. Burke noticed a barn, stables, and a bunkhouse before they were wriggling down behind the low bank that, as at the estancia, had been thrown up when the ditch was dug.

Paco was gesturing with his hand. Julio – a slim lad, barely out of his teens, slithered up the earthen wall and, crouching, ran toward the guard tower. Even knowing he was there, James could not hear a sound. After a few seconds, James followed the others as they, in their turn, left the ditch, bellies flat to the ground as they crossed the bank and made their way into the compound. They split up, like Julio running in a silent crouch, two to the bunkhouse, two toward the barn. Paco gestured James to move on a cabin set apart from the other buildings and which, he realised, must be the quarters of the officer commanding this tiny outpost.

The men who had gone to the barn now re-emerged, carrying bales of hay, which their comrades stacked against the outside of the bunkhouse. Meanwhile, Julio was climbing the tower ladder, one slow step at a time.

To James, every footfall and each creak from the ladder sounded so loudly that he could not believe that the place did not rouse itself into resistance. The only one of the garrison stirring, though, was the duty guard, whose feet James heard stamping from time to time in his tower. He seemed to be the single soul even half-awake. As James slipped through the night, he heard the sentry humming. He imagined that he was thinking of home and some Spanish sweetheart. For him, it would be one more dull night of duty and, if he heard the sounds at all, he must have dismissed them as the natural creaking of timbers or the scurrying of rats.

More straw was stacked against the bunkhouse door. Julio was ten feet from the ground when a bale dropped to the ground with a dull thud. The guard's face appeared over the side as he leaned out, the better to see into the yard below. As he did so, he was just five feet above Julio. The gaucho's knife was flying through the air before the guard could believe what he was seeing. There was a gurgling sound as the blade pierced his throat and a soft thump as his body fell back into the tower.

Still the alarm had not been raised, but there were sounds of restiveness from inside the bunkhouse. Paco decided that they could not rely on the advantage of surprise for much longer. Pulling a tinderbox from his pocket he struck sparks into the hay until it flamed.

The crackling of the fire finally awakened the men in the bunkhouse who, finding the door blocked with the burning bales, sought to escape through the window. The gauchos were waiting for them in the darkness. As they tumbled to the ground, the trap was sprung. The first two, still half asleep and with no clear idea of what was happening, were despatched with scarcely any struggle, but the others came out fighting. Inside the burning building, a few of the soldiers had loaded their muskets and fired from the windows, giving some sort of cover to their comrades.

The door of the commander's hut opened and the officer appeared, his unbuckled sword belt in his hand as he hurried to investigate. As soon as he saw Burke, he took his sword by the hilt and dropped the scabbard to the ground. James had no chance here of attacking while his victim was struggling to draw his weapon. Instead, he found himself armed only with a knife, while his opponent wielded a regular sword. His one advantage was that, until the Captain was through the door, the man did not have enough room to make full use of his blade.

James feinted toward his opponent who stabbed back at him. James swerved his body from side to side, trying to avoid the other's thrusts and tempt him into a swing with the sword. He wished he had a blanket to tangle the other's blade for, without one, he had no protection at all. As James swerved and feinted, feinted and swerved, the Spaniard was slowly forcing his way forward. James knew that, as soon as the man was clear of the building, the fight would be over in seconds.

None of the gauchos was in any position to help James. A shot from the bunkhouse had felled one of them and the others were engaged in a general melee around the window.

Burke was tiring now, as the officer forced him back. The sword cut into his sleeve and a second blow stabbed at his shoulder. At that moment, though, one of the soldiers in the fight at the bunkhouse let out such a scream that his commander, recognising the voice, turned his face for a moment toward the sound. That second's inattention was all James needed. Stepping forward he thrust once, hard and deep under his ribs.

The Captain half turned as if trying to see who had done this to him and, dropping his sword, fell dead at James' feet.

By now, the fight was almost over. The bunkhouse was well alight and the soldiers within were no longer able to provide covering fire for those outside. Paco and Julio ran to the stables and started those ablaze before calling for everyone to leave. The body of their dead comrade was left where it lay and the others melted back into the darkness. Only three of the garrison remained alive and they were in no state to mount a pursuit. Besides, they had no horses to follow with, as their beasts had fled in terror from the burning stables.

James was not sure that they would be able to find their way back to where they left the horses but the gauchos seemed to have an almost mystical awareness of exactly where they were on the pampas. In a few minutes, he heard the shuffling of hooves and the clink of harness and they were mounting up and moving northward. Only when the flames were no more than a flicker on the horizon did they stop and rest for what remained of the night.

The next day they travelled on toward the city. They rode quietly, their emotions mixed. The raid had been a success and their victory a dramatic one, but Carlos would never ride with them again.

They met up with the herd late in the day, as the drovers prepared to settle it for the night, ready to drive the last few miles to the slaughterhouses in the morning. Nothing was said about James' wounds or their missing comrade. Life on the pampas was hard and death an everyday reality.

They sat together round the campfire and talked about what price the cattle would fetch at auction and the girls they would be spending their time (and their money) with before they returned. Someone got out some cards and they played a few hands and James was so tired he allowed himself to win.

And then he slept.

The next morning they were up with the dawn, driving the cattle on the final stage of their journey. James' wounds were superficial and, in his borrowed gaucho clothes, his bedraggled appearance attracted no attention as they passed through the city gates.

He looked around for Paco and only then realised that Sr Iglesias was himself driving the trail wagon on this last stretch. If he had had any doubts as to where the captured silver was, they were gone now.

James kept a careful eye on the wagon and saw Iglesias turn away from the herd to head deeper into the city. For a moment, he considered following, but with the gauchos busy all around him, he could hardly expect to slip off unnoticed. He could only watch as Iglesias and his booty vanished away.

Any thoughts about the wagon were soon put out of Burke's head by the demands of driving the herd through the town. Although the streets were straight and wide, the cattle were frightened to be surrounded by buildings and kept trying to break away down the side streets. The gauchos had to force their horses past the nervous steers to get ahead and block off possible escape routes. The last mile of the cattle drive seemed more demanding than all the time that they had spent in the open space of the pampas.

When the beasts were eventually delivered safely to the stock pens, the gauchos were happy to leave Pedro to attend to the commercial side of their business while they went off to start their celebrations. They led James to a nearby establishment, which was obviously used to dealing with gauchos who had just arrived in town with their cattle. From the street, the place was nothing special but James was assured that here was one of the best *asados* in the city. He was led through the building to an open space beyond, where long tables were set out around a fire pit with great hunks of steak dripping fat onto the charcoal below them.

The owner set bottles of wine on the table. A couple of the men had brought guitars and sang songs of their pampas life as the drink circulated while they waited for Pedro to join them. As soon as he arrived, carrying a leather bag that jingled with the reassuring sound of silver dollars, plates of grilled meat and fried potatoes, black pudding, enormous sausages, and slices of ham appeared on the table, and the sound of singing stopped while the men concentrated on their food and wine.

Once they had done justice to the food, they relaxed with more wine. Toast after toast was made to 'our Yankee friend'. The guitars began to play again and everybody joined in singing long, slow songs about the loneliness and loss that seemed an inescapable part of living in this vast emptiness at the bottom of the world. The words were sad and the melodies plaintive but the singing evoked the beauty of the landscape and the passion with which they loved it.

As he sat amongst these men with their mix of European and Indian blood, speaking their own clipped Spanish and singing in a style quite alien to Iberia, James understood why they fought against their colonial masters with such ferocity. This, he felt, was the future of La Plata – a place that was unlike any European country and yet formed by Europeans. Not Spanish or French or English, but fiercely and proudly American.

At last, with their final farewells, the men were off back to the pampas they loved so much.

James waited until dark, when his condition was less likely to be noticed, before making his way back to Mr O'Gorman's house.

Mr O'Gorman, it transpired, was out for the evening but Mrs O'Gorman was at home. She screamed, prettily, at her first sight of James, dirty, his clothes torn and bloody. Then she directed that he should be taken to his room and, in the absence of William, she would take responsibility for his care.

And so it was that, after bathing him and dressing his wounds with a skill James was surprised to learn she possessed, Ana put him to bed, and, his condition demanding her continuing attention, slipped in beside him.

James had been in the saddle for three days; he had been fighting for his life and still carried the wounds; he had spent hours drinking at The Angel. Yet Ana's nursing endeavours seemed to restore him completely. So completely that a stranger, seeing Ana slipping from the room later in the evening, might have assumed from her dishevelled appearance that it was she who had returned from a long and gruelling journey while James' sleeping body presented a picture of rude health.

Chapter Five

William was at his master's bedside the following morning, full of remorse for not being there the night before.

'Don't be ridiculous, man. You had no way of knowing that I would be returning yesterday; still less that I would be any the worse for wear. Where were you, anyway?'

'I was walking out with a young lady, sir.'

'You dog, William. Who's the lucky lass?'

'Miss Simkins, sir.'

'And where did you meet Miss Simkins?'

William reddened.

'It's Molly, sir. Molly Simkins.'

Burke gave a burst of laughter.

'Molly! How can you be "walking out" with her? She's a whore.'

Too late, Burke saw the expression on William's face.

'I'm sorry, William. I didn't realise . . .'

'That's all right, sir. But you shouldn't hold the young lady's profession against her. We all have to eat.'

'Indeed we do, William.'

There was a short, embarrassed silence, broken by William.

'You look to have had an interesting time away, sir.'

James needed no more excuse to recount the details of his time at the estancia.

'I'm certain Iglesias and his men are just part of an organised revolutionary movement. If I can get to the man who heads this, I am sure that I can negotiate with him. I'd be representing the king, William. I can offer British help.' He paused for a moment, imagining himself meeting with the rebel leader and setting out with him the outlines of a new country: the country that Sr Igelesias dreamed of. 'I can do this, William. I can prise La Plata away from Spain.'

'Is that what we want, though, sir?'

'Of course it's what we want. With La Plata independent and hostile to Spain, Madrid can be cut off from its supply of silver. Spain boasts of its empire, but it is built solely on the income it derives from the Americas. It's the silver from here that buys her ships. It's American silver that pays her armies. Spain is little more than a great trader in silver with a government attached. Deny her the silver and she falls.'

'But aren't we supposed to be looking at the possibility of annexing the place ourselves?'

Burke paused to consider the question. Was his mission about painting yet more of the map of the world in pink? When he spoke again, his voice was thoughtful.

'That might be our ideal but I'm not sure that it is necessary. Britain has just lost most of its North American colonies and has no interests in South America south of Guiana – unless you include the wretched Falkland Islands, which are really of no interest to anyone.'

He took a sip of his wine.

'Britain doesn't need La Plata. It would tie down thousands of troops in its defence and we need those troops fighting Boney in Europe. And my feeling is that the likes of Sr Iglesias will make this country independent before too long, whichever European power claims title to it. No, the important thing is that we deny the riches of The Plate to the French, which, given that they are the allies of the Spanish, means denying the country to Spain. It doesn't matter who controls the place, so long as they are not inimical to Britain.'

'So tell all this to Mr Iglesias and your job's done.'

Again, Burke paused to consider the idea. It was simple, but not, in the end, that attractive. It was not right that the British plenipotentiary conduct negotiations with a humble rancher, however pleasant a man.

'I think not. Sr Iglesias is clearly an important man in this rebel army but he is not their leader. That is the man I need to talk to.'

'Ask Mr Iglesias who he is, then.'

Burke gave a humourless grin.

'When Iglesias took the money to this mysterious chief, he drove the wagon himself. He doesn't even let his own people know who this man is. He's not going to tell me. He already suspects that I am no cattleman. Were I to tell him that I am not a Yankee he would suspect me a Spanish spy.' He grimaced again. 'No, I am confident that the man is in Buenos Aires but we are going to have our work cut out to find him.'

Burke decided that William would again scour the drinking houses of Buenos Aires in his search for clues, though he should concentrate on The Angel and any others where the criollos drank. Burke would, once again, explore the more salubrious strata of Buenos Aires society.

Ana appeared delighted when James suggested another trip to the Societé Francaise. She wore her finest gown in honour of the occasion and chattered excitedly as James drove them to M Goriot's house.

She was carrying a fan and, as they entered the salon, she tapped James coquettishly on the chest. 'I know you must have your boring conversations with the merchants here, but don't you dare neglect me.'

James smiled and assured her that he would be at her side in only a few minutes, but soon he found himself engaged in one conversation after another about life on the pampas. His intention had only been to confirm his belief that the French merchants knew little and cared less about what was happening outside of Buenos Aires. Indeed, the most superficial discussion demonstrated their ignorance, but he could not resist showing off his own newly acquired knowledge. So engrossed did he become in these conversations that he remembered his promise to Ana only when he cast about the room to see her engaged in an animated discussion with Santiago de Liniers.

The sight of her flirting so obviously had him abandon the merchants and move toward Ana as fast as politeness would allow. He realised, too, that he had probably been revealing too much awareness of rural life for someone who, as far as the French merchants were aware, had scarcely ever left the town. He was irritated with his carelessness, but allowed the irritation to show by chiding Ana for her behaviour. Ana did not respond well.

'You are away for a fortnight and then you return and neglect me shamefully. You have no right to complain if I spend my time with Admiral de Liniers. He, at least, shows me some appreciation.'

They returned home in near silence. James had no more idea of where the silver might have gone than he had at the beginning of the evening, and Ana's ill temper added to his irritation. The day, he decided, had not been a success. He could only hope his efforts to establish links between somebody in Buenos Aires and the rebels in the countryside would be more successful in the days ahead.

The evening that Captain Witz spent with Colonel Calzada Castanio was more convivial. The colonel was sorry to have to admit that Captain Witz's purse was lost for good and he produced an especially good bottle of wine to try to drown that unfortunate memory. He had missed the company of his good Prussian friend and, as the two exchanged their news, it was clear that, as far as the Spanish authorities were concerned, nothing of note had happened while Burke had been away.

Each morning, James compared notes with William. William was drinking his way round every carter's tavern in the Buenos Aires – but no one seemed to remember a trail wagon on the day of James' return.

They continued their search for weeks, becoming steadily more irritated as the days passed. Burke's humour was not improved when he learned that Ana was dining with de Liniers while even William's cast-iron constitution began to suffer from night after night of drinking in the service of his king. After a month of fruitless effort, James called a council of war.

'We need to think out our next step,' said James, 'and I think a drink is an essential part of that. And we can't drink together here – it would shock the other servants. So let's find ourselves a tavern.'

James wore his plainest clothes and William his finest so the two could pass as companions. They found themselves a respectable tavern where they could sit over a bottle of wine.

'I'm at a dead end,' admitted James. 'This conspiracy is being organised from the city but I can get no clue as to where. The person we're looking for is intelligent and resourceful. It's not some merchant with a taste for adventure. It's a keen military mind and I want to know who it can be.'

'There's not a word in the taverns. I've been to dozens. I've been kicked out of a few for getting drunk and talking revolution but if anyone knows anything that matters, they're saying nothing. Most of 'em will happily join in any jokes at the expense of the Spaniards and there's a lot will talk about doing something about it, once drink has made them bold, but it's idle boasting. If there's any organisation, it's mighty quiet.'

'As secret conspiracies go, this one works well. It's organised in layers with people having contact only with the layer immediately above them. My bravado at The Angel may have got past Miguel to Iglesias but it's going to take more than that to get past Iglesias.'

The two men sat drinking in silence, thinking about what they knew already and how they could make progress. Finally, Burke spoke again:

'I think that most of those who are ready to strike against Spain are in the countryside. Iglesias's place is practically an armed camp and the raids we engaged on were in a completely different league from your window breaking. Captain Witz's friend the colonel was very definite that there had been no serious disorder while I was away, although he was prepared to admit that there was graffiti daubed on the Recova. Was that your doing?'

'I'm working on my letters, sir. You told me I should practise.'

'Well poor Colonel C is quite embarrassed by the incident. The Recova is practically outside his front door.'

'We worked on the far side, sir. In fairness, there's no reason why the guards in the fort should have seen us.'

'The guards on duty that night were cleaning latrines for a month.'

William pursed his lips.

'No accounting for the way an officer's mind works. Begging your pardon, sir.' There was the briefest of pauses before, changing the subject, he added, 'Perhaps we need to start looking outside Buenos Aires, sir.'

James considered William's comment while he drained his glass.

'I suspect that a peregrination around the estancias of La Plata looking for rebellion might be an unproductive venture. But you are right to remind me that there is more to Spanish America than Buenos Aires. There's a revolutionary from Venezuela who has been telling anyone who will listen in London that Spain gets fifty-five million pesos a year from its American colonies. If it's true, most of it is coming in silver from Peru. Colonel Taylor informs me that Mr Pitt and his government are anxious to know if these estimates have any truth in them. The simplest way to find out could be to go to the Andes and take a look.'

James' eyes were no longer focussing on the room. In his mind, the tavern had vanished, replaced by the sweep of the mighty Andes and the legends of the treasures of the Incas. His lips twitch into an unconscious smile.

'I'll pack then, shall I?' said William.

*

James had seized on the expedition as an alternative to inactivity in Buenos Aires, but it took only a few days to discover that organising an expedition would itself keep him tied down in the town. In the end, it took over a month to organise. It should have taken even longer, for James had no funding for such an adventure. He sent coded messages to England, explaining that a visit to Chile would let him examine the coastal defences on the west of the Americas. British ships were active in the Pacific and even a superficial survey of Spanish defences there could be invaluable. Could Colonel Taylor please ensure that a suitable sum was made available?

Rather than wait for a reply, James convinced O'Gorman that the trip was an essential part of his mission and that it would be in the national interest for O'Gorman to advance the money himself.

'His Majesty will be for ever in your debt,' James assured his host.

'Not for ever, I trust,' the merchant replied. 'I was rather hoping to see repayment in a matter of months.'

James laughed politely and settled down to obtain the proper papers, hire bearers, and buy provisions. With this in hand, he had to find a guide. That brought more delays as several refused, arguing that it was too late in the year for such an expedition and that they should not attempt to cross the Andes until the height of the next summer. Eventually, he found a wiry man, more Indian than Spanish, who looked him up and down and pronounced that he seemed fit enough to survive an autumn crossing. James and Apala (for that was his name) spent hours closeted together, poring over such maps as were available to work out a route while William arranged for mules and muleteers. James would not leave the purchase of horses to William but chose his own from those brought to the city by the gauchos. He found two high-spirited stallions like those he had seen roaming wild on the pampas. For days an enthusiastic James and a nervous William rode into the countryside around the town, familiarising themselves with the horses.

There were more difficulties in getting the internal passports allowing them to travel around the province and into Chile. There was no chance of the Spanish issuing such permissions to an Englishman but, with Ana's help, M Goriot was persuaded to request papers for that son of France, M Bergotte.

It was well into 1805 and summer was turning to autumn when M Bergotte, his valet, Apala the guide, and three porters drove their little mule train from the city and set off toward the Andes.

They travelled first across the pampas. After his time on the estancia, James felt at home in the vast emptiness of those plains. Indeed, he realised once he was out of the city, that he had missed the open countryside: the brilliant blue of the sky, the endless green of the landscape. He took a deep breath of the air, fresh and pure – free from the smells that filled the city streets. This was the land that Iglesias and his men had been prepared to fight and die for. Indeed, in his short stay with them, he had fought for this land. He had been there when Carlos had paid the ultimate price for the criollo dream of independence. Sometimes, James thought he saw the country through the eyes of the gauchos and had grown to love it.

For William, on the other hand, this was an alien world and he was not slow in letting James know how he felt about it. 'It's not right, sir. There should be hills or somesuch. Downland's well and good but grass has no business going on like this.'

James laughed and put his spurs to his horse. Soon William and his master were racing ahead of their mule train, leaving their cares temporarily behind them.

For two days they rode westward, seeing no one in that vast emptiness. On the third morning, in the distance, a plume of smoke rose against the clear blue of the sky. The next day they came across the skeleton of a horse and some feathers tied in a bundle on the ground, which led them to the conclusion that they had disturbed an Indian camp. Despite the apparent absence of any cover, the Indians seemed to have vanished, but when they woke after that night's camp, they found their resting place surrounded by the tracks of a party of horses. Here and there, too, were the marks left by the trailing of the *chuzos*, or long spears, of the natives. James was alarmed that anyone had been able to get so close to them as they slept and yet not disturb them. He was all for setting a guard at night from then on, but Apala assured him that the Indians there were not hostile, and that it was best simply to ignore them.

By the third week of their journey it seemed as if the plain might be literally, rather than figuratively, endless. They had passed through some small hills but beyond them the land swept onward, as featureless as before. The land grew drier and the grass coarser and thinner, until they were riding across bare earth, with only the occasional scrub to break the monotony. Summer was over, but it remained hot and the plains were devoid of shade.

They no longer saw herds of cattle in the distance, although here and there they would come across rheas, the ostrich-like, flightless birds that roamed the prairie. Apala would ride them down and shoot them, providing a welcome change of diet.

At last, though, the horizon was broken by a line of what James at first took for mountains. It was hours before he realised that what he was looking at was not the mountains themselves, but the clouds that hung about their summits. Only after another day of travelling did he get his first view of the Andes.

In all his travels, he had never seen anything like it. They rode all day and still the line of mountains, rising apparently sheer from the plain, seemed to draw no nearer. The range stretched from north to south as far as they could see, as if marking the very edge of the world.

Now, nearer, but dwarfed by the mountains beyond it, they made out the tiny cluster of buildings that marked the township of Mendoza. It was the first landmark on their planned journey. James had been told that the place had been founded from Chile over three hundred years earlier, and he was fired by the romance of this ancient town, between the empty plains and the majestic mountains.

As they approached, he left the road to look at the vineyards. He had seen wine from Mendoza sold in Buenos Aires and was puzzled how grapes could grow in such a barren land. As he rode past the rows of vines, he learned the secret: an intricate network of channels that carried the water that ran off the distant mountains. Even to his casual eye, it was clear that the system, though clearly recently repaired, pre-dated any European settlement.

The town itself was mellowed by age, the lines of its buildings softened by three centuries of wind and rain. Mendoza flourished here, in its splendid isolation. Its vineyards supplied both Chile and La Plata and its traders thrived on the travellers who set off from here to cross the Andes at the only pass that linked west and east for hundreds of miles.

They spent three days relaxing in Mendoza, enjoying the simple pleasures of bathing in warm water and sleeping in real beds. During the day, James suffered the inevitable bureaucracy associated with travelling from one Spanish province to another, for Mendoza marked the border between La Plata and the Captaincy-General of Santiago de Chile. He showed his papers and his passport, all the time maintaining the perfect French of M Bergotte. It was a chore but a necessary duty, and it allowed him time to explore the town. He visited the workshops of the jewellers who mounted Andean stones in local silver and discreetly enquired where the various mines were located. He strolled casually on the edge of the settlement where the straight roads just petered out into the plain, and he noticed the size of the barracks and the state of the men who guarded this vital pass. He sketched the vineyards, and estimated their value. Then, well rested and spectacularly well informed on the geography, geology, and economy of this strategic key point, James was ready to continue.

Though the trip across the mountains promised to be an adventure, he still found himself reluctant to leave Mendoza. Magnificent as they were, the Andes were unmistakably hostile. The days remained reasonably warm but there was already a nip in the morning air that reminded James that winter was on its way. He put off their departure for one last day of civilised comforts, and then the expedition left.

As they left the town, they were hardly aware of making any sort of ascent at all. The ground seemed as flat and featureless as it had for days before, but, as their horses trudged onward, Burke was aware of a slight, but steady, gradient. Nothing, though, prepared him for the sudden change from the plains to the mountains. For hours they had moved across the flat, if gently sloping, countryside and suddenly they were in the hills. The hills, to be fair, were not that high, but the contrast between the plain and the sudden mountainous terrain was dramatic.

Apala struck out confidently along a valley which twisted and turned until they were surrounded by hills on all sides. There was enough grass for cattle and horses to be grazing but there were cacti too, yellow and red flowers bursting from their green fleshy bodies.

After only half an hour, they were at the head of the valley, and in front of them they could see the towering heights of the Andes. Now the track that their guide followed rose more steeply, angling up slopes covered with tumbled rock. For a while they followed the course of a stream, carrying meltwater that would feed Mendoza's irrigation channels, but then they struck off, zigging and zagging up a track that was little more than a dusty trail on the bare rock of the mountain. By now, the Andean peaks blocked off their view all around. Facing back down the track, sheer walls of red rock blocked off their view, while ahead they saw the ominous white of the early snows already covering the mountain peaks. The sense of isolation was reinforced by the sight of the condors, circling in the brilliant blue of the sky.

'What do they eat?' asked William.

'They scavenge the dead,' Burke told him.

'They're following us.'

'We'd best remember not to die, then.'

It had been hot in the valley, but, already, Burke was noticing the chill of the air. He called to the guide to stop, so that he could unpack his greatcoat from one of the bundles of baggage hanging precariously from the mules' saddles. Apala, though, insisted that they press on.

'Soon we must stop. We cannot wait for the cold and dark before we make our camp. We will stop in less than an hour. There will be time for you to dress more warmly then.'

For another mile, they climbed still more steeply, the track doubling back on itself as they made their way up the mountain. At last it levelled off and, rounding a rocky ridge, they saw a patch of level ground with a shallow stream splashing across the rocky surface.

'Here we will camp,' their guide announced. Their porters set to unloading the tents, unused on their travel across the plains. Soon, the sound of mallets on tent pegs was echoing from the rocks as they did their best to secure their guy ropes in the stony soil.

Burke had freed his greatcoat from one of the baggage rolls but, as the sun vanished below the peaks, he felt himself shiver. 'We need a fire.'

Apala shrugged. 'Of course, señor. But first I will have to collect something for us to burn.'

Burke looked about him. There were no trees, not even any shrubs. The only greenery in sight was occasional clumps of what looked like moss clinging to some of the rocks.

He watched, astonished, as Apala strode to the nearest of these mossy clumps and tugged at it. Beneath the green coating some straggly wooden stems grew down into cracks in the stone. Burke heard them snap and realised that they were dry and brittle.

'They will not burn for long,' said his guide. 'We will need a lot. Do you want to come and help me collect it?'

Though he was tired from his day in the saddle, Burke was more than happy to explore the area around their camp. He remounted and set off with Apala, leading one of the pack mules with them. Every time that they saw any of the mossy shrub, they would dismount. The young bushes were no use to them but most had at least some older, dry parts that could be ripped from the ground and roped onto the mule's saddle. Each clump was small, though, and protected by sharp thorns that tore at their hands. It seemed to take for ever to collect enough and it was almost dark when they turned back toward their camp, the mule almost hidden under a great pile of brush.

The brushwood needed no kindling, burning fast and brilliantly. For several minutes they all huddled round the fire, enjoying the blaze. But, all too soon, the fierce heat was dying and they threw on more wood to protect themselves against the cold of the night. In less than an hour, what had seemed like a huge pile of fuel was almost exhausted. Reluctantly, they abandoned the fire. They took the sheepskins from their saddles to spread on the ground inside their tents and, wrapping themselves in blankets, lay down to sleep.

James did not sleep well. Several times, he woke and lay shivering in the thin mountain air. At last, the sky began to lighten and he heard the crackle of the flames as porters relit the fire to brew coffee and warm themselves before they started that day's ride.

When he left the tent, it was to find that it had snowed during the night. There was only a thin scattering of white on the ground, but it was a reminder of the dangers of travelling this late in the season.

'We must push on hard,' said Apala. 'We have to cross the pass before nightfall. It will be too cold to camp up there.'

The porters were already packing away the tents while James and William sipped at their coffee. Barely an hour after sunrise, they were back on the horses and pushing on up into the mountains.

There was no snow falling now but, as they climbed, the snow lying on the ground grew thicker. The path rose steeply and, after an hour, the landscape was distinctly wintry. As they neared the pass, the wind, moving through the gap in the mountain range, grew stronger, and the snow covering was blown about. In some places reddish or black rock lay bare to the sky while, in others, the snow was banking to the point where the horses would stumble, unable to see their footing beneath the white covering.

'We can't stay on the track,' Apala said.

He was right. The snow was drifting off the steeper rocks at the side of the track and banking on the path to the point where there was too much danger of a horse falling and breaking its leg. They urged their reluctant mounts from the apparent smoothness of the path onto the ragged rocks alongside it. Though these were steeper and, under other circumstances, would have made for more difficult riding, the snow lay thinly here and the horses could pick their way in comparative safety. Inevitably, though, leaving the path slowed them down and Burke saw Apala casting increasingly worried eyes upward as the day progressed.

Looking in the same direction, Burke could see nothing. Mist covered the top of the mountains and merged with the snow to make it a blank wilderness of white. He was astonished that their guide could navigate confidently through this emptiness but Apala pushed them on with no hesitation as to their route. His sole concern was that night might fall while they were still too high on the mountain.

The horses struggled as the snow grew thicker. Sometimes they would stumble in the steeper drifts and everyone would dismount to lead their beasts, which were less likely to fall when relieved of their weight. Climbing through the snow, even for short distances, was exhausting, though. The damp began to leak into Burke's boots and he found himself panting for breath in the thin air. He longed to rest and make a fire to be warm and dry, if only for a few minutes, but Apala drove them on.

Now the mountains closed around them and they were struggling through deeper snow, against a wind that howled through the gap between the peaks ahead of them.

Then the wind fell and Burke was aware that the path was dropping beneath them as steeply as is had been rising before. They were through the pass.

It was hours before Apala would let them stop, but at last they were clear of the worst of the snow and they pitched their tents once again. As they slipped from their horses, James and William were exhausted. When Apala went in search of fuel for the night's fire, neither offered to accompany him.

The next day dawned bright and clear and the spirits of the party rose quickly as they moved easily along the tracks down the mountains. The descent was, if anything, even steeper than the climb from the east and they dropped quickly. By midday, bare rock was already giving way to patches of grass. Tiny blue flowers began to appear and then cacti – first small and gradually larger, until they were passing spiny monsters taller than they were, bright with orange flowers. As they moved further down, myrtle and tamarisk began to fill the air with the smell of spice. It was still cold in the shade but they felt that they were, once again, entering a habitable world.

They camped for one final night before starting the last part of their descent. By now, the grass was thick enough to use as pasture. Soon after they broke camp they came upon an Indian shepherd driving a herd of llamas to graze beside the track. Burke had heard of llamas, but this was his first chance to observe them at close quarters. He was intrigued by their docility and the extraordinary beauty of their long eyelashes.

'William,' he decided, 'when we return, we shall purchase one of these creatures and drive it with the mules. The president of the Royal Society wrote to me asking that I report on the fauna of this region and I am sure he would rather have a living example of such a creature than a mere description.'

'Are you sure that's a good idea, sir?'

'It's an excellent idea. A collection of animals will distract attention from our primary purpose, it will serve the interests of the Royal Society and, finally, it will enable me to make a contribution to the Duke of York's private menagerie.'

'Oh well,' replied William, 'that's all there is to be said then.'

James Burke shrugged. That was, indeed, all there was to be said. The Duke of York was unlikely to forget a man who had given him a llama. For an ambitious officer without money, the goodwill of the Duke of York was well worth the inconvenience that the animals might inflict on William.

James looked at the beasts again. William would be able to manage them. He just hoped they didn't bite.

They continued to make their way down toward the Chilean plain. The descent, naturally, was faster than the climb up from La Plata. Their surroundings seemed to change with every hour. The vegetation grew taller and thicker and soon it was warm enough for butterflies to appear, at first in ones and twos but, as their little cavalcade moved downward, rising in their dozens to disappear between the flowers. On this side of the mountain, there was no shortage of rainfall and, for the first time since James had left Buenos Aires he was able to shelter in the shade of the trees growing beside their path. By the afternoon breadfruits, pawpaws, and mare's tails appeared. They passed a thicket of bamboo: a straggly clump – nothing like he had seen in Haiti. But soon there were more, growing thicker until the groves were filled with stems twice the height of a man. Streams ran alongside the path and waterfalls splashed down from the peaks above them. After the cruel emptiness of the mountains, they felt they were entering paradise.

Finally, they reached a valley, folded between the hills that still rose on either side. Here they came on their first evidence of cultivation – a patch of earth, laboriously scratched out among the trees and rocks.

James stopped to examine the plants growing there.

'It's a bloody potato patch.' He turned away in disgust. 'Might as well have stayed in Ireland.'

Beyond the potatoes, though, another field was covered with leaves amongst which trumpet shaped purple flowers struggled to reach the sun. This time it was William who peered suspiciously at the crop.

'That looks like a nasturtium,' he said. 'Only it isn't.'

Their guide stepped off the path to join him.

'Mashua,' he said. 'Like potato but spicy. But you shouldn't eat it. It makes you less a man.'

Apala turned back to the path and set their procession on its way again. Burke and Williams exchanged glances, shrugged, and followed him.

Barely had they started to move than the track veered around another spinney and they found their way blocked by three black cows. They were on the edge of a village.

This was no Spanish colonial outpost but an Indian village, such as they had not seen on their journey through La Plata. The houses were made of adobe bricks and smoke rose through their thatched roofs. Beyond the houses, the valley floor was a patchwork of tiny fields where the men could just be seen ploughing with piebald bulls. A woman, her baby in a wicker basket carried on her back, emerged from one of the huts and greeted them solemnly as they passed.

Spread below them were the fields of Chile. They stopped and looked at the wooded country ahead of them, so different from the plains to the east of the mountains. The smell of spice and damp in the air, the sight of Indians going about their business, cattle roaming in threes and fours instead of in hundreds.

James looked out over a whole new world. He took a deep breath, enjoying the air of Chile. As always, he was thrilled by the prospect of a new land. New places, new experiences, new people: in novelty, it seemed to him, he could re-invent himself, putting his past behind him.

'I think this was worth the trip,' he said to William.

Three weeks later, he was not so sure. When he had persuaded Colonel Taylor to finance the trip, he had promised that he would survey the coast in the south of the country. Though the possibility of a British naval expedition rounding the Horn seemed remote, he had set out intending to deliver on his promise.

'We'll start at the south and work our way up,' he airily informed William.

Now they had been trekking two hundred miles across the Chilean plain with its constant rain, he felt as if he had never left the perpetual damp misery of his Kilkenny childhood. And still they were hundreds of miles from the southern extremity of the country.

'This is ridiculous,' he complained to William. 'We're in the middle of nowhere.'

He spoke the literal truth. For the last two days they had seen no one and the supplies they bought in the last village they passed were running low. 'Even if the British Army got here safely, what would they do? Any landing is going to have to be made in the north.'

'There's Talcahuano, sir.'

James sighed. Sometimes he wished that William was not quite so efficient. He had hoped to forget Talcahuano.

'Yes, Brown, there is Talcahuano.' He sighed again. 'Very well, Talcahuano it is. But no further.'

So Talcahuano marked the southernmost point of the expedition. It was, Burke had to admit, worth the effort.

Although it had only been recognised as a port by the Chilean government less than fifty years earlier, a visit showed it to be flourishing. Half a dozen ships stood at anchor in the enormous bay, protected from any storms off the Pacific by a peninsular jutting northward. They saw whaling ships flying the flag of the United States, as well as Spanish merchant vessels whose crews filled the dockside taverns, readying themselves to face the rigours of a passage round the Horn. William spent a couple of evenings drinking with crew on shore leave and confirmed what James already believed. Talcahuano was the last decent harbour before the Magellan Straits. Any naval attack on Chile would need to make its first landfall here. James was happy enough with that prospect. A few days spent walking around the bay confirmed his first impression that its size made it impossible to defend. The entrance was too wide for any shore-based batteries to threaten ships out in the channel and a vast army would have to be tied down to protect all the possible landing sites along the shore. The Spaniards, sensibly in James' opinion, had decided that only a token presence was worthwhile. There wasn't even a proper fort – just a barracks, where a hundred or so troops represented the sole military force.

Satisfied with what he had learned, James led his caravan north. They moved slowly up the coast, stopping at every town they found. Burke would send William out with a butterfly net to encourage the idea that he was simply another European anxious to record the wonders of the New World for the learned societies of Paris and Berlin. It left him free to sketch, although far more of his sketches featured such Spanish fortifications as they came across than recorded the beauties of Chilean wildlife.

By the time they had worked their way back to Valparaiso, almost three hundred miles to the north, Burke was sick of the sea. The weather, though still mild, continued to be wet and the succession of small ports and even smaller villages between them had lost any charm it might once have had. He decided that they would spend the rest of the winter in Santiago. So the little caravan turned away from the sea and back toward the Andes that they had crossed almost ten weeks earlier.

Only when the mountains were looming over them did they finally arrive at the nominal capital of the province of La Plata.

James knew that Santiago was a relatively small place, overtaken by cities on the east of the continent, which offered easier sea routes to Spain. Even so, it was a disappointment. It was laid out on the same rigid grid pattern as Buenos Aires – a design that made only the smallest of concessions to the mighty Mapocho river which ran through its centre. The arrow straight streets and elegant squares, which were so impressive in Buenos Aires, looked stunted and ridiculous in this little town under the mountains. The only building that might have interested James was the mint – a palatial two-storey affair built around a central courtyard where orange trees promised that summer would come eventually. However, even this failed to live up to its promise. Parts were still scaffolded, with workmen dabbing paint brushes half-heartedly at the new plasterwork. William had, as usual, explored the local taverns to pick up what titbits he could, less because James thought there would be anything useful to learn as for want of something better to do.

'They've been building that place for the last twenty years,' he told James. 'I think some of them are hoping to spin it out until their grandkids can take over.'

After less than two months, James and William felt they had both walked every one of the streets a hundred times. Rain or no rain, it was time to be off.

The presence of the mint was a tangible reminder of the reason for the area's importance. If Britain was to be able to come to some well-founded view on the value of Spain's American possessions, it needed to know how much silver there was. So the focus of the expedition moved from Chile's military defences to its mineral worth.

They started with a return to the coastal plain but a month spent surveying the geology of the lowlands confirmed what Burke's masters in London already suspected: there was no silver there. The Spaniards' wealth came from Upper Peru and the near-legendary silver mines of Potosí. It was time to move north.

Soon they had left behind them the lush green of the farmlands and vineyards of the coastal plain and were entering the rocky desert of Atacama.

Even Burke's enthusiasm for new places was dented by the harshness of the world they now found themselves in. They had added three llamas to their mule train and all of the animals were loaded down with water, but still they had to ration their drinks in that great expanse of nothingness. The odd patch of scrubby grass made it through the rock, but everywhere they looked there was a glare of white stone reflecting the sun. Though full summer was still months off, the days were remorselessly hot. At night, though, they would shiver as the temperature fell toward freezing. It seemed almost as cold as it had been in the Andes. As he shivered in the morning chill, Burke remembered the fires that had thawed them out in the mountains. Here, their firewood had run out days ago and, in all that vast emptiness, there was no growing thing that could replace it.

James began to wonder if the Catholics had been right all along. Was this Perdition? Was he to repent his sins in an eternity of heat and thirst?

On the horizon, the Andes seemed to taunt them. The mountains formed a solid wall to the east and Burke's expedition had to push on until they reached the next pass, hundreds of miles north of Mendoza.

Each night, as they camped, James made a note in his journal, detailing the distance they had covered. Without his notes, he was sure he would have lost track of the time they had passed in that terrible place. When they finally left the great bowl of the desert, his notes said they had been walking for a fortnight. Without them, he could easily have believed it had been months.

Exhausted, and with their supplies almost gone, they were nonetheless relieved to be climbing into the hills again. The mountains here were lower and less rugged than where they had crossed in the south and the climb was relatively easy.

For the first time since they had entered the desert, they found water flowing in streams fed from the snow that covered the peaks of the Andes. There were oases of green amid the rocks, and, despite the harshness of the climate and the thinness of the soil, they found people eking out an existence on the slopes of the mountains. James delighted in the presence of Indian tribes he had not seen before, the men in brightly coloured woven ponchos, the women staggering under the weight of their multi-layered pleated skirts.

'They never take them off,' their guide assured Burke. 'And when they wear out, they just put another one on top.'

Burke, sniffing as he passed the next group upon the road, decided that he believed him.

Whenever they came to a village, William would enquire as to the availability of food and forage and James would look for evidence of mining or any mineral wealth. He often came across a craftsman working the local stones into silver mounts but the silver, he was always told, came from Potosí.

'There seems nothing for a European nation here,' he grumbled to William. 'The sole importance of this region is that it controls access to the mines and, beyond them, to La Plata.'

'That's as may be, sir, but I doubt you'll get an army across here. There's forage enough for a few animals like ours but nothing like what you would need for an army. Anyone crossing these mountains will have to bring their provisions with them.'

Their growing caravan (they had added two vicuñas and an alpaca to the llamas) continued eastward into the Andes. The air became thinner and the nights colder but they would still pass villagers, tending what little soil there was.

Seeing the poverty of the mountain settlements – too small, really, to qualify even as villages – Burke couldn't help feeling that the grandeur of the Spanish Empire was more apparent viewed on a ruler's globe than in its raw reality. The silver mined at Potosí, it was said, was enough to have built a bridge across the ocean from South America to Spain. Yet, the practical effect of colonial rule seemed to be that thousands of soldiers were tied down to maintain a hold on people the average Spaniard scarcely knew existed. James thought of the malodorous women, and the men, stolidly chewing the coca leaves that left them in a drugged semi-stupor that allowed them to get through the drudgery of their lives. Were these people worth the effort of colonisation?

His attitude changed, though, when they reached Potosí.

They had been climbing for over a week when they arrived at the city. They were now over twelve thousand feet above sea level and the air was so thin that they could move only with difficulty, yet the city of Potosí was huge. It was much bigger than Buenos Aires and laid out in the grand Spanish style, with great plazas surrounded by elegant porticos and well-built houses that would not have looked out of place in Madrid.

In fact, there was not one city but two – a European metropolis and, adjoining it, but kept entirely separate, a rambling slum where the thousands of Indians employed in the silver mines lived out a meagre existence under the rule of their Spanish masters.

Dominating the whole place was the Cerro Rico – the Rich Peak, a sacred mountain which, or so the stories said, was almost solid silver.

Burke's caravan made its way to the native quarter, where the animals were stabled and shelter was found for the porters before James and William crossed to the European town and found themselves rooms in an inn.

James slept that night in the first proper bed he had seen since they left Valparaíso and he woke with a renewed vigour only somewhat offset by the exhaustion resulting from any activity in the thin mountain air.

He spent the day exploring the town, gawking like any yokel at the magnificent buildings and the richly decorated churches.

'Perhaps,' he suggested to William, 'they really did come here to save the Indians' souls.'

'Indians can't use this church, sir. They've got their own on the other side of town.'

James looked across to the towers and cupolas of the church of San Bernito. The Indian church looked even bigger than this one and, he did not doubt, the interior would be lavishly decorated with silver and gold. He wondered if the Indians appreciated what had been done with the minerals they had dug from the mountains.

'Tomorrow, William,' he said, 'we must visit the mines.'

The next day they made their way toward the peak but, shortly after they left the town, they were politely but firmly turned back by a military picket.

'It's not safe up there,' a smartly turned out sergeant had told them. 'Not really the sort of place a gentleman like yourself would want to visit.'

James had to content himself with drinking in a nearby tavern from which he could see the traffic on the road – the files of Indians, trotting up the hill, harried along by mounted overseers; the carts carrying ore into the town for processing.

He left William spinning out another drink and counting the carts while he made his way through the town to the garrison.

The army's quarters at Potosí were built on the same lavish scale as the rest of the town but, even allowing for a degree of architectural extravagance, the building obviously housed a sizeable military force. From the size of the parade ground laid out in front of the barracks, James reckoned they could keep a whole regiment stationed there.

He strolled back toward the tavern where he had left William. Now he was looking for them, he saw soldiers everywhere. They mounted guard outside the mint, they manned posts along the road the ore took into the town, and they escorted mule trains heading east, their packs giving the occasional metallic tinkle. It was, he thought, like living in a bank – and an exceptionally well-guarded bank at that.

He decided that it was time for the amateur artist to take the air and so, after lunch at the inn, James could be seen here and there, working at his easel. He painted beautiful landscapes but each view would contain some detail of the approaches to the town or the position of guardhouses or the emplacements that protected the few cannon that Potosí possessed.

James' persona as an amateur painter was, by now, so perfected that he almost believed it himself. He was, therefore profoundly shocked, late that afternoon, to find his sketching interrupted by a young ensign accompanied by a sergeant and two private soldiers.

'Your papers please.'

James reached for his passport, which he carried always about his person.

'M Bergotte.'

'Oui. C'est moi.'

The officer switched from Spanish to a passable French.

'You have been observed at various points around the town, monsieur. I have been ordered to hold you on suspicion that you may be a spy.'

'Don't be ridiculous, man, I'm French. The French are your allies. Why would we be spying on you?'

The ensign was polite but firm: 'That may well be the case, sir, but I am to bring you before my captain. And I believe you have a servant travelling with you.'

Burke agreed that he had.

'We had best collect him on our way.'

That, Burke thought, was bad news. William was again ensconced in a tavern, this time keeping a record of the traffic to and from the mint. It was not a location designed to reduce suspicion. Nonetheless, he had no choice but to lead his captors there.

William seemed intent on his drink as they entered the tavern, though James noticed him pocketing the penknife with which he had been scratching a tally on the bench where he sat.

'Your papers.'

James stepped forward, ignoring the restraining hand of the Sergeant.

'If you read my documents, monsieur, you will see that he is included as being in my party.'

'And is he French?'

'He is from Corsica, monsieur. So, disreputable as he is, he is accounted French.'

The officer looked sceptically at William. His lips curled a little at the sorry specimen before him.

'Can you speak for yourself, man?'

There was a pause, before William stumbled out with: 'Oui. Je suis Francais aussi. Le valet de M Bergotte.'

William's French, though passable, was not fluent and his accent was poor, but the Spaniard, who had never come across an uneducated Corsican before, had no basis on which to judge him. He looked at Burke's documents and at the two men before him. Without warning, he switched to English.

'You're lying. You are English spies.'

Burke cursed inwardly that he had had the misfortune to meet up with one of the more intelligent junior officers in the Spanish army. None of this showed on his face, though, as he replied in French that he could not understand what the man was saying. But

William's expression had, for an instant, betrayed his alarm and the ensign allowed himself a grim smile of satisfaction.

'You are both under arrest. You will follow me.'

The Privates closed in either side of the two supposed Frenchmen with the Sergeant close behind as they followed the officer at a brisk march to the barracks. William was promptly thrown into the cells but James, in accordance with his presumed status as a gentleman, was left under guard in a comfortable room while men were sent to collect his baggage for searching.

It was late by the time the search was finished. It revealed nothing more than the sketches and landscapes that a gentleman travelling in strange parts might reasonably be expected to produce. There was also a journal of the journey in French. An officer with a good command of the language was brought in to read it but it would have taken a native French speaker to find the coded references to troop numbers and artillery emplacements that had been concealed in the most florid descriptive passages.

'What were you doing in Potosí?'

The question came again and again and always the answer was the same: M Bergotte was a gentleman visiting Buenos Aires. As a French citizen, he was a friend of Spain. He was innocently taking the opportunity of his business in La Plata to explore the Andes and to visit the famed city of Potosí.

After hours of this, Burke's interrogators were beginning to tire of the game and their prisoner's unfailing charm and good humour were beginning to win them over.

Burke explained again why he was in the town. 'I had thought it was a legend – like El Dorado. But the city really does produce that much wealth?'

'It does, monsieur.'

'But there is just one mine here. Surely the wealth of Spain cannot depend on just this one mountain.'

'One mine, monsieur but with a hundred shafts. The mountain is hollowed out with our digging. It is by no means trivial.'

'Of course not, señor. Forgive me. I had no intention of being insulting. I am sure that guarding this post is a most significant task.'

Something in M Bergotte's tone suggested that he was merely being polite and the officer, stung, could not resist sly indications of how important the place was.

The interrogations continued for two days and, at the end of them, the Spanish knew no more than they had when they started. James Burke, on the other hand, knew a lot more about the value of the mine and the disposition of the forces stationed to protect it.

William had been questioned separately but, after that first near-fatal slip, he was careful to give nothing away. He was surly, his accent was execrable and he appeared to his interrogators to be extraordinarily stupid – but then he was a Corsican. The island may have given birth to Bonaparte, but it was otherwise famous for producing fools.

'M Bergotte, you are obviously a man of culture. Why do you tolerate that man as your valet?'

'Jean? Poor man. His mother served my family well and her son is not that bright. I took him on as my valet and he serves well enough. Why, señor, is he troublesome?'

Not troublesome, it was admitted – just unhelpful. And, presumably, on account of his innate stupidity rather than any deliberate obstructionism.

By the third day, his interrogators were still uncertain what to do. M Bergotte had behaved suspiciously but his papers were in order and he certainly sounded like a Frenchman. His valet, though, did not sound French and the porters claimed they had heard the two talking in English. But, on the other hand, the porters spoke only Spanish and could well have been mistaken.

M Bergotte's papers had been examined by the Captain in charge of his interrogation and now they were scrutinised again by a major. By the time the troublesome Frenchman's case had been referred to the colonel, all that anyone wanted to do was pass responsibility for him elsewhere. The papers had been issued in Buenos Aires. Buenos Aires could sort it out.

So, M Bergotte was sent off to Buenos Aires. Technically, he was under arrest but, far from finding this an inconvenience, James found it a considerable benefit. Their escort (two troopers and a sergeant) kept them moving, and the fact that they were on government business meant that they were able to use the post houses set up for military communications. The soldiers were happy to chat and proved pleasant companions, as well as yet another source of information on the disposal of Spanish troops in the region.

Just over three weeks after leaving Potosí, James, together with his escort, rode up to the offices tucked away in the streets running off the Plaza Victoria. Here the clerks, messengers, copyists, and lawyers carried out the actual business of government and here M Bergotte's papers were confirmed as being in order.

'Are you sure?' queried the Sergeant. 'My Captain said we were to make absolutely certain that he's French.'

'The paperwork . . .'

'Yes, I know the paperwork is in order.' The Sergeant was meticulous and wanted more.

'Perhaps there's someone who could vouch for you?'

'Why not?' M Bergotte was happy to oblige. He was sure that his countryman, M Goriot, would tell the Sergeant whatever he needed to know.

M Goriot was sent for and immediately confirmed M Bergotte's identity and nationality.

The Sergeant was quite relieved. He had come to like M Bergotte. He shook hands with real enthusiasm and set off to ride to the local garrison for a night's rest before starting back to Potosí. James made a mental note not to visit Colonel Calzada Castanio until at least the next evening.

'What on earth was all that about?' asked M Goriot, as they made their way homeward.

'I don't really know. They seemed to have some fantastical notion that I was an English spy.'

'An English spy!'

The two men laughed. As M Goriot said to his wife that night: 'You can never account for the eccentricities of the Iberian mind.'

'But he's not a spy, is he?'

'Of course not, my dear.'

'Oh.' Mme Goriot didn't admit it but a part of her was disappointed. Life in Buenos Aires could be so dull. A spy would have livened things up.

*

At the O'Gorman residence, life was proving anything but dull. Three llamas, two vicuñas, and an alpaca had to be stabled alongside the two stallions with which they had started out on their expedition. Trunks full of jewellery and rock samples were sent to Thomas O'Gorman's warehouse and James' notes and drawings littered his room.

It was hours before some sort of order was restored. Thomas O'Gorman was finally left to his business, and the servants withdrew to their quarters to go about theirs. Only then did Burke finally find himself alone with Ana O'Gorman.

She was, James thought, rather quieter than usual, but she asked a few polite questions about his journey and then announced that she was feeling very fatigued and would rest a while in her boudoir. James smiled knowingly and, allowing her five minutes for propriety's sake, he followed to her room. He turned the handle and pushed gently at the door, only to find it locked. Puzzled, he knocked quietly. After a pause, he knocked less quietly. Another pause and he was about to hammer on the door when the sound of servants moving around downstairs reminded him that he had to exercise some discretion, and he had best return to his own room.

The next day, Ana contrived to ensure that she was never alone with James, so it was not until the day after that he managed to catch her as she was sitting at her household accounts.

'Ana, why are you avoiding me?'

'Avoiding you? Why, Mr Burke, I am here with you now. How can I possibly be avoiding you?'

'You know perfectly well what I mean.'

Ana looked up from the bills on her bureau and stared angrily at him.

'No, James, I don't know what you mean. I am here, in Buenos Aires, with you. I have not left you for over half a year to go gallivanting about the countryside.'

'Gallivanting about the countryside! Ana, I have been conducting a survey on behalf of our government. It was my work.'

'Phooey and fiddlesticks! You went because it was fun. You enjoyed yourself playing at explorers with your man William and now that game is ended, you expect to return to Buenos Aires and play your other games with me. Well, perhaps I have found my own entertainment while you were away.'

'Ana.' James tried to think of a response but she had already returned to her accounts.

'Don't interrupt me, James. I'm trying to add up.'

James, as a sound military man, decided to withdraw from the assault and regroup his forces.

For the next few days, Ana was polite but distant and James bided his time, watching and waiting, anxious to find out what new entertainment she might have discovered.

The answer came on the night of the next meeting of the Société Francaise. Ana spent longer than usual preparing herself for the evening's entertainment and was adamant that she would prefer not to be accompanied. She might as well, in James' opinion, have left a note for him: 'Have gone to meet my lover; do not wait up.'

Left alone in the house (Mr O'Gorman was conducting some business over dinner with another merchant), James told himself that he had not the slightest interest in Ana's doings. She was but a passing fancy. It had been fun while it lasted, but it was not as if she had ever meant anything to him.

He continued this internal monologue as he put on his boots and cloak. He was still telling himself that he cared not one jot for her as he heard Monsieur Bergotte being announced at the Societé Francaise soirée.

Monsieur Goriot hurried over to greet him.

‘I’m so pleased that you could come after all. Madame Perichon was explaining that you were a little unwell after your travels but I see you appear quite recovered.’

‘I was a little indisposed,’ Burke agreed, tactfully. ‘But I decided that the best physic would be an evening of your company and, you see, I am recovering already.’

M Goriot was delighted. M Goriot was pleased to hear that M Bergotte had suffered no real harm as a result of his arrest. (‘Such a ridiculous misunderstanding.’) M Goriot wanted to hear all about M Bergotte’s travels. (‘It must have been so exciting, monsieur. I only wish my business here allowed me to mount such an expedition.’)

M Goriot’s interests so monopolised M Bergotte’s attention that it was a good half hour before he caught a glimpse of Ana, deep in conversation with Admiral de Liniers.

As James saw the two of them, Ana looked away from the older man and saw James’ eye upon her. For a moment she blushed, before, with a defiant toss of her head, she turned back to de Liniers and carried on with their talk.

James watched them for a minute longer. All around him was the buzz of conversation but he no longer cared to listen. Abruptly, he turned away and, explaining to those well-wishers who would have detained him that he was not yet fully recovered from his journey, he returned home.

He did not sleep well that night. When William woke him, the tea that he brought was more than usually welcome.

‘Thank you, William. I needed that.’

‘Can’t go wrong with a good cuppa to start the day, sir. The others are already up. Mr O’Gorman is off about his business and Mrs O’Gorman is in the breakfast room.’

Burke hesitated. ‘Perhaps I should have my breakfast later.’ He had a vague recollection that Ana had featured in the dreams that had disturbed his troubled sleep.

He took his time dressing and almost an hour had elapsed before he made his way down to breakfast. But when he did, Ana was there waiting for him.

She gave him no chance to speak before launching into a furious attack. How dare he follow her? she wanted to know. What right did he think he had to behave in such a way?

James stood silent as she abused him. Her eyes flashed, her cheeks were slightly flushed. She was, he realised, quite, quite beautiful. And she was right. He had abandoned and neglected her and then expected to return and take up as if he had never been away.

She paused and, before she could add to her catalogue of complaints, he pre-empted her. 'I had no right, Ana, and I am truly sorry.'

He spoke as he did because, knowing he was in the wrong, he could think of nothing better to say. He had not adopted his approach as a cunning strategy. Yet nothing could have more completely won his way back into the good graces of Mrs O'Gorman. She kept up the pretence of anger for several more minutes but it was an act that was fooling neither of them. When Burke finally felt safe to sit and start on his belated breakfast, Ana insisted on heaping his plate for him and that afternoon, when she took her siesta, her bedroom door was no longer locked.

*

Buenos Aires at the start of September 1805 seemed not that much changed since he had left it. Spain had declared war on Britain at the end of 1804, but the news had not reached La Plata until just after James had left in February. Beyond the imposition of some extra taxes, the war had remarkably little effect on life in the viceroyalty. French, Spanish, and British merchants still lived and traded peaceably with each other. O'Gorman complained that new regulations were crippling his ventures, but Ana assured James that he continued to prosper.

'He's a lovely man, in his way,' she said, 'but he's never happy unless he's unhappy about something, and he's convinced that he faces ruin once or twice a month. He loves his business, James.' She sighed. 'I could never really compete with that.'

Burke looked at Ana who was, as she spoke, lying naked alongside him. O'Gorman, he thought, must have had an extraordinary commitment to commerce if he preferred to watch over his balance sheets rather than enjoy the prospect that Ana presented to Burke. He cupped one of her ample breasts in his hand.

'You may, at least, be assured of my full attention, madam,' he told her.

She giggled and Burke, true to his promise, put aside all thought of military plans and troop dispositions until, some considerable time later, she was lying asleep in a tangle of sheets with a contented smile on her face.

Burke slipped from the bed and made his way to his own room. He knew that he had come close to losing Ana, so he made sure that she did not feel she had to take second place to his business as well as her husband's. But now that the war that he had expected for so long had finally been declared, there was a degree of urgency to his mission. He sat up long into the night busy with invisible ink and codebooks. William's needle and thread stitched maps and drawings into leather goods, while troop numbers were hidden in the bills of account that accompanied them.

It was not until well into the next morning that Burke had William take the fruits of their labours to O'Gorman's warehouse, from which they would set off on their circuitous route to Whitehall and Colonel Taylor.

That evening, James and William relaxed over a congratulatory brandy and Burke reviewed their progress to date.

'We seem to have achieved most of what we set out to do. I have provided England with details of the coastal defences, both here and in Chile, and the state of the Spanish garrisons. With this intelligence, I am confident that Britain could, if it wished, mount a successful invasion. Our information on the geology and mineral wealth of the country will enable Mr Pitt to decide whether or not such a move would be in the national interest.'

William raised his glass in a silent toast and Burke continued. 'We have a menagerie of local wildlife for the Royal Society and a collection of jewellery for the Duchess of York. I think we can consider that a job well done.'

He sipped at his brandy, his brow furrowed.

'You're not satisfied, sir?'

'No, I'm not. There's no doubt that we can capture and hold La Plata and Chile and the amount of silver that the Spaniards are extracting here may make it a worthwhile exercise. But we are ignoring the political aspect of it. The Spanish are vulnerable at least in part because the people here do not support Spain. They will not fight for her. But we know that there are hidden forces out on the pampas. If the leaders of these rebels, whoever they might be, were to raise the people against any invasion, then the whole situation would be changed. We would need significant numbers of troops to hold down the province. But if the rebels were actively supporting a British invasion – or even just agreed not to intervene on either side – then we would be able to hand La Plata to His Majesty on a silver salver.'

'So we need to find out who is leading the rebels and win them over to our way of seeing things.'

Burke smiled at his companion. 'As ever, William, you see the situation and have summed it up in a nutshell.'

'So ask Iglesias for his help.'

Burke gazed into his brandy while thinking over what William had said. It might be possible. But suppose the mysterious leader would not reveal himself and, instead, chose to conduct his negotiations through Iglesias? Burke was conscious that he represented King George and the might of England. It was only proper that he talk directly to the future ruler of La Plata. And then again, Iglesias was a proud man and might well insist on conducting the business himself. James did not want to end up a footnote in history, talking to another footnote. Besides, there were practical problems.

He put his glass to one side and leaned forward.

'Easier said than done. He's seldom in town and when I find him here I have to tell him I'm not an American patriot but an Englishman and would he kindly entrust me with the identity of his leader – a man who seems to have gone to some trouble to protect his anonymity. And, of course, I have then exposed myself to him as a spy. Not perhaps the wisest move.'

'That's all very well, sir, but it could be the only move you have left to make.'

Burke whirled his brandy around the glass, sniffed, grimaced, and swigged.

'You could be right. But we'll try another week before we give up any hope of identifying the man behind all this.'

So for a week, William went back to trawling the taverns in the hope of hearing something while James courted Colonel Calzada Castanio, the Viceroy, and M Goriot. He even persuaded Ana O'Gorman that they should make another visit to the Societé Francaise together.

Their excursion to the Goriots' salon was the first time she had returned there since James had discovered her with de Liniers. Ana was nervous of being together with both of her lovers at the soirée and she decided to fortify herself by appearing at her very, very best. If a woman is to sin, she reasoned, she is less likely to be condemned if she sins in a truly beautiful dress. She tried one outfit after another, finally settling on a white creation in spotted muslin, so long that it effectively had a short train. To offset the plain white, she wore a silver brooch with a great red stone in it.

If the intention had been to make an impact on James, she succeeded beyond her wildest dreams. As she entered the room, he looked at her finery with a smile and then, catching sight of the brooch, he had stepped over and seized her arm.

'Where did you get that brooch?'

She had tried to make a joke of it.

'Mr Burke, I didn't know you were so anxious to have one like it.'

He was still holding her arm – so tightly she feared it would leave bruises.

'Mr Burke! James! Let me go!'

James released her arm and took a step back.

'I'm sorry, Ana. But I need to know where that brooch came from.'

'It was a gift.'

'From whom?'

Ana blushed and suddenly James realised.

'De Liniers!'

She nodded.

'Are you very angry?'

James laughed. He could not help himself. He laughed and pulled her to him and kissed her.

He had seen that brooch before, as Pedro emptied the treasure they had captured on their raid. De Liniers! A Frenchman, with nought but a mercenary commitment to the Spanish court. A military man, ambitious but unlikely to rise further in a military hierarchy where birth mattered. No wonder he was so anxious to keep his identity a secret.

'Ana.'

'James?'

'Do we have to call upon M Goriot?'

'I thought you wanted to.'

'I've changed my mind.'

'The chaise is waiting for us.'

He looked at Ana, a vision in white. Beautiful, vibrant Ana – who had just given him the answer to a mystery that had been tantalising him for the better part of a year.

'Then let's drive out. Only not to the Societé Francaise. We have something to celebrate.'

In the chaise, he remembered the inn where they had first made love and wondered whether he should not drive there. On reflection, though, the gown deserved more elegant surroundings.

'What's the best hotel in Buenos Aires?' he asked.

Half an hour later, they were dining in a private room at the Hotel Colón. And two hours after that they were lying in bed in the most luxurious bedroom Burke had ever spent a night in.

'I love this room,' said Ana.

James looked at the fine rugs, the elegant wallpapers, the polished mahogany tables.

'What do you like most?' he asked.

'Well,' she smiled, 'it has a very beautiful ceiling.'

*

James called on Sr de Liniers at his home early on Tuesday 10th September 1805. The admiral was at home and he was shown into the morning room by the butler, who announced him at the door.

'Mister James Burke.'

Santiago de Liniers was sitting at a writing table and he did not rise to greet James. Only after he had finished reading the note on the table in front of him did he address his visitor.

'Mister Burke.'

'Señor.'

De Liniers looked sharply at the Englishman. He was not wearing his wig. As James had deduced, he was going bald and this combined with the sharpness of his nose gave James the impression that he was being examined by a particularly intelligent eagle.

'I think we have already met. Only you were under the name of Monsieur Bergotte.'

James nodded his acknowledgement of the point.

'Or was it Captain Witz?'

'My apologies, señor. You will appreciate that I had my reasons for not advertising my true identity.'

'But am I to take it that you really are Mister James Burke?'

'Or Lieutenant Burke, if you prefer.'

'You are a British officer?'

'I am.'

'So you are a spy. Why should I not have you shot?'

'Because, señor, you, too, are not what you appear.'

The older man said nothing but simply looked at Burke.

James decided that he looked less like an eagle and more like one of the great Andean condors examining some creature on the point of death, deciding where to take the first bite.

'I know where Sr Iglesias received his instructions.'

No reply.

'Señor, I am here as a friend. I am an agent of the British government. I have the ear of the Duke of York.'

It was true, up to a point. He certainly had the ear of Colonel Taylor and Colonel Taylor was constantly at the Duke's side.

'Why would the British government want to be a friend to me?'

'Because you are an enemy of the Spanish.'

'I am an admiral in the Spanish navy.'

'But you are a South American patriot.'

Finally, de Liniers allowed himself a flicker of emotion. The tiniest inclination of his head suggested that he accepted Burke's point. Encouraged, James continued:

'La Plata will be independent of Spain. I have seen enough of this country to know that it can be no colony, yoked to a European master. Britain lost her colonies in North America and Spain will, as surely, lose hers in the south.'

'You are correct. Revolution will come. And sooner than anyone expects. But why would Britain support such a movement?'

'Because an independent South America cuts off Spain's supplies of treasure as effectively as a country garrisoned by British troops. If you would rise against Spain, then Britain will stand at your side.'

The admiral appeared to give this some consideration.

'Are you offering military support?'

'The British, as you must know, are contemplating a military expedition to South America. Such an expedition, by removing Spanish control, would allow you your independence.'

'Our independence from Spain, certainly. But only to exchange one master for another.'

So far, Burke had remained standing. Now, without being asked, he took a seat.

'You are in charge of the sea defences of La Plata.'

De Liniers nodded.

'Should you choose, you would be in a position to ensure that the British were able to land with no real opposition.'

'That would be to betray my country.'

'It would be to betray Spain. You are a Frenchman, living in South America. Your loyalty is to this land that you love, not to the Spanish crown.'

For a full minute, de Liniers sat silent. Finally, he rose and stood in front of Burke, looking down at him.

'I do not like you, Mr Burke.'

Burke said nothing.

'I do not like you and I do not like the English. But you offer our country the chance for freedom. Return here tomorrow at the same time. Then you will have your answer.'

De Liniers turned and returned to his seat. He did not offer to shake hands or bid his visitor farewell, but it was clear that the interview was over. James left the room, collected his hat from the supercilious butler, and made his way home.

The next twenty-four hours passed slowly. James could not settle to anything. Even Ana's flirtatiousness failed to elicit any response. Unusually, he slept badly and the next morning found him up soon after dawn, pacing his room until it was time to venture out to the admiral's house.

This time, he was shown to the library where Santiago de Liniers was waiting for him at a table covered in maps which themselves were submerged under piles of books and sheets of notes.

'Lieutenant Burke.'

James noticed the use of his rank and accounted it a good sign.

'Admiral de Liniers.'

The two men made polite, constrained bows. De Liniers motioned Burke to a chair drawn up opposite his desk.

The admiral wasted no time in settling down to business.

'You say you represent the Duke of York. Is that really so?'

'The Duke is the Commander-in-Chief of the British Army. I report to him on matters of foreign intelligence.'

'And you have his ear?'

'He has been kind enough to give some weight to my opinions.'

De Liniers made a play of examining the maps before him, moving piles of books and rearranging the papers so that the approach to Buenos Aires was clearly visible.

'I have considered your proposition. It is not especially attractive, but I think I have no alternative but to accept it. I am convinced that, whether I cooperate or not, the British will come. If they come in sufficient numbers, they will take La Plata and we will simply have exchanged one master for another. If I assist you, you will undertake to bring only a small force and you will guarantee us our independence under British protection.'

'What would you call a small force?'

'Fifteen hundred men should be enough, if you are confident of no serious defence.'

'Fifteen hundred would leave us dangerously exposed.'

'If the shore batteries fail to open fire and if a pilot were to guide you up the Plate to Buenos Aires, then fifteen hundred would be enough.'

James said nothing for a moment, reviewing in his mind all he had learned about the naval defences on the estuary of the Plate. Buenos Aires could not be taken with just fifteen hundred men if it were vigorously defended. On the other hand, he remembered the sketches he had made of Monte Video. Fifteen hundred men supported by a naval force could overrun the defences there. So, in the event of betrayal, the British would sack the town, justifying the expedition.

He offered the admiral his hand.

'Very well. Fifteen hundred men.'

De Liniers ignored the proffered hand.

'There is more.'

James sat back in his seat and waited to hear what the other had to say.

'The British will allow free trade. They will recognise that we must have our own government. Our laws, customs, and currency are to be respected. We will not pay taxes to the British. We will be a British Protectorate, not a colony.'

'But you will allow the British to garrison Buenos Aires and control trade on the Plate.'

'Subject to my conditions, yes.'

James smiled.

'Then I can see no problem.'

De Liniers did not return the smile.

'There is one final condition.'

James raised an enquiring eyebrow.

'I understand you have been concerning yourself in the affairs of Mrs O'Gorman.'

'Mrs O'Gorman and I are friends, yes.'

De Liniers' lip curled and he looked at James as if he were a peculiarly unpleasant insect.

'You and Mrs O'Gorman are lovers.'

'That is no concern of yours.'

'On the contrary. It is my concern. You will cease your relationship with Mrs O'Gorman.'

James was silent, digesting what he had been told. De Liniers sat motionless, his hooded eyes intent on Burke.

James tried to convince himself that it was a joke. It would be a joke in bad taste, certainly, but the idea that de Liniers was serious did not bear thinking about. He looked for any trace of humour on the admiral's face but the lips under that hawk-like nose showed no sign of a smile. Reluctantly, Burke was forced to believe that the future of La Plata was being bargained against the favours of the delectable Ana.

For a long moment, James seriously considered turning down the offer. He had, he realised, grown quite attached to Ana. It was, surely, unthinkable that he should, in effect, hand her over as a part of these negotiations. But then he had his own career to consider. He imagined trying to explain it to the Duke of York: 'Well, your Highness, we could have taken Buenos Aires from the Spanish, but I couldn't renounce the favours of a lady.'

'Very well,' he said at last. 'You have my word.'

'Your word, Mr Burke, will not suffice. There is a ship leaving for Rio de Janeiro this afternoon. You will be on it.'

The two men looked at each other in silence. Then, his face a mask, James rose to his feet.

'I will convey your regards to Mrs O'Gorman.'

De Liniers' lip twitched and, for a moment, James thought the admiral might be about to strike him, but he regained his self-control.

'Goodbye, Lieutenant Burke. I trust we shall not meet again.'

*

James was used to travelling light. It took William just three hours to have everything packed. It took him another thirty minutes to make his farewells to Molly Simkins.

Ana was visiting a lady friend. James left without saying goodbye.

Chapter Six

The *Santa Theresa* carried a cargo of gold, silver, and the inevitable leather goods. She did not normally take passengers but de Liniers was not a man to be trifled with and Burke's money was good. She was bound for Spain, of course, but she put in at Rio de Janeiro to offload some salt beef and wine and to take on board water and supplies for the months they would be at sea. Here, in Brazil, governed by friendly Portugal, James and William disembarked.

James looked up at the jumble of streets that ran down to the sea from the mountains that surrounded the city.

'It could be worse, sir,' said William.

James agreed. If he was to be exiled from Buenos Aires and Ana, there were far worse places to end up. After the geometric order of the Spanish towns in La Plata, Portuguese Brazil provided a welcome change. With its stunning setting, the sun shining on a sea of startling blue and the vivid greens of the jungle beyond the town, Rio de Janeiro would, James felt, proved an agreeable temporary base.

He established himself in comfortable quarters in the city and, for several days, concentrated on carefully composing his detailed report and his recommendations for the British to offer their protection to de Liniers and his rebels. Thus would South America be denied to the Spanish at little risk and for minimal military effort.

The day the report was completed, James retired to bed early. Usually a sound sleeper, he suffered an unusually restless night. He woke still tired and with a vague feeling that he had dreamt and that Ana had been in those dreams.

William entered with his morning tea to find him already up and pacing his room with unaccustomed anxiety.

'Shall I pack today, sir?'

'Yes.'

James reached the wall and turned abruptly.

'No.'

Five paces saw him at the other wall.

'Yes.'

William stood in confusion.

'Dammit, William. I don't know what to do for the best.' He paced the room again and then, abruptly, stopped.

'You're going home, William. I'm staying here.'

William was aghast.

'You can't mean that, sir.'

'I'm afraid I do, William. This report is too important to leave to a written communication only. It needs to be delivered by hand and by somebody who can vouch for its contents. I would take it myself but I do not trust de Liniers. Someone must stay near La Plata to keep an eye on things – and I'm the only person that can do the job.'

'It'll take me three months to get this to London, sir. And another three months to get any reply back to you. That's six months you'll be stuck here, sir.'

'I'm aware of that, William.' Burke smiled. 'But I think I might survive six months in Brazil. Even without your estimable services.'

A ship left for London a week later – a week that saw William fussing over his master's linen and polishing his boots as if to ensure that all would remain clean and in good order for the next half year. Then, finally, he was on his way and Burke was left to his own devices.

He had, he reasoned, more than six months to wait for any military response to his report. It made sense to use the time to establish good communications with Buenos Aires.

He sat at the desk where he had composed his report and began to write again.

My dear O'Gorman,

I am sorry that circumstances forced me to leave so very suddenly. I trust you were not too much inconvenienced.

I find myself now in Rio de Janeiro, where I intend to stay for some months. I recall that you have often spoken of the difficulty of exporting all your goods by way of Spain and have complained that Englishmen trading with Brazil benefit from the more friendly relations between those two countries.

It occurs to me that in my present situation, it should be possible for us to form a mutually advantageous relationship. If you were able to transport your goods to Rio de Janeiro, using simply local transport, I could then re-export them to England, taking advantage of the improved tariff regime that would thus result.

I am aware that there are many informal trade routes taking advantage of the contiguity of La Plata and Brazil and I am sure that we could develop these to our mutual advantage.

In the interests of discretion, I can be reached in Rio de Janeiro under the name of Scott. I trust that I will hear from you at your convenience.

Please convey my kind regards to Mrs O'Gorman.

I remain, sir, your always humble and obedient servant,

O'Gorman's response arrived barely a week later and Burke read it with some considerable satisfaction:

Dear Mr Scott,

You can imagine my surprise at receiving your letter when I expected that by now you would be well on your way back to England. I was, nonetheless, delighted to hear from you again – and with such an interesting suggestion. I am pleased that your mercantile instincts have been so stimulated by the time that you spent with us.

I must admit to finding your proposal has considerable attractions, but I will have to explore the possibilities of transporting my goods to you in a way that will minimise unnecessary bureaucratic obstacles. Once I have contacted persons of discretion who can attend to this aspect of the transaction, I will be in touch with you again.

Pray do not apologise for the suddenness of your departure. Any inconvenience was a trifling matter. Your horses were profitably disposed of. I would be happy to allow the sum raised as part of your capital for this venture. The llamas and vicuña are, I must confess, more problematic, there being little demand for such creatures here in the city. I am sure, though, that a solution will be discovered in time.

I have conveyed your regards to my wife, who expresses her gratitude that you remember her kindly. I think she is missing you. Certainly, since your departure she has been spending more time in Society and visits with her French friends almost every month. I have offered to escort her but she knows that, as I do not speak their damnable language, I should be bored, and she kindly excuses me from my duty.

Allow me to make my necessary arrangements and I will be in touch with you again as soon as can be.

I remain, sir, your always most humble and obedient servant,

He might have wished that Ana were spending less time with 'her French friends', but otherwise O'Gorman's response was all that James might have wished. The merchant was ready to make his 'necessary arrangements' to avoid tedious 'bureaucratic obstacles' like taxes, and then James would have a way in and out of La Plata. And should anybody discover it, they would simply assume it was part of the already substantial trade in smuggled goods across the border. They would be unlikely to associate it with espionage.

While he waited for O'Gorman to organise matters from Buenos Aires, Burke relaxed and explored the country. He could almost wish that Britain were not so firmly allied to Portugal for Brazil was a country he would welcome the chance to reconnoitre. With its wild jungle and fantastic treasures (he visited diamond mines and watched gold panned from the rivers), it was a country to seize the imagination, but the inhabitants appeared resolutely loyal to their European masters. It was La Plata and the Spanish domains that were his concern.

It took O'Gorman a month to set up a route for his leather to be shipped to Rio – a month which Burke spent persuading the British ambassador in Rio to advance the capital necessary for his scheme. Finally, the first hides were on their way, moving first to Monte Video and then on fishing boats up the coast until they could be put ashore a discreet distance from where Burke waited to collect them. All he had to do was to arrange for carts to pick them up and transport them to Rio, after which he could export them to England with no payment of Spanish tariffs. It was a profitable business and, on his lieutenant's stipend, it seemed to him that it more than justified his decision to stay in Brazil.

Throughout the southern summer, Burke was happy to spend his time in Rio. If only Ana were there with him, he thought, he would be happy to stay in Brazil for years.

O'Gorman's letters provided all the news he needed from Buenos Aires, although they were usually more informative for what they didn't say rather than for any positive information. The guerrilla warfare of the rebels was clearly making no significant impact. On the other hand, there was no news of the executions that would have followed any successful attempts by the Spaniards to put an end to them. The Spaniards were not reinforcing their garrison but neither were any men being sent home.

The smugglers were also able to give him news of Monte Video which, according to them, held only a skeleton garrison. All in all, it seemed, nothing was happening – which, as Burke enjoyed the Brazilian climate, Brazilian food, and Brazilian women whilst watching the profits mount in his trading enterprise, was exactly what he wanted to hear.

The one subject on which O'Gorman was a mine of information was the life and times of de Liniers. Ana's indiscretions (for such O'Gorman chose to call them) with the admiral had reached the stage where even the most self-deluded husband could not hide from the truth. Understandably reluctant to unburden himself to anyone in the small British community in Buenos Aires, O'Gorman chose instead to confide in Burke. So, week after week, James received letters detailing where de Liniers had been seen in town, how de Liniers' career flourished, why de Liniers was too powerful to challenge, how happy de Liniers was, how rich de Liniers was.

Although James tried to convince himself that Ana's affairs were no concern of his, he found O'Gorman's news would leave him unaccountably restless and prone to irritation. He was not surprised that Ana had turned back to the Frenchman. He could not object to her behaviour. He had, after all, abandoned her without a word of warning, but still he found himself hating de Liniers. He recognised his rival as clever, ruthless, and cunning. Their interests might have drawn them into an unnatural alliance for the moment but his instinct told him that one day the admiral would prove himself a dangerous enemy.

So life continued, with news of Ana the only cloud on his horizon, for over six months. Then, at Easter of 1806, news finally arrived from England. William had safely delivered his report to Colonel Taylor, who had passed it to the Duke of York, who had been impressed with it and passed it, in his turn, to Mr Pitt. Mr Pitt had smiled upon the strategy and an attack on Buenos Aires was to be set in motion as soon as the forces could be despatched.

Now Burke started the next stage of his plan. He wound down his trading concern and, as the very last delivery of hides was made, he was on the beach to meet it in person. When the fishermen started back on their journey along the coast, they took 'Mr Scott' with them.

The James Burke who disembarked from the little fishing boat that docked at Monte Video the following week was unrecognisable as the elegant officer who had left the city the previous year. He easily got work as a deck hand on the next ship sailing to Buenos Aires, where he disembarked to vanish amongst the stevedores of the port.

Stripped to the waist and wearing a pair of canvas trousers tarred against the wet, he was a fine figure of a man but with his hair crudely cut and without his elegant clothes, even O'Gorman didn't notice him as the merchant inspected the goods being unloaded. James Burke had vanished and Manuel Vincenza had taken his place.

Manuel Vincenza was a good worker. So good that, from time to time, he would be called out from the crowd looking for employment and ordered to work loading a ship of the Spanish navy. And if that ship ended up with leaking water barrels and rats among the flour sacks – well, these things happened all too often, and no one associated them with Manuel.

For James, though, despite the amusement that such escapades gave him, the weeks spent loading and unloading at the docks were mainly a mix of hard physical work, periods of immense boredom, and continual frustration as the British army resolutely failed to appear.

*

Commodore Riggs Popham read the Admiralty despatch one more time. He put it on his chart table next to the last despatch and weighted it down with a metal turtle he had bought when they were re-provisioning once on the Gold Coast. He'd bought a metal fish too but he'd lost that. Damn shame, he thought.

Popham looked out of the great stern window of the *Narcissus* to where Table Mountain dominated the view. He was a long way from London but his mind kept returning to his last visit there and his meeting with Colonel Taylor. Worrying sort of chap, Taylor. Very tied up with all that cloak-and-dagger stuff. Taylor had insisted that they meet at his club and there they had dined in private, banning the servants from the room. Taylor was a tall man, lean with black hair. He seemed somehow menacing, though he was doing his best to be affable. There was a plan, he said, to deliver South America to the British. A plan so secret that the details were not to be committed to paper. And then he had explained about de Liniers' treason (for, as far as Popham was concerned, that was what it was).

'You have only to take fifteen hundred men and Buenos Aires will be yours,' he had promised. 'When your orders come, be assured that our agent there will be ready to assist you. He's a steady man. Buenos Aires will fall and with it, La Plata. Within the year, Spain will be cut off from the source of her wealth.'

And now, in Cape Town, his orders had arrived. The problem was that the instructions from the government (marked 'Secret' and sealed with copious quantities of wax) not only made no mention of de Liniers or any rebel plot but made it clear that Popham was expected to invade South America and claim the land for Britain.

There was no suggestion that he would be liberating it on behalf of the inhabitants or that de Liniers and his rebels should be acknowledged in any way.

Popham blamed Pitt. The wretched man had no business dying like that. When there's a war on, you do your duty – and the Prime Minister's duty is to survive. Pitt was known to have been scheming with South American exiles for years. When England and Spain had been at peace, their ambassador in London was forever complaining that the city was swarming with Latin-American radicals. But now Pitt was gone and his successor, Lord Grenville, was desperately trying to reconstruct a foreign policy that had existed largely in the mind of his brilliant predecessor.

Finally, just to make confusion absolutely certain, there was a direct order from the Admiralty. Their lordships, it seemed, had not been made privy to Lord Grenville's plans, such as they were, and had issued instructions that Popham's squadron should stand by in South Africa ready to support a British invasion that was successfully completed even before the despatch had started on its way from London.

Another commander would have seen the confusion of different orders as a problem. But not Popham. For him, such confusion was an opportunity.

There was a knock at the cabin door.

'Colonel Beresford is here to see you, sir.'

Popham beamed and rose to greet his guest.

'Beresford, it's good of you to come.'

Beresford entered the room gingerly. He was a tall man and, like many soldiers, he seemed uncomfortable with the navy's low beams.

'You said you had a request you needed to discuss?'

'Can I offer you a drink? Some refreshment?'

Popham fussed over his guest until Beresford thought he would explode.

'Please, Commodore, just tell me what you want.'

'Well, I was wondering: as the army seems to have completed its task here, do you think I could borrow fifteen hundred men?'

*

Popham's fleet entered the estuary of the Plate on June 11th 1806. It was the middle of winter and, though the weather was warmer than an English December, the Plate was shrouded in fog.

Popham and Beresford were seated at the chart table in the great cabin of the *Narcissus,* arguing about what they were to do now they had arrived in South America. It was an argument that had been occupying them, on and off, ever since they had left Cape Town but now, inevitably, it was reaching its climax.

'You say you have intelligence that Monte Video is barely defended. You show me plans that demonstrate the exact position of their artillery. The town could be taken with the forces we have at our command and will provide a defensible base to fall back on should this venture not prove as successful as you assure me it will be.'

Popham scowled at the colonel. He found himself despising the army mentality that moved step by cautious step, losing the greater prize in its efforts to gain a foothold here or advance a line a league there. If it weren't for him, Beresford would still be in South Africa, achieving nothing. And now, with the navy putting the capital of La Plata in his grasp, he would delay so that he might take Monte Video.

'Colonel, we have clear intelligence that Buenos Aires will fall if we only march on the city. With Buenos Aires comes La Plata and with La Plata a foothold which will allow Britain to wrest the whole of South America from Spanish control.'

Beresford snorted with disgust.

'Your "intelligence" comes down to a promise from some dago that the Spaniards will not fight. Which comes as no surprise. They will not fight in Monte Video and, once we have taken there, they will not fight in Buenos Aires. But we cannot mount a campaign on the basis that the enemy will never fight. There is always the possibility that, one day, they might.'

Popham kept his gaze firmly focussed on the maps unrolled before him and took a deep breath. God save us from a soldier who sees the chance to lead a heroic campaign, he thought. Was there to be no end to this argument? On sea, Popham was in command and he wanted to move against Buenos Aires. But the military dispositions on land rested with Beresford. At this rate, the fleet looked set to remain in the Plate estuary for months.

Before the two men could resume their eternal rambling, a midshipman presented himself at the cabin.

'Mr Jameson's compliments, sir, and there's a boat making directly for us. Do we sink it, sir?'

*

James had almost given up hope of the invasion fleet ever arriving when a rumour started around the docks that British warships had been seen off Monte Video. A fisherman had claimed to see the men o' war riding at anchor in the mists, sails furled, waiting for he knew not what. This was not the first rumour of invasion and most people dismissed the talk out of hand. Gomez was known as a drinker: only last year he had claimed that his boat had nearly been taken by a giant squid. Even so, the story spread around the community of the sea front.

James laughed with the others and called Gomez a fool but, in his heart, he was sure that the story was true. He had been waiting months for this day: he could not bring himself to believe that the ships were not there.

That night, Burke sought out the fisherman. His boat was beached on the shore just west of the city and there, like most of his kind, Gomez spent his time ashore living in the shelter of its hull. Burke found him sitting beside a fire of driftwood. He had come armed with a bottle of wine and found Gomez more than happy to talk about the ships he had seen louring in the fog. From the description he gave, there clearly was a flotilla out there, though he had never got close enough to identify them positively as English. On the other hand, if the Spanish navy was in the area, there was no reason why they should lurk in the fog without sending a boat to announce their arrival. Certainly they were not expected in Buenos Aires, where the workers on the wharves would know about it even before the Viceroy.

'Can you find these ships again, Gomez?'

'Of course I can.' The fisherman took a hefty swig from the bottle. 'Gomez can find anything out there.'

'Even in the fog?'

Gomez laughed.

'I don't need to see. I can *smell* where I am on the Plate.' And he demonstrated with an enormous noisy sniff that reduced him to a coughing fit which, in turn, called for another libation from the bottle.

'Will you take me?'

The fisherman looked suspiciously at James.

'Why should I?'

James shrugged.

'It's no matter. I don't think the ships exist.'

'They exist.'

'Yes, old man. They exist in that bottle and all the bottles like it. They sail a sea of wine with the giant squid that nearly sank your boat the day you were so drunk you couldn't manage the sail.'

'The ships are there!'

'Prove it.'

Gomez squinted across the fire at James, a glint of cunning in his eye.

'I'll bet you five pesos that I can find those ships.'

Despite himself, James was amused by the fisherman's nerve. Five pesos was probably more money than he had ever held in his hand – and more money than any stevedore would have to gamble. Admittedly, James had secreted a hundred pesos when he returned to Buenos Aires. (He had buried it beneath the filth of one of the latrines. Things hidden in shit, he had discovered, are invariably safe from casual thieves.) Manuel Vincenza, though, had only five *reals* in the world, so now the haggling started.

In the end, Gomez agreed to show Manuel the ships for one peso. No matter that Manuel didn't have the money – James had no intention of allowing Gomez to return to Buenos Aires if a British squadron was, indeed, in the river.

Manuel returned to the hovel he shared with five other men and left Gomez to finish the wine, but the next morning he was back, prodding the fisherman awake with his naked foot.

Gomez, having slept on the bargain, had awakened with a dreadful suspicion that Manuel did not have the money and now insisted that he be shown this peso. Manuel retaliated by insisting that the fisherman produce his stake. As neither man had a peso, this produced an impasse that was resolved when Manuel offered to show Gomez two *reals* as evidence of good faith, if the fisherman would reciprocate. Grudgingly, Gomez produced two *reals* from the sand beneath his boat, Manuel showed the money hidden in his trousers and, honour satisfied, Gomez and Manuel pushed the boat out into the water.

Once in the current, Gomez hung out his nets.

'We'll be all day getting there,' he said. 'We might as well do some fishing while we're at it.'

As the hours passed, they drifted further toward the sea and the heap of fish in the boat grew steadily bigger. The morning fog cleared but there was no sign of any ships, British or otherwise.

By late afternoon, Burke was beginning to give up hope. Gomez, though, was still confident.

'Soon we'll hit the mists. Then the ships. You'll see.'

Not twenty minutes later, the fishing boat, as Gomez had predicted, slipped into a bank of fog hanging where the warm air from Monte Video hit the cold of the river and, half an hour after that, Burke saw the shapes of the warships looming toward them.

'There they are,' whispered Gomez. 'You owe me a peso.'

'They might not be British. Take us closer.'

Gomez looked at his companion as if he were clearly mad.

'If we go closer, they'll see us.'

Burke drew the knife from his belts and held it to Gomez's throat.

'Do it. Do it or I'll slit your throat and take the boat to them myself.'

The fisherman looked at the knife and then at Burke's face.

The little boat swung toward the nearest ship and started to close on it.

*

Popham headed for the quarterdeck, where the officer of the watch handed him his own telescope.

It was difficult to be certain in this infernal fog, but the vessel seemed innocent enough.

'It looks like a fishing boat. Just two men aboard.'

Popham glanced at the officer who had spoken.

'I can't see any place where men might be concealed. Can you?'

'No, sir. Unless they're under the fish.'

Popham looked through the telescope again. It seemed unlikely that the pile of fish in the boat could conceal a body of Spanish marines.

The officer of the watch looked troubled.

'But why are they running toward us? Any Spaniard should be fleeing for his life.'

And that, thought Popham, must be the explanation. The man in the boat must be their agent.

'Hail them. Get them alongside and get a ladder down to take them off.'

Five minutes later a jubilant Burke and a terrified Gomez were aboard the *Narcissus* and Popham was wringing Burke's hand with almost manic enthusiasm.

'I've heard about your work, sir. Sterling service! An honour to meet you.' He turned and looked quizzically at Gomez. 'Is this a colleague?'

Burke smiled. 'Hardly, Commodore. But he has performed a valuable service. He should be detained but have your men treat him well. And I owe him a peso.'

Gomez was hustled below while Popham led Burke to the great cabin, where Beresford, ignoring the general clamour on deck, still sat.

'Colonel Beresford, allow me to introduce Lieutenant James Burke.'

Beresford did not stand, but acknowledged Burke with a brisk nod.

Popham smiled. This was his moment.

'Lieutenant, can you show us how to take Buenos Aires?'

For two years, Burke had worked toward this. Now his hour had come. He looked at the maps on the chart table before him and at the two officers waiting for his exposition. He had lied and murdered and betrayed to get to this point.

He stabbed his finger at the map.

'We need to make our initial landing here . . .'

*

Popham wanted to start toward Buenos Aires the next morning but they woke to find the estuary still shrouded in fog. Even with charts based on the information Burke had gathered when he made the journey two years earlier, they dared not move further up the river with its treacherous shoals.

Popham invited Burke to join him for breakfast, where he did his best to give himself indigestion by staring at the opaque whiteness outside the stern window and cursing the weather.

'The longer we are here, the more chance of the Spanish blundering across us and scotching our plan. Or suppose that they send ships? We're trapped in the river if a few ships of the line were to turn up. Damn this weather!'

Burke helped himself to another slice of bacon.

'Why not get Gomez to pilot you up?'

The effect of his comment was electric. Breakfast was forgotten as Popham stormed from the room, calling for Gomez to be brought to him immediately.

Gomez's first reaction on being brought before Popham was fear. Then, when it was explained that his famous nose was to lead the British squadron through the fog, it was incredulity. This was rapidly followed by cunning as he saw the opportunity for pecuniary benefit presented in this situation.

'Ten pesos,' he said.

Popham reached in his pocket and withdrew a gold sovereign.

Gomez looked at it, weighed it in his hand, and carefully bit it. Satisfied, he moved to stand beside the helmsman and pointed westward into the fog.

'There!'

They waited another twenty minutes for the tide and then the *Narcissus* started to move, the other vessels in line behind her.

When they finally emerged from the fog, they were just two hours from Buenos Aires.

*

The first that Thomas O'Gorman knew about the invasion was when the alarm cannon roared out late on the afternoon of Wednesday June 25th, 1806.

He was at his office at the time and his first thought was for Ana. She might, he reasoned, not always have been as faithful as she promised at her wedding, but she was his wife. So, from a sense of duty and propriety as much as for any other reason, O'Gorman found himself hurrying home.

He was but one of hundreds of men who seemed to be rushing around the town with no clear purpose. At the fort, he saw Colonel Calzada Castanio mustering the garrison but, rather than taking up their posts for the defence of the town, they were preparing to depart. The Viceroy was evacuating his palace and a baggage train of his effects was forming up in the Plaza Victoria. As O'Gorman watched, he even saw a piano being manhandled onto a cart while chefs, still in their kitchen whites, oversaw the packing of casserole dishes and frying pans.

While the professional Spanish soldiers prepared to leave, civilians were hurrying into the fort to be issued with crude pikes and assigned to militia companies. Those who had their pikes joined the crowds filling the streets as they tried to find the muster points of their various units.

The bells of the town's churches were by now ringing the alarm, so everywhere there was noise: bells, the crash of pikes, the screams (for no reason he could see) of women, the anxious questions and answers of passing friends, the shouts of militia officers looking for their men.

O'Gorman was still chuckling over the undignified flight of the Viceroy when he got home to find Ana in great excitement. As he entered the door, she ran from the drawing room with her news.

'The Viceroy's left Buenos Aires.'

'I know. I've seen the wagons. But what's that to you? The British are on their way – we'll be all right.'

'It's Santiago.'

O'Gorman felt his good humour evaporating at the sound of de Liniers' name.

'What about him?'

'The Viceroy's put him in charge of the defence of the city.'

O'Gorman scowled but had, reluctantly, to admit that the appointment made sense. As the man in charge of shore defences, de Liniers was the obvious man to protect them against an attack from the sea.

'He knows a bit about artillery, I suppose,' he told his wife. 'But it's hardly a concern of yours.'

The main concern in O'Gorman's head at that moment was that de Liniers might know enough about artillery to drive the British off. Not that he cared that much either way: he had lived under the Spanish and he would live equally well under the British. It was uncertainty that was bad for trade, and de Liniers' appointment had introduced a considerable uncertainty into the equation.

It wasn't as if de Liniers hadn't introduced enough disquiet into his life already. O'Gorman watched as his wife fluttered ineffectually around the house, clearly torn between pride that de Liniers had been appointed as a war leader and fear that his position might lead to his being injured in the fighting. When he tried to calm her, she told him that he was a useless waste of space and insisted that that he sally out to bring news of what was happening in the town. Glad of any excuse to escape the house, O'Gorman wrapped himself in a cloak and ventured into the streets.

Evening was drawing in but the bustle was, if anything, more frantic than it had been in the afternoon. Militia men still roamed about uncertain of what to do or where to report, while those who had mustered were drilling in an amateurish way with much shouting of commands and clattering of weapons.

On the shore, where the fishermen kept their boats, men were dragging cannon into position, facing the British ships which could be seen standing a mile or so out. De Liniers himself was there, urging the struggling militia to more effort and O'Gorman was able to report to Ana that he looked suitably martial and in no immediate danger from enemy action.

Aboard the *Narcissus,* James watched the same scene through Popham's telescope.

'He's a cunning old fox, de Liniers,' he remarked. 'No one will be able to say that he didn't attempt to defend the town but those cannon are positioned on soft ground with no proper platforms. By tomorrow, they'll have sunk in enough to mean they're bedded where they are until the fighting's over.'

The weight of artillery that could be brought to bear on any naval assault was a matter of profound indifference to Burke. His observations of the landward defences of the fort had already made him decide that an attack from the sea was pointless. He would have the troops disembark away from the coastal defences and attack from the land.

The British fleet waited off Buenos Aires until the sun was dipping below the horizon. Then, in the gloaming dusk, Popham ordered his ships to sail the fifteen miles east to the little town of Quilmes. The troops started landing there the next morning.

All day boats rowed back and forth between the transports riding at anchor and the shoreline. A hundred marines from Popham's force accompanied Beresford's fifteen hundred men of the 71st Foot, so a total of sixteen hundred were landed over the course of day, wading ashore a dozen at a time. As the 71st was a Highland regiment, they were wearing kilts. These, ironically, proved more suitable for a beach landing than the trousers of the marines, which were soon heavy with mud and water.

Burke watched nervously from the *Narcissus.* If de Liniers were to break his word, this was the point where a Spanish attack could most easily stop the British. But as the day wore on and the columns formed up on the beach, Burke realised that the admiral was sticking to his side of the bargain.

As darkness fell, the troops settled down for the night and Scottish songs sounded incongruously on the South American air. Pickets were mounted around the bivouac but de Liniers was true to his bargain, and there was no sign of the Spanish.

Burke dined that night with Popham. The *Narcissus* had taken on no fresh provisions since Cape Town and Popham's hospitality was limited to salt beef and lentils, but Burke enjoyed the evening. The next day he would disembark to join Beresford and he was not looking forward to it. While Popham had been delighted when James had joined his expedition, and had never let the difference in their nominal ranks be a concern, Beresford's attitude was very different.

The colonel's irritation with Burke's mere presence showed as soon as James reported to him in the morning. Beresford made a great fuss about what he could do with a supernumerary lieutenant and how difficult it would be for Burke to fight with a Scots regiment if he was unused to Highlanders. James smiled gently and suggested that as the Duke of York had asked that he gather intelligence, he would be quite happy were he simply to be allowed to observe the progress of the invasion.

'Well, Lieutenant, if you feel that is how you can best be of use, by all means observe. I suppose you could be attached to my staff, where we will endeavour to make you useful.'

And so Burke found himself in the company of a small group of majors and captains who Beresford had chosen to designate as 'staff command'. Given that the sole military requirement (in the absence of any serious defence by de Liniers) was to march toward Buenos Aires without getting lost, Burke was unsure why a 'staff command' was necessary but, as his opinion was never asked on anything, he saw no problem with the attachment.

James, by now fitted out with a smart red tunic and grey trousers (he had been offered a kilt but had declined it), contented himself with marching alongside the troops while Beresford fretted with his captains and majors. It clearly rankled with the colonel that he was not mounted, but Popham had point-blank refused to transport horses to a country where so many would be available on their arrival. Unfortunately for Beresford, any of the inhabitants of Quilmes who owned horses had fled on them as soon as they saw the British start to disembark.

Burke found Beresford's desire to play the great commander quite amusing. It was, he thought, hardly as if the capture of Buenos Aires was going to call for heroic generalship. He had agreed with Popham over dinner that even Beresford was unlikely to be able to make a mess of it.

With the regular garrison committed to protecting the Viceroy, the only forces facing the British were the militiamen, many of whom were armed just with swords or pikes. As the 71st, their pipes skirling, approached the town of Quilmes itself, the militia gathered on a small hill looking down on the Scotsmen marching steadily toward them. With the enemy still some hundred yards away, those of the militia who had firearms discharged them but, being equipped only with old carbines, their shot fell short. The pipers marched on without a break in pace and the militia wisely decided to fall back to the city.

The clouds that had been building above them all day now burst and rain fell steadily as they marched on toward Buenos Aires. The water soaked steadily into Burke's trousers, and his jacket provided hardly more protection. After months of loading and unloading ships in all weathers, bare-chested and with only ragged trousers to protect him from the weather, James was at least better able to bear this than Beresford. The colonel by now looked as if he would exchange all his dreams of glory for a hot bath and a change of clothing.

The downpour might have taken some of the swing from the step of the troops but, after weeks at sea, they were at least on land and marching to victory. For the militia, it seemed as if the weather finished any fight that might have remained in them. The British advanced without any sign of the enemy until they came to the Río Chuelo, a small river that marked the southeast boundary of Buenos Aires. Here the Spanish had fired the bridge but the crossing was undefended. Beresford's engineers were soon able to improvise a pontoon from the smoking remains of the bridge and the boats that the fleeing Spaniards had abandoned on both sides of the river.

Before midday the British army were all across the river and drawing themselves up in battle order on the fringes of the city. Buenos Aires had no walls as such, but in front of the troops an embankment of packed soil ran down to the sea. This boundary had once been a defence against Indians and one or two dilapidated towers showed where troops had kept watch on the earthworks. Now, though, it was no more than a symbolic line with some shabby buildings already snaking along the shore outside the nominal town boundary.

James supposed that if he were in charge of the city's defences, he might decide that the embankment would provide as good a place to draw up his lines as any, but he was confident by now that de Liniers intended to honour his word. Besides, it was already clear that the only forces deployed in the defence of Buenos Aires were the militia and James knew there to be no more than six hundred men under arms. The city was essentially undefended. Even so, Beresford, not wanting to lose any chance to prove himself in battle, had brought up eight cannon, just in case, and these were, even now, being manhandled along the road by eight teams of sweating, swearing Scots.

Beresford, still without a horse, found himself uncertain as to how to proceed. His military career to date had not equipped him with the appropriate protocol for taking the surrender of a capital city and he was unwilling to bungle it. On reflection, he decided that here was a role for Lieutenant Burke.

'You know these fellows, Lieutenant. Find whoever's in charge and demand their surrender.'

Burke snapped a salute.

'Do you have terms, sir?'

Beresford snorted. 'I'm not discussing terms, Lieutenant. They're beaten fair and square. They can surrender or I'll burn their wretched city to the ground.'

James opened his mouth to speak and thought better of it. He saluted again and turned toward the city gate.

If his salute on departing was a little more thoughtful than the previous one, Beresford didn't appear to notice.

James gathered an escort – six men and a sergeant – but he need hardly have bothered. As they moved beyond the embankment, there was no sign of any defenders. The rain had eased off somewhat but the streets remained empty. They walked through the city as if it were a ghost town, the houses silent, the windows and doors all closed against them.

The Plaza Victoria was deserted. The Recova, usually packed with traders, lay silent and empty. Burke led his men across the square and through the Recova into that side of the plaza, which was the unofficial territory of the army. Here, with the fort immediately ahead of him, Burke finally saw some sign of activity. Militia stood beside the gate and, as he walked toward it, a messenger galloped into the building, his horse's hooves skidding on the wet cobbles of the courtyard.

No one tried to stop him as he approached.

'Who's in charge here?'

A man wearing the uniform of a militia sergeant, but with the bearing of a clerk, answered him nervously: 'The mayor, sir. Sr de Álzaga is in the Viceroy's quarters.'

James nodded curtly to the Sergeant and his party marched smartly through the gates and across the courtyard to the Viceroy's palace. There were no guards at the doors today and no one to announce him as he led his men into the Viceroy's residence. There, in what had been the Viceroy's audience room, a short man with a pale face sat waiting, accompanied only by a couple of civilian officials.

'I am Sr de Álzaga, mayor of Buenos Aires. Might I have the honour of knowing who I am addressing?'

'I am Lieutenant James Burke, currently attached to the 71st Foot. I represent Colonel Beresford of that regiment and I am come to request the surrender of your city.'

'Do you offer terms, sir?'

James thought of the agreement he had made with de Liniers. Beresford clearly either did not know or did not care about the details of their bargain. Burke hesitated. He was not a man who was that careful of the truth but he had learned the importance of honour and he was uncomfortable with the situation he now found himself in. When he spoke, he chose his words with care.

'Colonel Beresford demands your unconditional surrender, señor. But I can assure you that we will proceed with the utmost respect for the religion and property of the inhabitants. It is our intention, señor, to free you from the tyranny of Spain, rather than to impose a tyranny of our own.'

The mayor managed a tired smile in response to this little speech.

'Sitting as I do in an undefended city, I have no choice but to offer you our surrender and to thank you for the generosity of the sentiments that you express.'

'You say that the city is undefended. Is there no military commander who can surrender such forces as there are?'

'Señor, there are truly no forces here to surrender. The garrison has withdrawn to protect the Viceroy who intends to establish himself at Córdoba. I understand that it is a pleasant enough place. More to the point, perhaps, it is almost five hundred miles from here. The defence of the city was entrusted to Admiral de Liniers but he had only the militia and he has now left Buenos Aires.'

'I intend no offence to yourself, señor, but I am sure that Colonel Beresford would prefer to take the surrender from Admiral de Liniers.'

'I can well understand that but, alas, Admiral de Liniers is not at my command. The militia are stood down and, as the mayor, I am the only remaining authority here.'

Burke bowed.

'In that case, señor, I will convey your response to Colonel Beresford who will assemble his forces here to accept your formal surrender this afternoon.'

Burke bowed again, the mayor bowed back, the officials bowed, and only a sharp look from their sergeant prevented Burke's troops from joining the flurry of bowing. Instead, the Sergeant called them to attention, saluted the mayor, saluted James, and then saluted the mayor's companions for good measure before marching the squad out of the room with parade ground punctiliousness.

Thirty minutes later, James was reporting to Beresford that the city was his.

'But I'm to take the surrender from the mayor, rather than from the military commander?'

'Buenos Aires is now an open city, sir. There are no military forces to surrender.'

Beresford sniffed.

'That's damned irregular. Still, I suppose it's all you can expect from dagos.'

A corporal now appeared, leading a fine bay stallion. It seemed that while Burke had been away, Beresford had sent a foraging party through the houses outside the wall until they had found a horse that he considered suitable to his dignity. So much, James thought, for respecting the property of the inhabitants.

As orders were shouted and the modest army formed into parade order, James realised that the time he had been away had not been entirely wasted in looking for a horse. Beresford had also had his staff devise a suitable imposing triumph.

The colonel rode to the head of his victorious troops.

'You'd best walk alongside me, Lieutenant, as you're the only person here who knows the way.'

Behind the victorious commander, a piper led each of the columns. Beresford would have liked the martial beat of drums but, by tradition, the 71st eschewed drummers, so a piper would have to do.

The troops made their way into the city. Word of Burke's meeting with the mayor had obviously got out, for now windows were unshuttered. There were even a few girls waving at the balconies and, here and there, a muted cheer as the ranks marched past.

As the soldiers arrived at the Plaza Victoria, the columns spread themselves, each man marching a good yard from those on either side. The result was that the little army filled almost the whole of the square, allowing Beresford to accept the mayor's surrender whilst leading a force that, at first glance, appeared about twice its actual size.

The mayor came out of the fort and a colour party marched in. The pipes continued to play as the British flag was raised above the Castillo de San Miguel. Three cheers were given for George III and then three for the 71st. (Burke noticed a certain amount of fidgeting from the Marines at this point.) Finally, a toadying lieutenant called for three cheers for Colonel Beresford. The pipes skirled again, Sergeants bellowed their orders, and the British marched proudly into their new home.

*

Despite his initial qualms over Beresford's behaviour, Burke had to admit that, in the days following the invasion, everything seemed to be going well. Beresford installed himself in the Viceroy's palace and started to issue a series of edicts for the administration of the province. There were vague declarations about the freedom of the people and rather more specific pledges about free trade.

Burke heard mutterings that the French and Spanish merchants were concerned at the likely effect of British rule on their business. However, many of their fears seemed to be addressed when M Goriot organised a meeting under the aegis of the Societé Francaise, at which O'Gorman was one of the principal speakers.

Burke settled into his own offices in the fort and enjoyed the feeling of being at the centre of power. He wrote reports on every aspect of Buenos Aires life and suggested scores of ways in which the British troops could be made to look less like occupiers and more like liberators. As time passed, though, he realised that Beresford was not interested in the impression his troops created. As far as he was concerned, the British occupied the fort, their flag flew over the town, and the only question was how much profit could be extracted from the situation.

As the reality of Beresford's approach sank in, Burke's enthusiasm for his work diminished and he found himself spending more time thinking of Ana. It had been frustrating to be in Buenos Aires all these months without being able to see her, but his disguise as a humble stevedore had obviously made that impossible. Had he been seen in the neighbourhood of her house, let alone in her company, it would have been obvious he was not what he claimed to be. A meeting with Ana, he was sure, would have ended with a short interview with de Liniers and an intimate acquaintance with the public executioner. Now, though, he could see her without an immediate threat to his life. After two weeks he decided it was time to call on the O'Gormans.

He dressed himself carefully in his borrowed uniform and was the epitome of military elegance as he knocked on O'Gorman's door on a fine Tuesday afternoon. He was announced, and O'Gorman hurried from his study to wring his hand and greet him with all the enthusiasm of someone greeting a liberating army. James could not have hoped for a better welcome from Mr O'Gorman. Mrs O'Gorman was, though, conspicuous by her absence.

'I sent word up as soon as you were announced, but her maid came down to tell me she has just this morning been taken with a dizzy spell.' O'Gorman frowned as he spoke. 'And that's unfortunate because she was merry as a bird at breakfast.'

James did his best to conceal his disappointment and soon O'Gorman had him seated in the morning room while servants brought in tea and sandwiches. After some polite conversation about the business in Brazil (mutually profitable) and the llamas and assorted Andean livestock still stabled in Buenos Aires (which O'Gorman considered rather less satisfactory), O'Gorman explained about his public-speaking triumph.

'I told them they were being foolish. This was exactly what we had been wanting, I said. Britain had come to free us from Spanish domination, I said. No more being tied to the quarrels of the countries of Europe. I explained how England believes in free trade. When I told them that we would be able to trade anywhere in the world, they applauded. When I told them that we would be free of Spanish tariffs, they cheered.'

James, who was sipping his tea, spluttered audibly at this point.

'You told them what?'

O'Gorman looked puzzled.

'I told them that they would no longer have to pay Spanish tariffs. Surely that is true? The Spaniards have bled us dry with the tariffs they can impose because of the trade monopoly. But now, with free trade, those days are surely over?'

'I am not sure that Colonel Beresford has come to any firm conclusion yet on tariff levels.' Seeing the look of worry on O'Gorman's face, James sought to reassure him. 'The tariffs will, in any event, no longer be payable to Spain.'

In fact, Beresford had no intention of reducing tariff levels. As far as he was concerned, he had just conquered a new country for Britain and the conquest had to pay its way. 'In any case,' he added on one of the rare occasions Burke had been able to force him into discussion, 'they're no worse off now than they were before we arrived. What have they to complain about?'

Now that Beresford had installed himself in the Viceroy's palace, he saw no reason why he should pay any attention to Lieutenant Burke. In his view, the fact that Burke reported directly to the Commander-in-Chief's office made it difficult to get rid of him, but there was no need to encourage him. So James was left to look helplessly on as Beresford blithely led British policy toward disaster.

James was still welcome aboard the *Narcissus* but Popham also had other things on his mind. With Buenos Aires captured, his ships were lying idle and he was already laying plans to leave Beresford to his victory and take his flotilla to blockade Monte Video. When James went to him with his concerns, Popham was sympathetic, but unwilling to get involved.

'Old Beresford's got a point,' he admitted. 'We're not putting the tariffs up. War's expensive. We have to get money from somewhere.'

'But I negotiated a deal that saw La Plata free from financial exploitation. It was on that basis that de Liniers agreed not to put up a fight.'

'Well,' shrugged Popham, 'perhaps you'd better find de Liniers and discuss it with him.'

James grimaced. De Liniers had vanished from Buenos Aires and was rumoured to be in Monte Video. It left James feeling foolish and wrong-footed. This was not a feeling he enjoyed. So he kept his face impassive and said nothing as Popham sipped at his wine and watched him with one eyebrow raised quizzically.

Popham put down his glass and continued: 'While he remains so damn elusive, it's very difficult to take the agreement with him too seriously.'

Reluctantly, James nodded. What the hell was de Liniers playing at? He seemed to be just biding his time, waiting to see what the British would do. But why? And what was he planning to do next?

Burke nodded again, more definitely this time. He needed to find de Liniers and resolve the situation before Beresford made a political compromise impossible.

For the rest of the meal, James was distracted, his thoughts coming back again and again to the problem of finding de Liniers.

It was early when Burke went ashore. He went to his quarters in the fort and tried to sleep, but sleep was slow to come and, when it did, he dreamed of de Liniers, standing on the walls of Monte Video and laughing at him.

When he woke, it was still dark. He lay there for what seemed like hours, still with no idea where de Liniers was or what he was planning.

In the darkness, he found his thoughts turning to Ana. How close was Ana to de Liniers? Did she know anything that might help James now? The more he thought about her, the more he convinced himself that she might be able to tell him something that would give him an advantage over the admiral.

It had been a year since he had last seen her. There had been other women while he was in Brazil but, he realised, no one who had meant anything to him. Surely there could be no harm in meeting her again.

He called the next day. He knew O'Gorman would be at the warehouse so when he presented himself to be told, 'I'm sorry, sir, but the master is not at home,' it was easy enough to say, 'Oh, dear! Is Mrs O'Gorman in a position to receive me, perhaps?' And Mrs

O'Gorman did receive him. But this was not the passionate Ana of his recollections. She sat opposite him in the morning room, hands chastely folded in her lap, while the servants bustled in and out with tea and cakes, ensuring that she was always respectably chaperoned.

'You had business with my husband, I understand?'

'I would far rather have business with you, Ana.'

She sipped her tea and waited until the maid had fussed with the arrangement of cups and saucers and departed, at least for the moment.

'I have no idea what you might mean by that.'

'I thought we parted on good terms, Ana.'

Ana's eyes flashed.

'We parted on no terms at all. One minute, you were here: the next, you were gone! Did I mean no more to you than that?'

'I had to leave without delay. You were not here. I could hardly write a love letter for you and have it sent via your husband.'

'You didn't have to leave as quickly as that. You went to Brazil. I know because Thomas told me all about that and the way that you were smuggling hides with him so he could make a few extra pesos on each consignment. I thought you were a gentleman and you abandon me for this squalid money-grubbing.'

She knew him too well, he thought. Of every blow she could have struck, she had found the cruellest. It was true, he had been in trade but only incidentally. It had been profitable, certainly, but he was not a common merchant. Surely she knew that!

Ignoring the risk of interruption, he stepped across the room, and seized Ana by her shoulders where she sat.

'Ana, I had no choice but to go. I had negotiated an agreement with de Liniers that promised British success. He insisted that I leave immediately.'

She tossed her head and her dark hair moved in way that James found strangely affecting. He just wanted to kiss and caress her, but in her present mood he knew that would be fatal.

'Why would he insist on such a thing?' He could tell that she wanted to believe him but the whole situation was so ridiculous he could well understand why she did not. He decided that he might as well tell the truth and be damned.

'Because he did not want me to see you again.'

Ana stared at him, trying to take it in what she had heard.

'You see, Ana, you can honestly say that you were the price that had to be paid for this country.'

James had thought that this was quite a romantic conceit. It put Ana on a par with the great beauties of history – a sort of Helen of Troy for South America. To his astonishment, though, far from being flattered, she was furious.

'Are you telling me that you sold me to de Liniers for your wretched agreement?'

James retreated to his chair.

'You were hardly sold, Ana. And your husband tells me that you appear to reciprocate de Liniers' affection all too publicly.'

'How dare you! How dare you criticise my conduct after the way you took advantage of my husband's trusting nature when you were a guest under his roof!'

James opened his mouth to reply and found he could think of nothing to say. Ana, her eyes sparking, her cheeks flushed with fury, was a far more terrifying foe than any he had ever faced on the field of battle.

At that moment, the door opened and a servant entered.

'Is everything in order, madam?'

At once, Ana's face was a mask of icy calm.

'Everything is perfectly in order, George. But perhaps Maria could return in a few minutes to refresh the pot?'

So, James thought, Ana is even better chaperoned than was at first apparent.

As soon as the servant left, and taking care to keep his voice low, he tried again.

'Truly, Ana, if I did anything to cause you distress, I am humbly sorry. We were friends – more than friends – and I grieve that you have come to hate me.'

Ana sipped her tea and helped herself to a small slice of cake, which she nibbled daintily with her astonishingly white teeth.

The mechanics of eating and drinking seemed to calm her. 'I do not hate you, James. But I was disappointed in you. And I am, of course, much disquieted by the intelligence you have just offered me.'

'It wasn't what you imagine, Ana. De Liniers was jealous and he insisted I leave immediately. Everything hung on a knife-edge. I really had no choice.'

Ana dabbed at her lips with a napkin. 'And what was this agreement with de Liniers?'

When James did not reply, she answered her own question. 'He agreed to betray the city to the English, didn't he?'

'He's a patriot, Ana. He's saving his country from Spanish domination.'

Ana laughed. She had a very musical laugh. It was one of the things that James loved about her. Her laughter seemed totally genuine. 'De Liniers cares nothing for the country. Or the Spanish. Or the English. De Liniers cares only about the inexorable rise to power of Santiago de Liniers.'

'I had rather feared that you would say that. I don't trust him to keep to our agreement and I was hoping you might have some idea of what I might be able to offer him to ensure his loyalty.'

Ana was laughing again as Maria came in, bringing more tea. Only as the servant left did she respond to James' question. 'Loyalty is not a notion that takes up much of Santiago's time. He is loyal to me, because I am convenient and I am attractive and, in a town full of men and jealously guarded Spanish women, there is, frankly, little alternative.'

'Then why are you loyal to him?'

Ana smiled sadly across the teacups. 'You left, James. My husband is a good man and a fine husband in his way but boring beyond belief. And he has no ambition. He thinks that to be respected in our merchant community is to be a success.'

She left her seat and passed across the room to the window. 'Look at the world out there. There's a whole continent waiting to be conquered. There are men like you and de Liniers who will take this world and shake it and form it to their ends. There are men who will know power and fame and who will build nations here. And there's my husband, who will plot to turn a peso here and a peso there and who will account himself happy that men like you will acknowledge him in the street.'

She sat again. 'I'm a woman. I cannot fight. I cannot rule. But in de Liniers, I can touch that power. I can be a part of this new world.'

She stopped and the two looked at each other in silence for a while. 'You left me, James.'

'I'm back now.'

'You're a soldier. You're back because your duty has brought you back. And when your duty calls you away, you will depart. And I will be left here alone.'

Now it was James turn to take a slice of cake that and make a great show of eating it. Only after he had finished did he speak again. 'Where is he, Ana?'

'I don't know. Really, I don't.'

'If I find him, what can I offer him? Is there truly nothing that he cares about?'

'Just power, James. Not even the trappings of power – just the naked rawness of it.'

James thought of the ruby brooch that de Liniers had given to Ana. 'He may not care for the trappings of power, Ana, but I think he cares for gold. Money is, in its way, a measure of power.'

'It will take more gold than you will be able to lay your hands on if you seek to buy him.'

In an instant, it came to him. He leapt up and kissed her. 'You're a genius, Ana. I know where I'll find the gold. And when I've found it, I'll come back here and I'll take you wherever you want to go and I'll try to make you forget this whole damn mess.'

Ana smiled up at him. 'Yes, James, I think you will. And I think I'll let you.'

And then she rang for her man, and George presented Mr Burke with his hat, and the visit was over.

Burke made his way straight back to the fort and asked the duty officer for a sergeant and six good men. Then (fondly remembering when he was a real soldier who led troops into battle) he marched briskly to de Liniers' house. It was so obvious, he told himself, that he should have thought of it before. De Liniers had moved out of Buenos Aires only hours before the British attack. He had travelled quickly and he was now in hiding. It was unlikely that he would have been in any position to carry treasure chests with him. Therefore, James reasoned, they must still be in Buenos Aires and the most likely place for them to be was in his home.

James Burke might not have enough money to hand to buy de Liniers – but he intended to bribe the scoundrel with his own gold.

The squad arrived at the house where Burke had negotiated his agreement with de Liniers more than a year earlier. Their hammering brought the same butler to the door. James remembered him all too well. It gave him a distinct satisfaction to push past that haughty retainer and to watch the expression on his face as six burly Scots took the house apart. They dug up the ground floor, ripped open the mattresses on the beds, smashed into every chest, and tore down every tapestry. By the time they had finished the place was barely habitable.

Burke and the butler surveyed the damage. James had to admit that he was not displeased with the effect. There was only one small problem. They had not found as much as a single coin.

Burke found the lack of any money at all vaguely reassuring. Had there been the odd bag of gold or some pieces of jewellery, he might have reasoned that de Liniers did not, in fact, have the sort of treasure trove they were looking for. But the complete absence of anything valuable suggested that things had been hidden. It was just a matter of finding them.

The following day saw the same six Scotsmen destroy de Liniers' office in the morning and search his stables in the afternoon. The stables took a long time and when they had finished there was not a bale of hay that had not been scattered in the street outside. Of de Liniers' treasure, though, there was no sign.

Burke began to wonder if he might possibly be mistaken or if the cache could have been so cunningly hidden that he would be unable to find it. Perhaps he would be unable to celebrate his triumph with Ana after all.

And that was when it came to him. De Liniers was a senior officer in the Catholic Spanish forces. While men were men the world over, the Spanish had always liked to pretend otherwise. A Spanish officer might well take a mistress but it was frowned upon if it were too obvious. It was unlikely that Admiral Santiago de Liniers would, like James, be in a position to roger another man's wife in a dockside inn, and he would certainly be too discreet to take her to his home. Somewhere, there was a love nest that no one knew about. No one except Ana.

*

'Ana, when de Liniers bedded you, where did you go?'

For a moment, he thought she was going to strike him.

'It's important, Ana. I need to know.'

She saw he was serious. 'He had a little house on the edge of town. To the west. I can take you there if you want.'

*

The house was small and unprepossessing: a single floor built around a small courtyard. There was just one servant – an Indian girl, little more than a slave. She stood dumbly while the soldiers tramped through the rooms. They left her room untouched, and barely glanced at the bedroom. Next to the bedroom, though, was a locked door. When they broke the door down, they found an office.

James took one look at it and knew that he would find what he was after. This was the room where de Liniers kept his secret life. On the wall was a French tricolore, the ceremonial sword he had carried when he first joined the Order of Malta as a twelve-year-old page, and a portrait of a man in French naval uniform whom James assumed to be his father. There was little furniture: one chair, a bureau, bookcases, and a map table. The floor was of paving slabs, laid directly on the earth.

'Lift the slabs,' ordered Burke.

They had brought a pickaxe and went to work with a will, levering the slabs from the ground. The chest was under the third one.

*

Early in August, O'Gorman delivered a consignment of hides to the wharves to load aboard the *Santa Theresa*, only to be told that the ship would not be putting to sea.

He spent that afternoon making enquiries of other ships' masters, and then generally around the port. What he learned had him striding across the Plaza Victoria and into the fort, where he demanded a meeting with Colonel Beresford.

The next day he returned to the Castillo de San Miguel and asked to see Lieutenant James Burke.

When James was eventually located and had taken O'Gorman to his offices in the bowels of the place, O'Gorman told him what had happened.

'I asked to speak to Colonel Beresford, but they said he was busy. I spoke to a man who said he was an *aide-de-camp* to the colonel – some snot-nosed kid who thinks he's better than me because his family had the money to buy him a commission.'

'That kind of thinking isn't helping you, Thomas.'

'I'm sorry.'

The merchant made a visible effort to pull himself together. 'He said that La Plata had been Spanish, so that the ships owned there were Spanish ships and, being as England was at war with Spain, if they went to sea, they were liable to be seized as spoils of war. I went to him myself, Mr Burke, and explained the injustice of it but he said that there was nothing he could do. Even if he allowed them safe passage down the Plate, any British captain finding them on the high seas would seize them. I asked if they could not sail under our flag but he said that they were dagos and it would be quite improper to extend them the protection of our colours.' By now, O'Gorman needed a sip of whisky before he could continue. 'I ship my own goods on those vessels. There were never going to be enough British ships for all our trade. Shipping fees would rise; our goods would be stuck in our warehouses. Mercantile activity would cease. And could I make him understand this? The military mind, Mr Burke, can be remarkably limited in its outlook. Present company excepted, of course.'

Not only limited, Burke thought, but profoundly stupid. Beresford's latest pronouncement meant that 'free trade' meant only trade with England and her colonies or with countries allied with England in the war against Napoleon. The merchants, who had tacitly supported the occupation up to now, would, once they realised what was happening, turn against the British. And, Buenos Aires being built on trade, once the merchants opposed them, the city would take more than a garrison of fifteen hundred to hold it.

To make matters worse, Beresford was now isolated. After weeks of idleness, Popham had decided to withdraw his marines and all but one of his ships and move on to the business of blockading Monte Video. ('I might even bring de Liniers back for you, James,' he had joked.) Burke saw the situation moving out of control. Everything that he had achieved was to be undone by Beresford's stupidity.

O'Gorman had sat, uncharacteristically silent, while Burke thought over what he had been told but now the Irishman spoke. 'Can you not talk to Colonel Beresford?'

'I'm afraid, Thomas, that Colonel Beresford shows remarkably little interest in my opinions.'

'Is there nothing you can do?'

Yes, Burke thought, there was one slim chance that he could save the situation. He had to find someone who could negotiate on behalf of the criollos and try to reach some sort of settlement before Beresford's position became impossible.

'Go home and try not to worry, Thomas,' he said. 'I'll sort something out.'

The Irishman eventually left, somewhat reassured, and James paid a visit to the stables and demanded that they supply him with the best horse they had. The next morning he set off from Buenos Aires, heading northwest.

The British only controlled the city so James decided it would be wiser not to wear a uniform for the journey. He left the town dressed as a gaucho, with the broad-brimmed hat and wide trousers that he had grown so used to seeing during his time on the pampas.

He rode hard all day until he saw the familiar silhouette of Paco Iglesias's estancia on the horizon.

The guard in the watchtower must have recognised him because Pedro rode out to meet him before he reached the little bridge that led into the estancia compound. He had two men with him and they carried carbines in a way that suggested that they were not there out of friendship.

'What do you want here, Burke?'

James stopped his horse, sitting very still with his arms clear of his body and no weapon in sight.

'I want to see Paco Iglesias.'

'I don't think Sr Iglesias wants to see you.'

'I have urgent business with him.'

Pedro pushed his horse until he was just feet away from James.

'You're a spy, Burke. You are an English spy. Give me one good reason why we should not cut you down here.'

'Pedro, I fought beside you. I have spilled blood for your country. Nothing I have done has been to damage your cause.'

Pedro spat.

'The English are in Buenos Aires. It is their flag that flies over the town – not the flag of a free Argentina. They collect the taxes that the Spanish collected. They tell us where we can sell our goods. Their men steal from the people even more blatantly than the Spanish did. You have plotted with your Beresford to replace a Spanish tyranny with an English one. You have done nothing for Argentina. You are an enemy spy and nothing more.'

'I have come here, unarmed, to speak with Sr Iglesias. I have put myself in your power because I believe that I can help you free your country. If you are men of honour, you will not strike a man who has come peacefully for parley.'

Pedro backed his horse away. His companions fingered their weapons as the three men held an urgent whispered discussion in which the word 'honour' featured several times.

In his time with the gauchos, James had come to realise how important the concept of honour was to them. Now, it was all that stood between him and an ignominious death.

The debate between the three men seemed to reach a conclusion and Pedro turned his horse toward the farm buildings, beckoning James to follow.

They rode directly up to the clapboard house where, before they could dismount, Paco Iglesias exploded out of the door, yelling abuse. He seemed happy to vent his anger at both James and Pedro, who was informed that he should have killed the English spy rather than let him sully the soil of his home.

James dropped out of the saddle.

'Sr Iglesias, we don't have time for all this. I need to talk to de Liniers.'

Paco Iglesias stopped his tirade in mid-sentence.

'Get in the house and show some discretion.' And then, to Pedro, 'Take yourself away but keep an eye on his horse.'

Inside the house, Paco hurried James to the office where he ran the farm's affairs.

'What do you mean by mentioning his name like that?'

'Sr Iglesias, the admiral and I made an arrangement. I have not betrayed him. But things are moving out of control. I need to talk to him.'

Paco sat behind his desk, which was cluttered with paper. He picked up a sheet irritably, looked at it for a moment, and dropped it back.

'I don't think Sr de Liniers wants to talk to you.'

'Apparently not. But it is necessary.'

Paco fidgeted with his papers again and then seemed to come to a decision.

'We're riding to join de Liniers tomorrow. You will ride with us – but as our prisoner. If he wants to talk to you, you can talk. If not . . .'

He left the sentence unfinished and turned toward the window. Leaning out of it, he shouted for Pedro.

Burke was escorted from the room and taken to the feed store. Built to keep rats out of the grain, it was certainly sound enough to hold a man overnight – not that James intended to escape.

The next morning the estancia was the scene of frantic, but organised, activity. Thirty riders were preparing for a journey. Pedro released James from the grain store and led him to his horse.

'I'm not going to tie your hands,' said Pedro. 'We have a long journey and I want you able to ride fast. And we have broken bread together and I would not see you humiliated. But if you try to leave, we will bring you down and we will kill you.'

He looked James straight in the eye.

'You know we can do this.'

At that moment, Paco Iglesias appeared at the door of his house. A gaucho ran up, leading his horse and, as he mounted, cheers rang out from the men around James. Iglesias raised his hand in acknowledgement and started out of the estancia, the others falling in behind him.

They rode south. At first, the pampas was as deserted as ever but as the morning wore on, they saw other bands of horsemen in the distance, all riding in the same direction.

James realised that he was too late. This was de Liniers' army. He was being carried to the attack that would drive the British out of Buenos Aires.

*

De Liniers had watched from Monte Video as the situation of the British in Buenos Aires had deteriorated. At the beginning of the occupation, Beresford had decided that it would be good for morale if the Union flag were paraded around the square in front of the fort each day at noon, while the band played 'God Save the King' This had done nothing to improve the chances of the British being viewed as liberators rather than conquerors, but at least it had, at first, generated no particular animosity. With the passing weeks, though, resentment of this demonstration of colonial power had increased and the band had been greeted with boos and jeers. By now, when they ventured out, they were greeted with a hail of stones and rotten fruit.

Off-duty soldiers, who had had first been welcomed in the taverns of the town, found themselves waylaid by thugs and robbed or beaten. By the end of September, troops were confined to barracks after dark. Contact between citizens and soldiery was confined to searches by military patrols and exchanges of abuse at guard posts.

The mayor had taken no action at first, preferring to see the way the wind blew before committing himself. Once it was clear that the British occupation was bringing no benefits to the town, the people had turned against the troops. At first, Sr de Álzaga tried to meet with Beresford to explain the problems that his edicts were causing and to negotiate some compromise. But he was no more able to persuade Beresford to soften his approach than Burke had been. So, having no military forces at his disposal, the mayor took the only step he could. He called a general strike.

The collapse of British government was, as far as de Liniers was concerned, the best thing that could have happened. For a while, he had feared that the British might have established themselves successfully, in which case he would have had to negotiate with Beresford, trying to hold him to the bargain struck with Lieutenant Burke. The present chaos was much more satisfactory, though. Now, de Liniers was confident that he could unite the rebels of the countryside and the Spanish sympathisers in the town. They would make common cause to drive the invaders from La Plata. The campaign would leave Spain weakened, and the criollos on the verge of successful revolt. Most importantly, though, it was a war that would leave Santiago de Liniers, rebel leader and Spanish admiral, holding the power that came with victory – whichever faction ultimately triumphed.

De Liniers had seen Popham's ships anchor off Monte Video and decided it was time to slip back across the Plate. The Spanish forces in Monte Video were small and would be tied down defending the town. That, de Liniers realised, left him free to organise the liberation of Buenos Aires without the Spanish army being involved. Far from needing the troops for his plans, he wanted to see Buenos Aires liberated by the natives of La Plata.

Word went out to the rebel army that had been secretly preparing for years. Men like Paco Iglesias received their orders. Now, forty miles west of Buenos Aires, in the little town of Lujan, the rebels forces had assembled.

In one of the finest houses in the town, de Liniers stood in front of a mirror. He gave a tight smile of satisfaction at the image that looked back at him. He wore gaucho clothes, reflecting his role as the leader of the patriots. His Spanish uniform hung ready, if needed, in Buenos Aires.

Outside the house, a horse was waiting for him, its saddle a sculpture in leather, its harness and reins dripping with silver. The horse wore the decoration that, as a man of the people, de Liniers thought it wiser not to wear himself. Yet when he mounted, he was every inch a leader. He set off for the town plaza and the people cheered at his passing.

As he entered the plaza, the cheers grew almost deafening. There, filling the square, was his army of gauchos. From estancias across the nation, the likes of Paco Iglesias had ridden with their men to muster here.

De Liniers raised his hand and, slowly, the cheering died. Once there was silence, save for the stamping of hooves and the chink of harness, he spoke.

'Men of Argentina! You have ridden here to Lujan, where, for a hundred years, the people of this country have travelled to pray at the shrine of Our Lady of Lujan. This town is the spiritual heart of the country that we dream of. And from here, we set out to strike the first blow that will make us free! For, if we have known servitude under Spain, our masters have at least been of our blood. But those who would govern us now are alien to our ways. They do not speak our language. They do not share our religion. They have no place in our country.

'Men of Argentina! We ride to Buenos Aires and a glorious victory!'

The cheers echoed around the plaza again as de Liniers turned his horse and rode through the streets and out into the open pampas beyond the town. Behind him, the rebel horsemen followed, men from each estancia riding together under the natural authority of their employers: an arrangement that gave the rebels a structure and organisation that transformed them from a mob to an army.

In their midst, surrounded by the Iglesias's men, rode Lieutenant James Burke of His Britannic Majesty's Army. He looked around him and almost despaired. With the townsfolk against them and these rebels marching on Buenos Aires, Beresford's troops didn't stand a chance.

Burke pushed his horse closer to Paco Iglesias.

'I have to speak to de Liniers.'

'I can't get you to him now. We won't attack the city today. We'll camp for the night and attack tomorrow, so they can't regroup in the dark. I'll make sure you see de Liniers tonight.'

Burke had to be content with that and he rode on. Around him, voices were raised in song and the grasslands were green with the first promise of spring. It was a lovely day – but he rode with a chill in his heart.

They camped that night on the plain, still some miles from the city. Paco Iglesias left Burke sitting with his men and the evening reminded him of the evenings he had spent with these same men when they had worked the cattle on Sr Iglesias's estancia. The men were more relaxed with him than they had been, clearly unable to take him seriously as a threat to their plans. Still, there was a tension around the campfire they had built – a tension that was only broken when Paco Iglesias returned to tell them that de Liniers had agreed to see their prisoner.

Iglesias led Burke through the mass of horsemen to where de Liniers sat alone beside a campfire. He had clearly chosen to sleep on the ground alongside his men as a political gesture but was equally clearly missing the prospect of a real bed. The appearance of James at his fireside did not improve his mood.

'I told you I never wanted to see you again.'

'And a pleasant evening to you, Admiral.'

James sat himself on the ground as easily as if he was stopping for a chat with an old friend.

'I asked you once before why I should not have you shot and you talked your way out of that. Is there any reason why I shouldn't have you killed now, so I never need look on you again?'

James smiled pleasantly.

'Now you come to mention it, there is. I don't think you want Sr Iglesias to hear it, though.'

De Liniers sighed and gestured for Iglesias to leave before he turned his attention to Burke.

'All right, Mr Burke. I know you are not a fool. So tell me what you have to tell me.'

'You own a house on the west of Buenos Aires.'

'Do I?'

'It wasn't a question, señor. I've been there. And I've dug up your office floor.'

For a moment, James thought he had miscalculated and that de Liniers was going to kill him on the spot. But the admiral, with a visible effort, restrained himself.

'There is, presumably, a reason why you are telling me this.'

'Well, I had rather hoped that I could offer it back in exchange for cooperation with the British.'

De Liniers gave a short, mirthless laugh.

'I think things have, perhaps, moved rather beyond that, don't you?'

James nodded, sombrely.

'I think, perhaps, they have. But that is no fault of mine.'

'It's no fault of mine either, Lieutenant Burke. I fulfilled my part of the bargain. It is the British who failed to keep theirs.'

'Colonel Beresford has not been as diplomatic as we might have wished,' agreed James, 'but you didn't make it easier. You never presented yourself for negotiations. You left me claiming an agreement with an invisible ally. You set the situation up and you watched it fall apart. Why?'

De Liniers said nothing but his glance encompassed the army spread around them.

'I see,' said Burke and, for the first time, he did see. 'I thought you were cunning but I underestimated you. What do you intend to do when Buenos Aires falls to you?'

De Liniers shrugged.

'It depends on who makes me the better offer. This whole affair has left the Viceroy looking like a fool. He has no support here or in Spain. I think there will be a vacancy for the post soon.'

'And you think that these men will accept you as viceroy?'

'Why not? They know I am committed to the well-being of the country. And, without me, the rebels are leaderless. Should they decide to appoint a new leader – well, I know who they all are. And the Spanish army can be quite ruthless when properly directed.'

'And if the Spanish don't appoint you?'

'Then I will be in Buenos Aires with my army and they will be wondering how to get their province back. Either way, I win.'

'And where do the British stand in this?'

'They've served their part. Had they been true to our agreement, I would have treated them honourably. As it is, they are not my concern.'

'Let Popham evacuate them.'

'And have an army and a navy roving up and down the Plate wondering where to take revenge? I think not.'

'Britain will be avenged if you kill them.'

'Britain, as you well know, is a long way away and fighting a desperate war in Europe. I am confident that we can defeat any army they can spare, just as we can, if necessary, deal with Spain.'

The two men watched each other, each weighing their opponent. James was the first to speak.

'I want to buy their lives.'

'With my own money.'

James did not bother to reply.

'I will have the whole of La Plata. Why should I care about the money?'

'You're not a patriot, de Liniers. You're French. You betrayed the Spanish to the British and now you're betraying the British to these men here. And already, you are planning to betray them to the

Spanish. You live for power. And that money is the measure of the power you have. You don't spend it: you hide it. And there, in that hidden place where you take your women, you count it.

'Don't tell me you don't care about the money, de Liniers. It's really all that you do care about.'

Again, the two men sat silent, watching each other. After what, to Burke, seemed an interminable pause, de Liniers gave a slow smile. It was, thought James, the smile you would expect to see on the face of a snake, if snakes had lips to smile with.

'Very well. You may have their lives. And how do you suppose this exchange will be made?'

'You will accept their surrender and allow Popham to take them off with an undertaking that he will sail directly back to England. Once they are embarked, I will show you where the money is.'

De Liniers did not respond but sat watching the fire for a full two minutes before calling for Paco Iglesias to rejoin them.

'Paco, take Lieutenant Burke away. Keep him safe and keep him close. If he attempts to escape, try to bring him back alive. If you must kill him, make sure that he dies very painfully.'

Paco looked embarrassed by this order but led James back to where his men were gathered. On the way, he asked for James' promise that he would not attempt to escape.

'I know you are a brave man and I would not have you bound but de Liniers is obviously anxious that I keep you safe. Do I have your word?'

'Yes, my friend, gladly. Your commander and I need each other. I have no more desire to escape than he, at this moment, wishes me dead.'

Paco was clearly confused by the situation but, as they sat and ate together, he tried to put it out of his mind. James, too, concentrated on the moment – the smell of men, smoke, and horses; the sound of voices raised in song and, here and there, a guitar; the taste of the dried beef, and the rough red wine.

After they had eaten, James wrapped himself in a blanket and lay looking up at the night sky. Above him, the southern stars twinkled through a haze of wood smoke.

He drifted into sleep and a dream where he saw a condor fall on Buenos Aires and carry it up, up into the night sky to disappear among the stars, while an army of gauchos sang love songs to the tune of a Spanish guitar.

*

On the night of August 9th, 1806, Jorge and Gustavo met Miguel at The Angel. The place was strangely quiet. There seemed hardly any gauchos in Buenos Aires, but as the evening went on it filled with other young men. Usually these breakers of windows and daubers of slogans were a noisy crowd, but tonight they sat, nursing their drinks in nervous silence.

It was close to midnight when Miguel arrived. He opened the door and, without entering, beckoned those inside to join him in the street. There in front of the tavern was a handcart. Miguel reached into the cart and pulled out a liberty bonnet.

There was a nervous shuffling and Jorge stepped forward and took the bonnet. Miguel reached into the handcart again and passed a musket to Jorge.

Jorge stood, wearing the bonnet and carrying the gun, hardly believing this was really happening to him. Then, as if a spell had been broken, Gustavo cried out '*Viva La Plata! Viva Argentina!*' and suddenly everyone was cheering and pushing forward to be issued with their bonnet and their gun.

In the distance, they heard other young men cheering.

The people of Buenos Aires were preparing for battle.

*

De Liniers' criollo army arrived with the dawn.

As the gauchos rode in from the west, Sergeant Leonard was leading his morning patrol north from the fort. Half a mile from the Plaza Victoria, they were ambushed by young men wearing liberty bonnets and carrying muskets.

The rebels, though decently armed, had no experience of warfare and their first volley left the patrol unharmed. The British fired back but, outnumbered and uncertain of what the attack portended, Sergeant Leonard decided to withdraw to the fort and report.

Jorge, safely hidden in a side street, waited until the tramp of feet was a safe distance away before emerging to shake his fist at the retreating redcoats. That was when he saw a huddle of rags lying in the street – rags that looked pitifully familiar.

He ran, shouting, to his friend, but Gustavo lay still. The revolt had claimed its first victim.

Even as Gustavo died, de Liniers' cavalry encountered its first British forces. The main road from the west was guarded by a sergeant, a corporal, and just four private soldiers. Faced with the rebel cavalry, they did the only sensible thing they could do. They ran.

The pickets that Beresford had mounted at the city margins were overwhelmed within minutes and those patrols that were caught in the streets found themselves, like Sergeant Leonard, retreating to the fort, taking casualties as they fled.

By noon, the rebels had driven the British back to their headquarters. Beresford's men did not even control the Plaza Victoria because the Recova blocked their field of fire from the fort, whilst its colonnaded arcade provided the ideal cover for rebel marksmen.

De Liniers had set up his headquarters in a draper's shop – chosen because it was just out of range of the fort's cannons and its windows provided a vantage point from which, if you leaned far enough out, you could see the fighting at the end of the long, straight street. With the attack in full swing, Iglesias had relinquished his prisoner to de Liniers, and Burke now stood under guard in a corner of the makeshift command post.

'You should enjoy this, Lieutenant.' De Liniers was too refined to gloat openly but he could not resist this comment to his prisoner. 'I doubt you have ever had the opportunity to observe the staff command of an assault on this scale.'

Burke said nothing, but the experience did, indeed, hold an awful fascination for him. He was forced to admit that de Liniers was a brilliant tactician. He had a flair for urban warfare that the British, with their emphasis on set piece drill and battlefield tactics, simply could not match.

Although the ground in front of the fort was clear, the buildings on the sides of the square extended to the sides of the fort. Rather than bother with a frontal assault, de Liniers simply sent his troops into these houses, the flat roofs of which overlooked the fort's bastions.

While the gauchos busied themselves building barricades in the roads around the Plaza Victoria, trapping the British in their base, men in liberty bonnets were running along the roofs of the fashionable houses overlooking the square and settling themselves into firing positions that let them pick off the British soldiers manning the fort's defences.

Barricaded in by the rebels' blockades and unable to return any effective fire against their enemies on the rooftops, the British could do nothing but shelter in such cover as they could find. The walls offered no protection, and the troops were forced to withdraw to the Viceroy's palace. Trapped in the building, they could make no effective response to the withering fire of the enemy.

Around the middle of the afternoon, the British attempted to bring their artillery to bear on the rebel barricades, but they could not do this without exposing their men on the walls of the fort. De Liniers' militia were by now increasingly confident in their aim. A steady stream of reports came to the draper's shop of entire gun crews shot down at their posts. After an hour of carnage, the British abandoned the attempt to use their artillery without having succeeded in firing a single round.

Trapped in the buildings, the troops could not eat properly and, more importantly, had no access to water. The fort was equipped with its own well, but this was in a corner of the courtyard, and the sharpshooters on the rooftops made sure that any man attempting to approach it was hit before he could pump up a single bucket.

Burke thought that the best hope for the British was to attempt a break out under cover of night, but, as darkness fell, he realised there de Liniers had anticipated this danger. Horsemen passed through the Recova and galloped across the square with lighted brands that they threw toward the gates of the fort. De Liniers had had the dockyards raided for pitch, and wood soaked in tar burned well, keeping enough of a flickering light in the square to make any surprise breakout impossible.

The besiegers were confident and relaxed. They had as much food and water as they needed and knew themselves to be in little physical danger. There were so many of them that they could keep a watch through the night without any danger of the troops becoming over-tired and they would fire volleys into the darkness every now and then to disturb the rest of those trapped in the fort.

Colonel Beresford took stock of the situation at first light the next morning. A dozen men had been killed by enemy fire and, more importantly, over twenty had been injured. These now spilled out of the fort's tiny hospital, a mass of writhing suffering. Many were missing arms or legs where the surgeon had been forced to amputate and several were obviously not going to survive. The rest, pale from loss of blood, lay or sat stoically on the ground. Beresford was aware of horror bravely borne and of the hopelessness of their position.

Half a mile offshore, Lieutenant John Thomson had been enjoying his first command. The *Neptuno* had been captured in port when the British attacked the city and the Lieutenant, in his mid-thirties and overdue promotion, had been given the vessel when Popham took the rest of his command to Monte Video. His orders had been vague – he was to 'keep an eye on the place' and 'make himself useful' to Beresford should the need arise. It had seemed an easy enough task, but since he had heard the sound of gunfire across the water the previous afternoon, he had found himself completely at a loss as to what to do. The mud made it impossible to bring his ship up to the jetties near the fort. He tried positioning himself a few hundred yards from land and using his guns to support the men of the 71st but the fort, built to command the shoreline, blocked his guns from the main body of the enemy.

A signaller on the bows of the ship had tried to make contact with the besieged soldiers by semaphore but, with the garrison forced to stay under cover, there was no way that signals could be returned, even if they were being read.

While Beresford made his rounds ashore, aboard the *Neptuno* Thomson decided that he should try to land a party to establish the needs of the garrison and take in supplies. A second lieutenant was accordingly put off in a longboat with a dozen sailors and a midshipman and they set off toward the fort's seaward walls.

Thomson watched the boat pull strongly toward the shore until, a hundred yards from land, one of the sailors collapsed at his oar. Through his telescope, Thomson could see clearly as another fell, blood pouring from his chest. The Second Lieutenant half rose to urge the others to row faster but his action simply made him an easier target and he was next to fall. The midshipman gave frantic orders to go about and row out of range but with two rowers already dead and the other confused as to what to do, the craft floundered, allowing another three sailors to be picked off.

The mate was standing next to Thomson, pointing to where the fishermen had pulled their boats up on shore. The fire was coming from the cover of this little encampment.

'Man the capstan. Bring her round by the head.'

The crew, who had been lining the rails, watching as the longboat came under fire, hurried to their posts. As the anchor cable was tightened, the bow of the ship swung over, allowing the guns to be brought to bear on the fishermen's encampment. But all this took time and, already, two more of the men in the longboat were dead.

The first shot from the *Neptuno*'s cannon fell short but it served its purpose. Before the gunners had the chance to improve their aim, the rebels broke from hiding and sprinted for the cover of the houses beyond the beach. By now, though, it was too late for any attempt to land the longboat. It was already limping back to the *Neptuno.* Four of her crew were dead and four more were injured.

Thomson visited the injured in their quarters below decks. Stooping under the beams his face was inches from theirs as they lay in their hammocks, trying to find ease from their wounds. Two were lying still, breathing shallowly, and he saw death clouding their eyes.

Back on deck, he called the mate.

'Hoist sail and get us down to Monte Video.'

'Aye, aye, sir!'

A more experienced commander would have left it at that, but Thomson was young and felt the need to explain himself.

'They'll have other ambushes prepared. We can't bombard the enemy; we can't relieve our friends. All we can do is stay and watch. We're best warning Commodore Popham.'

But the mate wasn't even listening. He was giving the orders that would see the *Neptuno* set sail.

Ashore, Beresford was alerted by a shout from the seaward wall. He ran to an embrasure and saw the sails unfurling, white as they caught the morning sun.

Now he was utterly alone.

*

In de Liniers' headquarters, Burke followed every detail of the siege. There was a large table in the shop, used by the draper for laying out and cutting bolts of cloth. De Liniers had appropriated this as a map table and it was now covered with plans showing the approaches to the fort. The admiral pointed at the barricaded streets.

'Here and here, we could place cannon.'

There were fewer than half a dozen cannon available to him: weapons that had been positioned around the city, and which the British had abandoned as they fled. They were intended as static defences and were not mounted on carriages, so moving them would take time.

'But we have all the time we want.' De Liniers shrugged. 'We might as well bring them up.'

The cannon, he explained to Burke, were hardly a military necessity. He did not intend to storm the fort, so the cannon were not essential to his strategy.

'No, Lieutenant, an assault is unnecessary. We have them pinned down. The only forces that could relieve them are in Europe and cannot arrive here for months – by which time they will have starved. Meanwhile, every hour someone will show himself in the courtyard and my men will shoot him. So all the time men are dying in a futile effort to defend that which cannot be defended. I know your Colonel Beresford is stupid but he will work this out eventually.'

'So why bring up cannon?'

De Liniers shrugged again – a Gallic gesture that reminded Burke that the admiral was French, not Spanish.

'The navy put me in command of coastal defence. That's really an artillery command. You could say that the cannon are a sentimental indulgence.'

There was nothing sentimental about his prosecution of the siege, though. Throughout the day, James watched helplessly as runners brought details of more casualties in the fort. Once the besieged troops tried to sally out. They made it across the square but once in the streets they came under fire from the buildings on either side of them. They retreated long before they reached the barricades, dragging their injured back as the rebels poured fire into them from the rooftops.

When the news was brought to de Liniers, he turned to Burke.

'It seems your Colonel Beresford is more of a fool than I took him for. Perhaps we will have time to bring up the cannon after all.'

The first of the cannon arrived that afternoon. The musket fire from the roofs was silenced, allowing the British to venture onto the walls so that they could see the artillery being positioned.

The arrival of the guns was the last straw. As the crews laboured to fix them in position, the gate of the fort opened and an officer walked out under a white flag.

Five minutes later the man was brought before de Liniers who stood beside his map table. Although he was still dressed as a common gaucho, he had an unmistakable air of command and the Captain instinctively saluted him. As he did so, he noticed James for the first time, standing back toward the rear of the shop.

'Lieutenant Burke? What the hell are you doing here?'

Before James could reply, de Liniers cut in.

'Lieutenant Burke is my guest. He is here to ensure what you English call "fair play". I assume you are here to discuss terms.'

'Colonel Beresford is anxious to avoid more damage to the city and to relations between the people of La Plata and the British. He is willing to withdraw from Buenos Aires and be taken off by Commodore Popham's vessels.'

The Captain had the decency to look embarrassed as he made this offer. De Liniers laughed politely.

'So Colonel Beresford is kind enough to say that if we lift the siege he will march his men away. Commodore Popham will, no doubt, use them to take Monte Video.'

The Captain looked even more awkward.

'I really wouldn't know the colonel's intentions, sir.'

De Liniers smiled politely and sat down.

'Find the Captain a chair,' he commanded. 'Lieutenant Burke, join us, please.'

The three men sat and wine was brought.

'Captain, you have the advantage of me as I do not know your name.'

'Captain Henderson, sir.'

'Very good, Captain Henderson. Let me explain the situation to you. Colonel Beresford is surrounded. The fort will fall. The only question is how many of his men are allowed to die before this happens. Once the fort has fallen, his men are my prisoners to do with it as I wish. I certainly do not intend to release them unconditionally. Do you understand all this?'

'The laws of war, Admiral . . .'

'Ensure that you will be well treated if you surrender. But they do not demand that I release you unconditionally.' De Liniers paused and sipped from his wine.

'Fortunately for you, I have an understanding with Lieutenant Burke here. He has interceded for you. He has assured me that if Colonel Beresford gives his parole, his men will remove themselves to Europe and will undertake not to engage in any further military expeditions to the Americas. Do you understand this?'

Henderson nodded.

'Commodore Popham will lift his blockade of Monte Video and will send his transports to embark your men. The escort ships will remain out at sea and will not approach within a mile of the shore. Again, do you understand this?'

'Will we be allowed to retain the honours of war?'

'You may leave the fort with your colours and arms but you will pile your arms in the plaza and your colours will be surrendered to me.'

'I will put your offer to Colonel Beresford.'

De Liniers turned to Burke.

'I will check on the placing of the guns. While I am gone, Captain Henderson, I recommend that you talk with Lieutenant Burke. His rank may be junior to yours but I think he has a finer understanding of the position.'

De Liniers left the shop and Henderson turned on Burke.

'What the hell are you doing here, Burke? And why is de Liniers having you do his dirty work for him.'

Two days of watching as the men of the 71st died because of the stupidity of their commander had left James with no patience for that group of so-called 'staff officers' Beresford had surrounded himself with. This included Captain Henderson.

'Captain Henderson, I am here under the direct command of the Duke of York. Under his authority, I negotiated an arrangement that could have given us the wealth of South America without the necessity for this battle. Now you have thrown that away, I have negotiated a separate arrangement that will get the 71st out of there with no loss of life. If you turn this offer down, de Liniers will refuse terms and keep you fighting to defend that fort until the last man of you is dead. When Beresford sent me to demand the surrender of the town, he refused to offer terms. If you do not accept the arrangement I have negotiated for you, de Liniers will repay Beresford in kind. Tell your damn fool colonel that this is his last chance to get anyone out alive.'

'You don't talk to me like that, Lieutenant.'

'I'll talk to you how I damn well want. De Liniers hates me. He'll let you go because I can give him something he wants. Once he's got that, he'll kill me.'

Captain Henderson rose to his feet.

'You're in league with that man, Lieutenant. If he does kill you, I'm not sure that it's any more than you deserve.'

And with that, he was gone, shouting at the door for de Liniers to provide him with an escort back to the fort.

That night James was locked into a room on the upper floor of the house with a guard mounted on his door. He heard the firing continue through the night. He tried not to think about what life must be like in the fort but whenever he closed his eyes to sleep, the bleeding bodies of the men of the 71st filled his vision. He imagined that he could hear the screams of the dying on the night breeze.

In the fort, Beresford, too, was having a sleepless night. For him, the screams were all too real. Almost ninety of the men under his command were already dead with more than twice that number wounded.

In the morning, Colonel Beresford rode out of the fort and presented his sword to de Liniers.

James heard later that many of the private soldiers of the 71st had been in tears when they were told that they were to surrender. When the gates opened so that they could march out, the square was full of people: gauchos, merchants, servants. All were jeering as the Highlanders formed up behind their pipers. Even the whores had joined the crowd to pelt the soldiers who had occupied their city.

Looking at the crowd, one of the columns threatened to break away and charge into the mob in a final, futile act of defiance but their sergeants beat them back with their fists while the officers stood at attention and prayed to get the humiliation over with.

It would take over a week to get a message to Popham and arrange the practicalities of embarking the shattered remains of the army. Meanwhile, the men of the 71st were to camp in the stockyards where the cattle were driven on their way to slaughter. The officers fared better, being billeted in private houses around the city. Special provision, however, was made for Lieutenant James Burke, who found himself housed in a small cell in the liberated Castillo de San Miguel.

After nine days in the cell, James was brought to the walls of the fort to see the troops embark. The transports lay off shore under de Liniers' guns. All day, longboats rowed from the shore to the ships. In some, the men were silent; in others, those of the wounded who had not yet died screamed or moaned as they were laid into the boats. At the end of the afternoon, James saw Beresford shake de Liniers' hand and make his way onto the final boat. Half an hour later, the transports had hoisted sail and were already moving away from the shore.

De Liniers wasted no time but came straight from the beach to the fort.

'I have kept my part of the bargain. Where's my money?'

'When I tell you, you will kill me.'

De Liniers sneered.

'Your life was never part of the bargain, Burke. I have spared your countrymen. Your honour demands that you tell me where the treasure is.'

They were still standing on the walls of the fort. James looked toward the horizon and the vanishing sails of the transports. It had, he decided, been a good bargain.

'Ask Mr O'Gorman where the llamas are stabled. There's a dung heap there. Your treasure is buried in that.'

For a long moment, de Liniers looked at Burke. Then, swinging back his right hand, he struck him once across the face. A moment later, he turned on his heel and went to recover his fortune.

*

The next day, James was left alone in his cell. The day after, too, he was fed and the bucket left for his ablutions was changed but otherwise he saw no one. The situation continued for a week, during which he tried to discover something about his fate by talking to his guards, but to no avail.

On the eighth day, he was ordered from his cell and into the courtyard. There, a line of soldiers waited with their muskets. De Liniers himself was in command.

They offered him a blindfold, which he declined.

They stood him against the wall.

Muskets were raised to shoulders.

De Liniers held out his sword and, as he dropped it, six hammers fell. The priming powder exploded with six sharp cracks and smoke drifted from the priming pans.

Chapter Seven

I'm still alive.

James looked at the firing squad and saw them turn and march away.

De Liniers was walking toward him.

I'm still alive.

Now the Frenchman was just a foot from him. He leaned forward and spoke directly into James' ear.

'If I had my way, the guns would have been loaded. But you have been spared. The *Santa Theresa* is in port. I think you will remember her. You have safe passage to Brazil. When you get to Rio, you will write to Mrs O'Gorman in your own hand to assure her that you are well.'

De Liniers turned and stalked from the courtyard.

Dear Mrs O'Gorman,

I write to let you know that I have left La Plata and am now safe in Brazil. I will take an English ship from here, which sails tomorrow for London.

I humbly beg your pardon that, yet again, I have left Buenos Aires without first taking my leave of you. Our mutual friend arranged my departure and I was put aboard ship with scarcely any notice and with only the clothes I was wearing. I have no complaints, however, as my well-being required an immediate change of air.

Our friend suggested that I write to you to let you know that all has gone well. I was delighted to understand from this that you have interested yourself in my health and I thank you from the bottom of my heart for your good wishes and concern.

I remain, madam, your affectionate friend,

Lieutenant Burke arrived back in London at the beginning of December 1806. He disembarked at Tilbury and took the stagecoach through the rain to town. His nominal regiment was serving in India, but he had been provided with temporary quarters in the barracks at the Tower. There he settled to sleep on English soil for the first time in two and a half years.

The next morning he was woken by a familiar voice.

'Cup of tea, sir.'

'William, by all that's wonderful! What are you doing here?'

'Detached duty, sir. I'd missed the regiment – by the time I got back, they were already heading for India. So they kept me at the Tower doing this and that but mainly waiting for you, sir.'

'Well, it's good to see you.'

'It's good to see you as well, sir. Adjutant's compliments and you're expected at Horse Guards at ten o'clock.'

William had his uniform – stored in an army chest for the past thirty months – ready for him to put on. Burke had lost a little weight working as a dockhand but the uniform was still a good fit. William brushed off the jacket and fussed over the buttons and facings.

'I'm not turning out for inspection, Private.'

'No, sir. But I'll not have it said that my officer didn't leave my care the best-turned-out lieutenant in the army.' He straightened the tunic sleeve. 'Sir.'

Not wishing to soil his boots, which William had polished until they fairly gleamed, Burke rode from the Tower to Horse Guards and Colonel Taylor's office. To his surprise, though, the adjutant who met him escorted him, not to the colonel's office, but to that of the Commander-in-Chief himself.

The office from which the British army was run was an unassuming room that looked out over the parade ground. It was rather smaller than that occupied by Colonel Calzada Castanio, although it did have the advantage of a view of St James's Park in the distance.

Burke saluted the figure sitting behind the one desk in the room. Frederick Augustus, the Duke of York and Albany, was just approaching his forty-second birthday. Inclined to stoutness and already balding, he was widely ridiculed as the Grand Old Duke of York who had led his men to defeat against the Dutch six years earlier. James, though, knew him to be a sound organiser who, if not a great military tactician, was a man with a good strategic grasp of the political realities of war.

'At ease, Lieutenant.'

When Burke entered, the Duke had been poring over some maps showing the latest position of Bonaparte's forces in Europe but now he pushed these to one side and concentrated his attention on James.

'Bad business in Buenos Aires.'

'Yes, sir.'

'Not your fault, Burke, not your fault at all. You set the situation up for us and Popham and Beresford failed to exploit it. Bad show all round. Take a seat.'

Burke sat and a servant entered with sherry. The Duke made a show of pouring and passed a glass across the desk to James.

'I understand that you had more than a little to do with negotiating the release of the 71st.'

James summarised his negotiations with de Liniers, omitting the role that Ana had played in getting him out alive.

'You did a good job there, Burke – a very good job.'

The Duke searched among the papers on his desk and, finding the one he wanted, read through it quickly.

'It's unfortunate that Captain . . .' He looked again at the paper in front of him. '. . . Henderson seemed not to appreciate your position.'

He put the paper down and looked again at the Lieutenant sitting in front of him.

'The army operates on the principle of chain of command, Burke. Can't have a lieutenant ordering a captain about.'

Burke coloured.

'The situation was exceptional, sir.'

'Even so, Burke, it shouldn't have happened. You've been doing this sort of thing for me for years. I think I've rather overlooked your rank.'

'Sir.'

'So you're a captain with immediate effect. It will be gazetted tomorrow.'

For a moment, Burke could think of nothing to say and then, recollecting himself, he managed, 'Thank you, sir.'

Finally, he had been made up to captain. And he was not to have to buy his new rank. To be given the rank without payment was an honour he had never hoped for. The strange thing was that, after so many years of dreaming that he might one day somehow gain his captaincy, now that he had achieved it, it seemed hardly to matter. Already the Duke was talking about the future of the war with Spain, and James' next mission. Captain Burke put thoughts of his new rank aside and concentrated on what he was being told.

'Spain is now firmly allied with Napoleon and it is the view of the government that we require a decisive action against her. A victory in South America will damage her economy and draw troops away from the European field of battle. My staff officers are also anxious that the army should have the opportunity to redeem itself after such a humiliation.'

'So I am to return to South America.'

'In time, Captain Burke, in time. I am afraid that one thing that we have learned from our experiences so far is that if we are to attack the Spaniards in the Americas it must be done properly and with a proper army. No more half measures.' The Duke pursed his lips. 'Of course, given the military situation in Europe, finding the men and *materiel* for a proper army may be easier said than done. I do not anticipate any action before the end of the year ahead of us and it may well be longer. However, in the meantime, I think you can help us prepare by providing us with a proper understanding of the likely response to any invasion. Your skills will be invaluable in judging Spain's position to react to attacks by our forces, whether in South America or in Europe.'

He smiled, as if bestowing a favour.

'Captain Burke, I think it's time you went to Spain.'

*

Madrid in January was little warmer than London and definitely just as wet. The rain was falling in sheets as the stagecoach from Marseille pulled into the city.

The passengers got out and stretched, happy to stand in the rain after days of travel in the coach. They did not have to suffer the effects of the weather for long, though. Porters ran from the inn carrying umbrellas to shelter the gentry. The servants sitting outside the coach were already soaked, and it seemed of no concern to anyone if they got wetter.

Not that I could really get any wetter, thought William, clambering stiffly to the ground and calling for porters to help get Burke baggage out of the weather as his master hastened to the warmth of the inn.

'Monsieur Defarge?'

'Yes.' James turned to the innkeeper.

'Your rooms are ready, monsieur.'

James followed a potboy to his rooms, leaving William to organise the porters with his baggage.

By the time that William had joined him, James was already halfway through the hearty meal that had been served in front of the fire.

'Settled in, Jacques?'

'Oui, monsieur.'

William had been practicing his French religiously since James had told him he was going on this trip, but he still didn't sound like a native. If questioned, William was to claim that he was Flemish, forced south to escape the war. It wasn't ideal but James needed a servant to be credible and William probably spoke enough French to get by.

'I still don't understand why you have to be French at all,' he complained. 'After all, we're in Spain.'

'Just so.' James speared himself a piece of beef on his fork. 'And a fake Spaniard will be more easily detected in Spain than anywhere else in the world. Besides which, I need a reason to spend time around the court. Applying for Spanish citizenship gives me just that.'

'I thought the French in Buenos Aires managed very well without Spanish citizenship.'

'Ah, but I want to build my trade with Spain and I think this would be easier with Spanish nationality.'

James pushed his empty plate away from him.

'Anyway, we can start to worry about all that tomorrow. Find yourself some food and get some sleep.'

'Yes, sir.'

With the tiniest shrug of regret, he tore himself away from his position near the roaring fire and took himself to the servants' quarters at the rear of the inn, where a few logs flickered fitfully. The food was good, though, and the bed better than sleeping on the ground.

Half an hour later, master and man were both dreaming. In Burke's vision, he was leading a mighty army while George III and the Duke of York looked on approvingly.

William dreamed that he had dry clothes.

*

The bureaucracy that had so tangled any attempts to travel round La Plata was as nothing compared to the bureaucracy that Burke now faced in Madrid. He had hoped that at least some of the interminable delays and self-importance of the Viceroy's officials stemmed from provincial pettiness but he was fast discovering that their officialism was but a pale imitation of that prevailing in the capital of Spain's Empire.

On the first day, he attempted to arrange an appointment with the assistant to the deputy of the undersecretary who was responsible for matters of citizenship. It was patiently explained to him that an appointment was first necessary with the appropriate functionary whose job it was to confirm that you were worthy of a meeting with any higher beings, and who would, if he judged you fit, arrange such further appointments as were necessary. His immaculately forged letters of introduction from French officials eased the way but, even so, it was clear that he would spend weeks waiting for the appropriate formalities to be completed.

James was by no means unhappy at the delay. The longer he spent waiting to petition the various secretaries and under-secretaries, the more people he met who orbited the court of Charles

IV, and hence the more chance he had of gathering useful intelligence. As the weeks turned into months, though, he began to despair of gathering any useful information at all. It seemed to him that the Bourbon court knew little of the world beyond Madrid.

By March, James found that, far from gathering intelligence about Spanish forces, the officials he dealt with would ask him for information about conditions in their own provinces. When he admitted to having travelled across the Andes and visiting Potosí, the secretary for South American commerce was thrilled.

'Señor Defarge, I am honoured to meet someone who has seen with their own eyes the source of our country's wealth. To have travelled from coast to coast of our South American territories! So few people have done that!'

The secretary insisted that Burke join his family for dinner so that Sr Defarge could tell them about the wonders of La Plata from his first-hand experience. Word spread about the handsome Frenchman who had journeyed all around South America and – although James insisted that he had scarcely begun to explore that continent – he was soon looked upon as almost another Humboldt, whose fame as an explorer was just beginning. He began to receive invitations to soirées given by ministers and courtiers and finally, at Easter, he was summoned to present himself at an audience with King Charles himself.

Charles IV was almost sixty and showing his age. A small wig, perched high on his head, did nothing to conceal his baldness. His nose was prominent, as was his chin, reminding James irresistibly of Mr Punch.

His wife, Maria Luisa, was in her early fifties. She was running to fat and her yellowing hair and the missing teeth that she revealed when she smiled added to the suggestion that this was a Punch who had found his Judy. James, though, knew that appearances could be deceptive. Maria Luisa might be middle aged, ugly, and suffering from a range of ill-defined but enervating maladies, but she held the power in Spain.

Although she had lost her looks, Maria Luisa liked to surround herself with handsome younger men. There were several of them in attendance on her now. James recognised Godoy, the chief minister – who was widely believed to owe his position to his activities in the Queen's boudoir. Godoy was not the only one that the Queen bestowed her favours on, though. As James watched, she laughed flirtatiously at some comment from one of the other courtiers – an effect spoiled only by the gaps she displayed in her dentistry. None of the men around her allowed this to put them off, though. They fawned on her every word, laughed at her every joke and, as soon as the floor was cleared and musicians appeared, they almost came to blows as they competed to ask her to dance.

If Godoy was not happy with this state of affairs, he was wise enough not to show it. Looking on at the dancers, he smiled benignly – almost, James thought, like some pimp calculating the potential profit in his merchandise.

James sighed. Maria Luisa was known to have a fascination for South America and for men from that distant reach of the Spanish Empire. It was time for him to do his duty to his country.

*

James woke in a tangle of bed sheets. Beside him, the Queen lay still asleep. It was late afternoon and the light that penetrated past the shutters was kind to Maria Luisa. She opened her eyes, saw James looking at her, and reached to pull his face to hers.

When he kissed her, he was surprised to realise that he felt some real affection. It was hard not to like someone who was so open in their enthusiasm for a younger body lying on their own. Though she was a monarch and could demand attention, she was also a woman no longer in her first youth. Older women, James thought, were always grateful. That was part of their attraction.

The Queen pulled him closer to her, her free hand fumbling for his manhood. That was another part of her appeal, thought James. In the end, those women who most devotedly worshipped at Aphrodite's shrine could not help but give off an aura of eroticism denied to their less enthusiastic sisters. James would rather spend the night with an ugly libertine than with a beautiful woman who did not truly enjoy what he had to offer.

And then again, she was a queen.

*

James opened his eyes and peered uncertainly as William hovered over him with tea.

'What time do you call this?'

'It's noon, sir. I thought it best to wake you.'

'Noon,' he groaned.

James struggled to remember what he had been doing the night before. As he sipped the tea William gave him, the details began to sort themselves in his brain. He found himself rather wishing that they hadn't.

'I'm getting too old for this, William,' he said. 'The palace here makes a Roman orgy look like a little light relaxation after a bishop's tea party.'

'One must think of England, sir. The situation does seem to be providing a flow of useful intelligence.'

That was true, at least, James thought, massaging his temples. Maria Luisa's interest in South America was far from superficial and she was happy – in the brief intervals between her demands that they make love – to talk about the political situation and the various agitators who were travelling around the courts of Europe drumming up support for their various revolutionary movements. She was informative, too, about Spanish policy, including the logic behind de Liniers' recent appointment as viceroy.

'He's an awful man but the people adore him since he drove the English out. And he's ambitious. As long as he's viceroy, he'll keep La Plata loyal rather than risk losing his position.'

It was, James thought, an accurate summing up of de Liniers' character. She was less insightful when it came to Napoleon.

'Ghastly man isn't even French, my love. He's a Corsican and every inch the grubby provincial.'

'So why does Spain ally with him?'

'Because he's got a big army and he is fighting the British. I know you're French too but you must appreciate that your revolution can't last for ever. Eventually the monarchy will be restored – it's just the way things are. And then Napoleon's empire will fall and the old powers will rise again. And Spain with them.'

James found it difficult to give a careful political analysis whilst nibbling the Queen's neck but he did his best.

'I fear Napoleon may be more cunning than you give him credit for, Your Majesty.'

Maria Luisa wriggled against him in a way that made concentration on matters of state even more problematic, but James persevered.

'He does not want Spain as an ally but as a part of his empire. He plans to seize your throne and have Spain ruled by his brother.'

James brought his mind sharply back to the present.

'She didn't believe me, William.'

'Did you tell her about the Portuguese, sir?'

'As much as I dared.'

The Portuguese royal family, with Napoleon's armies already moving into Spain, feared a French takeover and was already preparing contingency plans. If Napoleon continued to threaten them, the court was to be evacuated to Brazil. The British were to provide ships to assist the evacuation. The Duke of York had made sure all this was passed on to Burke in the hope that the news might shake the Spanish out of their complacency.

'I can only hint at the Portuguese plans, in case the Queen takes it into her head to let the French know what's afoot.'

By now, James was out of bed and William was busy shaving him.

'Best not talk for a moment, sir. I like to shave close what with your being a courtier now – and I wouldn't want to cut you.'

For a moment, there was silence as William negotiated the blade around his master's neck.

'The Queen's daughter's married to the king in Lisbon, isn't she?'

'Not quite, William. Technically, he's not the king, but his mother's quite mad so he rules as regent. You're right, though. If she has the sense to talk to Princess Carlota, she might come to her senses and disentangle herself from the French.'

'Best keep trying, then, sir.'

'I suppose I had.' He sighed. 'It had better be oysters for lunch again, William.'

*

James tried for another month to convince Maria Luisa of the danger posed by the French but to no avail. By then he had sucked her dry of information and he feared that she was beginning to tire of him. It seemed an opportune point at which to invent a business crisis in Paris and leave the Spanish court.

Once back in France, James and William travelled to Brittany and thence they were smuggled across to England with twenty casks of brandy. It was, as James remarked, a good thing for the British spy network that smugglers would not let a little thing like continental warfare come between them and their profits.

James was allowed a week to recover after his exertions in Spain, before being ordered to Horse Guards again. This time he did not see the Duke of York but his *aide-de-camp*. Colonel Gordon had recently taken over from Colonel Taylor and was the new *de facto* head of British Intelligence. He had read Burke's report and had few questions to add.

'That seems most satisfactory, Captain Burke. A fine effort. It will substantially advance our plans for an expedition against the Spanish Americas. But I think we have probably exhausted your potential in that sphere.'

'I hope not, sir. I retain the strongest enthusiasm for British activity in South America.'

'That's as may be but we have, thanks to your efforts in Madrid, a detailed understanding of the Spanish forces in the New World and, after your adventures last year, fine charts of the defences they have in place. It remains only to put together an army.' Gordon grimaced. 'Of course, with Napoleon lording it over half Europe, finding the men to send to the Americas may take rather longer than we had hoped. Meanwhile, we have other things that are a more immediate concern. Speaking of which . . .' The colonel leaned forward, confidentially. 'There is another matter you could assist with. It's an issue of some delicacy . . .'

*

The 'issue of some delicacy' was to occupy Burke for almost a year. He moved from country to country, negotiating with allies here; spying on enemies there. All the time, it seemed, Napoleon's strength grew. Allegiances shifted and alliances crumbled and Burke would often find himself both negotiating and spying at the same time.

He was in Berlin when the message came. He was on attachment to Blücher's staff and he had been practising with a sabre in the gymnasium. As he wiped off the sweat, an adjutant came into the changing rooms and saluted smartly.

The Duke of York wanted to see him. He was to return to London immediately.

*

He was back in the familiar office in Horse Guards, sipping smuggled sherry while Frederick Augustus, Duke of York, made polite conversation about Burke's time in South America.

'My wife did appreciate the jewellery. I didn't realise that they produced diamonds in La Plata.'

'They do, sir, though these were purchased in Brazil. The mining region in La Plata is in the north east, near the Brazilian border.'

'Quite. Quite.' The prince sipped again at his sherry. 'Actually, it's your efforts in Madrid that are rather more pertinent to our present conversation.'

'Sir?'

'You report that you told the Queen that you had business in Paris. Do you think that it would be possible for you to return to Spain?'

'It would be quite possible, sir. My business in Spain was never completed and it would be quite natural that I should return.'

'Good. I thought that would be the case. And your relations with the Queen remain satisfactory?'

Burke thought of their last meeting. She had called him a naughty boy and told him that she would punish him, and had then proceeded to make love with a fierce abandon that had left him exhausted for the whole of the journey to Brittany.

'Quite satisfactory, I think, sir,' he said.

'Excellent. You will know, I assume, that Napoleon has moved his armies through Spain to attack Portugal. A lot of the Spanish see this as an invasion, and I can't say I disagree with them. They blame the court, and there have been riots.' The Duke smiled grimly. 'The people rising to protest against the product of the French revolution! It's rather wonderfully ironic, don't you think?'

James nodded politely and the Duke continued.

'There's pressure on the King to abdicate. Or he has abdicated. Or he's going to abdicate. The situation is, to put it mildly, confused. Anyway, there are those within the Spanish court who would like England to offer them assistance – though whether to resist Napoleon or to fly to South America like the Portuguese really isn't clear. We need a man in Madrid. Someone who knows his way around the court and who is trusted by the Queen. It the Queen that matters, not the king.' The Duke looked up reflectively. 'I met him once, you know. Nice enough chap. Rather vague. Not terribly bright.'

'Yes, sir.'

The Duke started, as if recalled to the present by Burke's voice.

'Well, you know the Queen. You're our man. Colonel Gordon will give you the details.'

Burke, understanding that he was dismissed, rose to leave.

'One last thing, Burke. The duchess really did appreciate the jewellery. And you did a good job in Prussia. You're being made up to major. It'll be in the *Gazette* next week.'

'Thank you, sir.'

'Don't thank me, Burke. You deserve it. Now get yourself to Madrid and let's see if we can stop Napoleon before he has the whole of Spain in his pocket.'

*

The trip back to Madrid went without incident, although James was frustrated by delay at almost every stage. First, the weather in the Channel was too rough for a crossing in the small boats the smugglers used. When it cleared, there was a full moon and no one was prepared to risk the run when excise men and naval patrols would find it all too easy to intercept them. When he finally made it to France, the stagecoach from Paris was repeatedly held up as the roads were closed to allow priority to Napoleon's troops marching south.

At the border with Spain, though, there were no delays at all. They were waved through with no checks whatsoever. It was enough that the coach and its passengers were French. The Spanish had clearly prevaricated for too long. Their French allies were now quietly annexing their country.

In Madrid, James learned that the royal family had left their palace. They had moved to the king's fabulously opulent new home, the Casita del Labrador at Aranjuez. While the Casita was undeniably lovely, James did wonder if its main attraction might be that it was built on the Tagus. Madrid had no direct access to the sea but, from the castle grounds, the King could set off directly downriver. The Tagus had provided the Portuguese with their opportunity to escape Napoleon. Perhaps the Spanish court was planning a similar evacuation.

James and William left Madrid early to travel the thirty miles to Aranjuez. The road was in good repair and the stagecoach rattled into town before noon, allowing them the opportunity to find accommodation and announce their arrival to the court that afternoon. To James' relief, a note arrived at his lodgings that evening, summoning him to an audience with the Queen the next day.

As he dressed his master in the morning, William made sure that every detail of his outfit was in the height of fashion. Spanish court style being quite formal, he even wore a wig, which William carefully powdered while James worked his way through a dozen of the oysters that had become his staple diet in Madrid.

In the event, though, these preparations were unnecessary. For once in her life, the Queen's attentions were not devoted to sex. After a year trying to convince herself that the throne was safe, she was now faced with the reality of a French takeover. Her sense of betrayal dominated everything.

She seized on James as a French friend who might give her some clues as to how she could, even at this stage, avert disaster.

'I know that most French men are like you, Alain. They are honest. They are loyal. In their hearts, they would see the monarchy restored. It's this Napoleon who is the problem.'

The Queen had invited him to share wine and *tapas* in her private apartments and, except for the servants, they were alone. She was so agitated she could not sit still, but paced back and forth. James thought that, though any beauty she had once possessed was faded, her anger brought a fierce attractiveness that made him almost regret that their meeting seemed to be concerned with the political to the exclusion of the personal.

She picked up an olive, biting into it so viciously that James feared she might break one of her remaining teeth. Then, pausing, she looked at the bowl as if it had given her an idea.

'Perhaps I could poison him?' She turned to James. 'Would that stop this whole wretched business? Napoleon dead of poison.'

'I think there might be practical problems, Your Majesty.'

'I could invite him to a state dinner. We could feast all night and I could have arsenic put in his wine.'

'I think he is unlikely to come. And, if he does, there will be precautions taken.'

'What can I do, Alain? How can I stop your countrymen from destroying us? The people are blaming Charles. They say he favoured the French and that it is because of him they are invading us.'

James felt that the time was right to push the Queen toward a commitment to take help from the British, but he had to move carefully.

'Your Majesty has always said that an alliance with France would, in the long run, work to the benefit of Spain.'

'I don't care about the long run! I care about what is happening now! There are pamphlets printed denouncing my husband. Sr Godoy – who, as you know, is a very dear friend,' (James was careful not to smile as she spoke of her one-time lover) 'says that he has been insulted in the street. Windows have been broken. The captain of my personal guard says that we cannot even be entirely confident of the loyalty of the garrison.'

‘Perhaps, then, it is time to turn away from France.’

‘That would mean turning to England.’

James shrugged.

‘Surely, madam, that prospect is not so utterly repugnant.’

The Queen resumed her pacing, her agitation somehow the more unnerving because of the careful elegance of the room, with its tapestry hangings and finely carved furniture.

‘The king’s policy has been built on enmity with England. England envies our South American colonies. They have seized the Malvinas Islands. They invaded Buenos Aires. They harbour rebels like Miranda and indulge their crazy schemes. England’s Nelson has destroyed our navy. How can we expect help from the English?’

‘In my business I have often dealt with the English. I know that they harbour no animosity toward Spain.’

The Queen continued to walk back and forth.

‘If France has turned against us, perhaps we will need to ask the English to intervene. But, Alain, is there no chance that France will behave honourably and remove her troops?’

‘The French are an honourable people, Your Majesty. But, alas, we are dealing here not with the people of France, but with Napoleon.’

‘So I must turn to England for help.’ She paused, as if trying to come to terms with the idea, before adding, ‘I must talk to Godoy before deciding on so dramatic a reversal of our policy.’ And then, remembering herself, ‘And, of course, the final decision would be the king’s.’

*

That evening James thought that something might yet be recovered from the wreckage. With Napoleon’s forces in Lisbon, evacuating the royal family down the Tagus would be difficult but, while the Royal Navy commanded the seas off Portugal, it was not impossible. In any case, if he were able to persuade the court to announce that Spain had joined the alliance against Napoleon, the Spanish people would be likely to rise against the French. This would tie down French troops, which would be an achievement in itself.

He was just congratulating himself that his mission seemed likely to bring England some real benefits when his thoughts were disturbed by the sound of shouting and breaking glass outside his lodgings. Opening the door to see what was the cause of the commotion, he heard shots.

The noise was coming from the direction of the palace. James hurried down the wide boulevards, which all converged on the royal residence. The riot (for that was clearly what it was) was centred on a house a few hundred yards from the palace gates.

The mob was not just the usual ruffians. Apparently respectable people were shouting, urging on the rougher elements in front.

'Drag out the traitor, Godoy!'

At the front of the crowd, James thought he could just make out some soldiers, apparently trying to maintain control. Other troops, though, were joining the mob, baying insults at the French and denouncing Godoy as a traitor.

Suddenly the crowd surged forward. Any attempt that the authorities might have been making to hold them back had clearly failed. There was the sound of more glass breaking and a splintering as the doors of the house were forced.

James had seen enough. He returned to his lodgings, uncertain what the morning would bring.

*

Maria Luisa was close to tears.

'They've seized Godoy! The soldiers ran away and left him to the mob. God only knows what will happen now.'

'He's alive, Your Majesty.'

'Oh, yes.' The Queen's voice was withering. 'He's alive. And held by a mob that is negotiating . . .' Her voice dripped with contempt. 'Negotiating with my husband. This band of puking peasants dares to make demands on their king.'

Then the haughtiness collapsed and she was again a frightened middle-aged woman, turning to an old lover for help.

'Charles is talking to them. He says he's trying to save Godoy but I don't know what he can do.'

In fact, Charles had already agreed to dismiss Godoy. The question was whether, if the Prime Minister was humiliated enough, the mob might spare his life.

'Madam, Sr Godoy is finished. His policies are finished. It is time to renounce the French and turn to the British.'

The Queen sat and looked hard at James. When she spoke, there was suspicion in her voice.

'Why, monsieur, are you so anxious to convince me to turn against your own people?'

It was time to tell the truth.

'I am not a Frenchman, madam. I am an agent of the English government.'

As he watched, the Queen's face seemed to collapse in on itself.

'I am surrounded by traitors,' she said.

'I am not a traitor, madam. I am here with your best interests at heart. The British want to help Spain and that means helping you.'

Maria Luisa drew herself up with a painful dignity.

'I think you may be telling the truth, Alain.' She paused, reflecting on what she had just called him. 'I suppose your name is not really Alain, is it?'

'No, Your Majesty.'

'Never mind. I will call you Alain nonetheless.'

James nodded and the Queen continued.

'I fear you are too late to help me, Alain. The people have rid themselves of Godoy. They have tasted power. They will rid themselves of Charles next.' She smiled. 'You should be pleased. With Charles gone, Ferdinand will be king. He will favour England. He has been plotting against his father and me for years, insisting that we break from France.' She shook her head gently. 'He has been a sad disappointment as a son.'

James knew that she was right. Charles was a weak king and this last blow to his power would destroy him. Ferdinand might turn to England as his ally against the French. The trouble was that he could never be secure if he were put on the throne by the mob. And with Napoleon already occupying half of Spain, a weak king could not expect to remain a king for long.

'We can get you out. Your Majesty.'

'I'm not worth it.'

James looked at the tired face of the woman who had ruled Spain for twenty years.

'You are worth it.'

Without thinking, he leaned forward and kissed her.

'I'll talk to the king,' she said.

*

That night, a French picket stopped a horseman on the road to Pamplona, a town now under French military control.

'What's your hurry?'

'Urgent message from a merchant in Aranjuez. Says it has to be in Brittany soon as may be.'

An officer sauntered over and demanded to see the message.

Your goods are almost ready for delivery but will need to be collected soon, as they are highly perishable. Please ensure you have transport arrangements in place. I would advise shipment by river.

He snorted. These merchants – so convinced that everything they did was so important.

'The man you are carrying this message for – French or Spanish?'

'French, sir.'

The Lieutenant shrugged.

'Better get on then. Never let it be said that the army got in the way of commerce.'

*

The next morning, James arrived at the palace early to find the gates closed and no one being allowed to enter. He waited with the crowds that were gathering in the plaza.

At noon, an officer crossed the gardens in front of the palace and read from a proclamation that he then fixed to the railings of the gate.

James could not hear the reading of the proclamation but there was no mistaking the chants of the crowd.

Viva el rey! Viva el rey Ferdinand!

He turned and walked disconsolately home.

*

'I'd have thought you'd be pleased, sir.'

'There's enough republican sentiment about without people thinking they can get rid of a king whenever it suits them, William.'

'He wasn't a very good king, by all accounts, sir.'

'King George is a pleasant enough man but hardly a shining star, William – but I don't want to see a mob pull him from the throne. Britain stands for stability in these difficult times and abdications don't bring stability.'

There was a long silence. When William spoke again, it was with an unaccustomed gentleness.

'You care for her, don't you, sir?'

'Let us just say that my duty and my inclination both lead me to say that we should get her out.'

*

The next day a message came from the palace that James should call upon Maria Luisa. When he was shown in, it was obvious that she had been crying. She looked older than he had ever seen her.

James hastened give her his good news.

'I've sent a message that we are to assist with your evacuation from Spain. We should be ready to move in a week.'

The Queen raised her hand to stop him.

'It's too late,' she said simply. 'I received word this morning that Napoleon's troops will be here in Aranjuez tomorrow. We will, in effect, be his prisoners. I don't expect to see you again.'

James felt as if he had been physically struck. To have come so far and then have failed. And never to see the Queen again.

He looked at her as if seeing her for the first time. Yes, she was vain and ugly and no longer young. But, as her world collapsed about her, what shone through was her pride and her fierceness in adversity. Now, as never before, she truly looked like a queen.

'There is one thing you can do for me.' There was a small table against the wall and on it there were two sealed letters. Now the Queen picked them up and gave one to James.

'I fear that I will not be able to have any private correspondence after today. This is a letter to my daughter, Carlota.' Burke nodded. Carlota had married the prince regent of Portugal and was among those evacuated to Brazil by the British. 'As you are an English agent, I am sure you can arrange for her to receive this.'

'I will be sure that she gets it, Your Majesty.'

Now the Queen passed him the second letter.

'I know you have been in South America and, for all I can tell, you may yet return there. If you do, I would have you see my daughter and tell her I was well when you left me. I do not expect to see her again in this life, but you have tried to be a true friend to me. I would have a friend take her her mother's love. This letter is an introduction to her Highness recommending you to her.'

James bowed.

'I'm afraid I am going to have to ask you to leave now.' Maria Luisa shrugged her regrets. 'There seems so much to do when one is being deposed.'

She took a step toward him and he reached out and held her. They kissed and he released her and he left.

He never saw her again.

*

James left Aranjuez the next day, as the French marched in. It seemed wiser to await events in the relative anonymity of Madrid.

In the weeks that followed, William was kept busy mixing his special inks, packing and unpacking cipher books from the secret compartment in the travelling trunk, or concealing the messages in whatever piece of innocent merchandise was to carry it back.

A few days after the French arrived in Aranjuez, the King and Queen were taken under escort to France 'for their protection'. Napoleon announced to the Spanish people that he would resolve the difficulties between Charles and Ferdinand and invited Ferdinand to join his father at a conference in France. To everybody's astonishment, Ferdinand went.

'His mother told me he was stupid,' James said, on hearing the news. 'But I really had no idea how stupid.'

Every day brought more news of French troops moving into towns around the country. William would prowl the streets of Madrid, complaining that the place was crawling with the blue uniforms of the enemy but that he was not allowed to do his soldier's duty and attack them.

Ferdinand and Charles were still held at Bayonne, just over the border. It seemed that Napoleon was playing with the future of Spain for it was clear that neither of them was going to be allowed to return to Madrid. The country was rife with rumour and counter-rumour. Units of the Spanish army were said to be mutinying; the French were supposed to have looted San Sebastian; Charles had been assassinated.

Crowds would appear on the streets to boo and jeer at French troops. With no clear notion of what was going on and without any leadership these demonstrations never came to anything. After an hour or two of catcalling, people would drift away, sullen and resentful but with no idea of what they could do.

William's frustration grew, as he and James lingered in Madrid, waiting, like everyone else, to see how things would develop. Waiting was not in William's nature and he spent more and more of his time on the streets, listening to the complaints of the people and adding a few of his own.

So things were on the first Monday in May, when William attached himself to a crowd jeering at a squadron of Moorish cavalry, trying to force a way through the streets for the carriage they were escorting. The Moorish troops, exotic in their turbans, were led by a French general. William asked a woman standing on the fringes of the crowd what the fuss was about. 'They say they've got King Charles' son in that carriage. They'll carry him off to France and he'll be murdered like his father.'

The crowd was growing angrier and now William heard cries of 'French assassins,' and 'king killers.' The press of people had briefly stopped the carriage but now the cavalry were pushing forward with their horses. They made enough space for the carriage to move again and it began to make slow, but steady, progress on its way. William prepared to report that, yet again, the people were protesting and, yet again, the French, utterly confident in their control of the country, were simply going about the business of conquest with no sign that they even noticed the opposition.

William pushed his way forward to see if he could make out whether the carriage did, in fact, contain the young Prince Francis. The crowd was all around him now, shouting and shaking their fists at the soldiers. Ahead he saw a young woman reach toward the carriage and, as she did so, one of the escorts reached down and struck her with his heavy riding glove so that she fell back with blood trickling from her lip.

The crowd shouted more loudly but the Moors simply ignored them.

'French bastards!'

William realised, in the heat of the moment, he had shouted in English. Curious faces turned to look at him and one of the riders seemed to be pulling his horse around toward him.

'Oh, well,' he thought, 'In for a penny, in for a pound.' He bent to the cobbled street, worked one of the stones loose, and flung it at the cavalryman.

The Moorish soldiers did not wear armour and, though the cobble only caught him a glancing blow, the trooper cried out with shock and pain. His cry was met with jeers and laughter from the crowd and, furious, he drew his sword and spurred his horse toward William. William bent to pick up another cobble and, as he straightened, he saw other men doing the same. The crowd, which had been angry but directionless a few minutes before, had suddenly turned into a mob, raining stones onto the soldiers who responded by drawing their sabres and laying about them.

Within minutes, there was chaos. The riders had cut down several civilians, including a young woman. Incensed, the mob had pulled soldiers from their horses, beating and kicking at them as they lay helpless on the ground. The General screamed orders and the remaining guards formed up in front of the carriage, striking at anyone in their path, as the coachman whipped his horses into a gallop. The carriage and its escort broke clear of the crowd and made its escape. By now, though, the anger of the mob was roused and people started toward the main square, looking for any Frenchmen unfortunate enough to be on the street.

William quietly slipped away to report to James that the people of Madrid appeared, at last, to be rising against the French. He decided not to dwell on his part in the incident.

That night, dozens of French soldiers were attacked and martial law was declared in Madrid. The next day, the French rampaged through Madrid, seizing any man found with a knife. Even boys with penknives or scissors were taken to the hill of Principe Pio on the edge of the city and shot. By the end of the day, the French had killed five thousand Spaniards.

On Wednesday, James made a tour of the city, careful to carry the papers that identified him as Monsieur Defarge. When he returned to his rooms, he started his last despatch from Madrid.

Sir,

I have the honour to report that the people of Madrid have risen against the French, who have retaliated with a brutality inconceivable among civilised nations. I am confident that as news of this massacre spreads throughout Spain, the people will unite to destroy the tyrant, Napoleon. Regardless of the outcome of the negotiations at Bayonne or the fate of the king, the Spanish people will call on our assistance. I am confident that any army that the British should despatch to the Peninsula will be welcomed as liberators and will enjoy the support and assistance of the overwhelming majority of the Spanish population . . .

Burke was recalled to London. There was, Colonel Gordon assured him, nothing more he could have done.

Back in Horse Guards, Gordon was brisk.

'Spain's a lost cause. Nothing you'll be able to achieve there now.'

'Yes, sir.'

'On the other hand, I think there may still be a use for you in South America.'

To Burke's delight, Gordon explained that, almost two years after Popham's abortive attempt at conquest, an Army of the Americas was at last being put together. This time, the plan was for multiple landings, striking at all the key points of Spanish rule.

'You're to be a staff officer, Burke. You'll be going back to Buenos Aires.'

It was, for Burke, a dream come true. At last there was to be a British intervention that was properly organised, and he was to be in a position to make sure that he mistakes of the past were not repeated. Even Gordon's news that the army was to be assembled in Ireland and that Burke must return to the country of his birth could not diminish his delight.

James landed in Cork on a fine summer morning. It was his first visit back to Ireland in seventeen years. His father had died while he was away on some secret mission, and he had returned to London to hear that the old man had already been buried. His brother owned the farms now, and the precarious economy of their family life was recounted to him in a yearly letter.

He sniffed the air but it was no longer the air of home. He was only eighty miles from the town where he had grown up but he doubted he would visit. The James Burke who had spent his youth dreaming of adventure and advancement was no more. Major Burke had outgrown Kilkenny.

The Army of the Americas was to be commanded by Sir Arthur Wellesley, a rising star, with a reputation as a careful strategist, but rather dull company. Sir Arthur entertained his new major on the day of his arrival in Cork and, after an evening that confirmed that the Major General hardly drank and did not gamble at all, James concurred heartily with the general view of his character. However, Wellesley did seem to understand what was needed to drive the Spanish from South America, and James considered that the fact that he was said never to have lost a battle was more significant than his lack of any social graces.

Wellesley believed in a scientific approach to warfare and made it clear that Burke was expected to produce detailed plans for taking Buenos Aires. Even more importantly, given Beresford's failure, he was to draw up a memorandum on how Buenos Aires was to be governed and defended after the initial conquest.

For James, this was an ideal employment. He recalled every detail of de Liniers' character and strategy to devise ways of outwitting him. He wanted to make it almost as easy to capture the city when de Liniers was defending it as Beresford had found it when Buenos Aires had been left open for the taking.

Even more exciting was the business of drawing up plans for British rule: plans that, he was sure could include a measure of self-governance. La Plata, he decided, with its dead Spanish bureaucracy, would be consigned to history. Buenos Aires would be the capital of a new Argentina that would go at least some way to fulfilling the dreams of men like Paco Iglesias, while still allowing Britain to benefit from the mercantile activities of the O'Gormans of this world.

For two weeks, James was almost entirely happy. Then a summons to Wellesley's office brought all his dreams crashing down.

'I've a message from the Commander-in-Chief.' Wellesley was sitting upright at his desk, uniform jacket immaculate as always, the despatch from London neatly squared on the desk in front of him.

'He mentions you by name. I understand you are to be congratulated on your work in Spain. The Duke considers your intelligence provides an important opportunity.'

James nodded, modestly.

'The Duke, after consultation with Mr Perceval, has agreed with your suggestion that a military force should be sent to the aid of the Spanish people. Fortunately such a force is readily available.'

Suddenly, James realised what Wellesley was going to say.

The Major General smiled. 'This one.'

'But –'

'I know you'll be disappointed, Burke, but the logic is impeccable. Your analysis of the situation in Spain demands that we send an army to the Peninsula. Striking at Napoleon in Europe is more important than any American adventure. In any case, we do not recognise the French impostor to the Spanish throne. So we are officially allied with Spain against France, which makes the idea of the British invading a Spanish possession . . .' (and here Wellesley coughed diplomatically) '. . . problematic. Indeed, I understand that you are to be detached from my staff and sent off to South America on your own to explain the new situation.'

Wellesley contorted his stern features into a look that James, rightly, interpreted as an attempt to appear sympathetic.

'I trust that possibility might offer you some consolation.'

Chapter Eight

James stood on the deck of the *Rochester*, enjoying the Atlantic wind in his hair. It was a beautiful day. There was no sign of the vicious weather that could make the crossing miserable at best and life-threatening more often than any sailor wished to dwell on. It was over four years since he had first stepped aboard this vessel: four years that had seen him move steadily up the social ladder. He was an adviser to foreign dignitaries, the confidante of dukes, the lover of queens. After all this, a return to South America – far from the London social scene and his useful contacts – should have been a disappointment, especially as his role was little more than that of a messenger. Yet Wellesley was right. The prospect of seeing America again was, indeed, a consolation.

For the moment, it was enough that the sea air was washing away the stink of London. Burke had spent a fortnight there, much of it waiting around Whitehall until the great men of the day should summon him to their presence. He had worked his way up the hierarchy of under-secretaries and secretaries and permanent secretaries until the day he had stood in the presence of the foreign secretary himself, George Canning. Canning had been in office for over a year by now. Though Burke was instinctively suspicious of all politicians, he admired the way that Canning was drawing together a web of alliances designed to cut Bonaparte off from his friends and to support his enemies. He especially appreciated the foreign secretary's understanding that the events in Spain offered an opportunity to bring South America into the war on the side of the British.

'What we need, Burke,' he had explained, 'is a chap out there who can ensure that the dagos are sound. Officially, your job will be military liaison but, unofficially, we want you to reassure the ones that fear the French, and keep an eye on the ones who see Napoleon as a potential liberator from Spain. The Spanish ain't steady, Burke.' He had shaken his head at this and consoled himself with a pinch of snuff. 'No, they ain't steady, and their colonies are worse. We want you there to give 'em some backbone, Burke. Make sure they know which side they're on and that they stay on it.'

Now, as the Foreign Office's most experienced South American hand, he was on his way back there. It was considered politic that for this mission he travel under a new identity, but he clung jealously to his rank, so it was Major Thomas James who was taking the air this fine day. William was again travelling with him. After so many years of service in so many countries, James had argued that William was overdue promotion, and it was Sergeant William Brown who had boarded the *Rochester*. He had learned from Helswig's mistake, though, and it was Steven Williams who now stood beside James on the deck.

'It's a good time of year to be travelling,' James remarked. 'We leave England at the end of summer and arrive in Brazil in time for the best of spring.'

'That's always confused me, sir. Spending Christmas in the hot didn't seem right.'

James smiled.

'Well, you'd better get used to it. Another hot Christmas is a definite possibility.'

'Christmas in Buenos Aires then, sir?'

'Christmas in Buenos Aires.'

The two men stood silent, each with their own thoughts of that city and the women they had left behind there. Each with their own reasons to return.

In fact, they were not to spend Christmas in Buenos Aires at all.

*

Admiral Smith did not like government agents. He had spent a lifetime in the navy, growing old in its service. Now, he represented the British Navy's interests in Rio de Janeiro. It was a shore posting, for all it was an important one. With Brazil allied with Britain, the port at Rio was essential to British naval operations off the South American coast. For years, it had been from Rio that

British warships had harried Spanish traders. For all that time, Admiral Smith had never felt the deck of a fighting ship move under him in the Atlantic swell. Instead, he had been forced to spend the war diplomatically ingratiating himself with one Portuguese official after another. He had done his duty and done it, he thought, damn well. And now some army major half his age was despatched from England to represent His Majesty's Government because Admiral Smith was, apparently, not up to the task.

'The situation in La Plata is too unstable to send you on there.' Smith scarcely bothered to hide his satisfaction at the news. 'You must bide your time a while in Rio until things are clearer.'

'Admiral, when I was last in La Plata, they were in the middle of a war. Just how unstable can it be?'

'They are on the verge of war now.'

'The people are rising against Spain?'

The admiral allowed himself a condescending smile.

'Hardly. News of Napoleon's usurpation of the Spanish throne has united the people behind the monarchy. No – the problem is that the Viceroy there is a chap called de Liniers. Have you heard of him?'

James' face was a mask.

'I believe I may have.'

'Well, he calls himself a Spaniard but he's a Frog. And that means he's not trusted – especially as the silly bugger has been talking to the French. So Monte Video has ceded from the province and Buenos Aires could be in revolt any day. My orders are to ensure your safety and I can't do that if you're in La Plata. So you're staying here.'

Life, Burke reflected, was simpler when you were just a spy. Now he was travelling, at least in part, as an envoy of the British government things could get very complicated. The foreign secretary, no less, had charged him to assure de Liniers of the security of the Anglo-Hispanic alliance and to stop exactly the sort of dalliance with France that the Viceroy was clearly suspected of. Burke enjoyed the prestige that came with being the Foreign Secretary's man in South America but the role meant dealing with lesser representatives of British power. Unfortunately, that meant having his plans interfered with by the likes of Admiral Smith.

Of course, Smith's injunctions didn't stop Burke from looking for a passage to Buenos Aires anyway but this proved harder than he had expected. It seemed that the admiral was not exaggerating the unrest in La Plata. Hardly any vessels were sailing to Buenos Aires or Monte Video and Admiral Smith had asked the authorities to ensure that no British subjects were allowed on any of those that were.

After a night spent drinking in the port taverns, William was confident that he could get the two of them aboard a vessel leaving the next week. 'But we'll be travelling as crew and there's no chance of smuggling any of the baggage aboard. So unless you want to represent His Majesty in a pair of tarred breeches and not much else, I think we're stuck here.'

James accepted the inevitable with good humour. He had enjoyed his stay in Rio de Janeiro before and he expected he would enjoy it now. Besides, he was here as a person of rank, and with the government to subsidise his visit. Things, he decided, could be a lot worse.

Given that the British government was paying, William had soon arranged the lease of a grand house near the town gaol. When James heard, he was at first unamused.

'Good God, William! For that sort of money, I'd expect better neighbours than the local felons.'

'It's all right, sir,' William explained. 'When the court moved here from Portugal, they had nowhere to put themselves so the gaol was cleared out, redecorated, and used to house them.' James looked uncertain. 'It's all very swanky now, sir.'

James agreed to take a look at their proposed new home and found the area very grand indeed. The gaol had been built next to the Viceroy's palace, now the official residence of the prince regent, and the two buildings were connected by an elegant glass-covered colonnade, allowing courtiers to pass to and from without exposing themselves to the elements.

James house itself was light and airy with tall rooms, which stayed relatively cool even in the heat of the Brazilian day.

'It wasn't easy to get anywhere,' said William. 'There's ten thousand people came over with the court less than a year ago, and they all had to be put somewhere. Nice houses are hard to get.'

'So how did you get this one?'

'Saw the undertakers carrying the body out and went to the agents with a bag of sovereigns before they had a chance to advertise it.'

'And the previous occupant died of . . .?'

'Best you don't know, sir. Not infectious though.'

James checked the bedrooms, sniffing suspiciously. The place smelled clean and fresh. He decided not to enquire about the previous occupant.

'We'll need a cook,' he said.

'Already arranged, sir.'

They moved in the next day. The place was certainly convenient for the court and James decided that he should spend some of his enforced stay in cultivating diplomatic relations with the Portuguese. At the least, he owed it to Maria Luisa to call on her daughter, the prince regent's wife.

When James made enquiries as to how one obtained an audience with Princess Carlota, it turned out that his house was not so well situated after all. The Princess was estranged from her husband – not for any simple domestic reason, but because the prince had taken exception to her attempting a coup against him a couple of years earlier. As a result, she did not live with the prince's court but in her own house on the sea at Botafogo – a few miles to the south. James duly hired a sedan chair (his time in Brazil had taught him that Europeans never walked) and four sweating negroes carried him to the Princess's residence.

James presented his letter of introduction to a butler, who passed it to a chamberlain, who vanished into the recesses of the large and well-appointed, if rather sombre, building.

James waited a good half an hour before being summoned to the royal presence by an usher in a livery so bedecked with gold braid and epaulettes that James worried that the poor man might collapse under the weight of his splendour. The walk from the small room where he had been required to wait to the Princess's audience hall seemed to go on for miles, one chamber leading from another, each elaborately decorated in the latest Parisian styles, for all that Brazil was at war with France.

When Major Thomas James eventually arrived in the presence of the Princess, he could not help but feel that it was something of an anti-climax. The figure smiling down at him from a throne mounted on a small dais was small and skinny. Although she could not have been much older than thirty, she had none of the beauty her mother must have possessed when she was young. Indeed, with her moustache and pointed nose and chin, she was straightforwardly ugly. Yet her remarkably dark eyes – so dark, they seemed almost black – sparkled with an intensity that made the rest of her features seem almost irrelevant.

As James was presented, the Princess left her throne. She scrambled down inelegantly, like a small girl, rather than the wife of one of the most powerful rulers in Europe.

'Mummy's letter described you well and said that you seem in the habit of changing your name. You were a good friend of hers, weren't you?'

As she spoke, directly and informally, James found himself reminded of the Spanish Queen. Mother and daughter shared a passion for court life – its scheming, its politics and, James guessed, its opportunities to combine these with a busy personal life.

Carlota took him unselfconsciously by the hand and led him to a side chamber where a table was laid with coffee and cakes.

'You must tell me all about you and Mummy.' For a moment, her face clouded. 'Napoleon won't let her go back to Spain. It seems so unfair after she favoured the French so much.' Then, with scarcely a pause, 'Have a croissant. They're delicious.'

James was there for an hour and left captivated with the lively young woman with the dark eyes. William, when he heard the story, allowed himself an audible sniff of disapproval.

'You've seen a different side of her from most, then,' he said. 'The people here hate her. They say that if you don't bow low enough when her litter passes, her guards will do you over a treat.'

James thought of the elaborate bow that he had performed when he was presented to her Highness and thanked his private deity that he had not skimped on the courtesy. Aloud he said, 'Well, she was perfectly civil with me.'

William sniffed again.

'Fancies you, then.'

James cast a withering glance at his servant.

'That hardly seems likely, William.'

William shrugged.

'Like mother, like daughter is what I hear. Though doubtless you'll tell me that's only servants' gossip.'

James made no reply. His years spying around the courts of Europe had shown him only too well that servants' gossip was seldom wrong about their masters and mistresses. Burke decided that he had best make discreet enquiries around Rio.

He soon realised that there was no need for discretion. The Princess's voracious sexual appetites were almost as famous as her arrogance, which itself was the stuff of legend. It was said that even the British ambassador had found himself knocked to the ground by her bodyguard when he failed to turn to her sedan chair and make the requisite full bow.

Burke found these descriptions difficult to reconcile with the woman he had met. He decided to risk accepting her invitation to another visit. This time he saw more significance in the wait in the hall and the interminable antechambers. He was certainly careful to bow in as low and fulsome a manner as he knew. Yet the Princess herself was again unpretentious and relaxed, chatting gaily about Spain and life with her mother. James did try once or twice to steer the conversation to events in Rio but, though she could be encouraged to talk about Portugal, she refused to talk about Brazil.

'Ghastly, ghastly country. Full of blacks and no one of fashion at all. Look at the dresses people wear here and tell me that the ladies of Madrid were not incomparably more elegant.'

James had to admit that people in Brazil did not reflect the height of modern fashion, although the influence of the Portuguese court was beginning to rid Rio of the worst excesses of eighteenth-century Parisian bad taste. Even so, it was still not unusual to see women wearing the high wigs that Marie Antoinette used to favour. These were often decorated not only with ribbons but also with scissors or little knives and even – on one notable occasion – with vegetables. The effect was made more ridiculous because the heat of Brazil meant that the glue that held these constructions together would often melt, trickling down the faces of the wearers, who would steadfastly refuse to acknowledge that anything out of order was occurring.

Despite the Princess's efforts to persuade him that she was little more than a guileless girl with strong views on clothes, James was not convinced. Her exile from the main court was because she had plotted to overthrow her husband – presumably over an issue more substantial than her dress allowance. And in between prattling prettily about Madrid fashions, she asked enough telling questions about the response to Napoleon's takeover to show that she had an intelligent interest in Spanish politics.

One afternoon, she suggested leaving the palace to walk on the beach. A litter was summoned and James was invited to share it as eight slaves carried the two of them towards the shore. A guard of six men walked in front of the litter with a bailiff carrying a silver-tipped staff ahead of them. James, watching from behind the curtains, saw that it was true that all the people they passed made obeisance almost to the ground. From the looks of sullen anger on their faces, it was clear that this was not out of any feelings of respect for royalty but rather from fear of the guards. James found it difficult to reconcile this ruthless display of raw power with the ugly but charming girl who was even now snuggling kittenishly against him in the sedan chair.

They alighted just where the grass gave way to a beach of astonishing whiteness.

'I love it here,' she said.

'It's beautiful,' agreed James. 'I've never seen sand so white.'

For a moment, the Princess's face contorted in a spasm of fury and James thought she would strike him. Then she checked herself and smiled.

'I don't come for the beach, silly. It's just that from here you can look out toward Europe. The sand is the only bit of Brazil that spoils the view.'

*

The time Burke spent with the Princess passed pleasantly enough but the prospect of an extended stay in Brazil still chafed. Having got nowhere with Admiral Smith, Burke decided to try his luck with Lord Strangford, the unfortunate British Ambassador who had been beaten by Carlota's guards. Strangford, to Burke's disgust, pronounced himself totally in sympathy with the admiral. After that, knowing of course that Burke was seeing a lot of the Princess, he decided to add to the Major's discomfiture by letting him have the benefit of his opinion of the woman.

'She's completely barking mad, Burke. Hates Brazil, hates her husband, hates pretty well everything and everybody here, if you ask me. She's obsessed with restoring the lost glory of Spain and sees herself as the last true Bourbon. You want to avoid her like the plague.'

But avoiding her was difficult. Burke didn't really have it in him to refuse an invitation from a princess and, by now, the invitations were coming in a steady flow.

'It's not like she's a regular princess, sir,' William pleaded. 'Her husband's the regent on account of how his mother's mad, and Carlota doesn't even live with him – on account of how she's mad too, only a bit less obviously, if you get my drift. And she's not the last Bourbon, begging your pardon. Her father's still alive and once we defeat Napoleon, Ferdinand will be back on the throne.'

'She is of royal blood,' Burke argued, 'and, more to the point, a charming young woman who has been kind enough to show me some friendship. Why should I not accept her invitations? More to the point, what bloody business is it of yours?'

William, understanding discretion to be the better part of valour, withdrew.

Things came to a head two months into James' enforced sojourn in Rio. He was spending the evening with the Princess. (Her invitations were increasingly to dine with her at dusk – a meal that she seemed accustomed to take with no other guests.) After dinner, they withdrew to her private apartments where they had become accustomed to playing cards together. Tonight, though, while she shuffled the pack from hand to hand, she seemed reluctant to deal.

'James.' (She had long ago established his real name.)

'Princess?'

'My mother is not a young woman, is she?'

'Your mother is a woman in the prime of life.'

'Don't be gallant, James. She's over fifty and, though I love her dearly, I know she is fat and ugly.'

James, unable to think of a diplomatic response, chose to remain silent.

The Princess ignored his lack of reply, chattering on: 'You were her lover, were you not?'

'The Queen was generous enough to allow me a degree of intimacy.'

'*¡Mi Dios!* You English with your delicacy. So, you were her lover.'

James shrugged and nodded.

'So, I am younger than her and prettier and I have my own teeth, yet you have not made love to me.'

James arrived back at his house early the following afternoon to be met with an obsequiously deferential servant and no remark at all on his absence the previous night.

After only an hour, the careful silence from William was far more irritating than any pointed comment could have been. Although he had sworn he would not mention the subject, James' resolve was broken.

'What else could a gentleman do, William?'

'I wouldn't know what you are talking about, sir.'

'She's a princess, William. And a very passionate lady. I can't just dismiss her.'

'I'm sure you can't, sir.'

*

It was about a week after they first became lovers that James had the first inkling that, while Carlota certainly appreciated his body, he might hold other attractions for her as well.

They were lying in her bed – a huge canopied affair in which the diminutive Princess could almost lose herself amongst the sheets – and Carlota asked how his plans to travel on to Buenos Aires were progressing.

'Frankly, my monkey, I'm stuck. La Plata seems on the verge of civil war and His Majesty's Government don't want anyone going in to negotiate with the parties until they are sure who is going to win.'

Carlota wriggled against him.

'The Viceroy doesn't seem very reliable. They say he favours the French.'

'The Viceroy is a treacherous, lying bastard.'

'But if he is still viceroy when you get to La Plata, you'll have to negotiate with him.'

James didn't want to talk about de Liniers. In fact, as Carlota wrapped her legs around him, he didn't want to talk about anything at all. But the Princess continued.

'I'm told that Monte Video will make peace with Buenos Aires.'

'It's probable. Monte Video can't survive on its own.'

'Then de Liniers will survive as viceroy.'

Burke reached to cup one of her buttocks in his hand. She squirmed in a delightful way, but would not be put off from her questions.

'Do the English want de Liniers to survive?'

'No, Carlota, they don't. But there's not a lot we can do about it.'

'There might be something.'

Burke rolled away from her and sat up. It occurred to him, for the first time, that Carlota was a shrewd political operator.

'You have something in mind?'

But now it was the Princess's turn to refuse to be drawn. She reached up to James and pulled him down to her.

'Later,' she said, wrapping herself around him.

*

The Princess's plan emerged slowly over the next few days, usually after they had been enjoying their now-regular intimacy. He wondered afterwards if he would have given it any consideration if it weren't that his judgement was not, perhaps, at its best in the afterglow of passion. He even wondered, briefly, if Carlota might not have been all too aware of this, but that was a possibility he did not want to spend too long considering.

'Monte Video is loyal to the Spanish throne and would like independence from Buenos Aires. It is my intention to offer myself as ruler of Monte Video. It would no longer be a province but a regency, under the direct control of the Spanish monarch.'

Even the memory of the Princess straddling him, her breasts covered in sweat, could not blind James to a significant omission in her reasoning.

'Carlota, you aren't the queen of Spain.'

She had dismissed his objection as barely worthy of consideration.

'Charles has abdicated and is now nothing but a tool of Napoleon. Ferdinand is just a prisoner of the French, whatever they say. What Spain needs is a monarch who is free to rule.'

It was an argument she often returned to. Even as they made love, she would stop nibbling at his chest long enough to insist that she was the last hope of the Spanish Empire. Then she would return to biting him with a passion that reminded him of the rumours that on their wedding night she had taken a chunk out of the prince regent's ear.

As the Princess elaborated on her scheme, James began to wonder if it might, in fact, be feasible. Monte Video had always held an anomalous position in La Plata. On the east shore of the River Plate, it commanded a strip of territory known as the Banda Orientale. Bordering Brazil, it was a perpetual source of dispute between the two Iberian powers. If it were ruled directly by the wife of the ruler of Brazil, Portugal could, presumably, be persuaded to guarantee its independence.

'Not just Portugal,' the Princess insisted, raking his back with her fingernails. 'If you negotiate such an arrangement, you could guarantee it on behalf of the British too.'

James doubted that he had any such authority, but, with the Princess bringing him to the point of ecstasy as she introduced this new diplomatic twist, he was not about to argue.

Strangford, though, was not under the Princess's spell. Burke was not so much of a fool as to let the British ambassador know that Carlota was trying to involve Britain in her schemes, but he did enquire discreetly as to what Britain's response to a Spanish principality would be.

'We'd oppose it,' Strangford said, speaking more bluntly than a diplomat might be expected to. 'We want the Americas kept out of the war, safely supplying the Allied treasuries. Nothing that stirs up the whole question of their status is to be encouraged by His Majesty's Government. And besides,' he added, 'that Carlota woman is quite mad.'

Mad she might be, thought James, but she was calculating, ambitious, and more politically astute than her enemies gave her credit for. And James was not sure that he didn't want the status of the Americas to be stirred up. He remembered his nights on the pampas and the courage and conviction of the criollos. They had had a purpose and certainty in their lives that he sometimes wondered if he lacked in his own.

He thought of the attack on the fort at Buenos Aires as civilians rose against the colonial occupiers and overwhelmed them. There was, he decided, an inevitability about the growing nationalism of the Argentines. When the war with Napoleon was won – as it must be – he could not imagine the people of Buenos Aires meekly accepting rule from Madrid. The question, to his mind, was not whether or not Argentina would gain its independence, but whether an independent Argentina would be an ally or an enemy of Britain.

In this context, the idea of a Spanish principality began to make sense. Whilst Carlota would rule nominally as a Spanish queen, the government would be in Monte Video and the province would effectively have self-rule. The Banda Orientale would become like

Brazil, a country where the population (though constantly grumbling about the extravagance of the court) showed no sign of rebellion because their rulers lived amongst them. True, the prince regent could be autocratic and Carlota – even the infatuated James had to admit – could be simply impossible, but James convinced himself that the Banda Orientale might be safe in their hands. Since the monarchs of Europe had seen Louis led to the guillotine, kings and queens ruled with a sensitivity to their subjects' interests that mere colonies could never experience. A Spanish principality under British protection could become a beacon of self-rule, lighting the way for the rest of Spanish America to establish its own governance under the benign watchfulness of the European powers.

Seduced by the Princess and captivated by visions of a free America allied to the British flag, James found himself agreeing that he would talk with the Monte Video rebels and try to negotiate the agreement Carlota was looking for.

There was only one problem. By February, when Admiral Smith finally decided that it was safe to sail on to Buenos Aires, the Monte Video revolt was over.

'Don't worry, my love,' the Princess said, exploring his nipples with her tongue, 'you'll think of something.'

*

Burke stood in the bows as they ran up the Plate on the tide. They passed San Pedro Telmo and he remembered the inn there and his first night with Ana. He was looking forward to seeing her again. Carlota had been fun, but her rampant sexuality was beginning to pall. Seeing Ana again would be a welcome return to a woman who had made a special place for herself in his heart.

William stood beside 'Major James' and he, too, was thinking of the girl he had left behind in his first precipitous departure from La Plata. Today, travelling as an official delegation from George III's government, he had abandoned his servant's clothes for his redcoat uniform. Self-consciously he flicked a speck of dust from the sleeve where his three stripes stood crisp and white and he found himself wondering what Molly would make of the smart sergeant he now was.

San Pedro Telmo slipped away aft and the towers and domes of Buenos Aires' churches appeared on the horizon. Soon Burke could see the fort, the Spanish flag once again flying proudly above it.

They dropped anchor near the fort, as they had on his first arrival. Looking across the waters of the Plate to the city beyond, he thought that the mud banks had grown perceptibly wider since his first visit, and that the ship was moored further out, but otherwise little seemed to have changed in the past five years.

James made certain that William was among the first to board the boats for the shore, carrying news of the arrival of King George's representative to the Viceroy while he remained on the deck. He watched the porters moving back and forth at the still-ramshackle quay. There was the usual mix of Spaniards, Indians, and Negroes hauling chests and barrels ashore. One tall, black figure caught his eye and he found himself recalling his meeting with the Book Man, all those years ago. For a moment, it seemed as if the Negro on the docks looked directly at him but he knew he must have imagined it. The man was too far away for him to see his features and he would scarcely have been able to make out Burke on the gently rolling ship. Yet James felt a momentary shiver and had a sudden conviction that the decisions he made in the next few days would somehow define him. He remembered the Book Man's words: 'You will walk with the rulers of the world and your actions will help to bring forth a nation.' He thought of the promises he had made to Carlota and his responsibility to Strangford. If he played his cards right, he could come out of this as the man who had delivered La Plata to the British. But where, he found himself wondering, would this leave Sr Iglesias and the rebels who fought and died for their own country, subject to neither Spain nor Britain?

He sighed. Things, he decided, were likely to get complicated.

Just how complicated became clearer when William returned. De Liniers, he told Burke, was delighted to hear of the arrival of Major James and intended to host a reception for him at the viceregal palace that evening. And, William had learned (for the habit of listening to servants' gossip died hard), the Viceroy's consort would be none other than a certain Madame Perichon.

'Ana!'

'Yessir. She's got her claws well into him, by all accounts.'

There was silence while James looked across at the city, as if hoping to see Ana there.

William watched him with an expression of concern. He seemed to start to speak, hesitated, and then said, 'She lives on Unguero, between Alzoga and Villanueva.'

Unconsciously, Burke's eyes swivelled toward Villanueva – a street that met the shoreline only a couple of blocks east of the fort. He saw William frown. The trouble with Sergeant Brown was that he knew Captain Burke too well. He had seen that glance and knew exactly what it meant.

'She's the acknowledged mistress of the ruler of the place, sir. I shouldn't have told you where she lives.'

James turned to him with a half-smile on his lips.

'Did your researches extend to where Molly lives these days?'

William's blush gave his answer.

'Take yourself over there, William. I think we both have some catching up to do.

*

Molly wasn't exactly sure how old she was but she doubted she would ever see twenty-one again. Too old, in any case, to be dancing the horizontal polka with anyone with a shilling to spare. Which was why she had invested the money that she had stored up, piece-by-piece, first under the floorboards and later, as her wealth had grown, in the strongroom of the local banker. Now she was the proud owner of a small tavern in San Pedro Telmo and, more importantly, of the four rooms above it. There, four good, honest, and, above all, athletic girls worked enthusiastically to increase the return on her capital.

South America, she thought, had been good to her. She'd had fun; she'd grown wealthy. Her tavern was popular – and not just with those who patronised her upstairs rooms. She still had admirers and, occasionally, for old times' sake, she would allow a gentleman to lead her to one of those rooms herself. But she'd insisted they all pay. There'd only been one man she would have let bed her without her fee, and he was long gone.

There was a knocking at the tavern door. It was barely ten o'clock in the forenoon. What kind of idiot would disturb her now?

The knocking continued.

She made her way to the saloon and opened the window. There were bars set in the wall so she could not lean out, but she put her face to the metal and shouted in Spanish for her caller to stop his noise.

'I'm closed,' she said. And, in English, she added, 'Piss off and come back in two hours.'

The banging stopped and a red-coated soldier came and stood at the window.

'Molly?' he said.

For a moment, she stared at the uniform and its sergeant's stripes.

Then she went to the door and let him in.

*

James had chosen to remain in civilian clothes for his call on Ana.

The house where she was living was small, but conveniently close to the viceregal palace. The door, like most of the doors in Buenos Aires, was tall and narrow and the upstairs windows opened onto little balconies with tubs of plants adding a splash of colour to the pale frontage. The building might be smaller than the home she had shared with O'Gorman but it was clear that Ana Perichon was doing well for herself.

A liveried servant opened the door. Though there had been plenty of servants in her old home, the appearance of gold-braided livery was more evidence that Ana's star was in the ascendant.

James handed over a card: 'Major Thomas James'. On the back, he had written, 'I would very much like to see you again. JB.'

The footman took the card in a gloved hand and placed it on a silver tray before leaving Burke in the hallway while he vanished into one of the rooms beyond.

Moments later, he was back.

'Madam will be happy to see you immediately.'

Burke followed the footman through the hallway to the tiny internal courtyard beyond. Tall doors opened off it to the principal rooms of the house and in one of these, Ana sat waiting for him.

The footman bowed his way out, closing the door behind him.

Ana sat, saying nothing, but staring up at James. James, in his turn, stood speechless.

When the silence broke, they both started talking at once, then both were silent as they simultaneously paused for the other to speak, and then both started together again.

Ana stopped trying to talk and burst out laughing, and the tension that had been palpable in the air was broken. It was as if James had left her but a week before and was now returned to tell her that his exile at de Liniers' hand was but a nightmare.

Before Ana had drawn breath, James had crossed the room and taken her in his arms.

'James!'

She pushed him away from her.

'Ana! Don't tell me that you don't want me!'

She flushed.

'Of course I want you. But Santiago will find out and he will kill you.'

'I'm here as an official British envoy.'

'Oh, yes.' Ana picked his card from the table where it lay. "Major Thomas James". Are the great men in London so very ashamed of you, James?'

'It was considered politic to separate this mission from any of my previous activities in South America.'

'Because you were a spy.'

James shrugged.

'And do the gentlemen who sent you here with this . . .' she paused, ladling sarcasm onto the next word, '. . . sophisticated alias expect that Santiago de Liniers will not recognise you?'

'They're diplomats, Ana. They expect him to behave diplomatically. I am here to let him know that England and Spain are no longer at war and to offer him the hand of friendship.'

Ana laughed again but harshly.

'This is Santiago de Liniers you are talking about, James. Do you expect him to offer you the hand of friendship?'

'I have an alternative proposition to put to him.'

He explained Carlota's proposal. Ana appeared unconvinced but James explained its benefits for La Plata.

'De Liniers would move to Monte Video and, in effect, rule the Banda Orientale as first minister at the court of Princess Carlota. He would not be running a colony any more but a principality, with its own sovereignty and sway over all the other Spanish possessions in the Americas – including La Plata.'

Ana shook her head.

'He won't accept it, James. He thinks Napoleon could win the war in Europe. He's happy for La Plata to remain a Spanish colony in name but he wants to be in a position to hand it to the French if they become the dominant power in the world. And, until then, he wants to enjoy the rule of La Plata. Don't you remember, James? It's all about power – and here Santiago de Liniers *is* the power. His title may be viceroy but there is no king in Spain. He runs the province how he wants, answering to no one.'

Burke thought of Paco Iglesias and his dreams of an independent Argentina, of the gauchos singing to the country of their birth, and of the citizens of Buenos Aires who had risen to drive the British from their country. The people of La Plata had put de Liniers where he was, and now he would betray their dreams to hold on to his position.

'So de Liniers is just to be allowed to walk away with everything he wants. He gets to keep the viceroyalty; he gets to keep his gold.' James stopped and looked at Ana who was sitting, flushed but trying desperately to regain some composure. 'He gets to keep you.'

'He doesn't own me, James.'

'No? You're to be at the dinner tonight – his acknowledged consort. A Spanish viceroy with a mistress he flaunts in public! It's unheard of. But it's not love, Ana. If he loved you, you wouldn't be hiding away here – you'd be in the palace with him. It's ownership.'

Now Ana was on her feet, her face tight with fury but James continued.

'You know what drives de Liniers, Ana. It's power. Having you sit beside him as his consort shows that he has the power to ignore protocol because his rule here is absolute. And keeping you here as his woman shows he has power over you.'

Ana's arm swung out and James felt the crash of a blow on his face. She had not slapped him: she had punched him.

'How dare you talk to me like that! Here in my own home.'

'A home de Liniers paid for.'

It was a guess but, in truth, where else could she have got the money?

Her arm swung back again but this time James caught her wrist. It would not do for His Majesty's representative to meet the Viceroy with a face covered in bruises.

'He owns you, Ana. You're bought and paid for.'

Suddenly the fight seemed to go out of her. She seemed almost to collapse where she stood and James found himself supporting her by the wrist that he had seized.

'I saved your life, James.'

James stood absolutely still. Then, carefully, as if handling something unbearably fragile, he released her wrist and set her down on her chair.

He remained standing and seemed to be struggling to find words. Finally, he spoke.

'Oh, God, Ana. I'm sorry. I'm so, so sorry.'

Ana looked up. She seemed to be smiling at him, though her shoulders shook with quiet sobbing.

'It was hardly a fate worse than death, James. He was already my lover. And he can be very generous.' The sobbing stopped. 'You're quite right: he paid for the house. I have an allowance twice what Mr O'Gorman gave me and considerably fewer expenses to meet from it. And I think he really rather likes me.'

She sat up, very straight in her chair speaking slowly, as if considering every word.

'But you're quite right, James. It's still about power. I am another proof of his authority. I am another man's wife and yet I am his acknowledged mistress. And I am sure part of my attraction is that he stole me from you.'

She paused and looked him in the eye as she continued.

'If you stay here, de Liniers will know. He pays my servants and they are not fools. If you stay, he will take his revenge on you.'

'And on you.'

'His revenge on me will be to have me watch as he destroys you.'

'Then perhaps it is wiser that I leave.'

Ana was still fixing him with her eyes.

'It's making the wise choice that has brought me here, James.'

One moment, it seemed to James that she was sitting there, watching him; the next she was standing and their arms held each other as if they were each clinging to the only thing that could save them.

*

On leaving Ana's house, James returned directly to the ship. There, William greeted him with more than his usual good humour.

'Miss Simkins was pleased to see you, I take it.'

William's broad grin was sufficient answer but his smile faded as he noticed James' sombre demeanour.

'Mrs O'Gorman wasn't pleased to see you, sir?'

'On the contrary, William, Mrs O'Gorman was delighted to see me. So delighted that there is a distinct possibility that I might meet with an unaccountable accident tonight.'

'Ah!'

'"Ah!" indeed, William. I think we had best tread carefully once we are ashore.'

William slipped a knife into his boots as a precaution but, despite James' concern, there was no evidence that de Liniers intended any assault as William escorted him to the fort that evening. The two arrived without mishap and William left his master at the entrance to the Viceroy's palace with instructions to return at midnight when the banquet should be ending.

A young officer greeted him as he entered the fort, snapping smartly to attention and saluting the night's guest of honour.

Burke followed him to a room where de Liniers was waiting. He could hear the buzz of chatter from the grand salon next door, but James knew he would be expected to wait, sipping sherry with his host, until the other guests had all arrived. Only then would they make their entrance.

De Liniers was wearing his dress uniform, but Burke hardly noticed him. For next to him, Ana stood, her dress cut as low as decency would permit. Around her throat was a necklace of diamonds that sparkled brilliantly in the candlelight. Matching jewels hung from her ears. She was beautiful, but a stiffness in the way she stood and a nervousness about her eyes told James that all was not well.

Servants were presenting him with a tray where a glass of sherry stood, waiting for him to take it. Surely de Liniers would not attempt anything as obvious as poison? James took the glass, watching Ana. Her expression did not change. Not poison, then. He sipped.

'Madame Perichon, you know.' De Liniers voice was without expression, but his face was a sneer. He took Ana's hand and raised it to his lips. The gesture was unexpected in the circumstances and de Liniers made it practically obscene.

James nodded an acknowledgement to Ana and she nodded back. She did not offer him her hand to kiss.

He sipped again at his sherry. Neither de Liniers nor Ana were drinking and de Liniers made no attempt at conversation, simply watching silently as Burke tried to ignore his obvious hostility.

Burke replaced his still half-full glass on the tray that a servant was still holding.

De Liniers broke the silence. 'Shall we go in?'

The admiral held his arm out to Ana and she took it, managing a sort of half-shrug of apology to James, who was forced to follow them alone.

In the grand salon, the cream of Buenos Aires society was seated at a mahogany table that now dominated the room. Light from the chandeliers reflected off the silver place settings. Soldiers in their dress uniforms stood at attention along the walls.

The hubbub quieted as they walked in. James noticed Thomas O'Gorman seated toward the foot of the table, his expression troubled as he noticed the Viceroy's snub in leaving his guest unescorted. As he seated himself, he heard the rumble of disquiet as others, too, wondered what de Liniers' slight might portend.

James found he had little appetite, which was unfortunate, as the banquet was designed to show the bounty of La Plata and consisted of a seemingly endless procession of courses as beef in all its forms was set before James. The banquet even started with ox-tail soup. Every time that James turned to speak to his host, more food would be set before him and de Liniers spoke only to insist that he eat. There were steaks, ribs, sausages, black puddings. When James was sure that he could face no more beef, whatever the diplomatic consequences, roast mutton appeared and mutton chops. There was some pork to add variety before the fish dishes arrived. To James' relief, fish were represented by just mackerel and trout. A sorbet of Andean ice was served to clear the palate before an array of desserts brought the meal to a triumphant conclusion.

After the eating came the toasts. A leather exporter – a deadly rival of O'Gorman – gave a toast on behalf of the British community. Señor de la Cruz Bringas represented the Spanish merchants. James had met him after his first communion as Otto Witz and hoped that the Spaniard's memory for faces was not as good as his own. A clearly confused Monsieur Goriot toasted 'peace between nations' in French (a nice touch, James thought) and an Italian – a man of no significance whatsoever – appeared to have been elected to give a toast simply to make up the numbers.

It was then James' turn to raise his glass to friendship between Britain and Spain and good fellowship between his people and those of La Plata. He kept his speech short, but throughout it, de Liniers watched with no flicker of reaction.

James sat to polite applause that was cut short as de Liniers rose to his feet. He held up an envelope and drew out a letter, which James recognised as the despatches from Admiral Smith.

'Major James,' de Liniers began, 'comes to us as a representative of the British government. He is recommended to us by men of honour in the British forces. Admiral Smith writes that he is . . .' De Liniers' made play of finding the reference in the letter. '. . . a "distinguished officer".' De Liniers turned to Burke with a look of contempt.

'Some of you may recognise this "distinguished officer". For we have seen him in Buenos Aires before. There I think he introduced himself to the Société Francaise as Monsieur Bergotte. Others may have known him as Captain Otto Witz. I think only our English friends were privileged to know him by his actual name. Is that not so, Mr James Burke?'

James sat silent. De Liniers was unravelling any possible working arrangement between La Plata and England. This went far beyond revenge because he had slept with Ana, though the public insult was presumably at least in part because of that. No, de Liniers was deliberately turning away the representations of the British Government and the navy's promises of support against any invasion. The Viceroy's sympathies for Napoleon went beyond meeting his envoys: he was leaving La Plata undefended so that he could hand it to the French.

De Liniers speech was now in full flow.

'Britain has sent this man – this spy – to represent them to our government. Of course, they can have had no indication of the sort of person that this James Burke really is.'

It was an oratorical flourish worthy of Mark Antony. If Burke had, indeed, been a British spy, how could the British themselves have been unaware of that? He was accusing George III's government of acting in bad faith. The angry muttering among his audience and the black looks thrown in James' direction showed that everyone understood what de Liniers was saying. Even O'Gorman, usually sublimely unaware of any political subtlety, looked worried.

'We are gathered here to do honour to the British Government and we must not forget that they have offered us their friendship, though the messenger they have sent has been no friend of La Plata. We thank them for their offers of assistance.'

Yes, James thought, but you are careful not to accept those offers. And while you refuse to talk to me, other Napoleonic envoys will be on their way. And all I can do is sit here and listen, while you blacken the name of England and plan to sell your country to its enemies.

By now, de Liniers seemed to be bringing his speech to a close. He reminded his audience of the way they had had to fight for their freedom. He did not have to remind everyone who they had been fighting against.

'And so, I raise my toast. Not just to our friends in Europe but to peace between all the nations.'

'Peace between nations.' It was no coincidence that de Liniers was making the same toast as M Goriot.

After the toast, de Liniers remained standing.

'Ladies. Gentlemen. I regret that I have to depart from traditional practice for I cannot finish my address with the toast. There is some business I think you would agree that I must conclude at once.'

James was conscious of a stirring amongst the soldiers stood nearest to his place and he knew, before de Liniers spoke, what was to come next.

'It is essential to the security of La Plata that the spy and enemy of our country, James Burke, should be held immediately. He has travelled here under the protection of his government and, respecting the norms of international conduct, I cannot punish him as he deserves to be punished. But he shall be escorted directly from here to the vessel on which he entered La Plata and I shall request that the ship sail to England on the first tide.'

Soldiers had fallen in behind his seat and a captain was placing his hand on his arm to raise James to his feet. He was to be arrested like a common criminal, taken under guard from a formal dinner where he represented the British Government and King George himself. The insult to man and nation was exquisite.

James looked at de Liniers, standing next to him. The Frenchman made no effort to disguise the sneer on his face.

James knew that he had to buy himself some time. Once he was back aboard ship, his mission was over. If he was to retrieve anything from the wreckage, he had to stay ashore.

He spoke quickly and quietly to de Liniers.

'You can't get her back this way.'

De Liniers flushed and James knew that he had swallowed the bait.

'Take him to my office. Hold him there.'

A soldier marched either side of him as the Captain led him from the salon, two more guards following. The whole of Buenos Aires society watched in silence.

At least, James thought, his insult to de Liniers meant that the Viceroy had rescinded the order to have James taken 'directly' to the ship. Instead, he and de Liniers were to have one final meeting. It was up to him to make the best of that.

He was kept waiting in de Liniers' office for a good half hour while the Viceroy took his leave of his guests. When the Frenchman finally arrived, he sent the soldiers out, ordering them to stand guard at the door.

James had sat while he was waiting. De Liniers walked to the chair and struck him across the face. It was the second time that day he had been hit, and his face felt as if it was on fire, but James made no response.

'Stand up!'

James stood.

'You're filth, Burke. You're a spy and a coward. If I could, I'd call you out.'

'There's nothing I'd like better than a duel with you, de Liniers. But I think that an affair of honour between the Viceroy and the British envoy would have complications.'

De Liniers stared at Burke as if trying to decide whether to hit him again. At last, as if he could no longer bear to look at him, he turned away.

'I said you were a coward.'

James ignored the insult. He had been so insulted already, he almost didn't care any more.

'We're both constrained by the rules of diplomacy,' he said. 'You can't kill me. You can't imprison me. All you can do is send me home.'

'I'll send you back to England with your name ruined.'

James allowed himself a humourless smile. 'And you can't even do that until tomorrow.'

'What do you mean?'

'Come, de Liniers. It's night. It's low tide. You can strike me here and deny it but you send me out across the mud, unexpected, in the middle of the night – well, any accident is going to be a little too public, is it not?'

'You are not expected back on board?'

'Certainly not.' James lied smoothly. 'I have lodgings arranged on shore and I would like to be taken there.'

If de Liniers agreed to his request, he would be in trouble as there were no lodgings but he was confident that the Viceroy would refuse him.

De Liniers was quick to show him that his confidence was not misplaced.

'If you stay ashore, you stay here, under guard.'

'Then I trust you can have a room made up.'

'You'll sleep in the cells like the common criminal you are.'

'I think not, de Liniers. There's only so much you can insult a representative of the king.'

'Very well. We'll tell the King that you spent the night in the Old Chapel. You can pray for your immortal soul.'

James had to admit to himself that the chapel was a nice touch. He knew from his visits to Colonel Calzada Castanio that the Old Chapel was in the block that now contained the guardroom and the fort's gaol. De Liniers would have the satisfaction of clapping him in the cells while being able to assert that he had done no such thing. The admiral, it seemed to Burke, had an eye for diplomatic niceties.

'One thing more, Burke. You have insulted me as the Viceroy and you have tried, yet again, to meddle in the affairs of my country. Because of that, you will be going home in dishonour.' He stepped forward so that his face was just inches from James'. 'But you have insulted me also as a man. This is for that.' And he brought his knee sharply up into James' groin.

James fell to the ground, vomiting the banquet as he lay doubled up in agony.

De Liniers stepped fastidiously away and called the guard.

'Mr Burke appears to have been taken ill,' he said. 'Take him to the Old Chapel and put him under guard there. He boards his ship tomorrow at dawn.'

Burke was half carried, half dragged from the room and cross the courtyard to the cellblock. The Old Chapel was the last room on the corridor. The guards stood supporting him while the door was unlocked and then dragged him to the threshold and let him go. He staggered for an uncertain step and slumped to the floor.

Lying there, he looked around him. No one had used the room as a chapel for years, though there was still a crucifix high on the wall. The furnishings had been removed but there was a camp bed in one corner and, as the guards stood by watching, he gathered his strength and dragged himself across to it.

The room was at least bigger than the common cell and he had it to himself, but he did not expect a comfortable night.

'I'll need my man,' he said, fighting the urge to throw up again. 'He will be waiting at the entrance to the fort.'

The Captain looked at him uncertainly. Burke, for all that he was covered in vomit, was still a gentleman and a diplomat. It might be best if his man was there to attend to him. A guard was sent to find William, and returned with him ten minutes later.

William was shocked to see the condition that James was in, and insisted that he was provided with water. For a while, the guards were kept busy fetching and heating water and finding cloths for William to clean up. They seemed uncertain whether they should treat James as a dangerous criminal or as a guest. William, issuing orders with the confidence of his new rank, was happy to keep them unsure of themselves.

Eventually, though, the guards left them alone, and James explained the situation.

‘What time is it now?’ he asked, once he had brought William up to date with events.

‘Just gone one, I reckon.’

Despite his bruised face, James managed a grim smile.

‘So the guard will change in about three hours.’

For a moment, William looked puzzled. Then, as he realised James’ plan, he, too, started to smile.

*

The new guard came on duty at four.

Captain Pepe Sampaulo looked smart and fresh, despite the hour, as his men fell in for duty.

‘I hear you had some excitement,’ he said to the Captain of the old guard.

‘We had that spy brought in. He’s in the Old Chapel with his servant.’

‘We’re holding the servant, too?’

‘No – just the officer. The servant came in to clean him up. He was a bit of a mess.’

‘How long do we hold him?’

‘Just until morning. Then there’ll be an escort to take him to his ship.’

‘I’ll keep a close eye on him.’

‘You do that.’

The Captain saluted his relief and led his men off duty, glad to be going to his bed.

Captain Sampaulo walked to the end of the corridor to check on the English officer. The only other prisoners in the gaol were a couple of drunks and a pickpocket. Captain Sampaulo felt safe leaving them to their own devices, but the Englishman should be watched.

A Judas window had been put into the door of the Old Chapel years ago, just in case it should be used in this way. Captain Sampaulo opened it, and looked in.

The officer was lying on the camp bed, his uniform showing clear marks of vomit, though it was damp from where the man’s servant had been trying to clean it. The smell carried through the opening in the door. Sampaulo wrinkled his nose in disgust.

The servant had the officer's jacket in his hands and was dabbing at it ineffectually while the Englishman berated him for his inefficiency.

'Can you not do better than that? I don't want to leave here tomorrow looking like the town drunk.'

'I'm sorry, sir. I need more hot water, and a scrubbing board and some soap would help. There's only so much I can do with a bucket.'

Now the Englishman seemed to become aware of the eyes on him and he turned toward the Judas window.

'You'd best send my man out to get my uniform cleaned up.'

Sampaulo looked at the servant – a wretched looking chap, with ill-fitting clothes and bruises on his face that suggested his master was vicious as well the traitorous spy everyone was saying he was.

'Come on, fellow, you'd best get your master's coat cleaned up before he finds another excuse to hit you.'

He unlocked the door and sent the poor man on his way, watching sympathetically as he shuffled down the corridor and out into the night.

*

Once outside, James set off toward the west of the town, heading for the house where de Liniers had kept his treasure. It was, he thought, a long shot but it was his only hope.

He arrived at the house with barely an hour to go before dawn.

The door was of solid wood but the keyhole was large and the lock crude. The knife was still in William's boot and the lock was large enough for James to work the knifepoint into the mechanism. He did not bother with any careful lock picking but just forced it open. It gave way with a snap that sounded loud in the darkness but no one woke to raise an alarm. He pushed the door ajar and walked in.

He remembered where de Liniers' study was and he found it easily enough, even in the dark. There was another lock but the door was flimsier than the one to the street. Forcing it was the work of a moment.

Inside, James took a flint from his pocket and struck a spark. Soon he had lit the lamp and could look around him.

He gave a grim smile of satisfaction when he saw the tricolore still on the wall. It was a dangerous symbol now that Napoleon had invaded Spain, and its presence confirmed James' belief that de Liniers favoured France. But he needed something more if he was to prove that de Liniers was plotting against Spain. He just hoped that he could find the proof here, where the admiral stored his secrets.

He opened the bureau. There were some letters from Ana, which he pushed impatiently aside, and some others, also in a feminine hand, which he put in his pocket to examine later. There was a book of accounts, showing that the Viceroy was drawing significant amounts of money from the public coffers, but James was sure that would be almost expected of a man in his position. It would hardly bring about his downfall. Beyond that, there was nothing.

James looked around the room again. It was furnished as simply as he remembered. It was possible, he supposed, that de Liniers still hid things under the stone slabs of the floor, but this seemed an unlikely place for the sort of documents that he was looking for. Besides, without a crowbar there was no way that he could lift them.

The first glimmerings of day were beginning to show through the shutters as James turned his attention back to the bureau. He pulled the drawers out and checked for anything that de Liniers might have fixed to their undersides but there was nothing. As he discarded the second drawer on the floor alongside the first, his eye registered something wrong. He looked at the drawers again, trying to work out what he had seen that was out of place. Suddenly his conscious mind picked up the detail that his eye had already noticed: one drawer was an inch or so shorter than the other.

He reached into the gap where he had taken out the drawers and rapped at the back panel of the bureau. On one side, the wood rang hollow.

It was growing lighter by the minute. He had no time to waste looking for secret catches or sliding panels. He forced his knife into the wood. With a splintering crack, it gave way. He reached into the concealed compartment, his fingers groping blindly until he felt the papers hidden there.

He drew them out and held them to his lamp. They were in French, sealed with the beehive seal of Napoleon. This, he was sure, was the evidence that would prove de Liniers to be a traitor.

There was no time to delay. James pushed the papers into his pocket and turned to the door. Even as he reached toward the handle he heard the street door open. He froze, as the sound of footsteps approached in the hallway. He willed the footsteps to move past the study door but they did not.

Burke stepped back, ready to face whoever might enter the room. He had little doubt, though, who it would be.

The door swung open. De Liniers stood there in his admiral's uniform. James' first thought was that it was an odd outfit to be wearing in his private house at six in the morning. Then he realised the significance of de Liniers' choice of dress. The uniform included a sword.

De Liniers did not advance into the room but stood in the doorway, blocking any possibility of escape.

'You know,' he said, conversationally, 'you're supposed to be locked up in the fort.'

When James made no reply, the other continued as if they were old friends chatting.

'Somehow I knew you'd be here. I thought, "He's in a cell. You really don't have to worry about him." But then I decided that while James Burke was in Buenos Aires, I wasn't entirely safe. So I came here.'

He looked at the drawers on the floor.

'It seems I was right to come.'

Only then did he draw his sword.

'You've done me a kindness really. Thanks to your status as a representative of the British government, I couldn't have you killed yesterday. But here you are, having broken into my house – and you were thoughtful enough to leave the doors with their smashed locks as proof that you were up to no good. Now I am simply an outraged householder. Fortunately, I am armed. And you are about to end your meddling for ever.'

He lunged forward. James was only just quick enough to dodge aside. He drew his knife, which elicited a mirthless laugh from de Liniers who lunged again.

De Liniers had room to move, though he was careful to keep himself between James and the door. James was being forced back, his knife no match for de Liniers' sword. Desperately he looked around him for a weapon. Even a cloak would help, as he could wrap it over his arm and use it to entangle his opponent's weapon as the gauchos did when they fought.

He grabbed the tricolore from the wall and swung it to trap the sword as it curved toward him. The flag, though, was not as thick as a gaucho's cloak. The sword ripped through the fabric, cutting James across the ribs.

'First blood, I think,' said de Liniers and moved in closer.

James pushed forward with his knife, hoping to take the Frenchman by surprise, but de Liniers brought the pommel of his sword hard down on James' hand and the knife fell to the floor.

James retreated to the far side of the room, as de Liniers closed in for the kill.

That was when he saw the sword mounted on the wall.

It was a ceremonial sword, given to de Liniers when he was just twelve, at the very start of his career. But de Liniers had been a tall child and the sword was a respectable length. And for all the gilt and the inscribed blade, it was still a serviceable weapon.

As de Liniers swung his blade to finish the fight, James grabbed the sword from the wall, bringing it down to parry the blow.

Now James fought back, cutting, parrying, and thrusting for his life. His sword was shorter than de Liniers', the events of the night had left him tired and weakened, and he was already wounded from his opponent's first blow. But he was younger than the Viceroy and his sudden counterattack had the advantage of surprise.

The noise of the fight had finally awakened the servant who stood behind de Liniers in the doorway, clearly terrified by what she was seeing. De Liniers glimpsed her from the corner of his eye.

'Get help, you little fool,' he called.

'I'll show them the despatches.'

'Wait!'

The girl stopped, trembling.

'I don't need help to finish you.'

De Liniers moved forward, using his longer sword to carve himself space and pushing James once more toward the far wall of the room.

As James edged back, his foot caught on one of the drawers he had discarded on the floor. He lost balance and fell. De Liniers raised his sword for the kill and the girl, still standing in the doorway, screamed.

The scream only distracted him for a second, but it was enough. As the sword came down, James was already rolling to the side. The blade slashed through empty air and into the wood of the drawer.

Now it was de Liniers who was off balance. James was already on his feet and moving to the attack. The older man had already recovered his balance, but his sword was embedded in the wood and he had to pull it free.

It only took a moment but it was a moment too long. James stabbed into his forearm. De Liniers had just freed the sword but, as he did so, it dropped from his hand.

De Liniers stood disarmed, blood pouring from his sleeve.

He drew himself erect and stared Burke in the eye.

'I will die with honour,' he said.

James held him at the point of his sword as he slowly manoeuvred himself toward the door.

'Actually,' he replied, 'you aren't going to die, and you will be left without honour.'

The next moment, he was through the door and gone.

*

James had to hurry. Even if William managed to maintain his masquerade until he was safely aboard ship, de Liniers would raise the town against him as soon as he had bandaged his wound. The traitor's only hope was that James might be hunted down and killed before he had the chance to pass on the French despatches.

James headed for Thomas O'Gorman's house. It was one of the first places that de Liniers would look for him, but he did not intend to stay there long.

The man who answered the door was new and, seeing a stranger in servant's dress, blood seeping through his shirt, he tried to shut him out. James blocked the door with a booted foot and shouted for Thomas. O'Gorman was in his bed, but James' shouts roused the household. One of the servants who came to the door to help eject the troublemaker recognised him and hurried him in.

O'Gorman, unshaven and hair tangled from bed was summoned to the morning room. He immediately ordered bandages and coffee ('But not in that order,' James insisted) and demanded an account of what had happened.

'There isn't time,' said James. 'I am pursued and must get out of the city. I need a horse.'

A servant was despatched to the stables while one maid brought coffee and another took off his shirt and started to wrap a torn sheet around his chest as a makeshift bandage.

Within minutes, the horse was at the door and James was pulling on his shirt and heading out of the room. He stopped only for long enough to take O'Gorman's hand.

'I doubt we'll meet again, Thomas. You've been a better friend than I deserved. God bless you.'

Then he was off.

He should, he knew, have headed straight from the city. It was his duty to his country to get the proof of de Liniers treachery to those who could stop him betraying La Plata to the French. But there was another duty he had to fulfil first, though it meant riding toward the fort and the risk of discovery.

Ten minutes after leaving O'Gorman's house, he pulled his horse up outside Ana's door. When the footman opened it, James ordered him into the street and gave him the reins to hold.

The footman protested that it was his duty to remain in the house and announce a visitor, but James was already through the door and heading to Ana's bedroom.

Ana was awake and seemed to James to have been awake for some time. Her eyes were red: she had obviously been crying. As James entered, she sat up in the bed, pulling the sheets around her with an uncharacteristic modesty.

'For God's sake, James, get out! He'll kill you!'

'I'm going. But listen, Ana, I can prove he is an agent of the French. He knows this and he will pursue me but I can finish him. You need to get out now, while there's still time.'

Ana looked at him blankly.

'Make for Monte Video. De Liniers has few friends there. I'll meet you there in a fortnight.'

Ana nodded dumbly, still clutching the sheets to her bosom. She seemed to James unnaturally stiff.

He reached forward and pulled the sheets from her. All about her breasts and body were the marks of bruises.

'He beat you.'

Ana said nothing but started crying silently.

James took her in his arms.

'Get out. Go to Monte Video. I'll meet you there and take you to Brazil.'

'You won't leave me?'

'I have to go now. I have to finish de Liniers. Then we can be together.'

She reached up and kissed him. It was a long kiss but, at last, she pushed him gently away from her.

'I want him destroyed.'

James nodded.

'You have my word.'

Then he turned, running for his horse.

He had realised as soon as he saw the papers. He held the proof of de Liniers' treachery and he had to give it to the man who would use it for the best.

James was a British officer but he had seen the British betray their trust already in La Plata. He knew, however much he tried to pretend that he didn't, that Princess Carlota was probably mad and certainly dangerous. The French were the enemy, the Spaniards would back de Liniers.

James rode from the city, heading for the home of Paco Iglesias.

He kept the horse at the gallop until he was well clear of Buenos Aires. Once he was sure that there was no one in immediate pursuit, he eased to a steady canter, eating up the miles between him and Iglesias's estancia.

He arrived, as he had the first time he had ridden there, just as dusk was falling. There was a cry from the lookout as he approached, and Pedro rode out with a couple of the gauchos to see who the stranger was.

Burke's wound had reopened with the effort of the ride and the gauchos were greeted by the sight of an exhausted man with his clothes covered in blood.

At first, Pedro did not recognise him. When he did, he reacted to the friend he had ridden with, not the British officer he had delivered to de Liniers.

'*Madre de Dios!* Let us get you in and your wounds dressed.'

Paco Iglesias was summoned. He, too, was concerned for Burke's welfare but he was also worried about why the Englishman had suddenly returned to his estancia.

James raised himself from the bed where Pedro had insisted he rest.

'I have come, señor, because I believe you to be a true patriot. I needed an honest man who loves his country to take these letters. You will know what to do with them.'

James reached into his pocket and withdrew the despatches, crumpled and bloody but still readable. He handed them to Paco Iglesias and then, his duty done, he fell into unconsciousness.

*

By the time he was able to leave his bed the next day, riders were already on their way from the estancia to the ranches of the other patriot leaders.

As James entered Paco Iglesias's study, his host leapt to his feet, crossing the room to shake him by the hand.

'Captain Burke, I always knew in my soul that you were an honourable man. Now you have repaid my trust a thousand fold.'

James was so taken by the other's expression of emotion that he didn't even bother to explain that he was now a major.

'You have exposed de Liniers as a traitor, unfit to lead our patriotic movement. I have already sent word to the other commanders. We will meet here to decide our new leader.'

'De Liniers is finished, then.'

'His power is ended. In a few days, he will know that we have evidence of his treason. His viceroyalty is finished.'

'What of the future? Another viceroyalty?'

Paco Iglesias looked out of the window at the pampas and James thought of the story of Moses looking out over the Promised Land. At that moment, he knew that there would be no principality in Monte Video. There might, he supposed, be one more viceroy. Great changes do not happen overnight. But with de Liniers destroyed, new leaders would arise: men like Iglesias who would lead their country to freedom and independence.

'This land,' said the criollo, 'is not Spanish any more. This land is ours.'

He clapped his hands and the Indian servant, Maria, entered with a bottle of the local wine. Behind her, James saw a tall man, almost a giant, standing in the shadows of the room.

'I didn't know you had a new manservant,' he said.

His host looked puzzled.

'There's still just Maria, though I suppose she could do with some help. What made you think there was anyone else?'

Burke looked again at the shadows. There was no one there but it seemed that there was a trembling in the air and James imagined a black giant of a man saying, 'You have found your road.'

He shook his head.

‘I’m sorry,’ he said. ‘It’s been a long journey.’

Paco smiled and poured two glasses.

‘To our country,’ he said. ‘To Argentina.’

James raised his glass and drank.

*

James stayed at the estancia to see the gathering of the criollo leaders. Trestle tables were set up outside the house so that they could all sit and eat together while they discussed de Liniers’ betrayal and how they were to deal with it. At first, he sat with them but he found himself feeling strangely detached. He had brought this meeting about but it was not for him to decide the future of the country. That was a task for its own people.

He began to think of what the future held for him. He had fulfilled the destiny laid on him by the voodoo priest all those years ago. Now he had to form his own destiny.

At the next break in the discussions, he spoke to Sr Iglesias.

‘Paco,’ he said, ‘I have to go to Monte Video.’

*

A week later, James was sitting in his room in Monte Video, looking out across the great estuary of the Plate. On the horizon, he imagined he could see a smudge of land that he already thought of as Argentina. He picked up the glass on the table beside him and raised it, echoing Paco Iglesias’s toast in his mind. His thoughts, though, were closer to home. That morning, he had visited the main inns of the town to see if Ana had yet arrived, but she had not.

James felt safe in Monte Video. The town had rebelled once against de Liniers, and the man who had escorted Burke on his journey had brought the news of the Viceroy’s treachery to the rebel leaders there. De Liniers was still viceroy in name but his authority was already slipping in Buenos Aires and any command to arrest James in Monte Video would be ignored.

James had argued that de Liniers should be dragged from office immediately but Sr Iglesias had explained convincingly why this could not be.

‘He was our leader against the British. He has ruled us with scarcely concealed contempt for Spain. He has allowed us to believe that we are strong enough to protect ourselves and to govern ourselves. If we tell the people that he was an agent of Napoleon, they will lose that belief. They will tell themselves that only Spain or England can protect us: that we are not fit to rule ourselves. No, we cannot take that risk. We will control de Liniers with what we know, and in a few months he will resign.'

The rebel leader had seen the disappointment on Burke's face and hastened to reassure him.

'Don't worry, James. His power is ended. Soon he will be driven from office and, be sure, we will be certain that, when he leaves, not a single *real* that he has stolen from his country will leave with him. This is a man who has lived for power and now he will be left powerless. Trust me, James; you have had your revenge.'

James smiled as he recalled that little speech. De Liniers was, indeed, destroyed, but James needed one more thing before he could be satisfied.

There was a knock at the door.

'Lady downstairs, sir, asking after you.'

James was on his feet in an instant. Pausing only to straighten his jacket, he hurried down the stairs.

The lady waiting downstairs was talking to the landlord as James entered the room. Her back was to him, but he knew at once that it was not Ana. Then she turned and saw him.

'Good morning, Mr Burke,' she said brightly.

'Molly, what are you doing here?'

'Looking for you, mostly.'

Molly saw the look of confusion on his face and took pity.

'When William didn't come by, I knew something must be amiss, so I made enquiries. I knew he had been living in the O'Gorman household when he was last there, and I thought they might have news of him. The servants there do gossip, so I made enquiries of Mrs O'Gorman. I found her about to leave the city and – well, she's an innocent in some ways, isn't she?'

James had never exactly thought of Ana as 'an innocent' before but he realised now that Molly was right. For all her sexuality and her pursuit of position, Ana retained a child-like naivety.

'I thought she had best have a travelling companion,' Molly concluded, as if there was really nothing else to say.

'Where is she?'

'At the Two Swans, half a mile up the road.'

James bent to Molly's face and kissed her.

'Best save that for her, I reckon,' said Molly. But she said it to herself. James had already left.

Afterword

James and Ana were reunited and travelled to Rio de Janeiro together. It would be nice to say that they were happy ever after and, perhaps, in their own way, they were.

William had boarded ship safely in Buenos Aires and waited for James in Rio. When he found Molly in their party, he was, as he put it, 'as happy as a man might reasonably expect to be.'

Burke's llamas never did make it to England. They stayed in O'Gorman's stables and he became quite attached to them.

De Liniers finally lost his position as viceroy four months later in August, 1809.

The next year, on 25th May, the citizens of Buenos Aires (including a prosperous and contented Thomas O'Gorman) met in the town hall and voted that they should no longer recognise the new viceroy, paving the way for independence. De Liniers was one of the leaders of a counter-revolution and was shot as a traitor later that year.

In 1816, at the Congress of Tucuman, the State of Argentina was officially founded as an independent country.

Historical Note

When I came to write this book, I started to research the early history of Argentina. What soon became obvious was that many of the incidents recorded by the chroniclers of that nation's birth either never happened or happened in ways that were significantly different from those described. Yet it is the stories, not the historical facts, that have defined the spirit of that still-young country.

In the end, it is stories that give us our sense of who we are and where we come from. Alfred never burnt the cakes, Harold didn't die with an arrow in his eye, but these are the myths that sustain us.

Which is my way of saying that when the historical facts and my feeling of what *should* have happened were in conflict, history went out of the window.

James Burke was born in Dublin, not Kilkenny. His early life seems to have been very comfortable but he did leave Ireland to join the Regiment of Dillon. This regiment was an Irish unit in the French army as described. He did sail to Haiti (then Saint-Domingue) to put down a slave rebellion but he couldn't have met the Book Man (or Boukman), who was killed a year earlier. The regiment really did surrender to the British and Burke's career as a spy started then. He was a very good spy, so we know very little about his life. I am very grateful for an article by Peter Pyne ('A soldier under two flags,' published in *Etudes Irlandaises* in 1998) as this seems the best source of information available on him in English.

The political background in Argentina is closely based on fact. The implausible romantic entanglements are based on truth as well. Ana O'Gorman, Princess Carlota, and Queen Maria Luisa were all real people and Burke's name was linked, more or less explicitly, with all three. The love triangle of Ana, Burke, and de Liniers also really happened.

A significant inspiration for this book was the city of Buenos Aires, one of the most exciting places on the planet. I am grateful to all the people I have met there who have made my visits so happy.

There are a few buildings from 1806 still standing in Buenos Aires and a walk around the backstreets off the Plaza Victoria (now the Plaza de Mayo) can give you an idea of what the town must have been like. Visits to the Museo Casa Rosada (on the site of the old fort – now the presidential palace), the Museo de la Ciudad, and the Museo Historico Nacional all helped. There is also an excellent small museum in the Cabildo (the old town hall) where, amongst other things, you can see the flag of the 71st Infantry, captured in 1806.

Fans of military history may notice that, although my account of the British invasion of 1806 is true (details of their defeat have been fictionalised), I haven't mentioned the invasion of 1807. Truth here, unfortunately, is not just stranger than fiction but so ridiculous as to be entirely implausible. The fact that one incompetent invasion of Buenos Aires ended with an ignominious defeat and the court martial of the commanding officer is just about believable. The fact that there was an exact repeat a year later (except that this time the British didn't even get as far as capturing the fort) would stretch the credulity of the reader.

The accounts of gaucho life draw heavily on the writings of Charles Darwin, who visited the pampas on his way to the Galapagos. Darwin is so identified with the theory of evolution that it is often forgotten that he was a brilliant writer and his accounts of his travels are well worth reading. There is nothing like direct experience, though, and my day riding with the gauchos at El Ombu is one I will treasure forever. The museum of gaucho life at San Antonio de Areco was also valuable (and the estancia there is my model for Sr Iglesias's home).

I spent an interesting couple of days recreating Burke's crossing of the Andes in similar conditions. We never made it to the pass: we were travelling in spring, rather than autumn, and the winter snows that still blocked the path made it too dangerous to push the horses on. As a result, my description of the walk down into Chile draws heavily on the account of Patrick Fermor, whose book, *Three Letters from the Andes*, describes just such a journey.

For a historical account of the liberation struggle throughout South America, I recommend Robert Harvey's *Liberators*, which helped me put Argentina's history in some sort of context.

Anyone looking for 'Upper Peru' on a modern map should turn instead to Bolivia. Named after Bolivar, the revolutionary leader, this country did not exist under Spanish rule.

The riot that William started in Madrid really happened (and did, indeed, lead more or less directly to the Peninsular War). The incident is the subject of one of Goya's paintings.

Tom Williams
June 2013

Burke will be back …

I hope you have enjoyed *Burke in the Land of Silver*. This is just the first of five books about James Burke that will be published over the next few months. The next one, *Burke and the Bedouin*, should be out in July 2020. It's set during Napoleon's invasion of Egypt (for some reason a campaign that isn't much talked about these days). It has evil French spies (of course), a beautiful woman, desperate night-time rides across the desert, and even pyramids. It's a lot of fun.

If you want to learn more about the books and the world that James Burke lived in, I recommend that you have a look at my website: http://tomwilliamsauthor.co.uk. You can also follow me on Facebook (https://www.facebook.com/AuthorTomWilliams) and Twitter (https://twitter.com/TomCW99).

I'm sure you've seen notes from authors before asking that you review their books on Amazon, but it really makes a huge difference. Without a huge marketing budget (and hardly any authors get those), Amazon reviews are crucial to getting books to an audience. If you have enjoyed *Burke in the Land of Silver* and would like other people to have a chance to enjoy it too, it would be so helpful if you could just write a few words on Amazon. Just a sentence or two saying that you liked it and you think others might is all it takes – we're not talking about the *Times Literary Supplement* here. I do read all my reviews (writers who say they don't are almost certainly fibbing) and I love getting them.

Thank you again for reading. I hope we'll meet up in Egypt.

Printed in Dunstable, United Kingdom

77973416R00170